Published 2010 by One Fine Day Reading

www.onefinedayreading.co.uk

For David and Dorothy Haynes, who epitomize the goodness in people that is worth saving.

LAST CHANCE

I feel so sad for all mankind
They cannot see that they are blind
They talk as if they own the earth
But do not know who gave them birth
They think they will survive for ever
But do not know that they will never
Know the ones who gave then breath
The same ones who will bring them death.

JR

Chapter 1

Michael Kelly woke with a start as the pilot announced they were starting the descent into JFK airport. His six foot four inch frame was not built for aircraft seats, and especially not for seven-hour transatlantic flights, so he pushed his legs into the aisle to try and stretch his cramped muscles. Glancing right he noticed both his parents looking out of the window, probably trying to catch a glimpse of New York on the way down.

He had been to America twice before on holiday, both times being looked after by his mother's sister, Jean. The first trip, when he was eight, they had stayed in Florida, and he had thought that Disneyland was the most fantastic place he had ever seen. It had proved to be even more wonderful than his dreams. The second flight, six years later, had been to Los Angeles and had been more of a beach holiday. This current trip was certainly no holiday. His mother Mary had been telephoned last Monday with the news that Jean and her husband Rui had been killed in a plane crash near the border with Canada. One week on and tomorrow was the day of the funeral.

The British Airways stewardess gave him a big smile, not for the first time in the flight, and asked him to move his feet so she could get her trolley past. Michael returned the smile and asked if he had time to freshen up before the seat belts sign was illuminated. She confirmed he had plenty of time as it was a long descent, and pointed to a vacant washroom. The twenty-two year old face looking back at Michael in the mirror was framed by a lion's long mane of blonde hair. Though not good looking in the normal sense of the words, with his big broken nose slightly bent to the right, his dark brown eyes seemed to light up whenever he smiled, which was often.

He splashed cold water on to his face, and wandered slowly back to his seat. His parents had seemed very tense and withdrawn since receiving the news, but he put that down to the loss of Jean and Rui. The sisters had never been particularly close, and since Jean moved to America to marry some twenty-five years ago, they had probably only seen each other two or three times. They looked up at him as he prepared to sit down, and again he had the feeling that there was something more about the trip that they hadn't told him. They had picked him up from Cambridge University on the way from the family home just outside Woodbridge in Suffolk en route to Heathrow airport. On the way down the M11 and round the M25 they explained that Rui's lawyer, Bob Haynes, would send someone to collect them from the airport and see them safely installed in their hotel.

Touchdown was very smooth, and the journey through immigration was nowhere near as bad as they had been led to believe it could be since the increased security at airports worldwide. They exited between the steel barriers into a sea of faces, but almost instantly spotted a white sign with KELLY written in bright red. The man holding the sign was dressed as a chauffeur, and Michael asked if he worked for Bob Haynes. 'No sir,' he replied, 'I work for the hotel, but Mr Haynes made the booking.' He helped them with their baggage to a huge black limo, and they took in the sights of New York on the way to Park Avenue. Pulling up outside the hotel, Michael's father whispered, 'I think we may be the wrong Kelly's, The Sandstone Hotel is definitely on the high side of expensive.' Inside, he checked with reception and they were indeed expecting Peter and Mary Kelly, together with their son Michael. They were shown to the penthouse, and were amazed at the views over the city and the size and quality of the apartment. The lounge was some thirty feet by twenty, with one of the longer walls full of French windows opening onto a large terrace. Four bedrooms were immaculately furnished, and the en-suite bathrooms were straight out of an expensive glossy

catalogue. There was a state of the art kitchen, and a swimming pool.
Peter rolled his eyes at Mary and Michael. 'Now I know we are definitely in the wrong suite of rooms. Let me give Bob Haynes a ring and sort out what's gone wrong.'
Whilst his father phoned, Michael wandered through the apartment. It really was an incredible place, and secretly he hoped that somehow they were in the right place, but opening a wardrobe and finding it hung with suits made him realise that his hopes would be in vain.
Peter put the phone down and grimaced. 'Right place apparently, and we have a table booked for dinner tonight at half past eight.'
'It seems someone else is staying here. There are clothes hung up in this bedroom.' Mary and Peter followed Michael through the bedroom and into a dressing room larger than most normal bedrooms. Slowly they opened half a dozen of the doors lining each side of the room. Most contained designer clothes that were obviously very expensive, but a couple were empty. Mary glanced at Peter. 'I will try reception.'
As she walked over to the internal phone there was a knock on the outer door, and she continued over to open it.
'Good afternoon, Mrs Kelly, I am Marcel Guthrie, the hotel manager.' Just over six feet tall, Marcel Guthrie was the epitome of the perfect host. 'Welcome to The Sandstone, New York. My condolences on your recent loss, and my apologies for not greeting you in person when you arrived. Let me show you round.'
'Hello,' replied Mary, 'something seems to be wrong. There are clothes in the wardrobes.'
The hotel manager gave a small frown. 'That is down to me. The clothes belonged to Mr. and Mrs. Rocha. After the tragic accident, I thought it would be best to leave the apartment intact until you arrived. Bob Haynes agreed it would be right.'

'So were Jean and Rui staying here when they died?' Peter looked puzzled.
'Mr. and Mrs. Rocha lived here when they were in town. I'm sorry, I thought you knew that.'
'We always used an address in Hampton to contact them,' said Mary.
'That is where they have their main house, but they spent most of their time here,' replied the manager.
'I am concerned that we cannot afford the cost of staying here,' Peter decided to be brutally frank. 'I am a school teacher back home, and I imagine the nightly room rate is probably about six month's salary.'
For the first time, Marcel gave a genuine smile. 'There is nothing to afford Your stay, meals, purchases, everything is covered.'
'By whom?' Peter pressed the point.
'I think you will have to take that up with Bob Haynes,' Marcel's expression changed to one of sincere apology. 'I'm sorry, but I don't have the authority to discuss too much about your sister and her husband.' He was almost stuttering. 'Please can we leave things until after you have met Bob?' His smile returned. 'Let me show you round the place, it has some interesting features but there is a manual in the desk drawer as well. If you get stuck, please use my internal number.' He placed his card on one of the coffee tables.
For over ten minutes he guided them round, explaining how everything worked, then left them to try out the apartment for themselves.
'There is something about all this that I can't quite understand,' said Peter, looking worried.
'While you are working it out, I am going to make the best use of it that I can, starting with the Jacuzzi,' replied Mary, moving towards the bedroom.

'I'm for the pool,' said Michael. Although it was only ten metres by five, he had already dipped his fingers in and the temperature was perfect.
'I will join you if we can find some trunks,' said Peter, and sure enough, after two minutes searching they had towels, bathrobes and trunks near enough the right size.
'I am going to see if I can get a pot of tea sent up,' came Mary's voice from the Jacuzzi, 'anything for you two?'
'Beer for me,' replied Peter.
'And me,' added Michael.
As he was about to enter the water, Michael noticed that the wall at the far end of the pool was curtained. Marcel had said nothing about the curtains in here but he soon spotted a remote control, and there was the button he needed.
He pressed and the curtains parted slowly, revealing the ultimate infinity pool. It gave the impression that the water was pouring through the window instead of in front of it. He swam up as near to the edge as he dared and looked out over Central Park. His father joined him and whistled slowly. 'I always knew Rui was well off, but this is getting crazy.'
'What exactly did he do?' Michael asked.
Before his father could answer, there was a knock on the outer door. Mary shouted to come in and a few seconds later there was a timid knock on the pool door, which was already open.
A chambermaid came in carrying a tray with two frosted glasses and two bottles of beer.
'I see you have found Mr Rocha's favourite view,' she smiled at the men, 'shall I leave the drinks here?' She settled the tray on a small side table. 'Please feel free to ring for service anytime, or the big fridge in the kitchen is well stocked as well.'
'Thanks very much,' Michael smiled back.
'You're welcome,' she turned and left them alone.
'What did he do?' mused Peter. 'Whatever it was he certainly enjoyed life. I have never seen anything like this. We knew he

had money, because he was always very generous, but we never had a clue how much.' He walked slowly up the steps at the far end of the pool. He towelled and pulled on a big white bathrobe. Picking up a beer, he turned to Michael. 'Come and join me in the lounge when you have finished swimming.'

Something in his voice prompted Michael to exit the pool and join him quickly. Mary came through with a cup of tea in her hand.

Peter looked across at her, then at Michael. 'We have been putting something off, Michael, but I guess now is as good a time as any to talk about it.'

Mary's eyes widened a little as her son looked at her.

Peter took a sip of his beer. 'There is no right time, no easy way, but Michael, you are not our son.'

This was the last thing Michael had expected, and he opened his mouth to reply, but words would not form in his mind. As he closed his mouth he nodded at his father and mother, and then slowly shook his head.

'For twenty-two years we should have told you, but life seemed so good for the three of us that tomorrow always seemed a better day to tell you. Your father was Rui, and your mother was Jean,' he dropped his gaze from Michael's face and looked at the floor.

Michael glanced at his mother. Two big tears rolled slowly down her cheeks, one from each eye.

Hundreds of emotions seemed to fly through Michaels mind. He knew the appropriate response was that it didn't matter, that they were his real parents anyway. Questions piled up one after the other, but all this happened so quickly that it was probably less than two minutes when he got up and walked over to Mary. He kissed her gently on the cheek, then crossed to Peter and did the same.

His father hugged him. 'Thank you,' he whispered. He looked across at his mother. 'Nothing has altered.' He even managed a small smile.

Mary smiled back, as she brushed away some more tears. 'Can you really forgive us for not telling you before?'
Again, Michael nodded at his parents. 'There is nothing to forgive. Given a choice I would pick you both again.'
Peter looked at his watch. 'We had better make a move if we have dinner booked for half past eight.'
Peter half rose from his seat, then dropped back. 'When I spoke to Bob Haynes earlier, he said that he would try to explain everything to us after the cremations tomorrow. A car will collect us at ten, take us to the service and then on to his office at about twelve. We will lunch together at Seventy Three, which I believe is one of the best restaurants in America. I know we have dropped a bombshell on you, Michael, but if we can wait until we see Bob tomorrow to discuss it, I think we will all learn a lot, and maybe Mary and I can then fill in any other details.'
'Call her Mum,' said Michael. 'I will always think of you as Mum and Dad.' He wanted to say more, but in his mind agreed that it could wait.
They rose together and went to get ready for dinner.
Michael decided he had time for a nice soak in the bath, and his thoughts drifted back to the life he had lead in England. Peter taught history at a high school in Woodbridge, and Mary freelanced as an economics consultant, mainly producing reports on large corporations for clients based in London. His father once confided in him that he would still do his job if he didn't get paid, as it was what he loved. He was called 'Pop' Kelly throughout the school, and his pupils seemed to love him as much as he loved them. He had always stressed on Michael the need to find a career that he loved, rather than chase money in an occupation he disliked. His parents had very seldom discussed finance with him but cash had never seemed to be a problem for the family. He wondered now if that was something to do with Rui Rocha. Although they were not short of money, his parents had always intimated that spending pointlessly was

pretty stupid. A favourite quote was 'You cannot buy who you are.' If you felt happy with what you were, then you didn't need designer clothes, lots of gold jewellery or overpriced cars to make you any happier. Yet they now seemed to be seeing some of that luxury lifestyle, and part of him admitted to liking it just a bit. From his parents, he had developed a love of history and economics, and had combined the two during his time at Cambridge, specialising on the economics of past nations, including the great dynasties of China, the empires of Rome, Greece, Spain and Britain, and the rise and fall of the nations of North Africa. It seemed that countries were unable to sustain a permanently good lifestyle, but reached a peak and then fell apart with the equivalent of sex and drugs and rock and roll. His life had been very easy, but this was the first time he had properly realised it. They had a lovely large house and grounds, two cars and a lady from the village who came in a couple of days a week to do cleaning and ironing. Holidays had been long and often, fitting in nicely with Peter's school terms. Michael had tried lots of different sports and had been good at all of them, but had never loved one of them enough to dedicate all his time to it. He played football, rugby and cricket at various age levels for Suffolk, and had even tried out speedway at the local Foxhall track on the outskirts of Ipswich. That gave him a huge buzz, and he liked to think he may have taken it further, only the best riders were all a lot smaller than him. His love life had followed much the same pattern. There had been lots of girlfriends, mostly initiated by the girls themselves, but he could not say that he had ever fallen in love. The kissing, and more, was great, but he could never make that total commitment. At twenty two he was still a virgin, but would never admit it to anyone.

His mind was still wandering when there was a tap on the door.

'It's just gone eight,' came Peter's voice.

'I'll be right out,' replied Michael.

The meal and service were both excellent, but there were ghosts at the table and the conversation never seemed to get above small talk. This was unusual as the three of them had always had very open and frank discussions about a wide range of subjects. Tonight it seemed that everything was on hold until tomorrow and it was almost a relief when they said goodnight and retired.

Michael was up quite early and took an orange juice from the kitchen with him into the pool. Peter was already in the water. 'I think the view seems even more spectacular this morning, and I have touched the wall of the pool in front of the window.' This was said with the grin of a Cheshire cat, as Peter was terrified of heights, and Michael was suitably impressed. 'I think you are right, the air is probably a bit clearer this morning.' He swam towards the window and discovered that it was actually about a foot beyond the wall of the pool, and was secretly pleased not to be as scared as he thought he may be last night.

'Would you like your tea in there?' Mary's voice came through from the kitchen.

'Yes please,' they replied as one.

Mary brought a tray through, and then joined them in the pool. 'I could easily be convinced that this would be a really nice lifestyle,' she smiled. 'I have asked them to serve breakfast up here.'

Michael felt pleased that the tension from the previous evening seemed to have eased, and they chatted away almost normally for a while until a knock on the door signalled the arrival of breakfast.

Despite the large meal last night, all three tucked away a substantial breakfast and ten o'clock found them waiting in the lobby at the front of the hotel.

Michael had formed a picture of Bob Haynes in his mind, and it was not the man who came out of the manager's office with Marcel Guthrie.

'Good morning, this is Bob Haynes,' he introduced Bob to each of them in turn.
Bob was about five foot six, with a medium frame that held no spare fat. His head was of normal size, but his face seemed too small to fit, giving him the look of a child's doll. His voice had only a slight New York accent, and was very soft and gentle. To Michael he did not give the impression of a high-powered lawyer, but rather that of a favourite uncle. He led them outside to the same limo and driver as last night, and they pulled out into the Park Avenue traffic.
There was no conversation at the start, as the three of them were too busy looking at the sights, and Bob seemed happy to sit back and relax. He started pointing out some of the buildings and sights as they progressed, and actually made a very good tour guide. His voice seemed soothing, and Michael decided he could be a tour guide or a salesman, but still held reservations about him being a lawyer.
After about twenty minutes Bob brought up the topic of the day. 'I have restricted the service today to yourselves and some of Rui's senior employees, and have pencilled in a date in three weeks time for a larger gathering. There would have been literally hundreds of friends and business acquaintances wanting to attend today, so I thought if you were happy to have a second service and general get-together, we could sort through the guest list between us.'
Peter nodded and looked at Mary and Michael. 'The idea sounds good, but we may have to leave it up to you, as we will have no idea who's who.'
For the first time since they had met him, Bob smiled. 'If you like music, then you will know a lot of the people on the list, as it includes most of the top recording stars of the past twenty or thirty years. Sounds exciting doesn't it?' he said in a soft voice.
'So what did my Dad do exactly?'

Bob glanced at Peter and Mary. 'We told him yesterday,' said Mary.
'Thanks a lot,' Bob whispered, 'I was dreading that most of all.' Turning to Michael he said 'Your Dad did a lot of things, but his first business was moving the equipment for rock bands around the United States and Canada, and virtually all of his customers have stayed loyal and remained good friends.' He glanced out of the window. They had arrived at a large chapel, built in Gothic style from the same brown sandstone used in so many buildings in New York. 'We are here now, so let's get this over with and I will explain the basic set-up of Rui's business to you, then I have set aside the rest of the week to go through it in detail.'
Michael's mind was running at breakneck speed. He was desperate to ask Bob for a list of possible invites, but he knew everything would have to wait. In the meantime he would try to be the perfect son at the funeral of his father, even though he was a man he had never met.
They entered the chapel, which Michael guessed held about one hundred people, and it was packed.
As they walked towards the front, he saw Marcel Guthrie, who nodded to them.
'Senior employees and us only,' thought Michael, 'but I suppose there are some friends as well.' He tried hard to concentrate on the service, but his mind was still in turmoil. He made all the right responses, but was relieved when they were finally outside again.
They stood around in small groups, and Michael reviewed his thoughts about Bob Haynes. He seemed to know everyone present by name, and was passing from group to group like a headmaster in charge of a school outing. Two or three times he passed Michael and his parents, and the soft low voice told them that he would be with them shortly. About ten minutes after they had left the service, Bob came over again; this time accompanied by a short lady, just over five feet tall, weighing

maybe one hundred and sixty pounds. She was in her fifties Michael guessed, and had short spiky red hair. 'Hello,' she beamed as Bob introduced her as Jessica James, Rui's right hand woman. 'Call me Jessie, everyone else does.' She was so alive, with sparkling eyes and a huge smile, that Michael took to her with ease. Bob went on, 'everyone else now knows who you are, and you will be meeting them over the course of the next few months. They are mostly in charge of businesses controlled by Rui, and I have taken the liberty of telling them that everything will work exactly the same as before. In the present economic climate, I thought we should emphasize that they and all the employees they look after are secure for the foreseeable future.' Bob looked Michael straight in the eyes. 'I hope that is in order.'

'At the moment I have no idea what any of this means and assume you feel that is the best way forward,' Michael nodded at Bob.

'Bob's right,' Jessie butted in. 'For the moment leave everything as it is until you get a feel for the whole of the business. It will look after itself pretty well, and I will make sure we remain on track.'

Bob smiled again. 'I wish I could afford Jessie to work for me, instead of the other way round. You can safely leave it with her. You'll come back to the office with us now Jessie?'

'I thought you were going through the Will,' replied Jessie.

'That's why you are coming with us,' smiled Bob.

By the time they reached Bob's office Michael had at least one hundred questions running through his mind, but decided to wait until later to start trying for answers.

Bob took his place behind a large desk, framed by a floor to ceiling wall of glass looking out over Central Park. Facing him were Peter, Mary, Michael and Jessie.

'Right,' Bob looked up, 'the Will.'

'There are three Wills, one for Rui, one for Jean, and a joint Will I insisted on as they always travelled together and there was the possibility they would die together. They are worded so that the joint Will is the one that is applicable. I obviously know the contents, so the first thing is for me to hand this envelope to Michael and await his reply. I do not know the contents of the envelope, only the Wills.'

Michael's hand was trembling slightly as he opened the thick envelope which had been wax sealed. He read;

'Hello son.

Do not read this letter out aloud, and try to maintain a fairly neutral expression.

For reasons I will explain to you later, your mother and I have had to stage an accident, but we are alive and well and look forward to meeting you soon. You can trust Bob and Jessie one hundred percent to look after the business until I contact you. Until then, please do not tell anyone that we are still alive. There are no financial problems with any of the businesses.

You can read out bits of the following if you wish.

Our apologies for being remote parents, but we knew that you would be perfectly brought up by Peter and Mary, and we were right. The fact that you are reading this letter means that we have left it too late to meet you in person. Please take advice from Bob and Jessie on what to do about the business, and give our love and thanks to Peter and Mary.

Lots of love

Mum and Dad'.

Michael read through the letter twice, then picked out bits from the second paragraph and repeated them in a voice shaking with emotion. As he was reading, he wondered if his parents were really still alive, as there had to be the possibility that they had had a genuine accident rather than a staged one.

Bob nodded towards him. 'O.K. The Will.'

He picked up the small document and peered over the top at each person in turn.

'One, we leave ten million pounds sterling net to Jean Kelly, and ten million pounds sterling net to Peter Kelly in gratitude for the way they have raised our son. Please enjoy it.'
Bob glanced again at Peter and Mary.
Peter was staring past him, his gaze going over the park. Mary looked pale. He got up and brought her a glass of water from the cooler. Peter looked up at him with a start. 'Same for me please.'
Bob obliged and sat behind his desk again.
'Two, we leave Jessie James one per cent of the value of the group, as agreed between her and Bob. She can take cash, part cash and a lower percentage, or leave her one percent in. Thanks Jessie, for giving us everything you have.'
'Three, we leave the balance to Michael Kelly, who we are proud to call our son.'
Again Bob looked over the top of the will. 'I figure the current group is worth, in US dollars, two to three hundred billion, what about you Jessie?'
'Yeah, two fifty is about right,' Jessie winked at Bob. 'If I was mean, I'd say three,' she laughed. 'But it doesn't matter; the cash can stay in the firm until we see what Michael is made of.' With that she leaned over and nipped his thigh. 'Seems to be made pretty well to me,' and her raucous laughter broke the tension in the room. 'We are multi millionaires,' Peter looked at Mary.
'I've still got a job,' beamed Jessie.
'I'm worth two to three hundred billion dollars,' said Michael.
'We are,' quipped Jessie.
Bob stood up and wandered round to the front of the desk. 'That's the formal business taken care of, and I guess everyone is pretty happy by the smiles. Any questions?'
'The figures you have quoted mean Rui has left an empire worth more than a lot of countries,' Mary was still finding it hard to

come to terms with the values involved. 'How long have you known him?'
'He was a client for twenty five years, and has built the fortune in that time. He certainly had the Midas touch, and from day one every investment he made has turned to gold.'
'You said he started with trucking?' Michael queried.
'He did,' replied Bob, 'he made money right from the start, and bought into the things his clients wanted to spend their money on. He talked about giving clients a complete lifestyle, so he bought good hotels and restaurants. The Sandstone is one of his, as is Seventy Three, where we will have lunch. He owns marinas, islands, two banks, gold merchants, oil companies, nightclubs, casinos - you think where you can spend money and he will be there. Sorry, I am still talking about him in the present tense.'
'However good you are, it is difficult to amass that amount, tax paid, in twenty five years,' insisted Mary.
'Tax hasn't been too much of a problem, as there are now over one hundred and forty companies registered in seventeen different countries, and we are able to move funds for maximum tax efficiency. My own group has received a retainer of twenty million dollars a year to act for Rui. His talent was knowing in advance what was going to happen. He could predict uncannily. Even in these present difficult times he increased the group value by billions. He was selling bank shares and oil he didn't own right at the top, and buying in right at the bottom. At the moment there is cash available in excess of one hundred billion.'
'So I am supposed to keep this whole thing going?' Michael sounded worried. 'Rock and roll was always the main part of sex and drugs and rock and roll, so where do the sex and drugs come in?'
'You own advertising agencies, nightclubs and casinos, so I guess that takes care of the sex side, but no brothels on the portfolio,' Bob smiled.

‘And drugs?’ Michael looked straight at him.
‘Initially I thought there must be something to do with drugs,’ admitted Bob. ‘Rui was from South America, and the cash just seemed to roll in. Back in those days he paid us by the hour, and I sat down with him one day, the intention being to release him as a client. It was not that I knew anything was wrong, but if something did go wrong I wouldn’t be able to explain to any inquiry how the money was being accumulated so quickly. I went through it with Rui. He promised me that he never did anything illegal and asked me to give him a month to prove how he made money. He gave me one million dollars as a retainer, and three tips. One was an oil company that made a huge discovery in the Gulf of Mexico. One was a gold mine that found a massive new seam. One was a bank which was taken over two weeks later at double the price. In the one month my one million dollars became two and a half million. ‘I work hard at what I do,’ was his response, ‘and what I do is make money.’ From that time we have never broken the law, although we do wring the last legal cent from it.’
‘I can second that,’ said Jessie, ‘your Dad will be a hard act to follow.’
‘A bloody impossible act to follow,’ muttered Michael.
‘The object at the moment is to keep all the assets from losing money, which in the current climate is far from easy,’ Bob had wandered back to his chair.
‘Mum is the expert on finance,’ Michael gazed in her direction.
‘Any help you can give would be greatly appreciated,’ said Jessie. ‘At the moment daily reports roll in twenty four seven, which are fed directly into a piece of software Rui designed. It flashes up anything outside the norm. All I do is look at discrepancies, query them with the company involved and report it to Rui if I am unhappy. If I could report to Mary instead...’
Peter spoke. ‘I think we all have to take stock of exactly what has happened and what we are trying to do in the future. Do any

of us three want to be based in the States? How was Rui making money so fast, and what was he trying to achieve? What do we all want to achieve? I think we may need to sit back for a few days before making any decisions.'

'I agree entirely,' responded Mary, 'except that we need to keep an eye on what exactly is going on in the current business. Someone has to be in charge of that.'

'I am unable to run the business and act as its legal representative,' said Bob.

'I am happy to keep doing what I do,' ventured Jessie.

'Then if you report to me in the interim, until we decide on a future,' Mary looked composed.

'That's fine,' said Peter.

'In the meantime I will try to gain an insight into how and why Rui made such brilliant business decisions.' Michael was secretly hoping Rui himself was going to give him the necessary information, 'but what I really need is half an hour outside just for some fresh air and to clear my mind.'

'Then why don't you walk round to Seventy Three, it's about half an hour away and we will join you there about one fifteen?' said Bob, looking at his watch.

'Fine,' said Jessie, before Michael could speak, 'and I will show you the way.' Michael wasn't sure he wanted company, but Jessie had seemed insistent, and he certainly wanted to keep her onside. She had turned down two and a half billion pounds in cash in favour of investing in and staying with the group. She certainly had more faith than Michael.

They said goodbye to the others and took the elevator forty floors down to ground level. They stopped one floor down for a smart, middle aged man to join them, so conversation was restricted.

Outside, Jessie turned along Park Avenue.

They were approaching the junction with East 61st Street when ahead of them what sounded like a gunshot rang out. A masked man ran from a store on the corner brandishing a gun, and turned to fire again at a woman who came out of the shop screaming at him. He missed, and continued towards Michael and Jessie, vaguely aiming the gun in their direction. Michael stood sideways on to the gunman on the edge of the kerb, as if trying to get out of the way. He moved Jessie slightly to the right, just behind him. He did not look directly at the gunman, but could see his progress in the windows facing Park Avenue. Suddenly everything seemed to go into slow motion. Into his mind came 'Stop. Immobilize. Disarm. Accomplice.' These thoughts came more as images than words. As the gunman approached, Michael stiffened his right arm down by his side. A second away from him, the gunman was in his peripheral vision. At the last moment Michael's arm swung up as fast as he was able, and he caught the gunman straight in the throat. Stop. The gunman left the ground as the speed of the blow coupled with his own speed exerted maximum force on his neck. Michael folded both his knees and dropped. Right knee straight into the stomach, left knee onto the bottom of the sternum. He heard ribs break. Immobilize. He grabbed the gun and pointed it back towards the shop. Disarm. There was no accomplice, only the woman from the shop staring at what had happened, and some pedestrians, wide eyed in disbelief. He pointed the gun at its owner and got to his feet. Time seemed to revert back to normal.

'Jesus Christ, you don't piss about,' Jessie was getting her mobile phone out.

Michael didn't feel anything for a few seconds, waiting for the adrenalin rush to subside.

Jessie was on the phone. 'Police and ambulance to the corner of East 61st and Park Avenue.' She went on to give a description of what had happened, finishing with 'the guy looks dead to me.'

She gave her name and address, and before she had finished speaking they could hear sirens arriving.

The traffic had all stopped to see what was going on. A patrol car arrived seconds before an ambulance. Two policemen flew out of the car with guns raised. 'Drop the gun,' shouted the driver, 'kick it towards me.'

Michael suddenly realised it was him the cop was shouting at. He laid the gun down and kicked it along the path and into the gutter. The driver's partner collected it. 'Now lay down on your front with your arms behind your back.' As Michael complied, an ambulance arrived. Two medics knelt by the gunman. The woman felt for a pulse and shook her head. Michael then lost sight of what was happening as he was handcuffed. The two policemen hauled him to his feet and bundled him into the back of the police car.

'Are you with him?' one of them shouted at Jessie. She was still talking on the phone, but nodded her reply. 'In the back with him,' shouted the driver.

'Where are you taking us?' she asked, still holding the phone to her ear.

'Mind your own business,' came the reply.

Michael could hear bits of her conversation on the phone. She looked at the car and he heard her say, 'The number is…' but the driver shouting at her to get in the car drowned out the rest.

Another police car drew up and the occupants conferred with their colleagues and the ambulance crew. They were still working on the gunman.

The two policemen who were first on the scene returned to the car, and the driver's partner turned to look at them. 'Now, what the hell happened here?'

Jessie gave a quick version of what had happened, pointing to the woman who had come from the shop and was still staring in amazement at the scene in front of her. The driver got out and went to speak to her. He then walked back with her to the shop, and came out a minute later. She had a coat on and they walked down to the ambulance crew. She spoke to them, then joined Jessie and Michael in the back of the car.

'Are you OK with the handcuffs for five minutes?' the driver asked Michael.

'What's the alternative?' he replied.

'It's only five minutes to the station and I can take them off there. I'm not sure about taking a chance on you.' He pulled away from the kerb.

'Then it's OK,' said Michael.

'No, it's not,' shouted Jessie, 'he's the hero, not the bloody villain.'

'That's for us to decide,' said the driver's partner.

Jessie could feel the woman from the shop shaking next to her. She took hold of the woman's hand and squeezed it gently. 'It's all over now.'

The woman was half sobbing and half talking. 'He could have killed me. I can't believe I chased him out of the shop.'

'What happened in there?' Jessie let go of her hand.

'He threatened the owner and grabbed money from the till,' she replied.

'Were you a customer?'

'No... I work there part time. I was just so mad,' the woman shuddered. 'He took a shot at me inside the store when I shouted at him, then another one when we got outside.' She started shaking again.

Jessie turned to Michael. 'I phoned Bob, and gave him the number of this car. He said he can find out where we are going and meet us there.'

'Bob who, that can trace police cars?' queried the driver's partner.

'Bob Haynes, a lawyer, though why I should tell you I can't think,' snarled Jessie.

'Jeez,' sighed the driver, 'how the hell do you know him?'

'In his own words to me this morning, he works for me, or to put it more accurately he works for Michael here,' Jessie's voice had lost some of its anger.
'Who the hell is Bob Haynes?' the driver's mate turned to face his partner.
'One of the top lawyers in New York,' was the reply.
'And this morning you…'
'We were at a funeral service,' interrupted Jessie, 'for Michaels Mum and Dad.'
'Jeez,' again from the driver. 'I am sorry, son. We are just about to pull into the station yard and I can get you out of those cuffs.'
Inside the police station the driver kept his word, unlocked the handcuffs and asked the three of them to take a seat. He went over and talked to the station Sergeant, who looked as if he was an actor in a TV police series. Just under six feet tall, he was well overweight and had just a touch of Irish in his New York accent.
'How long are you going to keep us here?' the woman from the shop was starting to feel better.
The station Sergeant glanced over. 'You can be first.'
The driver came over. 'Please come with me so we can get your version of what happened on the record,' he led her down a passageway and into a side room.
Michael had said nothing since he had hit the gunman, apart from his brief conversation with the police car driver. He turned to look at Jessie. 'Did you…'
'I don't know what happened,' she interrupted. 'I just seemed to feel your emotions from the time we heard the gunshot until the police arrived.'
'But did you want me to hit him?'
Jessie nodded. 'It all seemed to be happening so fast, and then time stood still for a minute or two. I think it was me who wanted to hit him, but it might have been me wanting you to hit him. It was a really strange sensation.'

The double doors to the station were pushed open and a policeman entered holding a woman by the arm. She was looking at the floor and he led her across to the counter in front of the Sergeant. 'This one was acting drunk and disorderly in the park. I think we need to lock her up for a spell.'
The station Sergeant looked up. 'Don't think so.' He smiled for the first time since Michael had entered the premises. 'Hello Brenda.'
The woman slowly raised her head.
'Ah,' said the Sergeant, 'I thought it was you.'
He sighed heavily and looked at his colleague. 'This is Brenda Casey. Just sit her down whilst I make a call.'
He picked up the phone, and the policeman turned Brenda to come and sit next to Michael and Jessie.
Brenda's face went from profile to full face as she neared Michael, and her vacant expression suddenly changed as her eyes locked onto his. She was probably about thirty, close to five foot six, with blonde hair in a ponytail at the back and a fringe at the front. Michael thought she looked pretty, but as their eyes met his stomach churned. It was similar to the feeling he had earlier with Jessie. Instead of words in his head, it was like thousands of cloudy pictures flashing by so fast that you had no time to see each one. He was left feeling terror, pain and sadness all rolled into one. Brenda was literally screaming for help inside his head. Nothing in his life had prepared him for the intense devastation he felt and he knew there was no other option but to help her in whatever way he could.
'Michael, what's wrong?' Jessie wore a worried look as she spoke.
As the policeman sat Brenda down next to Jessie, Michael lost eye contact with her. The intensity of the feelings subsided, but they were still there in his mind.
The station Sergeant put down the phone and walked round the counter towards the policeman who had brought Brenda in.

'Take her back to Century Fields. Do you know where it is?' he asked.
'Yeah,' was the short reply.
'Be nice to her,' said the Sergeant, 'I never thought she was guilty.'
Michael turned to look at Brenda again as the policeman gave her a hand up. Once again their eyes met, and there again was the intense pain and the cry for help. He thought his mind responded by offering to help her, but afterwards he could never be sure. 'Can I get you anything?' he asked, but by then she had disappeared through the double doors.
'What was wrong?' Jessie asked again. Michael shook his head. 'Where is Century Fields?'
Jessie shrugged. 'I've never heard of it.'
'Just outside Larchmont,' volunteered the Sergeant.
Michael looked up at him. 'What is it?'
'An institution for the criminally insane.' The Sergeant shrugged his shoulders.
'What did Brenda do?' Michael's brain was telling him not to get involved, but he knew it was too late.
'She was charged with killing her three year old daughter, but was sent to Century Fields as being not fit to plead.' The Sergeant was shaking his head as he spoke.
'And you think she didn't do it?' Michael whispered.
'It doesn't matter what I think. In four months I'm out of here with my pension intact.'
'What happened to you?' this time Jessie demanded a reply from Michael.
'You know back there with the gunman you could feel what was happening to me? Well, it just happened again,' Michael tipped his head back and looked at the ceiling, 'and I guess we can kiss lunch goodbye.'
As he finished speaking the doors swung open and Bob Haynes walked in.

He looked at Jessie. 'I believe 'I will show you the way' were the words you used. This is not Seventy Three.'
'Do you know anything about Century Fields, Bob?' Michael tried to keep his voice steady.
Bob looked as if he wanted to swear. 'Yes, it's a good place to steer clear of,' then, relaxing his expression, 'why do you ask?'
'We have a problem with one of the inmates,' Michael almost whispered.
'So was he the guy who got killed?' Bob looked as if he was losing patience.
'No, this one is there because she killed her daughter.' Michael was looking back at the ceiling as he spoke.
The door down the passageway opened and the woman from the shop came out, accompanied by the police driver and an older man in a grey suit. As they reached the reception area he called to the desk sergeant. 'Paddy, please arrange a lift back for Mrs. Sanchez.' He turned and shook her by the hand. 'Thanks for coming in. We will be in touch if we need anything else, but I doubt it. Look after yourself, and remember to hide in future, not chase.' Mrs. Sanchez managed a half smile and walked over to where Michael and Jessie were sitting.
'Thanks for helping me. I told them you should get a medal.'
Michael got up as she spoke and gently held her hand. 'I'm Michael, and this is Jessie. You were the brave one, chasing like that.'
'Or stupid, according to him,' she nodded in the direction of the grey suit, 'by the way, I am Monique, and thanks again.'
Bob introduced the grey suit. 'This is Detective Mitch Cameron; we've been friends for years. I expect he wants a word with both of you.' He nodded in the direction of the passageway.
'We should do this separately,' said Mitch, and in the direction of the Sergeant, 'did they say anything useful?' The Sergeant shook his head.
Bob nodded. 'Let's go by the book. Ladies first.'

He went off with Jessie, Mitch and the police driver. As they walked Mitch said, 'technically they should have been separated, but he has the sharpest ears in New York, and has solved a lot of crimes by listening in to people who think they can't be heard.'

As he waited, Michael reflected over the past twenty four hours. He had changed parents for ones who were supposed to be dead, but may be alive. He had become one of the richest men in the world. He had killed a man and become entangled with a woman who may have killed her daughter. And something had definitely altered in his brain. Like everyone, he had dreams and thoughts, but these two instances went far beyond that. He was still reflecting on the day when he realised Jessie and Mitch were stood beside him.

'Your turn,' said Mitch

Jessie just rolled her eyes in his direction.

'You were quick,' said Michael.

'Not much to talk about,' replied Jessie.

In the interview room was all the normal recording equipment and Mitch went through the standard procedures. He proceeded calmly through the sequence of events, taking notes, and Michael told him everything as it happened; only ignoring the thought sequence that had occurred within his head. Mitch agreed that it tied up with what Jessie and Monique had said.

'I will send in my report and in the meantime please bring in your passport until everything is tied up. I don't see any charges arising, but you may well receive a ticking off for using excessive force, just to pacify the do-gooders. Personally I think Monique is right, you should get a medal. Just two other things before you go. I can confirm that the guy you hit is dead. His name was Jaimie Spinetti, and he was a no good drug addict who had been in trouble all his life. A problem might be his big brother, Mikey, a really nasty piece of work who has spent a fair amount of time in jail, but not as much as he should have.

Although he is probably glad to be shot of Jaimie, family honour may mean he tries to get at you. Just keep your guard up until you finish your vacation.'
Bob had kept quiet all the way through the interview. 'Thanks for the warning, Mitch.'
Turning to Michael he smiled. 'Let's go get that lunch, and update Peter and Mary on your exciting life. I will give them a call to join us.'
Bob called a cab and the three of them were silent on the way to Seventy Three.
Michael's mind was a swirl of thoughts, mainly about Brenda and the vivid dream-like sequences that had run through his mind. He knew she was innocent, but he could not explain his thoughts to anyone without giving the appearance of being irrational. 'Bob, if you are able to find out all you can about Brenda Casey, who is in Century Fields, I would be very grateful.'
Bob smiled. 'You pay me a retainer of twenty million a year, you don't have to ask.'
He took out his mobile and spoke to his office. 'You will have everything by the end of the day.'
They were nearly two hours late for lunch and Michael was thankful for the large breakfast they had enjoyed. He was still famished when they arrived, and was surprised how busy the restaurant was half way through the afternoon.
They had only just sat down when Peter and Mary joined them. They were both very concerned about what had happened to Michael and Jessie, but Mary was especially worried. The conversation was interrupted as a waiter came to take their drinks order, and within five minutes the conversation was on hold again as the restaurant manager, Bernie Peterson, was saying hello to Jessie. She introduced the Kelly family to him, and it appeared that Bob already knew him well. 'How's trade?' asked Michael, thinking he should try to make the right noises.

'As ever, fully booked for the next three months and over eighty per cent for the following three. It has run like that for a long time now.' Bernie seemed pleased with his reply.
Jessie nodded slightly, as if in agreement.
'Now, what can I tempt you with this afternoon?' asked Bernie.
The lunch was delicious and most of the conversation centred around the run-in with Jaimie Spinetti.
Michael tried to make light of what had happened, but Mary was very concerned and told him to turn the other way in future and let someone else risk his or her life. Bob suggested they regroup back at his office and he would go through the main points about Rui and Jean. He checked with Michael that he was happy for his parents to sit in, which he readily agreed to.
Back at the office Bob took his customary place behind the desk and summarised what he had already told them about the empire. He had computer printouts available for them all, giving summaries of the one hundred and forty seven companies in the group. It was in descending order of current value and Michael noted that all had a company name followed by a 'trading as' name.
'All the companies were owned one hundred per cent by Rui and Jean, and now by Michael and Jessie. Each company runs to a formula that transfers what is considered excess cash to the two banks in the group. They again are formula controlled, maintaining cash in five different currencies, with the balance in short term lending. They have been untouched by the problems experienced worldwide by the larger banks. Again, I come back to my statement earlier that Rui seemed able to see what was going to happen tomorrow and take advantage of upswings and downswings. Have you anything to add to that Jessie?' Bob asked.
Jessie shook her head. 'They are all running well and are established businesses. Rui hasn't started anything for over a

year, he said there would be bargains to be had in the near future.'

'I suggest we start to work our way through the list. As I said before, I have set aside the rest of the week.' Bob's brow furrowed slightly as he spoke.

Michael concentrated as hard as he could, but his mother was the one asking all the pertinent questions and his mind drifted off a couple of times to Brenda and the vivid thoughts. They were interrupted once, when a young lady brought in an envelope for Bob. He read through it and passed it to Michael. It contained very full details of Brenda Casey, her life, (Michael noted she was twenty six), her marriage into an extremely rich old American family, the murder of her daughter, and subsequent incarceration. As the station Sergeant had told them, she had been declared unfit to plead.

Just after five Bob suggested they call it a day.

Michael wanted to get Jessie on her own and suggested they went back to her office together.

'Is it far?' he asked.

'One floor down,' she replied, 'we own this block.'

He explained that he wanted to see his future office, and agreed to meet his parents back at The Sandstone.

They all went in the lift together, with Jessie and Michael leaving one floor down.

The office suite was a lot smaller than Michael had expected. There was one office holding a dozen desks (of which eight were occupied), two other offices and a storeroom. Jessie introduced him to everyone, showed him Rui's office, which was fairly large, with the same stunning views that Bob enjoyed on the floor above, and then took him into her own office, which was identical.

She slumped in her chair. 'One hell of a day. What exactly happened to us?'

Michael sat opposite her. 'No, that's my question for you.'

Jessie looked him straight in the eyes. 'Jean and Rui seemed to be able to read other people's minds. When they took on staff, they knew within minutes whether the person was right or wrong and they always seemed to make the right decisions. Just occasionally I have had the same sensation as you, that I was feeling what was in their minds. It wasn't very often, but it happened with both of them. It was always when it was something very important.'
'Did you ever ask them about it?' Michael queried.
'One time recently when the feeling was really strong.' Jessie had screwed up her eyes as if she was trying to remember exact details.
'What were they talking about?'
'You taking over the business,' Jessie set her mouth in a thin line. 'What else did it say in the letter Bob gave you?'
'I hope I can answer that question within the next few days,' Michael tried to be discreet.
'After you have seen Rui?'
Michael gave Jessie a half smile. 'That question would mean that he is still alive.'
'So is Jean,' Jessie replied.
'That would be brilliant, and good for the business as well.' Michael was looking for a way out of the conversation.
'We have to work together and trust each other, Michael,' said Jessie.
'My belief is that they are both alive, but I am not one hundred percent sure.' At least I am telling the truth, Michael thought to himself. 'In the letter Rui said that I could trust both you and Bob one hundred percent, so I will only tell you the truth.'
'It's just happened again,' Jessie was shaking her head slowly, 'you are telling the truth. I felt it in your mind.'
'And you had the same with Rui and Jean?'
'Exactly the same. It seems a bit scary. Try to think something important,' Jessie waved her hands, trying to will Michael on.

'OK,' said Michael. He concentrated hard on what had happened when he hit the robber. Jessie looked straight into his eyes.
After a couple of minutes she shook her head. 'Nothing at all,' she exclaimed in frustration.
Michael shrugged. 'Let's just keep a note of when it happens, but make sure we always tell one another, whatever the consequences.'
Jessie nodded in agreement. 'Do you want to go through any more work, or call it a day?'
'If it's OK, I'll pack in now. I need to try and get my mind straight. What about you?'
'I'll probably do another hour or two and see you tomorrow.'
Michael rose to leave.
'Don't hit anyone on the way back to The Sandstone,' Jessie smiled at him.
'I promise,' whispered Michael.
He took the lift and on the journey down his mind was flicking from one thing to another. He wanted to get to grips with everything at once, but instead was sorting out nothing. 'A nice swim and a cold beer will probably be the best way to proceed,' he thought to himself.
Out in the street the light was just fading, but the pavements were well lit, mainly from the shop windows. He instinctively put his hands in his pockets, although it wasn't really cold, and as he did so an arm slid through between his elbow and his body, and squeezed his arm gently.
'Hello again, Michael.' He stopped and turned to see a smiling Jean grinning up at him. He flung his arms round her and hugged her as tightly as he dared. 'You survived! I thought you had, but there was always that slight doubt. This is wonderful, especially after the day I've had.'
'We both survived,' Jean tilted her head back to look up at him.
Instinctively Michael looked around for Rui.

'You will see him later.' Jean was still smiling.
'How did you know I was looking for Rui?'
'Jessie's not the only mind reader you have to contend with, except I can do it all the time. Make an excuse to come out later, the cinema or whatever, and get a taxi to this hotel.' She gave Michael a piece of hotel stationery with a room number written on it. 'About seven would be fine, but don't tell the others yet,' she reached up and kissed him on the cheek.
'Jessie already knows.' Michael raised his eyebrows.
'She's fine.' Jean squeezed his arm again and waved down a cab. As she got in she turned and waved. 'See you later,' she mouthed across to him. Michael's heart was pumping. He had been trying to sort out his mind before, but now it was running at one hundred miles an hour.
Back at The Sandstone, he asked at reception what was showing at the cinemas and picked out a title.
Upstairs he had a quick swim, then showered and changed, explaining to his parents that he was going out to see a particular film and would grab a bite to eat on the way. They were concerned, but he explained he would be taking a cab both ways and told them they deserved a nice meal on their own.
By twenty to seven he was back in the hotel reception and had a taxi ordered. The ride was quick and in less than fifteen minutes he was knocking on the door of his real parent's room.
Rui opened the door. He was much younger looking than Michael had expected, with dark hair and a tanned complexion. He looked different to the photos Michael had seen and he realised that the big bushy moustache had disappeared. Just about six foot, he was a lot slimmer than Michael. 'Come on in,' he beamed at Michael, grabbing his hand and shaking it as he pulled him into the room. 'It's great to meet you at last.'
It's a difficult thing to meet your father for the first time at age twenty two, but Michael broke the handshake and put both arms round Rui and held him tightly, just as he had done with Jean.

‘We have a lot of ground to cover,’ Michael whispered in his ear.
‘You have no idea how much,’ Rui replied.
‘Can I get you a drink?’ Jean stood up and walked towards him.
‘A beer, please,’ said Michael, ‘and something to eat if possible.’
‘They are serving us up here later, but one beer coming up in the meantime.’ Rui and Michael sat down and the awkward silence that comes with not knowing what to say was broken by Jean giving them both a beer and sitting down with them.
‘How did you survive the plane crash and what was in the coffins?’ Michael opened the conversation.
‘It’s part of a very long story.’ Rui smiled at him, ‘as for the crash, there are a couple of hospitals in the group and we had been waiting for a long time for male and female accident victims who fitted our size to come on the scene. As you probably know, all they found at the crash site was my arm, still wearing my Cartier wrist watch, and part of Jean’s leg with the engraved gold ankle bracelet. Both were badly burned. They were what was cremated.’
‘So you borrowed those parts from accident victims?’ Michael’s eyes widened.
‘It sounds gruesome, but hopefully it will all make sense in the end.’ Rui took a sip of his beer. He nodded at a side table. ‘I have some papers that you can take with you later, which will tell you about our past, but in the meantime let’s talk about the present and our futures.’
‘Just one more thing before that,’ Michael was curious, ‘can you and Jean read each other’s minds?’ Without thinking he looked at Jean. ‘I’m sorry; I should really call you Mum now.’
Jean looked across at Rui. ‘You are my son in my world, but would be my adopted son in this world.’
Before Michael could speak Rui butted in. ‘What did Jean just say?’

Michael repeated the words back.
Jean turned towards him. 'That's exactly what I was thinking, but I didn't speak.'
A cold shiver ran down Michael's spine. 'So I read your mind?'
'Yes.' The simple reply from Jean, coupled with the statement about 'her' world brought Michael up short.
'So you are not from Earth?'
'Jean and I are not from this Earth, but hopefully when you have read those papers it will all become clear.' Again Rui nodded towards the side table.
Further discussion was interrupted by a knock on the door.
Rui rose to open the door and an immaculate waiter pushing a hostess trolley entered. He crossed to the dining area and quickly had the table laid and dinner served. A magnum of Dom Perignon was opened and three glasses filled, then, bowing slightly, and with 'Enjoy your meal,' he was gone.
The food was very good, and the tension relaxed somewhat.
'One of my main worries is running the group, and especially making the right decisions.' Michael decided to stick to safer subjects.
Rui smiled. 'For the time being I will leave any recommendations on my, sorry your, computer in the office. Pass them by Jessie and she can instigate them.'
'And after for the time being?' Michael smiled back.
'By then you will know how to make the decisions.' Rui seemed positive.
'So how do you manage to get everything right? Bob was really impressed.'
'Imagine playing cards with someone and you were able to read his mind.' Michael's eyes widened again.
'Expand that to the world of business, coupled with knowing exactly where all the world's precious reserves are and at what depth. Oil, metals, you name it and we have the surveys to

pinpoint it.' Rui was shaking his head slowly, 'not really fair is it?'
'I suppose it depends on what you do with the proceeds.' Michael was getting stuck as to what to say.
Jean chipped in. 'That's the second part of the equation. Yes, we enjoy a lovely lifestyle, but the main aim is to spread the wealth more evenly and try to use it for good.'
'A sort of modern day Robin Hood?' Michael asked.
'Not quite the same. More to get world leaders elected who will try to run the world for the benefit of all the people, not just the rich minority,' Rui's face looked more serious.
'More like communism then?' Michael was trying to understand.
It was Jean's turn. 'A lot of people have had a dream of a world at peace, where there is no poverty or serious illness. That is what we are trying to achieve.'
Michael was stunned. 'I agree totally, but it's just not possible.'
'It has to be possible, because the alternative is unthinkable.' This time Jean looked really serious.
'So besides everything else, I will also save the world?' This time it was Michaels turn to shake his head.
'See,' Rui turned to face Jean. 'I knew we could rely on our son. He is just as good as Peter and Mary told us he was. All the problems solved… although seriously Michael, it is one hell of a task, but we believe it has to be possible. Hopefully when you have read those notes, you will believe it possible and worthwhile. We will meet on Saturday at the house in Hampton and you can tell us how you want to go forward. For now though, let's hear about growing up in England.'
Michael relaxed as he entered familiar conversation and it was well after ten when Rui ordered a taxi for him.
They hugged again before he left; feeling that he had at least started on the road to knowing his parents, or were they adoptive parents? He had forgotten to ask.

The large buff envelope felt hot in his hand and he started to worry about the enormity of the task his parents had set for him. Self doubt weighed heavily upon him, as although he agreed with the sentiments, he really thought the desired result was impossible. He fervently hoped there was some help or a solution in the notes Rui had given him, and he started reading as soon as he got into bed that night.

EARTH
The story of Mark and Maureen
A

Mark had entered the Memory Builder, where he received the bulk of his tuition, in good spirits that morning. He switched on the machine, which had already been set by the University to install directly into his brain the next lesson in his learning programme. He settled back into the easy chair and his lesson commenced. Mark felt his stomach muscles start to tighten as his breathing became shallower. There was no way he could help the other victims of the last missile attack. His legs were trapped beneath him and although he knew he should be trying to free himself, his eyes would not leave the young woman in front of him, clutching what was left of her baby with her one remaining arm.

He had never met her before, but in that one moment he loved her and the child more than anything in life. As the sickness forced its way through his parched throat, his lips formed the words "Stop the war," and his brain cut off any further pain.

Kneeling on the toilet floor with his stomach still heaving, Mark felt anger that his present condition could be cured instantly by a modern drug, but this thought was over-ridden by the certainty that what he had seen in the Memory Builder would never leave him and would make him unable to ever contemplate war or violence.

As his suffering subsided, he reflected on the past of his people. How the last of the Great Wars had reduced both sides to the very brink of extinction. How, just in time, the leaders had realized that to continue would mean that both sides had lost.

The meetings that had resulted in the "Declaration of the Future" all those thousands of years ago and had formed the present existence of the whole universe. The primary declaration, although recognising the opposing beliefs, stated that never again would war or violence be tolerated; that truth was sacrosanct and that the total knowledge of each group should be available to the other.

The intention of that primary declaration had been upheld and the only contest now was to sway the minds of the other believers.

The total population was limited to what was then seen as an easily supportable number. One hundred times that amount could now be supported, but the discussions on whether the limit should be changed had been running for hundreds of years and were one of the few distractions to the eternal struggle to recruit the minds of the opposition.

He wondered briefly what it must have been like in that first era of peace, when the finest genes were used in the production of babies to ensure the continuation of the races. How each side had concentrated on developing the minds to the exclusion of all else and then passing those minds and memories directly into the next generation. It was now possible to prolong life beyond two hundred years, but most people entered the rebirth chambers at about one hundred, when the body was beginning to suffer too many aches and pains that could only be eased by stronger and stronger drugs.

That exit also meant that the next couple on the waiting list could have "their" child. In the first days of peace, that child had the total knowledge and memory of the person who had entered the rebirth chamber. He or she knew that they would be able to live forever in that re-created way. Those minds became brilliant and totally non creative.

The desire to stimulate new ideas had resulted in one of the major alterations to the Declaration of the Future: that no memories could be preserved beyond death. The immediate result had been a drop in the use of rebirth chambers and there had even been talk of compulsory euthanasia, but a small amendment had allowed name retention, which gave the impression of eternal life, so anyone could trace himself or herself back through many previous generations.

As he left for home that evening, Mark felt an elation he had never experienced before. Today's session in the Memory Builder had been the last in the compulsory series designed to eradicate in everyone all feelings of violence or hostility and he knew that tomorrow he had a free choice programme. He understood the need to maintain the world in it's present form, where the "perfect" society had been created, a world where sickness was unknown and injury extremely rare. Crime had long since gone. Work was a thing of the past. Robot workers, who maintained and eventually replaced themselves, provided every necessity of life. A world where the atmosphere was controlled, where pollution did not exist, where poverty and hunger no longer raised their ugly heads. A world where, after a history session in the Memory Builder, he had remarked that they had created the "Green Dream;" a reference to a political group of the pre-war, as everyone called the time before the last Great War. No one at the University had appreciated the comment, and as his elation subsided, Mark realised that the small, almost dream like part of his mind that had niggled him before, was telling him the truth, that no-one actually cared. Yes, they had the greatest minds that had ever lived, men who could play three dimensional chess without a board, just using thought transfer; women who's brain capacity was so enormous that they could relate exactly any piece from any book ever written; pianists who could play different pieces perfectly for ever; and none of them cared. As long as the world did not change, 'perfection' was maintained. There had to be something else. There was the eternal struggle to find a way to convince the opposition that they were wrong, but would anything change anyway? A cold shiver brought goose pimples onto his arms. These thoughts were almost treason, but he knew that something in life was missing. A feeling much like panic gripped him. If his feelings were real, then the very knowledge that they existed meant his acceptance of life was a lie; a thought in direct conflict to the primary declaration; something to be reported to the local committee. But if what he felt was the truth, then the world that he lived in was the lie, and should he then report a truth? He tried to analyse his thoughts. If he felt that there was something missing in life, then there had to be change. There had been no changes to life for thousands of years. Even the introduction of the law on retaining memories at birth had brought no new ideas that he knew of and had certainly changed nothing. So, was it possible that he was having a new idea, that he was intended to think differently, that he was not thinking a lie, that he need not report himself, as no one had ever done before him? Comforted by this arrangement of his thoughts, he waved to his mother as he entered the apartment and told her that he would be going to the party discussion that evening.

The term 'mother' had lost its historical concept before the time of the last Great War, as no one was expected to accept any form of unnecessary pain and all babies had been created in hospitals, although the 'parents' could select the genes that would help in the creation of their child. Immediately after the war, that right had been suspended in an effort to produce perfection. The resultant children had been placed with parents who matched most closely the requirements of that child.

That 'suspension' was something that had never changed.

He could relate well to his parents as he, like them, had been created to look at history, in the hope that something could be learnt that would give a slight edge to his side in the eternal conflict. His evenings were normally spent discussing what the Memory Builder had taught him that day, or accompanying one or both of them to the party discussion. Was he close enough to his parents to discuss his feelings that something was wrong? A fear that he might be the one who was wrong made him wary of bringing up the subject head on. He would try to introduce it to them gradually.

His father was in excellent spirits when he came home. He had served on the local committee as a history adviser for one year, one of the few distinctions in life. Mark knew immediately what his happiness meant, although his father could not tell him in advance of that evening's local open meeting. The party share of the population had increased.

As they entered the hall that night, Mark knew that he had guessed correctly. Everyone was smiling and talking excitedly about the future. The chairman's opening remark that "the latest opinions are that we have increased our share of the following of the people by thirty three to give us over fifty percent of total populace" was greeted with great applause. Mark could not help feeling that although this was happening in another hundred meetings, the opposition was hearing a similar loss situation, and that in three months time the next opinions would show the reverse to be the case. Just occasionally, one side increased twice in succession, but it had not happened in his twenty years of life.

The meeting heard reports from all the committee on their ideas to encourage the opposition to join them and would then break up into small working groups to discuss these ideas.

As he walked with his parents to the history lecture theatre, he noticed a new face in the discussion group entering the hall. He touched his father's elbow and asked why he had never seen the girl with the black hair before. His father's smile expanded as he replied 'wait for the announcement.' So, there had been a double reason for his father's earlier excellent spirits.

As the group settled down, his father took the lecturer's rostrum and announced that tonight, instead of looking at history, they may be making it. He explained that in another history group adjacent to theirs, a young lady had suggested that it may be beneficial to encourage new ideas by members visiting other groups as guests, and tonight he welcomed Maureen Adams as the young lady in question. The girl with the black hair took the rostrum to polite applause. Mark glanced around him. This was the most significant thing that had ever happened in the lives of all these people, yet there was no questioning, no surprise, just a total acceptance of the situation. He inwardly revised his previous assessment of his fellows. It was not that they didn't care. They didn't know how to care. He glanced back to the front of the hall as Maureen began a short speech. His mind suddenly exploded as he realised the implications of what had happened. She had thought of an original idea and had carried it out. But that was impossible. Like the idea of increasing the population, it would have to be dealt with by the full council and would never be agreed upon in a lifetime, so how had she..? He picked up the words 'and so tonight I intend only to come as a guest, to listen and learn so that I might take any new ideas back to my own group.' Once again the polite applause and his father offering a warm 'thank you' for having chosen their group.

Mark knew he had to talk to her, if only to find out how she had managed to have her idea accepted. Something told him to be very careful. He was entering an area he did not understand, and he had never seen black hair like that on someone with such a pale skin. As the formal meeting was ending he would take his chance. Most people stood in groups waiting for the time to re-enter the main party meeting. He missed the rest of the speeches as his mind wrestled with the question; how did she get a discussion on her idea? He suddenly realized that people were moving about and he had not even thought about an opening remark, or how to tell her that he felt different. He found himself on the edge of the little group surrounding Maureen, and almost stuttering 'Good evening Miss Adams. I hope you will let me return the complement you have paid us by visiting your group next time.'

Maureen detached herself from the group of people and guided Mark to an area away from the rest. As she turned to face him he felt he was looking through her eyes into a world he had never dreamed of. He felt his flesh crawl as he tried to focus on her face. 'My name is Mark. My father is leader of the historical group.' His words seemed stilted, but there was little else he could think of.

'What do you study in free periods?' her voice was level and calm. Suddenly there was so much he wanted to ask her. Did she feel different? Why was her hair so black? Why did no-one else seem to care?

Instantly her mind reached into his. This was unheard of! Thought transference was acceptable when pre-agreed, such as for chess and collective working sessions, but uninvited! His panic subsided as her thoughts gently eased his mind. 'I am sorry, but I had to be sure.'

As Mark's mouth opened to reply, Maureen said softly. 'Please answer my questions and we can talk about other things in the future.' There was part threat, part warning and part tenderness in the gentle statement.

'History,' replied Mark.

'On your next free choice, select biology,' said Maureen. 'Try this reference.' She pressed a piece of card into his hand. 'Let me know when you would like to attend our next meeting.'

As Mark searched for a reply Maureen was gently guided away from him.

He glanced at the card in his hand. On it was written 'Biology' followed by a long reference number, together with her personal contact number.

As he raised his eyes, Maureen was leaving the hall, but glanced his way and smiled. Once again his flesh was creeping and he wanted to run and stop her from leaving, to tell her he understood, to tell her... As she left he realized that he understood nothing, but he wanted to know.

That night in bed his mind twisted and turned as he wondered what the biology reference number was going to reveal to him. The origin of everything? A wonder drug to prolong life even further? A breakthrough in gene culture? As he drifted into sleep, his last thought was: why was her hair such a different colour to normal?

Next morning his father was still in excellent spirits and Mark felt that he must have been affected by the presence of Maureen, but it soon became obvious that it was the lead in the opinion polls that mattered to him.

Mark ventured that he would be going to Maureen's group to see if he could gain anything useful. Both his parents thought it was a good idea, but the full committee would have to give permission. Mark pondered on this as he left for his studies.

Although time in the Memory Builder helped to take his thoughts from Maureen, as the mind was very quickly taken over by the lesson, Mark was left with the in between periods to again wonder what the magical biology reference was going to tell him. It had seemed to be the longest time in his life until the last period of the day, but that free period eventually arrived and he entered the door of the Memory Builder which was allocated for his studies. His excitement was at fever pitch as he punched in the commands Maureen had given him.

The machine quickly took control of his mind and he was standing on a road bridge over a river that ran into the distance towards the square tower of a church. The main teaching aid of the Memory Builder was that the student did not have to read or listen. He was part of the programme and therefore knew everything contained within it, which in turn became part of his memory. He was approaching a small wooden style next to a sign marked ‘footpath.’ As he walked along, his senses were bombarded with the sight and smell of the wild flowers, and on his left a cottage garden full of daffodils was a yellow carpet of beauty. A sudden movement caused him to jump, as an Old

English sheepdog bounded against the gate let into the fence surrounding the cottage. His inbuilt terror at seeing a live animal for the first time in his life was quickly calmed by the Memory Builder, and although his history course had briefly explained that animals were the greatest carriers of disease in the pre-war, he found himself reaching over the gate to make a fuss of the dog, which looked up at him with one pale blue and one pale brown eye. His hand felt the gentleness of the long hair and moved down the side of the dogs face. Suddenly a big pink tongue was noisily licking at his hand, but instead of revulsion he felt that he had just made a friend for life.

Passing the cottage, he turned his head to see a lapwing performing the most incredible display of stunt flying. He sat on the bank and thrilled to the most wonderful sight he had ever imagined. Twice he feared the bird would crash head first into the river, but each time it managed to flick itself out of trouble, and almost laugh at him with a strange pee-wit call.

Again, his eyes followed a movement at the edge of his vision. Swimming in front of him were a dozen mullet, on their way further up the river.

He was in paradise as he sat on the bank, never wanting the moment to end. He glanced up the river again and saw that the sun was starting to set, burning the water to a deep orange and the sky to a... His fury exploded. Who had put electricity cables across a valley like this? He had not noticed them earlier from the bridge, but now in the setting sun the wires stood out against the natural beauty like...

Suddenly he was back in the entrance part of the Memory Builder. It had aborted the programme. He knew it was possible, but never imagined it could really happen. The screen in front of him read ‘The high intensity of feeling in your mind prompted a premature close. Please discuss this with your advisor.’

As far as this was concerned, Mark knew immediately the advisor he would discuss it with. Although she was not an official, Maureen had occasioned his visit, and had produced in him the most intense feelings that he had ever experienced, albeit feelings that turned so quickly from pleasure to anger. Anger that anything so beautiful could have been so thoughtlessly altered by man.

He was still seething when he entered the apartment and picking up the videophone he punched in the private number Maureen had given him. Her face appeared on screen, but it was a recorded message that apologised for her absence. He was about to try and explain his feelings when Maureen went on to say 'if it's you calling Mark, please just agree to meet me tonight at the entrance to your classes at six thirty.' Mark left a message that he would be there and wandered through to the kitchen. His mother looked up and asked, 'what's wrong?'

Immediately Mark's mind put him on the defensive. Everything was wrong, but how could he even start to explain to his mother what had happened in the last twenty-four hours?

'I'm fine, Mum,' he replied, 'I was just deep in thought about today's session in the Memory Builder.' Another lie?

'Tea will be in about half an hour when your father gets home,' said his mother.

Mark glanced at his watch. Just before five. Time for a shower and change before tea, then it was only a short walk before he met Maureen; and why was her hair so black?

He was so excited at the prospect of seeing her again that he found it difficult to concentrate on the conversation of his parents. He wanted to bolt the food down and leave early, but knew that if Maureen had said six thirty he might just as well enjoy his tea and arrive on time. As it was, he was waiting outside the classes at ten past six. He was feeling slightly breathless at the prospect of seeing her again, although he had walked the short distance from the apartment slowly and was in prime physical condition. He made a mental note to have a check up in case he needed drugs of any kind. His mind flicked back to the free period in the Memory Builder and his automatic assumption that he had not reached the important point of the teaching before the programme had been aborted. Perhaps he should have re-entered and tried again. He knew, however, that the message to contact his advisor should take preference. He was still wondering what he had missed when a tug on his sleeve and the words 'Hey, daydreamer,' brought him back to reality.

It was Maureen, definitely, and yet with brown hair. His expression of amazement caused her to giggle and him to blush, another thing he had never experienced before.

'How...' his words tailed off as she giggled again and linked her arm through his.

'Come on, we'll walk through the park.' The nearest park was a perfect garden, much like all the others, with the flowers in regimented rows. As each flower died it was replaced, by a robot worker, with an identical new plant so that the perpetual beauty was never altered.

'The flowers are beautiful,' remarked Maureen.

'Yes, but not...' began Michael

'I know,' interrupted Maureen, 'but we can talk about that later.'

'Everything was "later" with her,' thought Mark, but he had to admit that just walking along with her had made his breathlessness vanish. He was just not sure what had replaced it.

Ignoring any seats, Maureen guided him onto the grass and they sat down facing each other.

'Now,' said Maureen, 'tell me why you contacted me at the meeting.'

Suddenly a cold chill passed through Mark. His defences were alerted. What if Maureen was not a friend? She might be investigating him. His previous thought that something was wrong, that things might be lies, that he had not reported himself to the committee; that she might be from the committee! His horror at the electricity cables across the valley, when he knew

that science maintained their present perfect world. What if she had lied to him? He had never imagined that he could think that of anybody. It was unthinkable, and yet he had thought it of her.
Maureen waited patiently. 'Look into my eyes, Mark.'
He raised his head to look at her. 'Please enter my mind.' With that simple statement she ended all his doubts, and although he slowly shook his head, she smiled.
'I apologise,' said Mark, 'I should not have doubted you. It's just that so much seems to have happened so quickly. There is so much that seems wrong. Why are our gardens all the same and in straight lines? Why are there no birds or animals? Why does nobody care? Why do we never talk to people from the other side? Why is somebody telling lies in direct contravention of the prime directive, and why was your hair so black?"
Maureen burst out laughing, 'which question was first?'
Mark felt the laughing was at him, but joined in. 'All of them' was his reply, 'but why did you make it black?'
Maureen's expression changed to one more serious, and again the goose pimples arrived on Michael's arms.
'You are at a crossroads, Mark. I can answer nearly all the questions, but if I do you will never return to the life you have known. Yes, you will still live at home but you will live a permanent lie for years. You will have more knowledge than you ever thought possible but may never use any of it. Believe me, it will be difficult. I know because it is the life I lead. Alternatively you can return to the happy life you led up until a month ago, with no worries or effort.'
'Do I lose you?' Mark's question surprised him. He had been offered an amazing choice and his first thought had been Maureen. Maureen smiled. 'I knew I was right, you are coming with me. It is imperative that you discuss our meeting with no one. Present this envelope to your adviser for delivery to the committee. You can read the contents.'

Mark opened the small buff envelope and read the contents. It was a letter from him to the committee.
'Please note that I shall attend lectures in different groups to further my education, unless the committee disagrees.'
'Easy, isn't it?' smiled Maureen.
'They will discuss it forever,' laughed Mark.
'Now let's drink to celebrate our meeting.' Maureen passed him one of the standard orange drinks available everywhere.
'Thanks, but I really prefer lemon, the orange is too sweet,' replied Mark, although he took the proffered container.
'The taste doesn't matter. It's the contents, or the additions to them that really count.'
Again Mark felt slight apprehension, but this was quickly surpassed by his previous acceptance of Maureen. 'I'm taking added drugs?' he questioned.
'No, you are having previous drugs reduced.'
Mark stopped drinking. 'Then you are wrong somehow. I have had no drugs for years now.' Then, as his memory jogged him, 'although earlier today I thought of going for a full check up because I was quite breathless when I was waiting to see you.'
Again the giggling from Maureen. 'I will explain that later.'
'Again,' thought Mark, 'later.'
Suddenly her expression changed to one so serious that Mark thought he may have upset her. 'You have been drugged every day from birth,' said Maureen, 'as has everyone else.'
'But that is a kind of lie,' retorted Mark, 'and as such is in direct contravention of the primary declaration that truth is sacrosanct.'
'Now, my history professor,' chided Maureen, 'what was the greatest event in the history of our people?'
'The last of the Great Wars, or the fact that it stopped just in time?' Mark immediately felt an expression of puzzlement cross his face. The first part of his reply was the set standard, so why had he added a rider to it?

‘There was no last great war. Look into my eyes Mark. Enter my mind. Accept the truth.’ Later, Mark convinced himself that he would have accepted the truth without the mind link, but he was never quite certain.

‘But what about the opposition?’

‘There is no opposition,’ replied Maureen.

In two short sentences she had destroyed history as he knew it and the whole reason for the existence of the population.

‘You have much to learn,’ said Maureen, ‘and it will be more exciting than you can imagine.’

Suddenly her manner changed again as she stood up, pulling Mark with her. ‘I will make the necessary arrangements for your tutorials but in the meantime, one of the 'later' moments has arrived.’

‘Stand close and face me.’

Mark prepared to enter her mind again, but the next order threw him completely.

‘Put your arms around me and press your lips gently to mine.’

Although thinking Maureen was slightly crazy, Mark complied with her request.

The tip of her tongue trembled its way between his closed lips and immediately the goose pimples he had felt before covered his body; the previous breathlessness was now a total breakdown of his lungs and the short blush was now a top to toe beetroot colour.

Maureen eased herself away from him and again the smile and giggles enchanted him.

‘That is called a kiss,’ was her simple explanation, ‘and you do not need to go for a check up.’

As he stood awkwardly, trying to regain regular breathing, a million thoughts rushed through Mark's mind, but uppermost was the knowledge that he would have traded his world for that kiss, and hopefully another.

‘Remember, you have entered a different world.’ Again Maureen was serious. ‘Please do not try to discuss what has happened with anyone but me, or the people I shall introduce you to. It will be very difficult, but I know you can do it. I must leave you now but will be in touch very soon.’

‘Can't I come with you now?’ Mark didn't want to rely on a 'very soon.’

‘That's not possible at the moment, but believe me; I shall see you again soon.’

Mark knew what he had to ask, but again felt the colour coming to his cheeks. ‘Please can I ... would it be possible ...would you...’

Suddenly Maureen was laughing again. ‘OK, but this time just open your mouth slightly.’ Maureen moved her lips against his as they kissed, and for the first time, her tongue touched his. Her mouth then gently drew his tongue between her lips, which applied a slight pressure. Again Mark was taken on a wild journey that ended with the now familiar goose pimples and breathlessness.

B

Maureen smiled as she let herself into her apartment. The kisses had been part of the programme for Mark, but she had to admit that she had enjoyed them both. Was it possible that she...? She immediately dismissed the thought as irrelevant.

After dinner she made her way to the university and entered a room marked 'Private - Special Meeting'. A quick glance confirmed that the other sixteen were there. Joanne, who had been the original member, smiled and opened the meeting with, 'most important things first, did we find anyone out there?' Maureen rose at the same time as two other members, Paula and Elena. 'Right Elena,' said Joanne, 'you start.'

'A twenty-four year old studying maths.' she replied. 'He got up the river as far as the new bridge before the programme aborted. His anger was over the size of the construction for the width of the river and unnecessary use of resources. The kiss didn't seem to do much for him.'

Maureen rose and reported on Mark's trip up the river and his fall at the first hurdle. She then felt herself blush as she described the kisses, finishing with 'I think he may work.'

Paula had a similar description of Nicky, finishing with 'But one of you men can try the kiss test on her.'

They all laughed. Joanne said 'do you think they will be able to join us?'

Three affirmatives followed, and Joanne confirmed that they should soon be up to twenty in number.

Maureen let her thoughts run on to the new world that Mark would soon discover. Not only did he have to re-learn all history, but some of the alterations to the present would seem impossible at first. She glanced up as Joanne sought confirmation, saying 'so we are agreed that they will attend tomorrow's meeting. We had better have a two o'clock start.' When she had returned to the apartment, Maureen used the videophone and dialled Mark's personal number. She had guessed correctly that he would have arrived back from the evening meeting. 'Hi Mark.' His delight at the call was obvious as he told her he had been worried she wouldn't call. 'Your first lecture in a different group will be tomorrow at two. How would you like to spend the morning with me instead of using the Memory Builder?' She knew the reply before he agreed. 'I will meet you at the university, near your class's entrance at about nine. Look forward to seeing you in the flesh.' The standard videophone ending suddenly seemed to take on another meaning to them both and the call finished with laughing on both sides.

Next morning, Maureen was first to arrive, only a minute before Mark, and she greeted him with the words 'look, I even remembered to get you lemon this time.'

'I really don't need a drink at the moment,' said Mark, then looking at Maureen's face he added 'but I expect I'm going to have this one.'

'Right,' smiled Maureen, 'from today all your eating and drinking will be controlled by me. Tell your parents that you are undertaking special food and drink for your group. They will be quite happy. We have all this morning to ourselves, and I will try to explain some of the puzzles that have been going through your mind. You will find that most of what you have been told is untrue, but that it was originally done with the best of intentions. No one had ever questioned what they had been told, until about fifteen years ago a woman called Joanne felt that things were not correct and started to try and find the truth.'

'I have never heard of anyone ever questioning the system before,' Mark's interest was acute. 'I would like to meet her.'

'At two o'clock your wish will come true,' Maureen smiled, 'but don't expect too much of her; she is just like you and me, but the rest of us feel she is special.'

'Rest of us?' queried Mark.

‘At the moment there are seventeen of us and the three new recruits, including you, make twenty.’
Mark suddenly felt a bit deflated. Up to that moment the two of them had been special, now they were only two of twenty. ‘New recruits?’ he ventured.
‘You have been fed drugs from birth, as I told you before,’ said Maureen. ‘Over the past month we have gradually reduced the quantities to see if anyone starts to question what is happening. We have a set formula now. We approach other groups, which is in itself a gigantic happening for the people in those groups. We dye our hair to an unnatural colour to make us stand out like sore thumbs and we drop hints in our address to the group if no one has queried our presence.’
‘So your hair was black for that reason.’
‘Yes, do you think it suited me?’
Mark suddenly realised what he had felt was an interest in Maureen's appearance, something that had never concerned him before in any other woman. ‘I think the brown is better, but we are talking about feelings between a man and a woman, which are of a sexual nature, and sex problems sometimes caused wars.’
‘And religion. And wealth. And power. And drugs, which you have been taking all your life, so why not discuss the others?’
Mark felt uncomfortable. ‘But you said you were giving us the drugs.’
‘No.’ replied Maureen, ‘I said we had reduced the quantities added to the water supply in the first place. Maybe I am not making myself as clear as I should. I am trying to give you a brief idea of the changes that are going to happen to your ideas of history and the future. Up to the period just after the second of the Great Wars, history as you understand it is not far from the truth, but then events took a different course. You will find from the Memory Builder the exact course of events, but suffice to say, at the moment, that there had always been conflict -

black and white, rich and poor, capitalists and communists, different religions, but mainly the oppressor and the oppressed. The world was full of these problems when two groups decided, at the same time, on a course of action which had catastrophic results. Not the third and final war as you have been taught, but a simple solution to a major problem. However, you will discover much of that in the Memory Builder. Let's try you with a few questions about the present. How many of us live here?'

'I, I, I'm not sure,' stuttered Mark. He felt acute embarrassment that such a simple query had never crossed his mind. 'I suppose about two hundred thousand or so,' he guessed.

'So how big is this place we live in?' responded Maureen. 'One mile across, twenty miles across, one hundred miles across?'

Mark knew that people were not cramped in at all and ventured, 'fifty miles across.'

'So that would be the furthest we could travel in any direction?' said Maureen.

Mark knew instinctively that he was way out. He tried again. 'Well, say two hundred miles across.'

'Wrong way,' laughed Maureen, 'there are less than one thousand of us and this so called city is less than two miles across.'

'But we would see the edges,' Mark interrupted,' I know we have to live in a dome, but at that size the sides would be visible.'

'One of the great inventions you will discover in your time in the Memory Builder is the Bendelec,' said Maureen. 'It is one of the prime examples of the rings. Nothing can be a straight line, so it must be a curve. If it is a curve, it must eventually form a ring. Everything forms a ring.'

'But light is a straight line.' Mark was sure of his facts.

'As I told you before, you will have a lot to learn and a lot to unlearn and that is one of the things to unlearn.' Maureen giggled at her choice of words and Mark laughed with her.

‘As I know I can trust you totally, I believe that you believe what you are telling me,’ he grinned.
‘But,’ went on Maureen, ‘I may be wrong. Turn ninety degrees right and tell me what you see.’
‘The path we are on goes into the distance,’ replied Mark.
‘And next to the path?’ queried Maureen.
‘Grass, flower beds and some trees in the distance.’
‘Right, walk over and touch the nearest tree,’ demanded Maureen.
‘But I would have to cross the grass, and we always walk on the paths.’
‘We walked and sat on the grass before,’ said Maureen.
‘Yes, I worried about that at the time,’ replied Mark, and then, realizing that nothing had happened before, set off across the grass. He walked straight towards one of the trees, although from behind his progress was more in the shape of an arc.
‘Now stop,’ directed Maureen, ‘and put out your left arm as far as you can.’
Mark glanced back at her with an expression that said ‘I will try, to please you, but this is really stupid,’ and raised his arm.
‘Now look at your left hand.’
He turned his head very slowly as if he was going to see nothing, and immediately snatched back his arm in terror as it did indeed end in nothing, from the elbow down. He looked down at his hand, which was solid enough again. Gingerly he poked his hand towards where it had disappeared before and sure enough his fingers, then hand, then wrist, just disappeared.
‘Now come back to me,’ called Maureen.
‘I just want to...’
‘Come back now.’ The urgency in her voice immediately drew Mark back towards her.
‘You are starting to think and experiment for yourself, which is fine,’ Maureen told him, ‘but we don't particularly want anyone else to get worried about it. That is the edge of your world at

present, but bending the light gives it the appearance of going on forever.'
'What else is there to unlearn?' Mark was earnest in his enquiry.
'About fifty percent of what you know, and here is as good a place as any to start.' They had walked all around the city to the entrance of the university, and Maureen suggested that they went to get some lunch. Mark was still anxious to discover what else he needed to know. Maureen asked him to wait until he had met Joanne and the rest. Most of lunch was occupied with small talk. They left the café and were soon at a room marked 'Private - Special Meeting,' and entered just before two o'clock. The first couple inside the door were Paula and Nicky, who introduced themselves to Mark and Maureen.
'Nicky is one of the three newcomers like you, Mark,' said Paula.
As Mark shook hands with Nicky, his eyes looked straight into hers and again he felt a blush tinge his cheeks. 'I guess us new ones had better stick together, so we don't get overawed by our more experienced friends.' As he spoke, Nicky's hand stayed clasped to his for just a second longer than necessary.
'That's a great idea.' smiled Nicky.
'She is pretty,' thought Mark, 'really pretty, and with such a gorgeous smile.' Once again he felt goose pimples on his arms and legs.
Maureen touched his arm. 'Let me introduce you to Joanne, if you can tear yourself away,' she almost snarled, her voice tinged with jealousy.
Mark looked at her in amazement. 'Maureen, I...' his voice tailed off.
'I am confused would be your best reply,' came the frosty retort.
Joanne flung her arms round him, kissed him on both cheeks, and squeezed him tightly. 'Hello Mark. Maureen has told me all about you. Welcome to our little group.'

Again Mark was captured, but differently this time. His hours with Maureen were so special and when they were together he wanted it to last forever. On meeting Nicky, he had felt the same sort of happiness; ease, contentment, pleasure, wanting to stay. Now with Joanne he had been welcomed as a friend, but not as an equal. It was a different sort of wanting to the other two but he needed to be on equal terms with her. He wondered if he kissed her as Maureen had kissed him, or if he kissed Nicky, which would be best. Joanne was not so pretty but there was something about her strength. When she had held him he felt totally under her power. Maybe if they were alone. He was jolted out of his thoughts by the sound of laughing. It was Joanne. 'Obviously Maureen has not told you about me. If you think it to me you might just as well say it. I don't have to be invited into your mind, you project into mine.'

'But that's not fair.' Mark was scarlet at the thoughts he had been enjoying. 'If you can see my thoughts and I can't see yours.'

'You did,' replied Joanne, 'I did not speak to you.'

Immediately Mark looked round for Maureen to give him re-assurance and took hold of her hand. 'What is...?'

'You have so much to learn and unlearn,' she whispered. 'It is very difficult to start with, but everyone at this meeting will be happy to open their mind to you fully. Believe in what is happening. Don't doubt it for one minute. All you will learn is the truth.'

'I understand that and there is no problem,' replied Mark. 'It's the other things. You are my ....best friend,' he decided, 'yet I think that Nicky is really nice and Joanne is something special.'

'Joanne is special, as I told you earlier, but as far as you are concerned, remember that I am very special.' Her grip on his hand was so tight that his fingers were full of pins and needles. He felt he should say something, but was at a total loss for words.

Elena came over and introduced her new member to them. Brian was much taller than Mark and seemed very serious. Elena had very long blonde hair. Mark was studying her intently when the sound of laughing once again brought him out of his thoughts. It was Joanne. She was speaking to Maureen. 'When you said that he may work, I think it was the understatement of the year.'
Again Maureen squeezed his hand.
'What have I done now?' Mark was almost afraid to speak.
'Nothing that less orange juice won't cure,' was the tart reply.
As Joanne walked over to the lectern, Mark glanced round at the other people who had entered the room. They all seemed to be in their twenties to early thirties.
'Welcome to our new friends; Nicky, Mark and Brian. You will gradually meet all the other members of the group, which now numbers twenty. You have months of tuition in the Memory Builders in front of you, which will explain in detail our past, and our discussion groups will relate that to the future we are now able to consider. For the time being, suffice it to say that after the great disaster one man took charge to ensure the future of our species. His name was Li Po. He was eminently well suited to the task, as you will discover. I, or rather we, believe that he intended the present order to be challenged at some time in the future. Now, nearly ten thousand years later we are able for the first time to look at the past truthfully, to analyse it, and to try and arrange our own future. Just because my mind was the first to be sufficiently unresponsive to the drugs at present administered does not give me any more power or knowledge than anyone else. I have simply had that knowledge for longer. As you have probably guessed by now, the minds and most activities of the population are controlled by centrally administered drugs. We have used very small quantities of an antidote in the fruit juices given to you. From now on you will only eat and drink meals prepared for you by our members. Your bodies will gradually recover as the power of the drugs

still in your system reduces. We have discovered what we believe to be the truth of our history stored in the computer records, which is why we believe that someone was eventually meant to overcome the drugs that have been administered. The three of you have been told of the alteration to your lives that membership of our group will entail. You still have the choice to return to your previous existence. We do not intend to alter that existence, for it is the closest thing to paradise that man has ever created. Everyone is well cared for and can have anything they require within the confines of the drugs that control them. Joining us will expand your minds and bodies, but will lead to problems that you would never have encountered in the life you are leaving. I take it that you still wish to be with us?'

Three heads nodded in unison.

'Very well, have you any questions?'

Nicky was the first to respond. 'What happened to reduce us to our present numbers if the third Great War did not take place?'

Joanne was silent for a few seconds, then 'The poor of the world were expanding at a far greater rate than the comparatively rich. Despite years of trying to limit the third world population explosion nothing had succeeded. One of the major powers decided that the costs of supporting the rest of the world were becoming too great and that their electorate would not subject themselves to the lower standard of living necessary to maintain the other nations. They developed a totally safe drug, which they would add to water supplies rendering both males and females infertile. It would not react with anything else and was completely harmless. They had the antidote which they would use when the populations of the areas they meant to adjust were at the level they wanted.' Mark could not contain himself. 'But that is the most awful thing possible,' he blurted, 'to treat mankind as some sort of plant, to be pruned at will.'

'You haven't started yet on what is bad,' replied Joanne. 'Anyway, as usual with politicians, they forgot one of the first rules of life. Even if you think you are doing something new, it usually means that someone else is doing it, has just done it, or is about to do it. Of course the unthinkable happened. One of the smaller religious groups were at the same time concerned at the rapid increase in the numbers of their adversaries, and developed a very similar drug to make people infertile. If they had developed the same one, things would not have changed, but again, in their eyes, it was perfectly safe. They could introduce it to the water supplies in the countries concerned, and like the other one, it was broken down by sea water, so that after it passed through the population, it went via the drains into the rivers and eventually to the sea. One was introduced within six months of the other, before the effects of the first were noticed. The effect of the two together was catastrophic. They were not rendered harmless by the seas and the clouds soon carried them worldwide. Not only did they render impotent all forms of life which drank the water, but anything that breathed the tiniest amount of water in the air. At first it was thought that there was no great problem. A few weeks and they would find an antidote, which changed to a few years, which went on and on. The whole planet was wiped out in one fell swoop, not in a war, as you supposed, but something even more deadly.'

'Then where did we come from?' asked Brian.

'You new lessons start tomorrow,' was all that Joanne would tell them.

C

Next morning, Mark joined Nicky and Brian for breakfast at the university, which was where Joanne met them.
'Back to the familiar routine I'm afraid,' she explained. 'The Memory Builder for you three, only the lessons will be different.' She passed each of them cards with codes for their own machines. 'Meet here for drinks just after eleven.'
Mark wanted to ask about meeting Maureen again, but Joanne gave the impression that things had altered slightly and they were now her pupils. He felt it was better to leave the matter for the time being.
Joanne was the first to appear in his mind, again taking the teacher-type role to explain that most of the lessons to come had been taken directly from the main computer, with additions and explanations as the group thought necessary, but they believed that all he was about to learn was the truth.
He moved into a laboratory and, as was the way with Memory Builder learning, knew that he was in a Space Station. A man came into the room. He was grey haired and had narrow, oriental eyes. 'Greetings, my name is Li Po. I am the director of Space Station M1. The object of my colleagues and I is to try and create on this planet conditions which will enable some sort of life to exist without artificial life support systems. With this in mind we have gathered all combinations of plant and animal cultures presently available. As well as trying to alter the climate to accept life as we know it, we will also try to compromise by altering life to suit the planet. At the same time, exploration goes on to try and find habitable planets where the future increase of mankind can take place.'
There then followed a technical explanation of the way they were starting to try and alter the climate, mainly by altering the composition of plant and animal life in relation to the basic properties of the environment.

A suitable break found Mark back at the controls of the Memory Builder, and a short walk took him back to 'their' room at the university, where Joanne, Nicky and Brian were waiting.
'Any questions so far?' asked Joanne, passing drinks to them.
'Are we all using the same programme?' Brian looked very serious.
'Yes, and you will right through,' replied Joanne.
'How relevant is what we have learnt?' queried Nicky, 'or do we find that out as we go along?'
'The seventy people who were the staff of that original space station, plus fourteen crew from interplanetary transporters, were the survivors from the end of the planet. Li Po, because of the work he was doing with climate and genetics, was the first one to recognise the possible outcome of the drugs which had been developed and released on the planet. He monitored the situation as well as he was able, and made a decision to restrict all transport from the planet to the Space Station until he could be sure of the safety of his staff. That was the decision which saved mankind. We still live on the planet which housed that Space Station. The climate outside does not support life as we know it, although a lot of work is undertaken out there. Our original home planet is, as far as we know, still contaminated.'
As Joanne handed them the next set of Memory Builder instructions she glanced round. 'Any further questions?'
'We have been drugged from birth, and you are now taking us off those drugs. Are we having any others substituted?' Mark looked at Joanne.
'Why do you ask?'
'I don't feel ill at all, just different. I seem to go up and down in my feelings,' replied Mark.
'Part of that is your body starting to return to its original state. As you were told before, your new life is not as easy as the paradise in which you were held, and yes, you are being given a few extra drugs. It is a great help not to arrive too quickly in

your new world. Believe me, I did that to start with and found it very difficult to cope. Your learning time should coincide with your total freedom from drug dependency.'

As Mark made his way back to the Memory Builder he reflected that he hadn't asked about seeing Maureen again.

The next session followed on from the first, with detailed explanations of the way efforts were being made to improve the atmosphere of the planet. It mainly centred on trying to increase the output of any life form that emitted oxygen and reducing the need of anything that used it.

Lunchtime saw the four of them together again, discussing their second session.

Mark felt a little tired and was quite relieved when Joanne told them that the afternoons were not spent in machine learning.

'You have to assimilate large amounts of knowledge. This was relatively easy before as your mind had no other material distractions. As your brain gradually opens up you will find learning progressively more difficult. From a one track process you will become the hub of a large ring, pulling information in and pushing opinions out.'

As she finished speaking Elena came into the room. Mark noticed that her blonde hair was now gathered up instead of falling loose over her shoulders. A frown crossed his features as he tried to think what difference that made.

'Good afternoon everyone,' smiled Elena, before adding 'you don't have to look so pleased to see me, Mark.'

Mark smiled back. 'I'm sorry; it is nice to see you again. I just felt that I was missing something.'

'Maureen?' queried Joanne.

Mark thought back to the embarrassment and laughter following the first meeting with Joanne and Nicky. 'I think so,' he ventured.

'You'll be seeing her again this afternoon. Don't worry about the slight confusion. The drugs are doing their work and seem to be at about the right strength. At least we've cured the blushing and breathlessness.' Joanne was gentleness itself as she lightly squeezed Mark's arm. 'Everything will work out.'

'Right,' said Elena, 'you are mine for this afternoon. When you have finished lunch we will have a wander round part of the city with a map so you can become accustomed to what is where.'

'The city is less than two miles across.' Brian wore his usual stern expression. 'I'm twenty-four and in all those years I have never looked at all of it, or more importantly never even wanted to. Why?'

'Li-Po was a brilliant scientist, and his knowledge of psychology was very deep, but the scientific brain will always be more logical and cautious than any other.' As Elena replied she was unfolding a map of the city. 'He harmonised a multi-coloured, multi-religious, multi-political group of eighty four people into a survival unit. He must have been extremely strong as we think everyone agreed to stay for the future of the species. Joanne believes that there were probably more, and that some who could not overcome their family ties returned to Earth on a transporter, but we are not sure. What we are sure of is Li Po knew that if people can think, then they will enquire. If they enquire they will have to find out. If they find out they will need to change things. Some things for the better, some for worse. Whether any of the original eighty-four were given medication we do not know, but certainly the second generation were drugged. He foresaw the need for a period of stability, and being the scientist he probably overdid it a bit. Having said that, the right result has been achieved in that our group has emerged and recognises the need to maintain this world as it is to preserve the species in case we go wrong. The answer to your question, Brian, is that the drugs you were receiving stopped your brain from questioning everything outside the strict areas it was limited to. As your brains open up there will be thousands of basic questions to ask. Where does our food come from is one?'

Nicky interrupted. 'Where does it come from?'
'You'll see part of that this afternoon,' replied Elena.
As she smoothed out the map they could see a circular city with spokes radiating out past the edges of the paper.
'Which part is two miles across?' asked Nicky.
'The inner circle, which is basically the limit of our territory without breathing aids. The pieces radiating out from it have various functions, including the growing areas. As you can see, the city streets are all curved, so you have an impression of continuance. The edges of the dome have the light bent more than normal to give the impression of depth, except where specific functions take place, such as the rebirth chambers,' Elena rose as she finished speaking.
As they set off Brian automatically fell in line with Elena. Nicky and Mark were close behind. Quite when or how it happened Mark was not sure, but he found himself holding hands with Nicky.
'I will give you maps when we get back with everything marked,' said Elena. 'None of the streets are named, but at every junction we have colour coded the path on the corner of a building. It corresponds to the map, so you can't get lost.'
'Would it not be easier to letter or number them in sequence?' Brian's logical mind came into play.
'The less information you give, the less the chance for it to be queried, etcetera, etcetera.' Elena smiled as she glanced round at the two holding hands behind her.
She stopped and took out the map. 'Here is the university,' and moving her finger, 'here we are at the edge of the city.'
They stood in front of an apartment block, no different from the others. A quick glance at the back of the map and she pushed some different areas of the wall close to the door, which opened inwards. She stepped inside a room no more than two metres wide in either direction. The others followed and made room for the door to close behind them.

‘This is part of the double wall of the dome of the city,’ Elena explained. ‘We are going into one of the growing areas that radiate from the city. We can enter these without breathing aids or the fear of contamination.’ She pressed her hand flat against the wall in front of them, which slid effortlessly to one side.
Mark’s chest heaved as he looked through the clear walls of the tunnel at the most beautiful sunset, seen live for the first time in his life. His mind flashed back to the aborted session in the Memory Builder and his breathing was suspended as he took in all the different colours.
A cry from Nicky brought him back. ‘Your grip!’
Mark glanced at his companion. ‘I'm so sorry, it's just so beautiful,’ he relaxed his grip. ‘See the pinks and the oranges and the purples?’
‘Of course,’ said Elena, ‘you blew out the Memory Builder at the cables in the sunset.’
‘What was that test for?’ queried Brian. ‘I went on past that up to the footbridge.’
‘It was partly to start an introduction of how life used to be and partly to determine how sensitive you are. Mark is very sensitive.’
‘Is that good or bad?’ Mark was puzzled.
‘Neither, it's just that you will probably have deeper emotions than most people.’ They stepped into the tunnel, which was about thirty metres across and disappeared into the distance.
As they walked, admiring the rows of vegetables, the sun dipped below the horizon and Elena pressed a switch to light the tunnel.
‘Please,’ said Mark, ‘just hold the lights a little bit longer.’
Elena pressed the switch again and turned to look at Mark. He was staring intently upwards and suddenly pointed with his free hand. ‘There, Nicky, see it?’
‘My very first star.’ Nicky's expression was one of sheer disbelief.

Brian and Elena followed Mark's outstretched arm. 'Just wait for ten minutes, but in the meantime have a look at the landscape outside the tunnel before the light goes totally.'
On each side they could see other tunnels radiating from the city, but looking towards the end of the tunnel they viewed a flat, barren landscape.
'For ten thousand years the robots have been trying to cultivate anything outside the dome or the tunnels, directed by the instructions left in the main computer. We think that some new thinking is really what's needed to give them any chance. Ten thousand years, and alas, still nothing,' sighed Elena.
'So we are stuck here forever?' questioned Nicky.
'Possibly not,' replied Elena, 'but now look at the stars."
As their eyes went up, gasps came from three throats simultaneously.
'That is the most wonderful thing I have ever seen in my life.' Brian's normally serious expression had been replaced by one of rapture. 'There must be thousands.'
'Is our original planet visible?' Mark ventured.
'These are not planets, but suns, although where our original one is I don't know.' Brian replied.
Mark was still amazed at the vast galaxy of stars.
'Nor do I,' laughed Elena, 'we will have to ask when we return.'
As she switched the lights on again the stars seemed to dim, and they slowly made their way back to the city wall.
'Just one more time, please...' But Nicky didn't have to explain what she wanted as again they all gazed at the glory of the heavens.
Out of the main door, their eyes quickly adapted to the night lights of the city which, although less than daylight, meant there was never total darkness. Elena led them, again showing where they were going on the map, until they came to one of the rebirth chambers. She pushed open the door to reveal a room with the same depth as before, but probably twice as wide. Some

chairs and a small table were set to one side. The door swung to behind them, and a robot worker stood near the table glided silently towards them.
'How can I help you?' his slightly metallic voice enquired.
'We wish to have a look inside the tunnel,' was Elena's reply.
'Place your hand flat on my breastplate,' again the inhuman voice.
Elena did so and the sliding door opened to reveal another tunnel as wide as before, but with a wall on the right going some forty metres into the tunnel.
'Oh no!' Brian was obviously startled, as he stared into the front of a huge machine filled with compost.
'What originally happened to all living things?' asked Elena.
'They died, broke down, and returned to the soil,' said Mark, his historical training at the ready.
'Oh no.' Again, Brian found it hard to accept what was obvious.
'All the flowering plants and shrubs from the parks that are replaced come into one of these recycling machines,' explained Elena.
Mark suddenly felt Nicky's nails bite into the flesh of his hand as she asked, 'and the people that enter the rebirth chambers?'
'When it has been agreed that they are the genuine ones, by their handprint agreeing with the original request to the computer, they are asked to wait for two or three minutes, until everything can be prepared for them. Their bodies are then removed to the re-cycler. It seems drastic, but for a child to be born, someone has to die. Don't forget that nothing arrives in our world from outside. Everything has to be recycled, including the dead.'
'They are gassed?' Nicky seemed close to tears.
'They never know,' replied Elena.
Mark slipped his arm round Nicky.
'It seems horrible,' she sobbed.

'Death always is, its just that we never had to think about it before.' He gently squeezed her and as she looked up he could see tears gently welling from the corners of her eyes.
Again there was the elusive little niggle that he was missing something. It was a sombre group that made its way back to the university.
'We will meet all the others for a meal when we get back and you can start to get to know them all. You are really lucky to have joined the group. There is so much to discover, so much to look forward to.' Elena was trying to lift the spirits of the little party.
'If it's like that I don't know that I want to find out,' Nicky was still feeling very low.
Mark gently squeezed her hand. 'I think if we had gone into the rebirth chamber first, and then seen the sunset and the stars it might have been better.'
Nicky looked up and gave Mark a quick kiss on the cheek. 'Thanks, I needed reminding that I had also seen the most wonderful sight ever.'
'I think we all did.' Brian seemed to have overcome the distress he felt in the second tunnel.
As Brian spoke Mark's mind flicked back to that earlier moment when he had wondered what it would be like to kiss Nicky. The little peck on the cheek had started him thinking again.
Before he had time to give it any more thought, Elena was opening one of the university corridor doors, into a room where the other sixteen were waiting patiently for them.
'How did your first field trip go?' Joanne seemed pleased to see them all.
They all started at once, until Brian bowed low and, looking at Nicky, said, 'Ladies first.'
'I may have to revise my thoughts about him,' Joanne made a mental note. 'He seems to have suddenly eased up quite a lot.'
Nicky glanced round. 'It was the best and the worst day of my

life. The sunset and the stars were the most wonderful things I have ever seen. The dreadfulness of the rebirth chambers was the worst.'

'I thought you were going to say holding hands with Mark and kissing him were the worst.' Elena looked straight at Maureen as she spoke.

Maureen started to rise when Joanne's thoughts entered her mind. 'Don't let her wind you up. You found Mark, but that doesn't mean you are entitled to him. You may not even be allocated to him. Just wait and see how things develop.'

Maureen smiled at Elena. 'That's funny; I thought she was going to say that was the best.'

There were one or two laughs in the room, and what tension had arisen seemed to fade. Again, Mark knew he had missed something.

Joanne was talking again. 'You mentioned the best and worst day. We will discuss that over dinner, which I believe is now ready next door. I have split us onto three separate tables, with one newcomer on each, so would you all look out for your place-names?' They went through into the next room, and Mark's worry at being split away from the other two was only relieved when he saw Maureen's name next to his own on the table.

As he sat he felt Maureen quickly nip the side of his thigh. 'I let you out of my sight and you have to start kissing someone else,' she whispered angrily.

'It wasn't the same type of kiss that we had.' For the first time with Maureen, Mark felt that he had said something right. 'She was crying and I tried to cheer her up.'

'So if I burst into tears I can expect a big passionate embrace.' As she spoke, Maureen realised they were the centre of attention at their table. 'I'm sorry, everyone, please let me introduce you to Mark.' Round the table, Mark was introduced to Greg, a huge man who seemed to wear a permanent smile. With his long blonde hair and beard he reminded Mark of the pictures he had seen of polar bears. Then there was Cynthia, who was so thin Mark thought she might break in two if she fell over. She had short, dark hair and bright red lips. He remembered that women used to colour their lips in the old days and although he had never seen lipstick before, he thought the result was great. He also met Sophie, who was the opposite shape and had masses of dark curly hair. Her whole face lit up as she smiled at him when they were introduced, and he just knew she would be wonderful to cuddle. Of the men there was Clive, who was even darker skinned than Mark, slightly shorter than him, but very muscular under a tight fitting top, then Wendell, who was about five foot four tall and gave the impression of being very well educated.

The food was served by robot waiters, and Mark suddenly realised how hungry he was. Waiting for someone else to start, he realised that everyone had lowered their heads and the room was silent. Wendell looked across at him and Mark closed his eyes as he said 'Please God, bless this food and all present here. May their future be as You would wish.'

Mark felt a shiver go down his spine and opened his eyes as he heard the sound of conversation start again.

Joanne's voice came across the room. 'For Nicky, Brian, and Mark, we feel that the best way to introduce you to God is not to explain, but to be part of what we believe.'

'But God was one of the main causes of war in the old times. How can we believe in someone like that?' Mark was the first one to reply.

'Each table can explain to our newcomers,' Joanne seemed quite serious.

As Mark started to eat, he automatically knew who would explain on his table. Wendell's voice had dropped in both depth and strength as he started to speak, measuring each word slowly. 'Religion caused many wars and much death. It was not God, however, but man who was ultimately to blame. There has always been God, but He took many names and many forms to the different people of the world. One of the great gifts to mankind was the ability to believe himself to be right, so he would pursue an idea to the end, very often for the benefit of everyone. It was also his greatest downfall, as he could also insist that his belief was the only one, and try to make sure that everyone else should share his belief. When Li Po started this world that we know now, one of his major problems was religion. Working together on a space station was never a problem to the differing religious groups, but saving mankind gave religion a whole new meaning. It was agreed that there was only one God overall. As English was the universal language of space, the name 'God' was accepted in it's widest sense to mean the original. Religion was deleted as far as the process of saving the species was concerned, because of it's previous troubles and possible controversy. Now that we are a thinking, feeling group, it is felt that we should recognise all truth, and God is part of that.' Wendell's voice was so soft, slow and low that Mark used all his concentration to make sure he did not miss a word. He was still deep in thought seconds after Wendell had finished speaking. What he had known all along had just been confirmed. The rest of the table watched his face and waited for him.

Slowly Mark lifted his head. 'Thank you Wendell. I have waited a long time to hear that.'

Sophie smiled at him. 'It also means that there is another area of possible trouble that you have to think about. Nearly all the problems of the past were caused by things for which there was no tangible proof. Religion, politics, sex, greed...'

Mark interrupted. 'Surely greed was wanting a tangible thing that someone else had?'

'Only if you look at it in the short term. Having anything is only relative,' Greg seemed sure.

Sophie took up the conversation again. 'Joanne said earlier that we would discuss Nicky's best and worst day. Everything, and I mean everything, is a ring. I think you already know that there is no such thing as a straight line, so there can only be curves, and curves must form rings. That does not only apply to physical things such as light rays, but to abstract things like colour or opinions. Take black and white. You think of a straight line going from black to dark grey to pale grey to white. In reality it is a ring with black opposite white. If you move from black towards white you are also moving towards black. Take good and evil. Move in any direction and you move towards both. Now that the ring is in your mind, imagine that it has good at the top and evil at the bottom. Half way down each side is half way between the two. Now put another ring across the first so that you use the half way marks again. Now put more rings in so you end up with a globe made of hundreds of rings all packed tightly together. Because if you move on a ring you are moving away from the place you started and towards the place you started, all the rings will be set differently. If you move from one ring to another, you can move directly from good to evil, and back. You do not necessarily have to go half way round the ring. The rings apply to everything and everyone. Hence Nicky's best and worst day. Not opposites, but possibly side by side.'

Mark spent the rest of the meal engaging in small talk, but mainly trying to absorb the new information he had been given. God he had no trouble with, and could easily accept, but the rings? As the dinner started to break up he decided to question Maureen about his difficulties with the concept of the rings.

They left together, and as they walked towards her apartment he asked her about the rings.

'It's simple,' was her reply,' when you hold me and kiss me I love you. When you hold and kiss Nicky I hate you. You could hold me and kiss me, but if I thought of you with her I would love you and hate you at the same time.'

D

It was a long time before Mark went to sleep that night. Everything had been so ordered and logical such a short time before. Hard facts had been his diet in the historical environment, or at least what he then believed to be hard facts. Now it had changed to things that were hard to define. Religion he was perfectly happy with. Either there was a God or there wasn't, and he was now convinced that there was. Politics he was not so sure of. He had felt that the way forward for the group was something that was being argued about behind the scenes, yet he had no real evidence, just a feeling that he was missing some vital points. Love and sex, which in his mind were the same thing, were a total puzzle. He could remember the first kisses with Maureen, and how wonderful he had felt at that time. He still wanted to be with her, but she did not seem to be the same person that she had been, or maybe it was him? Perhaps the added drugs were having that effect on him? He would ask Joanne in the morning. And as for the rings - he could understand the first part, with black at the top and white at the bottom, so at each side was grey. If you then put another ring through to use the greys, you then had two blacks, two whites, and two greys, which was fine, except that the black and white had moved but not the greys. So if part of the ring had moved, and part had not... he fell asleep still wondering.

Maureen lay awake for a long time as well. Elena had obviously taken great delight in telling her about Mark and Nicky, and she could not understand why she had been so nasty. They had not been particular friends but as with most of the group they had got on well together, with no arguments. She wondered if Elena was jealous of the relationship she had with Mark, yet she had not tried to get close to Mark as Maureen had done. Maybe it was just that they were all finding things so different to the life they had known. They now had to think, and there always seemed to be different answers to the problems they encountered. She shivered as she remembered what Joanne had said, that she might not be allocated to Mark. She knew that the future lay in choosing the most compatible couples, but she also knew that Mark was the man for her, even if he didn't know it yet. She slept fitfully, and in her dreams the man she wanted was always paired with someone else, and that someone seemed to change from Elena to Nicky to Joanne and even to Sophie.

Next morning Mark was woken by his mother. 'Maureen is on the videophone for you, she says it's urgent.' Mark scrambled into his dressing gown and walked through to the living room. Maureen smiled as he came into view. 'Hi, how are you?'

'Still a little confused about everything, but I guess it will all work out. Anyway, what is so urgent?'

'Just me wanting to see you in case we don't get to meet during the day. Have a nice time today, and think of me.' As her picture faded Mark tried to make sense of what he had heard and, shaking his head, wandered into the bathroom.

The sessions in the Memory Builder that morning were mainly concerned with the reasons that decisions were taken to dampen the minds of the people with drugs. There was a great emphasis on the violence that had taken place over the centuries, not just the physical violence that Mark recognised from his other sessions, but the mental violence used by individuals, groups, and whole nations to get what they wanted. He was sickened at the way man had behaved towards his fellows, the other animals and towards his world as a whole. There had been some outstanding individuals, but they seemed to be fighting a constant war against worldwide corruption. The thought came through that the release of the two drugs may not have been an accident. It was suggested that the same corporation had sold the drugs to the different countries knowing that the result would be mass genocide. From what he had seen Mark felt it was a distinct possibility, and he could even understand the motives behind it.

Li Po explained that they had to take the second chance that had been offered to them. If they had been able to use the entire planet then they may have approached the situation differently, but restricted as they were to occupying what they could build, it was considered paramount that there should be no friction. He almost apologised as he said 'Please do not think too badly of us if things have not worked out well, we took the decisions with the knowledge we had at the time.'

Mark wandered back for lunch feeling weighed down by the new knowledge that he had acquired. How Joanne had coped when she first realised that things were not as they should be he could not imagine. She had the same dominance as Li Po, and he wondered if some of his genes were in her. She had not met them for breakfast, so he had been unable to ask about the effects of the drugs he was taking, but as he opened the door she was there to greet him, and he made that his first question.

She laughed when he explained about his feelings for Maureen. 'Yes, the drugs you are taking will suppress those feelings, only gradually releasing them.'

'Could you release them a bit faster, please?'

She laughed again. 'You have had no feelings at all for twenty years and now you can't wait a few months? If a man was starved of food for a long time, the worst thing you could do would be to give him a big meal. You would have to slowly build him back up again. It's the same with emotions.' As she spoke her eyes met his. 'Believe me Mark, I went through it myself, and you are better off this way.'

Mark felt that no one, not even Joanne, could have felt the way he did with those first kisses, but he was prepared to wait, for a time anyway. As they ate lunch he asked if there was any possibility that she was related to Li Po. She wanted to know

why he suspected that possibility. 'I think I would have been scared of him too.'
Again Joanne was laughing. 'Surely you are not scared of me, Mark?' she asked.
'Just a little,' he replied, 'not so much scared of you, as scared of the power that you seem to have.'
Her expression hardened almost imperceptibly as she said, 'I am not a dictator. Our group is a democracy, and we make all our decisions as such.'
'I know that, but it's just that you seem so much wiser that everyone tends to agree with your views anyway. In the Memory Builder session today it appeared that even some of the old democracies weren't really that, but were dictatorships that were made to appear otherwise.' Joanne looked a little sad. 'You are probably quite right, and it's something I must try to overcome. As for your question about Li Po, it's quite possible that there is part of him in me, or in you for that matter. They selected as best they were able to produce a society to retain brain power and physical health, while trying to hold that brain power in check.'
'They seem to have done a good job, as there is no sickness and the group seems very intelligent' said Brian as he joined the discussion, having arrived shortly after Mark, quickly followed by Nicky.
Joanne's expression suddenly became very serious. 'That is fine for the way the Happies live. We call the ones outside our group 'the Happies', because they live in paradise, so they are permanently happy."
'There used to be a group called the Hippies in the old times.' Mark remembered history well. 'I believe they also took drugs, so it's probably a good name.'
'It's only a name, and not meant to be derogatory at all. Remember that all those people are just as intelligent as us, and are the future of mankind if we fail.'

'Fail in what?' Nicky was inquisitive.
'As I was saying before we became involved with Hippies and Happies, the way that people have been created is fine for the current state of affairs, but we believe that we have to go further than that. We have to re-introduce feelings if we are to succeed, and most of those come naturally as the drugs leave our bodies. Some of them are the result of something else happening, such as the feelings of parents when they have a child.'
'Surely you are not suggesting that women should go through all that pain again just for a baby?' Brian looked shocked.
'As Li Po explained to you in this morning's session, we were given a second chance to achieve the potential which we have. The first attempt ended in near total tragedy, and we have then had the artificial world of the Happies. Although this has maintained mankind, no progress has been made at all, except by the computers and robots, independently of anyone else, just following the instructions laid down nearly ten thousand years ago. As you know, we believe we were meant to break free and question the system, although probably sooner than we did. We will of course maintain this world as we know it but at the same time we have to use that second chance to create a world where man can flourish as was originally intended. We can watch over the people of that world and hopefully not interfere in their progress towards a truly wonderful life. Obviously it means going back to basics, and part of that is having children in the original way.'
Mark was wondering if the 'hopefully not interfere' was part of the division he suspected was there when the group discussed the politics of the future. 'So that means sex will be re-introduced?'
'And love,' replied Joanne.
'I thought they were one and the same thing, and one of the main causes of trouble.' For once Brian seemed a little unsure.
'Most of the causes of trouble are not in themselves what creates

a problem,' Joanne had adopted her schoolmistress approach. 'The trouble has always been how man has reacted to them. Hopefully the problems will be less second time around. That is one of the areas under discussion at the moment. How much help should we give to a new society? Should we leave it to progress naturally, or help it where we know the answer?'

'Or think we know the answer,' the words came almost without thinking from Mark.

'I believe we were told that the original world was still uninhabitable,' said Nicky. 'Does that mean that the computers have solved the problem of living outside on this planet, or will this new society be an extension of our present living conditions?'

'The planet outside is still inhospitable to man without protection,' replied Joanne, 'and you are correct in saying that the original world still has the infertility drugs present as far as we know.'

'So when you spoke of the work that was still being done in response to the original computer instructions, you meant that another habitable planet has been found?' Nicky looked at the others with amazement.

'Twenty years ago, and this seems too much of a co-incidence when we arrive shortly after. I feel one triggered the other.'

'So you intend to populate a new world, and then make sure it runs according to your rules?' Brian did not disguise the sarcasm in his voice.

'Before you say it,' interrupted Joanne, 'I am not playing at being God.'

'I'm sorry,' Brian dropped his eyes momentarily.

Mark's mind had raced ahead. 'A new world will be populated, and we expect it to succeed, when it's obvious we can't agree amongst ourselves about things.'

'That is progress, if it is handled correctly. If, as we have been doing, we discuss things and arrive at a sensible conclusion before we take action, then that is the way forward. Brian just apologised, probably for the first time in his life, because before he would never have been so involved as to give a forthright opinion.' Turning to Brian, Joanne went on, 'What you said was quite true and if criticism can be taken in the right way, then it makes a contribution. Whether we should interfere is still under discussion, as I said before, and just for the record I believe we should not interfere at all."

'I'll second that.' said Brian.

'Thank you, but please give it lots of thought, as I am not convinced that I am right,' and as she looked at Mark, Joanne added, 'and if I'm overruled, so be it. No, Mark, I don't know everything.' As Mark opened his mouth to ask more questions about how they were to go about populating a new planet, the door opened, and one of the group members came in. 'Sorry I'm a bit late, Joanne.'

'Hello, Sheila, you probably came in just at the right time. We were starting to get involved in discussions that I want to save for a while.' Joanne stood up as she spoke. 'Just to refresh your memories, this is Sheila, who will take you for this afternoon.'

All three nodded in her direction, and eventually Brian broke the silence 'I'm starting to feel like a baby, being taken for an afternoon walk by my governess.'

Sheila burst into a fit off giggles. 'I don't think anyone would want to produce a baby your size.' She moved over to Brian's side. 'But if you are very, very good, then I may get you a lollipop.'

Even Brian started laughing, and the others joined in.

'I suppose you three are the babes of the group, and I'm just the person to help you through adolescence.' Sheila winked at Brian as she started giggling again.

'There is a rumour that someone somewhere saw Sheila when she wasn't laughing, but we have no hard evidence.' Even Joanne's mood seemed to have lightened.

Mark immediately felt at ease with Sheila. She was certainly no lightweight, but was good looking all the same. She had that quality of happiness and fun that made her the ideal person to spend time with. He was looking forward to the afternoon session. Once more his mind wandered to the past and the kisses with Maureen. His thoughts were starting to progress when he heard Joanne. 'Maybe I should not cut the drugs so quickly.' As he glanced in her direction he realised she had used thought transfer, and her smile told him she was joking.

'Come on, you three Musketeers,' said Sheila.

'Who the heck are they?' Nicky asked.

'They were literary characters from the old days.' Mark could vaguely remember something about them.

'In good books you always had the goodies and the baddies, and they were goodies.' Sheila had the simple explanation. 'There was a lot of evil at that time, and their job was to alter things for the better. You three are the final members of the group for the time being, and although there is no evil, we are certainly going to alter things.' She glanced at Mark. 'I took history as well, so we have more than one thing in common.'

As Mark started to ask what the other thing they had in common was, Sheila was leading the way out. She stopped outside the door to show them where they were going on her map. Before Mark could ask, she was off again, talking over her shoulder 'You three can navigate us there.'

They were now quite used to the maps and the city, and were soon outside a door leading into the city wall. Sheila went through the usual procedures, but this time they found a small monorail waiting for them when they entered the greenhouse. They were soon at the end of the plants, and again Sheila used palm prints to open a door into the end of the tunnel. Once inside, the door closed behind them and they followed Sheila's example in putting on helmets and back packs, before she opened the outer door. There was another monorail waiting and

as they climbed aboard Mark noticed that the sun, which was getting close to the horizon, was even more vivid than when they had seen it previously. They went straight across a fairly featureless landscape before dropping slowly into a tunnel going straight into the earth. As daylight faded, it was replaced by the artificial light they normally lived with. Sheila's voice came into the helmet. 'This was one of the original excavations. There are five in all, which provide all our needs in the city. As far as we can make out this was a world similar to our original one, in that it has most of the fossil remains that were natural there. It is a lot older, however, and for some reason has died. There were a vast variety of plants, and a fairly limited number of animals, but we believe there was nothing with any large degree of intelligence.'
As she finished speaking, they slowed down and entered a huge cavern, where the monorail stopped. The sight was impressive as they watched robot workers mining and transporting material by conveyor to a central processor. The monorail lead into the distance.
'Where does the rail go to?' asked Nicky.
'That one is just to remove soil to the surface,' Sheila's reply came through to all of them.
'So we are desecrating something else,' Brian interrupted.
'If we lived out there, then we could backfill as we went along, but as things are at present, we will leave it until we exhaust the mining. There is actually very little work done in the mines, because everything is re-cycled, and as we have not expanded, there has been very little need for most things.'
'There seems plenty of activity at present,' Mark was quite amazed at the sight, and realized how restricted their minds had been before, that he had never wondered how anything new was produced.
'Most of this is routine inspection and maintenance work, but we thought you ought to see the scale of the operations that exist just to maintain our small world. We could actually live for a

very long time without anything from outside the dome, but re-cycling is not quite perfect, so all these facilities exist.' As she finished speaking, Sheila motioned them all back onto the monorail and they came out of the tunnel into darkness, and again the stars were a blaze of glory against the black ink of infinity.

Nicky was the first to speak. 'Joanne told us that another habitable planet had been found. Which direction is it in?'

Sheila slowed the monorail to a stop. 'If you follow my arm, you can see a group of six stars that roughly make the shape of a sword. Straight through the middle of the handle will take you there, although the sun is not visible with the naked eye.' Sheila eased the monorail forward as she finished speaking.

'What's it like?' Nicky asked for the three of them.

'That's part of the learning that you still have to undertake, but at the present time we believe it would be perfectly suitable. Just imagine being the first people to go there.' As Sheila spoke Mark could almost feel the romance in her voice. He looked round, and although her face was partly masked, her eyes were shining with a passion he had never seen before. 'Imagine being the mother or father of a new world; discovering all of its secrets; living as our ancestors once did, and shaping your own future.'

Mark felt himself shiver with excitement as his imagination ran riot. He was back on the path next to the cottage, with the dog, the fish and the birds. The sun was just setting, but this time there were no cables to spoil the view.

They reached the end of the line, removed their protection, and were back on the monorail through the greenhouse.

He was sitting next to Sheila, and as Brian and Nicky were talking, took the opportunity to ask 'What was the other thing we have in common besides history?'

Again an outburst of giggling preceded her reply. 'Why, kissing of course. Apparently we both enjoy it.'

Mark knew that without the drugs he was taking he would have been blushing again, and as it was he felt very uncomfortable. 'How did you know about my kissing?' he muttered.
'The group has to know everything about everyone in order for it to progress,' again the slow wink that he had seen before, and more laughing. 'I personally think we ought to practice together to see if we can make kissing a perfect art form.'
Mark was taken aback by Sheila's forthright manner, but he had to admit that the idea was very pleasant. Her lips were slightly larger than normal and although she had dark hair, her eyes were a pale honey colour. The closer he looked, the more he liked the idea. He suddenly realized that they were back at the wall and Brian and Nicky were waiting for them to get up.
'I thought you two were using mind transfer,' said Nicky.
'No,' laughed Sheila, 'we had been discussing what the future might hold and dropped into deep thought.'
As they passed through into the street Sheila whispered, 'and I bet my thoughts were way ahead of yours.' She squeezed Marks hand as they set off back towards the University.
That evening they again all ate together, although the group had been re-arranged so that at his table Mark met: Tanya, who seemed very serious, and spent much of the meal talking to Cocho, who seemed just as serious; Sue, who had lots of freckles, and talked to anyone who would listen; Murray, who was the darkest member of the group; Sven, who spoke very little at all, and Earl, who sat immediately to the left of Mark.
Mark looked round, and noted that Maureen was on the next table. She smiled back as their eyes met. He would rather be sat next to her, but his thoughts were interrupted by Sue. 'What have you seen of the outside world so far?'
'We went into one of the greenhouses, through a rebirth chamber, and today we went out to one of the mines,' he replied.
'What was the best bit?'
'I can't decide between the sunset and the stars,' replied Mark.

Earl turned to look at him. 'Definitely the sunset,' he said in a very slow, deep voice. 'The colours are pure magic, and they are so soft that they all end up eating into one another and you can't really tell where one starts and another ends. It is the most beautiful sight in the universe.'

Mark was convinced he was right and was opening his mouth to agree, when Sue butted in. 'Don't do it, Earl.'

Earl totally ignored her as he went on. 'The stars are very beautiful. When you can watch them from early on, from the first one or two, and the backdrop slowly fades to that midnight blue. Some stand out like diamonds, some with a touch of emerald. All the most beautiful colours are there. But instead of being just one sunset, they are millions, and together they are the most beautiful sight in the universe.'

Mark knew he was right, and agreed with him. 'Earl, you are so right.'

Earl smiled and glanced towards Sue.

She claimed Marks attention. 'Which is right?'

'How do you mean?' Mark was confused.

'He just told you that both the sunset and the stars were the most beautiful, and you agreed.'

'I'm sorry, Mark.' Earl looked apologetic; 'I just can't resist seeing if it works on someone new.'

'How do you do that?' queried Mark.

'It's that voice of his,' said Sue, 'it's almost hypnotic. He can charm anyone.'

'Except Joanne,' replied Earl,' she hears what I'm thinking as well as what I'm saying.'

'She told us earlier that this was a democratic group, and that she accepted decisions that she disagreed with.' Mark was interested to find out more about Joanne.

'I think she would accept a decision that she didn't agree with, but I don't think it has happened yet,' said Murray, and Sven nodded in agreement. 'She is vastly more experienced than the rest of us and we do tend to follow her. I think she has probably been right so far as well. As you come off the drugs, your minds will be much more alert and questioning, but they are also more reasoning. What she has achieved in fifteen years is truly remarkable, but nothing compared with what is intended.'

'Starting a new world.' Mark was still surprised how much the four words meant.

'There are massive decisions to be made about that, and they have to be collectively done.' Sue seemed to be almost saddened as she spoke.

'But it will be wonderful,' said Mark.

'So who and how many are going?' queried Murray.

'And for the ones left behind, who have just as many feelings, and would want to raise their own families, what happens to them?' Sue's feelings seemed to have deepened.

Mark realised he was only starting to touch the tip of the iceberg as the dinner party started to break up.

Maureen was waiting for him at the door, and as they walked home, his happiness at being with her was tinged with sadness at the thought that decisions in the future could not be made to please everyone. They spoke about what he had learnt that day, especially the future, and as he left her that night their lips met briefly and she gave him a gentle hug.

E

Next day they were met at the university by Cocho. 'All work today,' was his opening remark as he handed them the programme details for the Memory Builders. 'Come back here for lunch as normal, but after that you are back on the learning curve.'

Again the sessions in the Memory Builder were used in tracing their past, and trying to explain the reasons why various decisions had been taken. It seemed that everything had been done to try and guarantee the future of the human race at the cost of taking it forward. Given the circumstances, it was easy to agree with the decisions that had been made.

As Mark returned for lunch, his mind wandered forward and again the question came as to whether they should interfere in the future of a world they created. As he tried to decide, he realised that no-one interfered with them: no-one outside altered the way they arranged things, so presumably God let them get on the way they wanted to. What was good enough for God was good enough for him. No interference. Just as he was about to confirm the decision in his mind, the old niggle returned. How did he know that no-one interfered with them? Just once or twice in the past he had felt that he was not totally in control, or totally alone. So maybe God did interfere, or if it wasn't God, was it possible that there existed already a set of people like them? What if Li-Po was wrong and they were not being given a second chance, but a third, or even a fourth?

He was still deep in thought as he reached the lunch room. He was the last of the three to get back and Cocho was waiting to greet him. 'Anything you want to discuss on this morning's session, Mark?'

'No, it all seemed fairly straightforward and fitted in with what I expected.' Cocho smiled at the three of them. 'If you don't mind,

I'll leave you to lunch alone as you have no questions. Please use these programmes for this afternoon.'

'There is just one thing,' said Mark, 'Li Po said that we had a second chance. What if it's a third chance?'

'Go on,' replied Cocho.

'Say what has happened to mankind has already happened before. Not necessarily in the same way, but with the same end result. A group similar to us then started our original world. At the moment they might be deciding on our future, as we decide on the future of the world we intend to create.'

'When you finish lunch, don't go before I get back,' Cocho rose as he spoke and quickly left the room.

'You seemed to upset him,' Nicky remarked.

'I don't think you upset him so much as shocked him,' said Brian, 'I wonder who he's gone to see?'

'Apparently there's a meeting going on all day, that's why we're in the Memory Builders.' As she spoke, Nicky's expression changed to one of puzzlement. 'But do you think there already exists a layer between us and God? A group like us who control what we do?'

'The thought of it seemed to worry Cocho,' Mark felt faintly pleased with himself.

'I don't think it was whether they existed, but the fact that no-one else had thought it possible,' Brian had reverted to his usual stern expression. 'It will be interesting to see what they decide to do about it.'

As he finished speaking Cocho came into the room and sat down. 'A change of plans for this afternoon. Instead of the Memory Builders, you are invited to join us at our meeting. If you have all finished lunch, then please follow me.'

A short walk brought them to the meeting room. Joanne smiled as she asked them to find seats. 'Thank you for coming so promptly. As you probably know, we were having a full day meeting, which was why you were scheduled for the Memory

Builders this afternoon. The main topic of discussion was the way we were to progress in the future, especially with regard to the new world. Because you three are still fairly heavily dependent on drugs, I had taken the decision, and I apologise for this, that it would be unsuitable for you to be present. Cocho came and reported Mark's comment, and we have unanimously agreed that you should join us now and in any future discussions. It seems that it is possible you may have insight for some things at your present level. Any comments please?' With that Joanne sat down.

Mark rose first. 'I'm sorry. I didn't mean to mess things up. I don't even think that there is some other group.'

'There is no need to apologise, Mark. It wasn't what you said, but the fact that none of us here had thought of the possibility of another group existing,' Joanne seemed eager to appease Mark.

Tanya stood up. 'I propose that we suspend the normal learning for Nicky, Mark and Brian, and invite them to join in the work we are at present undertaking, so that we can progress without waiting for them to catch up.'

A quick show of hands agreed the motion.

'I propose that the reduction in drugs is suspended in case there is anything further for us to learn at this stage,' Cocho was speaking,' especially for Mark, as he came up with the new idea.'

Mark's stomach was churning as he rose. 'But I want to come off the drugs sooner, not later,' he glanced at Joanne as she got up.

'Before we take a vote on that I would like to plead the case for Mark. As we all know, he went through the kissing routine in a rather spectacular fashion. He is particularly anxious to return to that state as soon as possible and I think Maureen would second that.' A small ripple of comment went through the room as she spoke. 'If Mark agrees, I would suggest that we hold him as he

is at present for say two weeks, but then hasten his withdrawal so that he reaches normality at the originally proposed time.'
'That seems fair.' Mark was not sure, but felt he could not argue.
'I further propose that we alter the rates for Nicky and Brian in a similar fashion,' Joanne was back in control, and a quick show of hands again confirmed her unanimous support.
Earl stood. 'I think it's probably best left to the three original minders to explain the up to date situation, and then get them started into work first thing tomorrow. If we finish now, they have the rest of today to catch up.'
Mark could have kissed him there and then. He was proposing Mark should spend the rest of the day with Maureen, and that suddenly seemed very important. His hand was the first in the air as they took a vote.
As everyone started leaving the room, Joanne joined him. 'I'm sorry about all that, but we are trying desperately to get all the possible angles we can before we decide on the new world.'
Mark was so pleased at the thought of spending the rest of the afternoon with Maureen he would have forgiven her for just about anything.
Maureen joined him as they left the room, and by the time they left the university they were holding hands. 'I thought if we went back to my place and I brought you up to date there it would be easiest,' she suggested,' then we could have dinner together."
They were soon back at Maureen's apartment and after she had dealt with a couple of videophone messages they sat facing each other across a coffee table.
'This is probably the easiest way for me to explain where we are, but I think it would be better if you laid out on the settee and put your head on my lap.' As she spoke Maureen patted the seat next to her.

Mark thought it was the best suggestion she had ever made, moved round, and having made himself comfortable, gazed up at Maureen's face as she started to speak.

'From what you have learnt generally and in the Memory Builder you know that there are twenty of us who want to create a new life for ourselves and at the same time maintain the present system intact. It is our intention to populate a world that the computers have discovered.' As she spoke Maureen was slowly tangling and untangling her fingers in the hair just above Marks left ear. He never wanted this moment to stop, so in spite of all the questions he wanted to ask, let her continue unchecked. 'It has already been agreed that there are three options. Number one is for us all to go there and leave this place exactly as it is, with no outside interference at all to alter the way life has been for the last ten thousand years. Number two is for us to all stay here, using the outside resources to create another world under cover similar to this one. We can then keep an eye on what happens here without interfering in it. The third view is that we split into two groups, with one going to the new world and the other remaining here.' Her voice seemed to have gained an almost ghostly quality, and while it was not hypnotic in the way that Earl had used his words, Mark nevertheless didn't want to move an inch to break the spell. His mind seemed to be floating, with her voice gradually ebbing and flowing like the tides on their old home planet.

'The thought is that the third view is the one which will probably be chosen. That then brings the crunch decision. Who stays? Who goes?'

Mark heard himself almost whisper. 'I don't care as long as we are together.'

'That is where the main problem lies.' Mark looked up to see two silent tears slowly caressing down Maureen's cheeks.

The pain in her voice brought Mark out of the semi trance like state. 'But surely there is no way we are going to be split up?'

Maureen sniffed as she replied. ‘The obvious way for the future of any race to succeed is to use the genes that are furthest removed from one another to give the best possible chance of success together. At the moment one group is gathering all the information possible to give the best pairings for the future. It’s further complicated by the fact that probably some of us can't have children anyway. What we agreed to do was to look at the results when they are known, and in the meantime hope against hope that we end up with the right result. If I could only end up with you... but the odds are stacked against us.’
Mark was uneasy. ‘But we can't be made to do anything against our wishes. That wouldn't be right. Whatever happens we have to agree it is right for us.’
‘I know. It's easy to say, but when you are talking of creating a whole new world for mankind, it seems so petty to talk of love,’ Maureen stuttered on the last few words, and the two teardrops turned into a deluge.
Mark sat upright and hugged her. ‘Let's not worry about a result until we know what it is.’
They clasped each other tightly and Maureen eventually murmured, ‘the other thing that Joanne said was that very often in the old days couples who fell in love and married often then fell in love with someone else. She said we might as well start with the best possible chance and hope love fell into place along the way.’
Mark found it hard to argue with the logic of the statement, but felt it wasn't the right time to say so.
They hugged for a long time and as Mark relaxed his embrace, they were once again face to face. They kissed long and tenderly, and the moment was only broken by tears from Maureen which Mark tasted touching the corner of his lips. He gently pushed her away from him.
‘To hell with those rotten drugs.’ Mark was amazed at the ferocity in her statement.

'I'll be off them before too long,' he apologised.
'By then we will have had to vote on who is to accompany whom, and where they will be going.' Maureen was having great difficulty stringing words together and her breath came in short, sharp spasms. 'If you had to vote straight after those first kisses I know which way it would have been.' Mark thought back to the time concerned. He could remember every detail of the kisses but his mind couldn't replay the pleasure and magic involved. The kiss a few moments ago had been lovely and he knew the drugs were holding back his emotions, but a small voice made him wonder if this was the way of love. It gradually started to die as soon as it was born. 'Let's wait and see what happens,' was all that he could contribute.
Maureen tried to break the downbeat mood. 'I'll start making some dinner for us.' Although it was possible for all meals to be provided by a combination of computer and robot, most people liked to take pleasure in the preparation process. 'Besides, we've got something special to try.'
She made a sauce based on dried tomatoes, onions and herbs, and used it as the base to heat some chunks of protein rich vegetable which were from the number one flavour range. The nearest description to taste would have been chicken, if they had ever tasted chicken as a comparison. The potatoes she sliced very thinly and interspersed the layers with chopped leeks, finishing them off with a good seasoning and then covering them with a little stock and milk. For a second vegetable she had chosen some purple sprouting broccoli.
As Mark helped her lay the table he noticed there were two large jugs of water. Maybe there is more spice in there than I noticed he thought. That must be what she meant by special.
It was only as he sat down that he noticed that they both had two water glasses. Maureen filled up one of the jugs and poured a glass each. 'Try this very carefully.'

Mark smiled as he slowly shook his head at Maureen telling him to be careful with water. He had remembered a quotation from a book written in the old days. He didn't know what it meant, but he somehow felt it was right. ‘Rum cattle women. You've got to winter and summer 'em.’

Maureen reached forward and gently touched her glass on his. ‘Cheers.’

He should have known then if he had remembered his history. Instead he sipped at the drink, which had a delicious flavour, although much drier than the drinks he was used to. ‘I like it, but whatever is it?’ he asked.

‘Three guesses,’ laughed Maureen.

All of a sudden his memory came to his help. ‘It's alcohol,’ he blurted out, ‘another cause of trouble,’ he added without thinking.

‘It's actually white wine,’ said Maureen, ‘and really quite good for a first attempt. It isn't a cause of trouble, but I think it might have helped in the old days.’

‘But who made it, and how?’ asked Mark.

‘Sheila,’ replied Maureen.

‘I might have known. Come to think of it, she might have been drinking it for some time the way she acts.’ Mark knew that alcohol loosened the responsibilities but he admitted to himself that the taste was good and as the meal progressed the second glass tasted better than the first and the second jug tasted better than the first.

Next morning he was still in Maureen's apartment, and felt dreadful. She was nowhere to be seen and he decided the first thing he should do was to call his mother to say he had been delayed. She must be worried. As he picked up the videophone, Maureen came in from the bedroom wearing a dressing gown. She was very white and sat down heavily as soon as she reached a chair.

‘Maureen, you look awful, is there something I can get you?’ He put the videophone down and walked towards her.
‘Look in the mirror before you decide who looks awful,’ she replied.
‘I'll just call mother first, she'll be worried,’ Mark wandered back towards the videophone.
‘It's okay, I told her yesterday you would be out all night,’ Maureen shivered as she spoke.
‘How did you know we were going to get drunk?’ Mark asked.
‘That's not what I had in mind, but not to worry. She isn't expecting you home until this evening.’
Mark rose and came back from the kitchen with two steaming mugs of black coffee. ‘Until we can work out what drugs we need to get us better, I think this is what they used to take in the old days.’
They sat in silence for a few minutes, sipping at the coffee. ‘We must try and find something for this condition. I can't face another meeting feeling like this,’ Maureen walked over to the videophone. ‘I'll ring Sheila. She must know the best cure.’
Sheila's face came on the screen, and at the sight of Maureen she burst out laughing. ‘How much did you drink?’
‘We had two jugs between us and we feel dreadful.’
Sheila was still laughing as she said ‘I had two bottles to myself the first time, so think what I felt like. There is no actual cure, but if you take some K18 tablets, they will take away the headache and sickness. You'll be fine by lunchtime.’
‘What are K18 tablets?’ Maureen had never heard of them.
‘I believe they were originally used on the old space transporters for some types of sickness, but they work anyway. I didn't know we still had such things available, but apparently unless someone decides otherwise, everything we have is replaced forever. It took me ages to work through the computer to find them. Just punch the code into the food controller, and they'll arrive. See you in the flesh later.’ Sheila's image faded.

As Maureen switched off the videophone, Mark was already entering the code for the tablets, and it wasn't long before the pills arrived and were quickly swallowed. 'I'm sorry about yesterday afternoon,' Maureen looked a bit sorrowful. 'I was supposed to bring you up to date on everything, but I seem to get stuck when I get to the bit about who partners who.'
'Give me a quick update over breakfast.' Mark felt a bit better, although he didn't believe the pills could have had any effect yet.
'You can fancy food?' clearly Maureen didn't feel much better.
'I'm starving,' was the reply.
'After all you ate last night! I don't see how you can be hungry.' Maureen glanced at the clock as she spoke and started giggling. 'Have you seen the time?'
Mark looked at his wrist. 'It's not five yet. That white wine does funny things to you. Mind you, it was nice, and the meal was delicious. But the best thing was the company,' he gave her a little hug. 'Let's get showered and changed, and then I'll make breakfast.'
Maureen started giggling again. 'I don't think my clothes would quite fit you, although you can try if you like.'
The standard clothing was identical for men and women, but everyone's was made to measure for them, and as Mark was nearly twenty centimetres taller than Maureen, and about twenty five kilos heavier he joined in the laughter at the mental picture of him in her clothes. 'I could still use a shower, even if I put these things back on. I can call at home on the way to the university and change. You go first. I'll get us some more coffee.'
As he went back to the kitchen, Mark thought about the previous evening. He had enjoyed being with Maureen, enjoyed the meal and the wine, although he decided next time just one bottle for the two of them might be better. If he lived with Maureen, and moved his things in, they could eat like that every night, and he

wouldn't have to go home to change. He was short of the normal age at which he would leave home to join in partnership with a woman, and would normally have no choice of partner. If he moved in now, it would solve a lot of things.

'I thought you were getting us some more coffee?' Maureen came into the kitchen.

'I'm sorry. I was just thinking about last night. If I moved in with you we could be together all the time,' Mark handed her a cup.

Maureen avoided his gaze. 'Yesterday I planned for you to stay the night. I wanted to go to sleep in your arms, and wake up with you beside me. Now I'm glad it happened differently.' She looked up at him. 'I want something more than that.'

Mark was confused. Women were certainly strange. 'What do you want?'

'I'm not sure, but at the moment I don't want anything to change.' Maureen was not making sense, even to herself. 'Go get in the shower and I will make some breakfast.' As they ate Maureen started to fill him in on everything she could think of. The planet the computers had discovered still held some life, but was previously very populated, although they didn't think by anything of high intelligence. The distances involved were huge, but travel times had been cut by use of the rings before their world was created. There were two ways to travel using the rings. The permanent way was to move from ring to ring at junctions. The exact course was plotted in advance and the new planet was seventeen days away, although it would once have been measured in thousands of light years. The second way was to use the bendelec principle with the rings to move almost instantaneously to somewhere else. Mark made a mental note to find out more about the rings, as they seemed to affect everything. He picked up Maureen's voice again as she explained that with the temporary travel system you could go somewhere and see everything, but it was very difficult to do anything. You were not visible, so had no effect on your surroundings. If you wanted to do anything at all you had to become visible, but the transporter would only hold this state for seconds before pulling you back. In theory there should be a way to make the temporary movement permanent, but no one had discovered how. Greg was the only one who had made temporary trips to the new planet. There was a limited amount of plant life in the six locations he had tried, but he saw no trace of animal life. Most of the planet was water and they believed from the computer findings that if there was animal life on the planet, then it would be found there. The computers had been amassing data for a long time now on the temperatures, winds, rainfall, seasons and everything else they could read at such a distance to try and assess the best areas for man to survive. The six picked so far were the ones Greg had visited. They all had abundant water and plant life and were in regions where the temperature never dropped too far. The day was longer than the one they were used to. All Greg's trips had been fully recorded and Mark would be able to see the results. There had been no permanent travel to the new planet as this would make use of one of the old freight transporters. Greg had offered to take the chance of using the temporary transporter, but as this was direct and moved only him, a malfunction was unlikely. When they used the old freighters, although they had been perfectly maintained and were as good as new, a seventeen day voyage was much more of a gamble. The first time they were used would not be a practise run. Who was going to be on them was the point they had reached last night.

Mark realised he had not touched his breakfast. He had been spellbound as he listened to Maureen. 'When can we see the recordings?' He started to eat.

'After today's meeting if you want to, and talking of meetings, it's time we were on our way.' They called in at Mark's home for him to change, and his mother remarked that they both looked very pale. Maureen explained that they had not taken the correct quantity of a new food, and that they would be fine by lunchtime. Mark was amazed how quickly his world had altered from one in which the truth was sacred to one in which lies could be told at will. Before they left the apartment his mother took him gently by the arm. ‘I know what you are doing is right and for the good of us all, but please ask them to be careful with you. Your father and I both love you very much and never want to see you come to harm.’

Mark was saddened as they set off to the meeting. When Maureen was describing the new world he had thought of nothing except being there. Even the chance that he would not be selected had never entered his mind. That other people would be affected by him... and that of course included Maureen. If he had to choose between a new world and her?

‘When do they expect the results of the tests to find out who is best suited to each other?’ He suddenly realised that this could be very important.

‘The details are held for everyone except you three newcomers. Accurate figures cannot be obtained until the drugs have been reduced in your bodies.’ Maureen was feeling a bit better after the effects of last night.

‘But that wouldn't affect my genes.’

‘It affects whether you could ever pass them into another generation. Until you three are done, the best matches cannot be made.’ They entered the university as Maureen spoke.

‘The computer will have our gene patterns anyway, so it could give a temporary result.’ Mark wanted to know the future. ‘If we asked it for two results, one with me being a father, and one without.’

‘And for Nicky and Brian?’ Maureen asked. ‘Already you are reducing the present situation to ifs and buts. It has already been decided that the whole group will wait and get one result.’

‘Wait for how long?’ Mark decided he hated waiting.

Maureen stopped and squeezed his hand. ‘One month.’ She looked up at him, and her eyes caused some of that original feeling when he first kissed her to return. ‘We have one month to be in love. Then we find out if it can be forever. Let's make the best of that month.’ She kissed him very lightly on the cheek before they made their way into the meeting.

F

It wasn't long before the meeting room filled up and Joanne suggested they take comments first from the newcomers.
Brian glanced round at Nicky and Mark and then rose to his feet. 'I assume that the three of us have been filled in with the same information.' Joanne nodded slightly as he glanced in her direction. 'Three options have been suggested. All go to the new planet, all stay here or we split into two groups and one group go.' Again Joanne confirmed with a nod of her head.
'Taking the second route first, I see it only as a stopgap. If we extend the present world we have it will only be a matter of time before our presence is discovered by the new people we create and we will be back to square one.'
'The idea was to create a larger number of people in conditions identical to the ones they would find on the new world. We could then help them to find immediate answers to any problems before moving them to the new world, probably under the influence of drugs, so that they never knew their origins.' Joanne interrupted. 'So the stop gap principle is right, although I can see some slight advantages in being close at hand.' A slightly puzzled expression on Brian's face cleared as he went on. 'I believe we should aim to set up the new world from day one. There is less chance of us being discovered like that and I earnestly believe that some of us have to remain here. The chances of survival on a new planet are increased by larger numbers, but I think it would be potential suicide to all go there. If there is present even the most innocuous virus that mankind had not encountered before, it could wipe out the whole group. It might be another ten thousand years before a new Joanne came along to start the next group. I think we have no alternative but to split our ranks.'
Although Brian's voice did not carry the almost magical quality that both Joanne and Earl possessed, his logical argument was

hard to challenge. Mark was convinced his was the correct line, but felt he had to speak out.
'What Brian has said is of course correct, but I would like to play Devil's Advocate if I can borrow a phrase from our past. When I first heard about the new planet, I didn't give a second thought as to who else would be going, assuming that I would be one of them. That doesn't mean I think I should go, just that I hadn't considered the possibility that I wouldn't go because of the excitement involved. I would still like to go, but realise now that it may not be possible. There may be others who do not relish the thought of going but would be the best logical choice. I feel a new generation would be less likely to succeed if it did not have the pioneering spirit of the people who opened up our old world. People who wanted to go, whether to try and find a better life, or just for the adventure involved, would have more chance of success. I do not believe that anyone should have to go just because they are the most logical choice. I think they would be less likely to succeed. I agree with Brian that a split of the group is the most logical way to proceed, but suggest we get the results from the computer before we discuss the new world further. I think whoever goes should have the biggest say in how we proceed.'
Mark sat down as Nicky got up. 'I agree totally with what has been said. I can't see why there is the rush to get things decided, when another month will tell us a lot of what we want to know.'
Joanne rose and was silent for a few moments, 'Yes, you are right Nicky. It's just that some of us have been waiting for so long that we are probably too eager to proceed. We thought we could sort out a lot of the details before the big decision. I think it would probably be more sensible to revert to your original drugs withdrawal programme and call the next meeting when the results of the computer analysis are known. If in the meantime you have any more original thoughts, we can re-convene.'

A quick show of hands gave total agreement to this proposal and the meeting split up soon after.
Cocho rounded up the three newcomers with the news that they might just as well resume their studies in the Memory Builder, and they set off for their lessons after Maureen said she would meet Mark when his final session was over.
The bulk of the time in the Builder was spent looking at the politics of the old world, how Communism had only succeeded in any sense at all with relatively small populations, but how capitalism had contributed to the eventual disaster because of the reluctance of the wealthy to keep on helping the poor. The first had been practised for centuries before being grasped by a large part of the world as the new way forward. Its own size had destroyed it and its people started on the capitalist way of life. Capitalism itself became more and more profit conscious, and the successful multinationals became larger and larger as they either took over their competitors, or reduced them to bankruptcy. Eventually three giant corporations controlled the wealth of most of the world. These were owned by the employees and pension funds of the same three corporations. The power of these giants was controlled by the workers, and Mark smiled at the sly reference to the way in which a type of Communism had won the capitalist world, with no-one realising it. He finished the session for the day unsure of the way in which he would like to see the new world develop, but knowing that he would not allow it to decline in the same way as the old one.
Maureen was waiting for him outside, and they linked arms as they set off.
'I wish this month would hurry up. There is so much to be planned for the new world,' Mark's mind was still full of the days learning. 'Now you know why we are so keen to get on with it, even though we agreed to your delay of one month,' Maureen could not resist a gentle piece of sarcasm.

'Touché.' Mark accepted with good grace.
'Anyway, please don't wish our time together away. I just cannot have any optimism about the results to come.'
Mark squeezed her arm as they walked, 'You're right. Let's concentrate on us. Tonight I'll cook the dinner, and we can try a lot less wine. We can listen to some of the old music and you can twiddle my hair like last night.' Maureen smiled. 'Did you enjoy it that much?'
'It helped my mind to just relax and float. It's hard to explain, but it really is a wonderful sensation,' Mark could almost sense the feeling it provided.
'Then I had better try it tonight instead of you, although it must be mighty powerful to affect your memory as well.' As Maureen laughed Mark knew he had missed something. 'You wanted to see the pictures of the new planet that Greg brought back.'
Mark was instantly torn. He desperately wanted to see the new pictures, but he also felt he would be disappointing Maureen if he made that his choice. 'How long are they?' he asked.
'The six cover just over three hours, but you could watch a couple while I make dinner if you like, then decide if you want to see the others tonight.' Maureen pulled him right at a junction. 'I thought we'd pop in to see your mother on the way to my apartment. I think she was worried how bad we looked this morning.'
Mark realised that his hangover had disappeared without him noticing. The headache had gone, and the tight, empty space in his stomach had disappeared. The decision he made surprised him at the time, but afterwards he was sure it was correct. 'I can watch those whenever, this evening is just for us.'
They arrived at Mark's apartment, and as Maureen had guessed, his mother was pleased to see them looking so much better. 'I think I had better take a change of clothes with me, I may be out all night again.' Mark started towards his bedroom, but Maureen brought him to a standstill.

'No, it's okay tonight. We will both be at home.'
Mark glanced at his mother, then Maureen. 'Oh, I thought we would be going right through again.'
'No, it's another experimental dinner, and tonight we had better get the quantities right.' Maureen smiled at his mother.
'I do worry about him you know, with this new type of work he does. He looked so bad this morning, in fact you both did. I bet it was your idea to pop in and let me see you had fully recovered. Girls seem so much better at understanding feelings than boys. I sometimes think he'll be just like his father. More feelings for what goes on at work than what goes on at home.'
Mark was feeling embarrassed, and interrupted his mother. 'Don't worry, mum. I'll be fine. Maureen will make sure nothing happens to me.'
'That's a promise,' said Maureen as they left.
On the way to her apartment Mark asked about the evening to come. 'I thought you wanted me to stay the night.'
'I do, but not yet. I know it sounds silly, but this isn't the time.'
'So when is the time?' Mark couldn't resist giving a bit of torment.
'I don't know, but I'm sure I will at the time.'
'Let me know, and I'll try to be around,' Mark was enjoying the situation.
'Oh don't be so awkward, Mark,' it was the first time either of them had shown anything but loving feelings towards the other. 'You're still well under the control of drugs, so you have no idea yet of the feelings I'm going through. When you've grown a bit more perhaps you'll understand.'
Mark didn't know how to reply. He felt slightly scared of the Maureen he had never seen before. Would his feelings grow like hers?
She stopped and turned to face him. 'I'm sorry, Mark. Please forgive me. It's just that I love you very much, and don't know what to do about it. I need your help, but until the drugs have

been reduced a lot further, you won't be able to give it. Remember those first kisses? Those are the sort of emotions I have all the time.'

'If I say or do anything stupid, just give me a good slap,' Mark felt that a little humour was his best way out.

They started walking again and the atmosphere had lifted before they reached Maureen's apartment. Mark was still not sure if what was between them was the drugs, or if men and women were fundamentally different. He had never before seen his mother get so upset over a minor problem, but then realised that she had never had to deal with a problem in her life before. Everything was taken care of. Paradise existed, and he wanted to escape from it. Perfection exchanged for problems. If he wanted to exchange it, then it couldn't be paradise in the first place. Except that it had been paradise before. A small part of him wished just for a second that none of this had happened. That Maureen had never come to the meeting. That he had never met her. If he felt pressure from the problems facing him now, what would it be like when he was off drugs completely? What must Maureen be going through all the time? Even as the thoughts raced through his mind, he knew that he couldn't go back, and didn't want to. If for nothing else, he couldn't chance losing her, and had to try everything in his power to keep it so.

In the apartment he flicked the screen onto old world recipes, and chose stroganoff. He punched in the request for number three flavour range, together with onions, mushrooms, stock, butter, soured cream and nutmeg. Salt and pepper were already there. As he started to cut the meat substitute into thin strips, he remembered that alcohol was often used in the old days to enhance the flavour of food. What if he tried white wine instead of the stock? Discretion eventually persuaded him to try half stock and half wine.

The meal was a great success, and they finished the bottle of wine he had used to enhance the flavour of the sauce. Mark was in favour of starting another bottle, but Maureen reminded him of how bad they felt that morning, and how most of last night had become a blank. She joined him on the settee, but this time lay with her head on his lap. Mark's mind had drifted into the same sort of pleasure he felt when Maureen had been stroking his head. It was a wonderful sense of well being. As he gently tangled his fingers in her hair, his thoughts eased along with a feeling that gave little prickles of pleasure in his head.

'I hope we get selected together,' Maureen was murmuring rather than talking. 'Just think how we could plan the future. We could create a nice world. One where everyone was happy. One where we could be proud for our children to grow up.'

'A world like the one we used to live in,' Mark didn't make the comment with any malice, and Maureen understood what he meant.

'Just like that, but with the freedom to make up our own minds,' she gently raised herself on one elbow and looked into his eyes. 'The two of us together for all time, and our children with us.' She raised her lips to his, and the kiss this time was soft and tender. For a long time their lips embraced each other. Not in the way of those first kisses which had produced such a reaction in Mark, but in a way that made his dream like state even more wonderful. Was it the wine? Was it the reduction in the drugs starting to take effect, or was it just him and Maureen? Was it a combination of everything?

They kissed again, and the pleasure was just the same. A little shiver ran down his spine. Moments like this never existed in the old paradise. As soon as that thought passed through his mind, he knew that the opposite was true. In the old paradise, although this intense type of feeling never existed, nor did the pain of it having to end. If they were not selected together........Mark's mind ran on. If they didn't go to the new planet, then they could stay here. They could live together like this for ever.

He gently broke the kiss. 'If we don't get selected to go, then we live here together. If we have children, that's fine. If we don't then that's fine as well, because we will always have each other. How stupid we've been. Either way we win.'

'I wanted you to say that, but I also want you to say it when you are clear of drugs. The problem comes if one of us is selected to go and the other isn't,' Maureen gave him a quick kiss on the lips as she spoke.

'My little pessimist. The chances of that are remote. We will be together, never you fear,' Mark felt confident.

'The chances depend on how many stay and how many go, but we've agreed to wait and get the results, so let's forget about the problems, and concentrate on us.' Maureen was determined to keep the evening going.

They kissed again, just as long and just as tenderly, but it was impossible to re-create those first few minutes as they both thought of the possible future.

That night Mark lay awake for a long time. His mind felt clearer as the effects of the wine left him. He was sure of two things. He wanted desperately to be part of the new world, and he wanted Maureen to share that with him. When he was with her it was difficult to think of anything or anyone else. Alone in his room he found it more easy to rationalise his thoughts for her. He felt sure that he loved her, but nagging little doubts sometimes crept in. What if part of the love was because she was the one who had found him? What if some of the interest he had shown in the other women in the group was fuelled by love rather than by curiosity? They all had their own attractions, but he was sure that Maureen was the one. Perhaps if they were the only ones to go to the new world, then any other thoughts would be banished as they were on their own. As he drifted into sleep his mind went back to the session in the Memory Builder when he looked up the river into the setting sun. The cottage with the daffodils in the garden. What would their house be like? The dog with one blue and one brown eye that had licked his hand. They would have to have a dog, and he knew just which sort.

Next morning he called Maureen on the videophone, 'Just to tell you that I love you.' It seemed important to do it, and she seemed very pleased with the call. 'Snap,' she replied, 'the more I hear you say it, the more I like to hear it.'

The sessions in the Memory Builder were concerned with the spread of humanity throughout the world. The most successful emigrants took a lot of the items they considered necessary for life with them. Mark made a mental note that whoever went in the future should do the same type of thing. He noticed that there was an almost deliberate vagueness about the origin of mankind. The majority view was that man was descended from the primary life forms on that planet. The exact link had never been found. The religious view was that mankind had been placed on the planet by God. In between were a number of minority views, including those who believed that man came from the stars. Most of history was black and white, although a little colour had sometimes been added either accidentally or not. He was more at home with facts, and didn't care for the grey areas. As he was convinced of the existence of God, he decided that was the theory he would accept for the time being.

Maureen was the one to meet them for lunch that day, and they discussed the morning lessons. Brian was convinced that man was descended from primary life, through the great apes. Nicky was not sure either way. As he listened to their arguments, Mark was again troubled by his previous thought. What if the things they were contemplating now had been done previously? What would you tell your children about their origins? Certainly not the truth, that they were the remnants of a failed civilisation that had lived as zombies for ten thousand years, and were still living, being watched over like children in a nursery. That God had put them there? That could be true, as if they were carrying out God's will then that was true, and it could well be the truth in any case. That they had come from the stars? True again. That they had descended from the apes? Brian would believe that was true. Or would they present a mish-mash of half truths to cover their exact origins?

'Back to work,' said Maureen, 'I'll meet you later at your Builder, Mark. Mum and Dad have asked us over for a meal, and I accepted for both of us. I hope that's OK with you.'

'That's fine,' Maureen had spoken very little about her parents, and Mark was looking forward to meeting them. 'Tell me, what do the rest of you do while we are beavering away, now that there are no meetings to attend?'

'It depends on the education we had. Most of those with a scientific background of any sort are trying to discover all they can about the new planet from the computer. The rest of us are attempting to put together the ultimate survival package for whoever goes there,' Maureen seemed to include herself as one of 'the rest'.

'Did you like the sunset scenes from the new world?' Nicky asked Mark.

'I haven't had time to look at them yet. Perhaps tonight,' but as he caught Maureen's expression he realised they would be out that evening, 'or tomorrow,' he added lamely.

'You'll be number one volunteer when you see them,' Brian looked across at him, 'absolutely fantastic!'

'I thought nothing was being done about the new world until we had the computer results?' It seemed to Mark that he was missing out on some important and interesting work.

'Nothing is being done as far as selecting the people who should go, but we are getting on with anything that could be of help in the meantime. You can trust us, Mark. Some of us have a bit of intelligence,' Maureen's laugh as she spoke taking any possible upset out of her words.

Mark felt a bit sheepish. 'It's just that it sounds a lot more exciting than some of the stuff in the Memory Builders. It also

doesn't seem to run in a logical sequence. We go from the start of this world right back to the start of the original one and all the stops in between.'
'It's done like that to make you think about what took place, instead of learning it in sequence. It's very easy not to think about things if they are presented in a straight line. The programme will have been altered from the time I looked at it. Not in content, just in sequence, to try and gain anything else that might be there. I know it's not as interesting as some of the work we are doing but believe me, some of that is fairly mundane as well. Looking at everything we do at present, and trying to re-organise that for a world without most of the basics is not the top of scientific aims,' Maureen glanced at the time as she spoke, 'now back to lessons.'
'Yes ma'am,' Nicky was grinning as she used the phrase from the old times.
The afternoon session continued on from the first, looking at the spread of civilisation. A lot of it was well documented, but some of it had obviously been guessed at to coincide with other events. Parts of it again set Mark thinking if someone else had been concerned in the start of that world. There were lots of unexplained areas that had been accepted because they existed. Parts of huge building works remained from a time when civilisation was not sufficiently advanced to have constructed them. No definite explanations were given, just a few possibilities that were accepted universally. He soon realised that they could very easily conceal any trace of the past. A few half-truths handed down from generation to generation would cover everything.
Maureen was waiting for him as they left the building.
'How much can we actually tell about the new planet from the information we are able to get?' Mark's mind was never far away from his possible new home. 'Not as much as the scientists would like,' replied Maureen, 'there was a lot of

discussion that we should send one of the freighters to take as many pictures as possible and return. The proposal was only narrowly defeated, and I'm still not sure about it. If you go as Greg did, using the Bendelec, then as long as you don't materialise at all on the new planet nothing can come back with you. As it is, he was still given a check for everything we could think of while we held him in quarantine. If you send one of the freighters, the safe zone for contamination would keep it far enough away as to be ineffective. It's an area of research that hasn't been updated for ten thousand years, because we don't know how to go about it. If we knew what to look for we could identify safe distances, but from the research that was done by Li Po it would seem that some contamination can spread across vast areas. To enable it to be studied, we would have to first populate another space station to use as a Guinea Pig. We could then pull exploratory missions back to that base and write it off if there was dangerous contamination. If we could link travel using the rings with normal time, then it would be possible to send a freighter which could transmit back all the pictures we need but the pictures would take light years to travel back. If we could combine rings travel with Bendelec travel, then we could put a freighter into close orbit without it materialising, and get the information we need that way. Two problems for that one. Bendelec is only useful for small objects, as large ones tend to break up, and everything sent has only a very limited range of travel.'

'I keep meaning to learn all about these rings,' Mark felt he couldn't contribute enough unless he had all the facts.

'There are major sessions to come in the Memory Builder which will give you all the information we have. It's pretty logical; you just need a very open mind to accept its principles. The main problem is that the Bendelec also bends time. If you take that area to its logical conclusion, then time is also a ring. If we stay here instead of going to the new world, you will be free to sit in on the discussions that take place on the possibility of time being a ring. They are suspended at the moment as everyone is concerned with the new planet, but if you want a real headache, then you can look forward to some interesting meetings. Most things to do with rings are fairly reasonable, but when you decide that you are going backwards and forwards in time at the same time, and the thing that you did yesterday was actually tomorrow as well, you have got major problems. It also means of course that we have already been to the new world, and we came before the old world. Great isn't it? What we do know is that if you use the Bendelec principle, and then materialise, you have only a very short time to do anything, as the power fades very quickly. In the tests that were done in the past, volunteers were lost in time or space, we don't know which. The main computer will not handle any theories connected with time travel as it is logically impossible. Li Po was, we think, the only person who could have taken the present knowledge further. Although we could retain his memory, we could not re-create his thought patterns. It's another area that hasn't advanced for ten thousand years.'

As Maureen finished speaking she stopped outside an apartment block similar to the others, and they were soon being welcomed by her parents.

They were very interested to find out about the work Mark and Maureen were doing, and Mark found it easiest to let Maureen start the reply and he would finish it off. How easily they had become accomplished liars. It saddened him that they were going to start a whole new world on the basis of lies, but he could think of no sensible alternative.

The meal was very pleasant, and it wasn't a strain to keep the conversation on topics that were safe and easy to deal with. The only situation that surprised Mark was after the meal, when they were sat with cups of coffee, and the conversation was starting to wane. Mrs. Adams said that she too, like Mark, was a student

of history. She had concentrated her efforts on historical fiction. The theory was that nearly all fiction contained historical facts and part of her work was trying to reconcile fiction with known facts, where possible. She enjoyed the work immensely, as she would have studied fiction in her spare time anyway. 'If I didn't know differently, I would swear you two were in love, just like some of the characters from the novels I study. The way Maureen carries on is exactly the same as some of the heroines who fall in love, and when I met you, Mark, I could see why.'
Mr. Adams shook his head, 'Forgive your mum, Maureen, she sometimes does go on a bit.'
Maureen was quick to respond. 'I'm not surprised that it seems like that. We've been studying so much together, and especially with the new diets we've been trying out, I think we have just become very used to one another.'
Mr. Adams had not even noticed anything out of the usual, but Mark felt sure that although his wife gave the impression of being satisfied with the explanation, she felt there was more to the situation than she was being told.
Her only comment was that it was a shame that they did not have the good side of love from the old days, although she knew the problems that it raised. She didn't mention the subject again until just before it was time to go. Maureen was saying goodbye to her father when Mrs. Adams whispered to Mark, 'take care of her.' A little squeeze on his hand told him far more than any words. He returned the squeeze with the words, 'for ever.' He knew that he was letting out something which should remain a secret, but the look in her eyes told him that the chance was worthwhile.
As they walked back to her apartment, he told Maureen about the little exchange that had taken place.
'There isn't any reduction of drugs going on at the moment is there?' he asked.
'No, that is all suspended,' she replied.

'I just don't see how she could have understood so much without a reduction in drugs,' Mark was now slightly worried about his indiscretion.

'I don't expect men will ever understand. I know she is not my natural mother in the old sense of the word, but that doesn't stop me from being her daughter. When it comes to very deep feelings, she could be under drugs twice as powerful, and would still have part of my feeling in her. It's the same thing that your mother feels for you. Your heartache is hers. If you were a girl, then her heartache would be yours. It is something that mother and daughter can feel together. I think just very occasionally a son could sense some of it, but it would be very unusual. Don't worry about it having any effect on life outside her. That is another part of being a mum. There is no way she could do anything, or say anything, that could mean problems for me.'

Mark looked at Maureen afresh. Not only did she have the problems caused by the world outside drugs, but she had to cope with other feelings he could only guess at. In his historical studies he had sometimes been surprised at the choice of a woman as leader, and at the strength that woman had shown. There seemed to be a lot more to women than the history lessons had told him, although quite what the total truth was he wasn't sure. He resolved to be just a bit more careful in his dealings with women in the future.

G

Next day was back to the routine of the Memory Builder, and the first session seemed to be a continuation of the previous one on capitalism.

Mark found himself at the start of mankind on earth, approaching it as if in a spaceship, and immediately his mind interposed the old and new worlds. The beauty of the planet as he approached was incredible and he was taken on a tour of its natural splendours. From rugged mountain ranges to massive forests. From lakes that sparkled like jewels to endless plains where the moon and stars seemed so close he could reach out and touch them. Down rivers that held him captivated at every turn to the mighty oceans and beneath them to the life they held. Even the massive deserts had their own beauty, with the wind playing tricks that made them move like ripples on a golden pond. 'This is all for you. You are the only one in the world. This is yours, and it is free. It has no value but its beauty.'

As he wandered the world, man gradually appeared. He could walk unnoticed among the different peoples. He became a part of the history of each land. The men and women at first seemed content with their lifestyle, and took only the excesses of nature for their own use. They tried to replace something in the land for anything they took out of it.

He was present when man first exchanged crops he had grown for timber to help improve his shelter.

He saw the start of the concept of money, and the way it affected the world.

He saw the droughts and the famines and the floods. He saw how from every disaster someone increased his wealth.

He saw the wars which were fought to obtain more lands and peoples. He saw the way those people were never totally dominated, and eventually freed themselves again.

Huge houses of power arose, and counted their wealth in diamonds, gold, antiques, and their cash value. He saw those houses fall, only to be replaced by others.
He saw misery, poverty, and filth. He saw children die by the million. He saw oppression because of colour and creed.
But all the time he saw everything that was bad was fuelled by greed. Greed for wealth, greed for possession, greed to have more.
He saw mankind die. He saw the rich man become as the beggar, infertile. He saw the richest women reduced to the same level as the outcasts of the world, unable to reproduce.
He watched as the wealth so important became so worthless. The riches of the world changed hands as promises of cures were claimed.
He saw the mountains, the plains, the lakes, the deserts, the rivers and the oceans. The voice said again, 'this is all for you. You are the only one in the world. This is yours, and it is free. It has no value but its beauty.' Mark came out of the Builder pale and shaking. He knew that the programme had been put together to affect him as it did, but he also knew that it was true. He felt sick at what had gone on in the past. Not the physical sickness that came from the indoctrination designed to end the violence, but a far deeper sickness that the rape of something so beautiful had occurred. As he wandered back for lunch he remembered the suggestion that the end of mankind had been planned by a chemical distributor. Whoever he was could well have been right.
As he entered the room they used for lunch, Nicky threw her arms round him, and at the sight of her tears Mark began to cry uncontrollably as well. Brian came in at the same time as Clive and it was some time before peace was restored. Only Clive wanted anything to eat, the other three were content with a drink. Nicky was still sniffing. Mark was just about in control of

his feelings. Brian was fairly composed, but his voice sometimes wavered as they talked about the morning.

'If that is the future of our new world, then I don't think I want to be part of it,' Brian spoke for the three of them.

'That was the past of our old world. It is up to us to forge the future for the new one.' Clive was very dark, and Mark realised that much of the oppression of that old life would have been against his forefathers. None of them were white skinned, although Greg was fairer than most, and Mark wondered if they were more affected by the persecution they had seen because they all had some colour in their genes. He thought again about the morning's programme and realised that there had been massive oppression of all colours, by all colours. Did it really matter who had done what?

He glanced across at Nicky. Her lips were still trembling, and her eyes were red. She was not going to say anything for a while.

'You are part of it, Brian,' Mark remembered his previous feelings. 'I wished with all my heart that things could be back as they were, but only for a while. There is too much that we have now that is good to go back. We have to make it work.'

Nicky opened her mouth to speak, but the words got mixed up with more tears and she shook her head.

Brian took a large breath. 'I know you are right. I'm not sure what we are learning is doing us any good for the future. If our world goes at the same pace we'll all be long gone before trouble starts. I was against any interference in the new world, but now I'm not so sure.'

'What you have seen has been agreed by us all as being as near to the truth as we can possibly tell,' Clive was very serious. 'The obvious worry is that by putting together a programme of lessons, your minds can be affected, as millions were in the old world, to produce the type of result we want. That has not happened with the programme that you are undergoing, although it does in the normal sessions that the Happies have. None of us are sure that it is the correct thing to show you, and if you can think of areas to improve it, please let us know.'

'What is this afternoon's session about? I don't think I could face another one like that,' Nicky had managed to speak at last.

'I don't know how yours have been mixed, but this morning's was one of the worst.' Clive seemed fairly positive.

As they walked back for the afternoon session, Nicky walked alongside Mark. 'Thanks for holding me so tight when I needed it. I had no idea of the past really, and seeing all those children starve to death was awful. I think I would rather not have any children if I thought that was to be their future.'

'What if you are the only one able to have children out of the ten women in the group? Could you say no?' Mark knew it was a hard question, but it was also one that concerned him. If he ended up as the only man, and there was only one available woman, and it was not Maureen, he was not sure of himself.

'It would be alright if it was...' Nicky stopped and glanced up at Mark in alarm.

'We are all hiding secrets from one another, when we should be trying to share them. Who is the lucky man?'

'I'm not sure if it's a good idea. I don't think he suspects, and if I get selected for someone else it might be a good idea if he never knew.' As she glanced up at Mark, Nicky suddenly realised that she could be starting a dreadful mistake. 'Oh, it's not you, Mark. Oh, I'm sorry. That sounded really pompous. I think you are ever so…'

Mark cut off her embarrassment. 'I know it isn't me, silly. That hug would have been a lot different.'

'What's it like to be in love with someone who loves you back? That is... like you and Maureen. Oh, I'm sorry, I'm doing it again,' Nicky had gone red as she spoke.

'It's wonderful. It's the most wonderful thing in the world. It's awful facing the thought that we might not be together in the future. I don't know if I could cope. Look, we have to get on with the next lesson. Maureen will be coming to pick me up. Wait here and we'll collect you. You shall be our first guest for dinner. We can tell you together what love is all about.'

As Mark entered the Builder he was not certain he had done the right thing. His love for Maureen was a very personal thing, but he somehow wanted to share it as well. He knew he should have asked Maureen first but felt sure she wouldn't mind. As he sat down he realised another evening was going to pass without seeing the pictures from the new world.

The session started in exactly the same way as the morning one. He was again approaching earth and was thrilled again at the shear beauty of the planet. Again he saw the mountain ranges, different ones, but just as beautiful. The lakes, deserts, everything he had seen that morning thrilled him again. Mankind appeared again, and he started to feel a dread fear of what was to come. This time the emphasis changed, and concentrated on individuals. The scenes switched from great composers to artists, to poets, to sculptors and writers. Each was interspersed with pieces from the lives of ordinary people, but this time good people. He saw men and women who devoted themselves to helping their fellow human beings, without thought of fame or reward. He watched as aid was given freely, because it was right. Some of those he saw were recognised for the work they had done. Some were made into saints, but the majority were fulfilled by the good they had done, and that was their true reward. Because of the speed it used and the impressions the Memory Builder could create, Mark finished the session sound in the knowledge that billions of people were good, and that humanity need not be the sights he had seen that morning. The only thing left out was the knowledge that all that goodness had failed to save the planet.

Maureen was waiting for him. 'That must have been a good session; you look on top of the world.'

'I think I am at the moment. It was the session showing all the goodness and beauty that there can be in the world. After this morning I think we deserved that one.'
'What did you have then?' Maureen asked.
'All the worst things about mankind. The wars, the misery, but especially the greed.'
'No wonder you feel good. Just make sure the second memory doesn't blot out the possibility of the first. I didn't have the two one after the other like that,' Maureen seemed quite serious about the subject. 'Because of the time limits involved, the Memory Builders tend to give the end colours of the spectrum, when the middle is nearer the truth, but not as spectacular.'
They had walked some distance when Mark suddenly remembered Nicky. He stopped. 'We've left Nicky standing outside her Builder waiting for us.'
He started to run back, and Maureen joined him. 'I think maybe you have left her standing, not me.'
'I invited her to join us for dinner tonight,' Mark had not wanted to explain it like this.
'That's fine,' Maureen replied as they slowed to a walk.
'She wants to find out what it's like to be in love.'
'She wants what?' Maureen grabbed him before they rounded the corner to greet Nicky.
'She thinks she loves someone, and wants to know what two people being in love is like.'
'She might not get the chance to find out if you try anything else like this. It's our love, Mark. It's precious and not for other people to look at and decide if it's good or not.'
'I can tell her that tonight's off if you like,' as Mark spoke Nicky came round the corner.
'Hello you two. I thought Mark had forgotten me, so I came looking for you.' The afternoon session had obviously cheered her up.

'He had, but I somehow got the impression it was my fault.' Maureen linked arms with Nicky. 'Lesson number one on being in love is that women have to be a lot more in love than men.'

'How do you mean?' Nicky looked slightly startled at the forthright approach Maureen had used.

'They fall in love with us, and that can't be very difficult as we do nearly everything for them. We have to love them in spite of all their imperfections.' Maureen didn't glance at Mark, who was trailing along behind them.

Nicky was obviously embarrassed at the delicate situation she had been drawn into. 'Perhaps we should leave dinner until another night.'

Maureen burst out laughing, and turned Nicky round so she could hug both Nicky and Mark. She planted a noisy wet kiss on his lips before speaking. 'I think we really love them because of their imperfections.'

'You mean you weren't really upset with him?' Nicky was obviously relieved that the tension had been lifted.

'Whether you are upset with them doesn't matter. Loving them and forgiving them is what counts,' Maureen still had her arms round them both as they set off for her apartment.

'Rum cattle,' Mark muttered under his breath.

'What was that, darling?' Maureen was enjoying her role as tormentor.

'Nothing. Just thinking about a bit from one of the Memory Builders.'

They wandered in silence to Maureen's apartment.

As they entered Mark asked Nicky if she had seen the pictures from the new world.

'Yes, I thought it was very beautiful. Did you?'

'I haven't seen it yet, but I'm looking forward to it a lot,' Mark was making small talk on something he felt safe with, as he was still not totally sure of Maureen's mood.

'It's very much like the old world that we saw in the Memory Builders today, although possibly with not as much vegetation. Mind you, we only see a very small part.'
'What would you like for dinner, Nicky?' Maureen was opening a bottle of wine as she spoke.
'I haven't seen that type of bottle before. What is it?' Nicky added. 'Anything for dinner is fine. I usually have the day's menu.'
With the availability of anything through the system, some people never bothered to cook, and most tried the menu for the day unless it was something they disliked.
'Haven't you tried this before?' Maureen asked as she poured a glass, 'Sheila invented it.'
'Hang on just a minute,' Mark walked over to the videophone, and soon had Sheila's face on screen.
'Hello, we've got Nicky round for dinner, and I suddenly realised we weren't sure about giving her a drink.' He wasn't sure quite what had been decided about Sheila's wine.
'No problem. Just don't give her too much. It's not sort of official yet. I suppose I ought to bring it up at the next meeting. Mind you, by then most people will have tasted it. Enjoy your meal.'
Maureen passed a glass to Nicky. 'It's white wine, made by Sheila. It's a nice taste, but the alcohol can give you a nasty hangover if you drink too much.'
As she tasted the wine Nicky gave an involuntary shudder. 'It's not very sweet, is it?'
'No, but it gets better as you go on.' Maureen walked over to the control panel, and after calling out some options, punched in the instructions for their dinners. They were soon sat round the table, and Mark noticed that Nicky's glass was not going down at all. 'Can I get you a different drink?' he asked.
'Please. Any of the orange flavours. I don't find Shelia's wine very nice, but please don't tell her.'

'I'm sure she wouldn't mind. It was her first attempt, and I think in the old times you could get sweet wine,' Maureen looked to Mark for confirmation.
'There were all sorts of alcoholic drinks, but some people didn't like any of them.' Mark smiled.
'I thought alcohol was a major cause of trouble in the old world.' Although Nicky used the word 'thought,' she was sure of the fact.
'It seems that a lot of the pleasures caused a lot of the troubles, and that is one area that needs a great deal of thought for the future. Take love as an example. It is the greatest pleasure in the world, to love and be loved.' Maureen spoke from experience. 'But the thought that love can be taken away is painful, very painful. If I was to be the only one who could have children, and had to go to the new world with someone else, I don't think I could cope.'
'That's my problem,' said Nicky. 'I think I love someone, but I don't know what to do.'
'Asif is lovely. Those big dark eyes. Maybe if he was the one to go to the new planet with me, it wouldn't be so bad,' Maureen looked directly at Mark as she spoke.
'You wouldn't. How did you guess?' Nicky was very flustered.
'No, I wouldn't, and the way you look at him, I should think most of the women in the group know how you feel.' Maureen reached out and squeezed Nicky's hand as she spoke.
'That is amazing. How can you tell by just a look?' Mark took a sip from his wine.
'That's one of the differences between us. Women can feel things, whereas men have to talk about them to try and understand. I suppose that's what makes us love one another. Vive la difference.' Maureen surprised Mark with her phrase from the past.
'What would you do if you were me?' Nicky spoke very quietly.
'I don't know.' Maureen and Mark spoke together.

'Well at least you're unanimous in not knowing,' Nicky laughed. 'I thought you two out of everyone would know the answers.'
'I think the answers alter as you go along,' Maureen was not quite sure what she wanted to say. 'If you had asked Mark directly after our first two kisses, which everyone knows about…'
'The answer would have been love and let the future take care of itself,' Mark interrupted.
'And if you ask him when we are told we must separate, if it comes to that,' Maureen continued.
'It's better to have loved and lost than never to have loved at all,' Nicky quoted from the old days.
'I think we are back to don't know,' said Mark. 'We have survived so long without the type of love you are talking about; I think it may be impossible for us to tell what is what. I think we are as much in love as we know how to be at the moment, but whether that is the one great love, we have nothing but old history to judge it against.'
Maureen found herself nodding in agreement as he went on. 'If we remain together, either here or on the new planet, then I think we will be together, in love, for ever. If we do have to split up, I think it will make any new relationship difficult, especially in the early stages. It might have been better for the sake of that relationship if we had never been together in the first place.'
'Could you split up?' Nicky posed the question very softly.
Maureen answered. 'We have asked ourselves that question a thousand times, and fear that at some stage we may have to answer it for real. One problem is that the whole group knows we are in love, so if we do end up with a different partner it will be very difficult for that person as well. Hardly the stuff to build a new world on. Maybe Joanne is right. Pick the right person and hope for love to come later. I think it worked for some in the

old world, but I'm not totally sure. If you haven't loved before it must be a lot easier for it to work.'

They sat in silence as Mark poured coffee for them.

'Li Po was undoubtedly a brilliant man,' Maureen broke the moment, 'but I think even he didn't have the answers. He took all the contentious issues and put them to one side. That was his way of producing paradise. Perhaps with more time he could have sorted some of the problems out. I think we have to make decisions that we are happy to live with afterwards. I suppose however the new world progresses, we should try to mirror the principles of that world in the tiny part of this one that is ours.'

'Live your life that you are proud of your words and deeds,' Nicky produced another quotation from the old world to fit the occasion.

'I think that could well be the starting point for the new world, and hope that ideal is kept forever,' Maureen poured some more coffee. 'We seem to have sorted out everything but whether you should let yourself fall in love.'

'But you've told me the answer. I can wait less than a month to find out if he can be mine, then if he can, just watch me go,' Nicky was smiling as she stood up. 'Thanks very much for a lovely evening, and for straightening out my thoughts. See you tomorrow, Mark.'

'Hang on, I'll walk down with you,' Mark stood up.

'No, you stop and say goodbye to Maureen.'

Both women were giggling as Maureen answered. 'See what I mean about men.'

When Nicky had left, Mark asked why they had been laughing, and what the remark about men meant.

'This,' replied Maureen, and taking him in her arms, kissed him and held him tight.

Mark was suddenly very conscious of the shape of her pressed against him. He wanted to be closer to her than ever, and moved his body very gently against hers. As her grip relaxed, he opened his eyes. She swayed gently away from him and he saw she was biting her top lip. His previous decision to take care in dealing with women flashed across his mind like a blinding light, and he remained silent.

Suddenly she opened her eyes and kissed him lightly on the cheek. 'I love you. See you tomorrow.'

H

When he got home that night Mark was still very much awake, and called up the first of the videos that Greg had taken on the new planet. He was looking along a beach of very pale golden sand. The view was altered to give the impression of walking along the beach, as far as a headland which was at first in the distance. Climbing the small hill gave him a view right down the coast, and the view panned round to show an area of vegetation which ran back to the foot of a small mountain range. It was very hard to judge distances or heights, and the view continued along the side of the mountain until it picked up a stream, which the camera followed down to cross the area between mountain and sea, broadening as it did so. It eventually reached the sea at the far end of the beach where the film had commenced. No documentary was given to spoil the effect, and Mark could hear the whisper of the wind as it sighed through reed beds at the back of the beach. He thrilled to the music of the stream as it chattered over the rocks before plunging into a pool at the base of the mountains. He felt the movement of the river as it silently slipped between small trees and bushes on its way to the sea. He sat spellbound as the tide caused waves to roar onto the beach, only for them to fade into a soft caress as they died and pulled the sand back with them.

He had seen all this before, but in a world that was gone forever. This one was real and obtainable. The beach faded as the statistics of the area came onto the screen. It was an island over two hundred kilometres long, and seventy kilometres wide. He flicked back to the start. He would pick up the facts and figures later. Right now he wanted to walk that beach again, and listen to the wind and the sea. The fifth time he played the video he fell into a deep sleep.

He wandered along the beach, and he thought it was Maureen with him, but he was not certain as she seemed to change

continuously. He delighted in seeing their shadows going ahead of them. This time he crossed the fertile area and climbed the mountains. He looked round over his world and knew he had indeed found paradise.
He awoke with a terrible crick in his neck and the facts about the island filling the screen. He glanced at the time. Just after six. No point in going to bed. He made some tea and was just about to go back to the screen when he picked up the videophone and dialled Maureen's number.
She looked puzzled and half awake as her image cleared. 'Just to say I love you. See you later today.' He flicked the screen off as she opened her mouth.
He was going to run the number one location video again, but changed his mind and put number two on.
This time there was far more vegetation, with taller and stronger trees. Again Greg had used a panning technique that gave the impression that for part of the time you were walking in the area. The view changed from the woodland and crossed some gently rolling meadows that gradually descended to a broad, slow moving river. The fields were full of the most gorgeous flowers he had ever seen. True, they were nothing in size compared with the plants he regularly saw in their own parks, but their quantity, brightness of colour, and the way they were spread in such a haphazard fashion over the landscape made them a thousand times better than the regimented lines of flowers at home. He felt he could almost smell the perfumes which he knew must be there. The image changed to the river itself, and he caught a small movement close to the surface of the water. Although he ran the sequence a dozen times, it was impossible to make out what it was. The view changed to the opposite bank of the river, and climbed through meadows very similar to the ones he had crossed earlier. He was again captured by the beauty of the flowers. He could imagine Maureen sat in the middle of all that beauty, and he was surprised when he

visualised her in a dress, something that no one wore any more. The vista rose to take in a row of trees marking the edge of a wood that formed the horizon. It ran down to the river, and up, and the impression was one of a carpet of beauty held together by the woods on either side, and fed by the river running through the middle. A carpet of beauty that ran on forever.

He skipped the details and ran through the scenery once more. The video hadn't finished when his mother joined him.

'What a beautiful place, Mark. Is it part of the old world?'

'It's how the old world used to be in parts. A pity we can't create the same type of thing here.'

'I think it's safer on images, really. There used to be rats wherever there was water, and they used to spread a lot of disease. The field insects spread disease, and some of them carried lethal poisons. No, we are a lot better of here.'

Mark had a sudden desperate urge to shout at his mother, to tell her that her mind had been doctored, and was still being doctored, to believe that she lived in a paradise. He wanted to say that the new world she had just seen was real, and was what he wanted. That was the true paradise, and that what they lived in now was a prison by comparison.

He took a deep breath. 'Of course, you're right, mum. Look what happened to it in the end. I'll grab a shower, and then we can have breakfast together.'

His father joined them for breakfast, and although he enjoyed the time with his parents there was always a slight unease on his part as they asked questions about the work he was doing. He didn't like to tell then downright lies, but in some cases there was no alternative.

Breakfast finished with his mother expressing her pleasure that they had managed to get his food right. 'You looked so pale that morning. I wish I could get you a proper meal, instead of you having that special stuff, even for breakfast.' He told her he was

fine, and that the paleness was a very temporary thing that hadn't even needed drugs to cure.
She seemed happy as he left for the university. He felt just a bit sad, however, as he thought of them as part of a pet collection. He knew people used to keep animals, and he had a sudden vision of his present world as a huge aquarium. The people were fish, swimming contentedly through their world. They had plenty to eat, were kept warm and comfortable, and their whole life was meaningless. All they did was maintain the species, but as long as they were happy, did it matter? He wanted to escape from the aquarium into the ocean. The trouble was, he didn't know who lived there already: beautiful and harmless angel fish, or beautiful and dangerous sharks.
Again the vision flashed through his mind of them not being the first to start again. What if the old world was already a second chance? He shuddered at the thought. Instead of an aquarium he saw the earth as an ants nest in space. People as insects rushing forwards and backwards in a never ending pursuit of they knew not what. Then one day the park keeper came past. 'Drop some poison on that ants nest sometime,' he told his assistant. The end of the world. He felt sure that wasn't the true story, but just the thought sent another shiver down his spine.
Sven was the one to greet them that morning. 'Any problems with what you have learnt so far?'
Nicky was the first to reply. 'Not so much problems, as trying to tie everything together, especially as far as the future is concerned.'
'That's why everyone is in such a hurry to get something done. I read once a quotation from the old days: 'If you have a problem and can't see the solution, try not to do anything about it. As various options come up and they are not acceptable, discard them. The final option is the solution.'' Sven grinned at them.
'The trouble is in knowing when the final solution comes along.' Nicky was thinking about Asif, Mark decided.

'I believe he must have been a very wise man who said it, so he would know when the problem was solved.' The grin had not left Sven's face, and Mark decided there was much more to this very quiet man than you first realised.
'I seem to be finding it more and more difficult to handle conversations with my parents. I am forever on my guard against saying anything which might jeopardise the group.'
Sven became more serious as he replied to Mark. 'That is a problem which most of us encountered, and why we now live apart from the Happies. We also did not take anyone who had already entered a relationship into our group. Joanne thought the complications would be immense. When you want to have your own place, just let me know. We have two or three apartments in reserve all the time.'
He handed out the instructions for the morning's programme, and they set off for their lessons.
Brian seemed very quiet, and Mark asked him what the trouble was.
'I think it's something to do with coming off the drugs. It doesn't seem to be a smooth process at all. One minute I'm looking forward to the future so much it hurts, and the next I don't really want to let go of the past. I have feelings that are difficult for me to cope with, but they come and go as well. I didn't want to say anything to Sven, as they seem sort of private, but I wondered if you two had felt anything like it.'
'Don't tell us who she is; just believe that I have exactly the same trouble. Mark's lucky. At least his feelings are out in the open,' Nicky smiled up at Brian as she spoke.
'How did you know someone else was involved?' Brian stopped walking as he spoke.
'They are different to us, Brian,' said Mark, 'I sometimes think they are like Joanne, all seeing, all hearing, all knowing. They say they can feel things. We have a lot to learn about women.'

Nicky was making funny faces at them. 'I'll get my black hat and broomstick if you like.'

Even Brian had to smile. 'Thanks, you two. I just felt so alone.'

'I went through it all, but Mark and Maureen helped me out over dinner last night. Remember, we three have to stick together, so any problems and we ask one another.'

'I know, I just feel awkward talking about them,' Brian left them to enter his Builder.

'Thanks again for last night. It helped me a lot with my problems,' Nicky left him.

'I wish I believed we were sorting out problems, instead of just scratching at the tip of them,' thought Mark as he sat down.

The programme again opened with the flight to the planet earth, and a quick trip round its beauty. This time it concentrated on the romances of history. Some of them were the great, well documented love- lives; some were unheard of couples who had none the less loved each other so much.

For every man or woman who loved, their partner in life was everything to them. No one person could be loved as a partner by anyone else. There were the problems of break-up and resettlement, jealousy and infidelity, but in the main, each man loved one woman, and each woman loved one man.

They saw their partner in a slightly different light to everyone else, and yet that partner was still only a man or woman. The difference was in their perception of what they saw, not a property of that partner.

What you loved was what you believed your partner was.

The subject changed to religion and in the first instance the wars that had been fought for so long and so often in religion's name. Most of them used religion as an excuse for something else, but the truly religious wars were the result of someone's belief. That belief, or love, was so powerful that it had to be forced onto the rest of mankind. That love had to be shared with everyone. The programme flicked backwards and forwards between love of a partner and love of God. Love of a partner was often broadcast in notices and newspapers, but was kept secret between the couple, and not shared with anyone else. Love of God was often a very private thing, sometimes just a thought during the day or a prayer at night, but it was then shared with everyone.

Yet the two loves were identical. They were both a perception of what the other meant, whether it was God or a partner.

Sometimes that love was so strong it hurt. Sometimes it was difficult. Sometimes it fell down altogether. In both cases it was seeing with the mind and not the eyes.

With the love of a husband or wife there were billions of potential partners, each one waiting for that mind that would see them with love. With God, love took the same shape. There was no specific body to focus on, just a partner waiting for a mind that would see them with love.

Because there was no point of focus, believers had God in their mind, and loved their idea of what they saw.

As it is always more difficult to deal with the abstract, man gave his fellows his impression of God. There could have been billions of different Gods, as everybody held a different idea, but as is the case with mankind, the leaders gave their own definitions, and the masses folded those figures in with their own ideas to create their own God.

It was incredible, looking at it in retrospect, how few religions were created by man to cover so may impressions of what one God could be.

It was like every man on earth loving one woman. Although woman, or man, was only one thing, she or he had to be different for everyone else on the planet.

God, too, although only one, had to be different for everyone.

Mankind had always used their eyes to see, instead of their minds. Their eyes had told their minds what to think, and except for a very few, they had spent their lives in darkness. They were able to see God with their minds and paint a picture to help them, but they were unable to see things with their minds that their eyes had already focused on. Instead of seeing a leper as a person, their eyes told the mind to see that person as a leper.

Very few people were able to see the goodness in everything, yet it was there as part of the brain. You looked at the one you loved with the mind. You looked at God with the mind, yet nearly everything else you looked at with your eyes.

The scene switched back to the cottage by the bridge, in Mark's first Memory Builder session of his new life. Again the dog was licking his hand, and the question came across: was the dog good or bad? Mark knew the answer was good. The dog was good because it had shown love, and Mark had felt that love and given it back.

Love therefore became the answer.

Did you love someone because they were good, or were they good because you loved them? The two grew and fell together.

Whether it was God, a partner, a leper, or a dog: whatever it was in the world, if it was given love it became better, and if it was given more love it was better still. If that love started to fade, then so did the love that came back.

Very few on the old world had learnt to love like that. To love because something was there, rather than to love because of what was seen.

Again the scene switched quickly between a man who had taken everything he wanted in life, and a woman who had spent her life giving everything to the sick and needy in the gutters of one of the poorest cities on earth. He owned a large part of that city, but seldom went there, preferring his other homes around the world. She was often as hungry as the people she tended, but never left the city.

Mark then entered her mind. Love was so strong that tears of joy crept from the corners of his eyes, and he swallowed as his throat constricted. She had everything in life right there. Just as quickly he was inside the man's mind. The emptiness changed his tears of joy to tears of pain as he felt the nothingness. How could anything be so empty? No love ever went out, so none ever came in.

He was still feeling very low as he made his way back for lunch. Sven was there to greet them. 'I know there will be questions on this morning's programme, so who wants to start?'

The three looked at one another before Nicky spoke. 'What if your love is not returned?'

Again Sven had the grin on his face. 'Are we talking of someone special?'

Nicky nodded.

'Don't get confused between general and special love. Somehow we have to try and improve the presentation of that sequence. There really ought to be two words to describe love. Let's call the love you have for me love. Let's call the love Mark feels for Maureen true love, if he has no objection.'

Sven had such a lovely manner about him that Mark didn't think he would have objected, even if it were not true.

'If you can direct love to everyone and everything, then the improvement in your quality of life will be immense. I wasn't too sure about it before I decided to try it out. It has not altered the way I am. I know I am a very quiet person. I still am. I do not go round telling everyone I love them. I just try to make them feel it.' Mark felt that Sven's description was perfect. 'Use that same love for everyone, including that person you feel should have your true love. If that true love develops, then so be it. If it doesn't, at least you still have a good and loving friend.'

'What about God?' Brian seemed to have lifted his spirits from earlier in the day.

'Whether it's love or true love?'

'And about this return of love.'

'Right.' Sven looked at each of them in turn. 'Love or true love. I don't know. I think it's different for different people. Personally I don't think it has to matter. Whichever way you give that love, the more of it you give, the better you will feel. That great feeling you experienced in the programme when you entered the mind of the woman was the result of her loving. That is what God gives you back. If you were the only person in the world to give love, and no one gave any back, you would still get back all that love from God, because every time you give out love to anyone else, it goes to God as well.'

'So if the people in the new world all loved their companions, and really tried to keep that love going, then they would be in paradise,' Nicky looked like a child with a wonderful new toy, her eyes wide open in amazement.

'If it was as easy as that, then I think the old world would still be going,' Sven looked more serious as he spoke. 'To truly love some people is not always easy. Sometimes they don't want to be loved. It's easier to love the ones who want to be loved, who are the loving ones anyway. Ignore the warts and they'll go away. Believing that a wart is just a beauty spot is sometimes difficult. Even God comes in for trouble when things go wrong. Sue is one who can do it naturally. She loves everything and it shows. She is also loved.'

'What about the Devil?' Mark had never heard this subject raised before in his life.

'If you have to have some hate, or bad feelings in your life, it's a lot easier to channel them outside your own world. Throw all the bad things you feel at him, rather than at someone else. If you can get along with no bad feelings, then you are very lucky, but if you can't, then throw them all his way. If things go wrong, blame him. If someone else has a problem, chuck it on his heap. Stick with the love aspect, and throw the rest at the devil. He is one great guy.'

'You can't mean that.' Nicky was shocked.

'Of course I can. He absorbs all the hate, all the bad feelings, and never sends any back, because he doesn't exist. Very early on, someone realised that you need a fall guy, someone to take all the blame, so he invented the Devil. The only bad feelings that exist are the ones expressed between people. The Devil never dishes any out because he's not there to do it. The trouble is, most people blame anyone but themselves, and anyone but the Devil. As soon as you throw blame around, you get some back, and the whole thing goes downhill. Throwing love around doesn't seem as easy, but it's a whole lot better way to go on.'

'You make it all sound so easy,' Nicky was not so sure.

'It's the easiest thing in the world to talk through. All you have to do is love everyone and everything in spite of their blemishes. Any problems belong to the Devil. That's Sven's philosophy for life. Actually doing it is a lot more difficult, but it can be great fun trying, so why not give it a go?' The big grin was there again as he finished speaking.

'I think it will be easier in the new world,' Mark started to speak.

'It will also be easier tomorrow. Easier still next year, and easiest of all a hundred new worlds away in a thousand years,' Sven was laughing as he spoke. 'This is not a problem to put off, it's something good to try out here and now, so take your tabs for this afternoon, and get out there and love everyone and everything!'

I

Mark returned to his lessons that afternoon with very confused feelings. His original certainties in the old life that he had led had been replaced with uncertainty about everything.
His relationship with his parents, once so stable, was now mainly a tissue of lies.
With most of the group except Maureen he felt like a new boy at school. Everyone else knew what to do except him.
His relationship with God was apparently not enough to be just an acceptance; it had to be based on love. How could he love someone who had so nearly ended mankind? Or had he? With Nicky and Brian he at least felt a little more at ease.
With Maureen he was not totally sure how he felt. If there was love and true love that Sven spoke about, was his love for Maureen true love, or just first love? How much were his feelings dictated by the drugs that still coursed round his body?
The afternoon session in the Memory Builder looked at the discoverers of the past who had opened up the old planet. Those who had set out with the aim of finding fame and fortune: those who had been running from the circumstances in which they lived: those who were just curious to see over the next hill: those who wanted to create a better place for their children to grow.
As with all the Memory Builder sessions, the time allowed for a huge subject was limited, so the programme concentrated on the extremes of each area. Fame and fortune could be removed as far as the new world was concerned, as whoever went would not be coming back. The ‘what does it look like’ syndrome could go, as Greg had already provided the view. They didn’t have to run away from the world in which they lived, which left the reason for going as wanting to create a better place for their children to grow.
Mark felt that this was only partly the truth. In his history studies he had been amused by a remark made by a

mountaineer, returning from a particularly difficult ascent, suffering from quite severe frostbite. 'Why do I climb the bloody things? Because they are there.'
This was the main reason, Mark felt sure. If you are given a glimpse of what is possible, then you have to try for it. It was something different, and that in itself would never be available to most people in the world he now knew. Did everyone in the group of twenty feel the same way, or would some of them think the risks were too great? Did Maureen feel the same way as him? Up to now he had assumed automatically that would be what she wanted. As he decided to find out that evening, he was startled by a tap on the shoulder.
'Are you going to sit all evening in a switched off Memory Builder?' Maureen had come in looking for him.
As they walked back to her apartment, Mark searched for the words to ask if Maureen felt the same way as him. He realised that his previous assumption that she would automatically want to go may not be correct, and while he wanted it to be, didn't want her to be pressured by him.
'How do you see our future, given the best hopes?' he ventured.
'The two of us together for all time, hopefully with children of our own,' she stopped and slowly turned to face him, 'in the new world.'
He put his arms round her and held on tight.
'I did wonder when you would ask if I wanted to go,' she murmured.
'But I didn't. At least I hadn't, although I was going to. Anyway, how did you know what I was talking about?'
Maureen smiled up at him. 'Men don't feel, they have to hear it spelt out. If you had never joined the group, I would still want to go there, for much the same reasons as you. The difference is that even if I hadn't wanted to go before I met you, I would now because of the feelings I have for you and the fact that you wanted to go.'

As they entered Maureen's apartment, Mark felt that what he had heard was what he wanted to hear, or at least he thought so. Maureen suggested that they should watch the scenes from the new planet, much like people in the past would watch videos of resorts before deciding where to go on holiday.
They both helped to prepare a simple meal of tomatoes and herbs on pasta before settling down on the settee with a jug of Sheila's wine.
'Have you managed to watch any of them yet?' Maureen asked.
'Just Sites A and B, as Greg called them, although I would quite like to run through them again to see if I get the same thrill, and have an immediate comparison with the other four.'
Once again spellbound, they ran through the first two, and this time Mark read the details of the second location. It was set three hundred kilometres back from the coast in part of a huge land mass in the northern hemisphere of the planet. Although it was very beautiful, the feeling of walking along the beach in site A was an experience that Mark felt was too good to miss. 'Site A so far I think.'
'There are four more to come, but I agree so far,' Maureen replied as she moved closer to him and laid her head against his shoulder.
The third area was a vast expanse of prairie, again with a slow moving river. Clumps of trees and bushes dotted the area, and a three hundred and sixty degree turn by Greg gave an unbroken horizon in all directions. As when he first watched, Mark spent a lot of time going over pieces again, and they were both convinced that they saw something move on the skyline, but couldn't agree if it was alive.
As they ran through the details of the location, Maureen pointed out that they had taken over an hour to watch that one. 'It might be a good idea to let your mother know you're going to be late if you want to watch the other three.'

‘Or I could stay the night,’ volunteered Mark. He was sitting with his arm round Maureen, and the feeling of relaxed contentedness that he had experienced with her before had prompted the suggestion.

Maureen thought hard before replying. She knew that one of the last programmes Mark would run in the Memory Builder was the one attempting to explain about sex. As a Happy, there was never any information available except that sex had been one of the causes of war. All sexual feelings had been totally eradicated by drugs, and she had gone through the bumpy ride from total innocent to sexually mature woman at the same speed as the rest. It was not an easy ride, and although she wanted the feelings available beyond the kisses she had shared with Mark she was not sure how far she wanted to go. If they were to be together after the selection process at the end of a month, then her mind might be clearer, but even so she knew that Mark would not be able to love her fully at the present time. He didn’t even know anything about sex, and she was not sure how his feelings would cope with partly wanting something he didn’t know about, and couldn’t manage anyway. She wondered how far the drugs had released him, and decided that no great damage could be caused by a more passionate kiss than they had had before.

She pulled his head towards her and as their lips met slipped her hand inside his top so her palm gently rubbed his side just above waist level.

The effect on Mark was electric. Besides the intense feelings he had experienced before, he was also trembling violently with the most wonderful sensation he had ever experienced. His body felt pain and pleasure mixed together in random proportions, and as their lips parted he managed to gasp, ‘How do you do that?’

Maureen smiled as the ache inside her started to ebb. She knew he could not yet respond to her advances, and that he would end

up confused, and she would end up frustrated in knowing what may happen one day, but couldn't happen yet.
'How do I kiss you?' she teased, as innocently as she could.
'No,' Mark's breathing was coming back under control, and the violent trembling had subsided to small tremors, 'how do you make me feel like that?'
She knew that he had not realised that her hand had touched his bare side, as it was an area previously unacceptable in society. He had experienced the effects, but not the cause.
'As you come off the drugs the kissing gets better, but you have to be patient. Now, let your mum know you will be late,' she kissed him quickly on the lips. 'I'm going to have a coffee. Want one?'
'After we kiss again,' Mark grabbed at her, but she skipped out of his reach.
'Before you go home, ring your mum,' Maureen moved into the kitchen.
Mark reached over to the videophone and called his mother. 'I might be a bit late, as we have some reports to go through.'
Are you with Maureen?' his mother asked.
'Yes.'
'That's fine then. Give her our love, and see you in the morning,' his mother's smile faded as the screen darkened.
Maureen came back with the coffee, and called up Site D.
This time they were beside a large lake in heavily wooded country. Greg used the same techniques as with the other areas, and they had no difficulty in picking up the geography of the location. Apart from the lake itself, there were only small open areas, so views into the distance were fairly limited. The sounds were very few, and it was difficult to imagine what some of them were. On one view of the lake a bright reflection flashed momentarily, but as before, they could not decide if it was the movement of the surface, or something in the lake. The facts and figures gave it as part of a continent in the southern hemisphere,

and Greg voiced over that there appeared to be a lot of potentially edible plants and fruits in the area.
This was an area Mark had not even started to think about. 'Of course, we will have to feed ourselves.'
'Drink is the most important, which is why each location is near what we believe is fresh water. We will have to grow crops, make our own clothes, mend and eventually renew the tools we take. Make some sort of house for ourselves. It will not be all fun and walks on the beach.'
Mark started to think for the first time about what was really involved in starting a new world. Up to that moment it had been a great adventure, with nothing to do but explore, watch the sunsets and call it paradise.
'There will be no central computer to call on. There will be two people, cut off from everything for the first time in their lives. Relying on themselves to look after each other, and hopefully the children that they create.' Maureen looked him straight in the eyes. 'It will be extremely difficult to cope and survive, as none of us have the slightest experience of what must be done.'
'Water, food, fire, shelter,' Mark remembered the basic requirements to survival from his history lessons of the old days.
'It's what most of us are working on at the moment. It might be a good idea to bring you three newcomers up to date with how far we have got. You are still at the stage where you don't automatically think something through, because you have spent your life being prevented from doing that. As the drugs wear off you will discover the need to see something through to the end, and the frustration involved in not being able to sometimes.'
'So a place near the sea would be the most useful, as if there is any life it is likely to be there,' Mark was starting to think ahead. 'We would be able to catch fish to eat.'
'What a good idea,' the reply from Maureen was heavy with sarcasm. 'You will be able to kill the fishes, and take out the

guts before we eat them. Even better if there are some birds or animals, as you can kill those as well.'
Mark went pale. 'I couldn't do that. It's not nice, and besides, we don't have to eat flesh. We can always...'
'As I said before, we will need to do everything, and it won't be easy.'
His flesh tingled as he watched the screen. It was almost a feeling of coming home. This WAS paradise. Again, Greg was on a beach, which formed a complete semi-circle holding the brilliant blue waters of the sea. The tops of the small waves which hissed up the narrow beach sparkled with a thousand colours. A tiny island was a dot on the right hand side of the bay, near one of the headlands which rose probably thirty metres from the beach. Trees and shrubs dotted the landscape, but not so thickly that the view was blocked. The ground rose very slowly away from the beach, and then more steeply on each side. Greg aimed the view at the wide gap between the hills some two thousand metres behind the beach, and followed a very small river. The shrubs were a riot of colours. Pinks, reds, yellows were mixed gloriously together. Mark could almost smell them. As they proceeded, the river, although not much more than a stream, rose more steeply to the left. As they reached the crest of the saddle between the hills, an almost mirror image came into view as the far slope ran down to another beach. The view then swung round to the bay they had first seen. The sea was now golden in colour. Mark thought of his first trip along the river when the water was burnt to a deep orange. The view was raised slightly to show a golden sun dipping into the ocean. Greg turned the scene to show his face, and as he smiled, even his teeth were golden in the evening light. He returned the view to the setting sun, which disappeared ever more quickly into the sea.
Maureen had watched his face more than the screen for the thirty minute show, and could sense his feelings. She put her

arms round him and squeezed as hard as she could. ‘Welcome home, darling,’ she whispered.
‘We have to get there. Just imagine - did you see - Oh, Maureen, I love you.’
Again they kissed, but this time Mark's thoughts were on this new paradise, and as they broke apart he asked ‘Is that the one for you as well?’
Maureen nodded her agreement. ‘But we should watch Letter F.’
They ran through the details of site E. It was a comparatively small island, just over fifty square kilometres. It was quite hilly, but these were of no great height. Mark missed most of the information as his mind kept rushing ahead.
They ran through the view of F, another inland site, but Mark's mind had already been won over. He took in the site, but was comparing it all the time with E.
His mind whirled with what he had seen that evening, and sleep was a long time coming when he eventually got home. One of his last thoughts was that he had missed out on the second 'special' kiss that had been promised before he went. He couldn't actually remember whether they had kissed good-night at all. As he drifted off to sleep he was swimming out to the tiny little island in the bay. The fact that he couldn't swim seemed unimportant.
Next morning at breakfast Mark was still hanging on to all the good memories from the evening before. His mind was subconsciously holding back on all the negative areas, such as what if he was not selected for the new planet, and how difficult it would be if he was.
His parents were pleased to see him in such good spirits, and his mother remarked that it was lovely to see him looking so much better than the morning he and Maureen looked so ill.
‘That was just some testing we had done on various foods,’ Mark lied. ‘Yesterday we were working on areas of the past that could affect our present and our future. It was very interesting,’

he felt easier telling his parents a close version of the truth rather than outright lies. As he looked at them he realised that they would always be Happies, and resolved to try never to look down on them for not being able to share the life he led.

'So your history studies are being of use in your special project?' His father was making small talk.

'Yes, I think that's why I was selected,' again Mark lied. His father was far more experienced than him in history, but the drugs would prevent him from questioning why he couldn't help in special projects. The minds were so affected that nothing was ever queried. Nothing seemed strange. Mark thought back to last night, as he drifted off to sleep. He was swimming, yet his mind accepted the fact. He must have been asleep, as in dreams nothing is strange. Looking at his parents again he realised that dreaming was the nearest he had come to explaining the world they lived in.

'How long do you expect the special project to go on?' asked his mother, 'it's not that I mind, I just don't want them testing things out that can upset or harm you.'

Mark smiled at his mother. 'The main project has another month to go, but I hope to be chosen to continue with some other work.'

As Mark answered his stomach heaved. How would he tell his parents if he was selected? His euphoria quickly subsided as he realised how awful it would be never to see them again. His mother especially would be heartbroken.

He walked part of the way to the university with his father, and met Brian and Nicky as he entered.

'Have you both seen all the places on the new planet?' Mark's feelings were buoyant again as he pushed thoughts of possible partings to the back of his mind.

Two heads nodded in unison.

'Which one did you like the best?'

'Site E was the most beautiful,' said Nicky.

‘Though probably not the most practical,’ interrupted Brian.
‘Why?’ challenged Mark.
‘The island where it's situated is probably too small to have all the necessary requirements for a couple to start a new civilisation,’ Brian seemed glum, but then smiled as he added, ‘but it is certainly the most beautiful.’
Mark realised that Brian was ahead of him on thinking of the future, and for a moment wondered if his drugs were being reduced faster, but then worked out that Brian had seen the new planet before him, and had more time to think.
He was still pondering on the different sites as Asif met them at the door.
Good mornings were exchanged and they were handed the tabs for the next lessons in the Builders.
‘Which of the sites on the new planet is the best one?’ Mark wanted someone to agree with him, and thought Asif might be the one.
‘D,’ replied Asif, ‘it seems to have all the basic necessities.’
‘But if you were going and had to choose for yourself,’ Mark persisted.
‘You mean to sit with your arm round Maureen and watch the sun go down on site E,’ Asif smiled.
‘That's not hard to work out for me, but what about you?’ Mark wasn't sure if he was pushing too hard.
‘To sit on the bank, next to the big tree, with the one you love, as the sun heads down behind the little island,’ Asif sighed, ‘but we must wait and see what happens.’
Mark wanted to go on, but a kick on the back of his leg changed his mind. ‘I suppose we had better find out what you have in store for us this morning.’
As the three of them walked down to the Memory Builders, Nicky asked crossly ‘What were you trying to get him to say?’
‘Better to have loved, and all that, and as one of the Three

Musketeers, I felt I should get the ball rolling for you. All for one and one for all you know.'

'Not when it comes to my love life,' said Nicky, 'I don't want him pushed into anything. If he feels anything for me, I want it to come from him without any help from you.'

Mark felt suitably admonished.

'Snap,' said Brian as they came to the Builders.

The lesson for the morning was concerned with the discovery of the new planet and the work that was still going on to find any others that may be habitable.

All the details of the solar system containing the new world were fed directly into Mark's brain, along with vivid images of the sun and other planets, and their relationship to one another. Full details of the new planet filled Mark with awe at possibly existing in a place with such extremes of temperature. The images were intertwined with details of the plants and animals that had existed on the old earth. Although none of the new plants had been proven to be identical to the old, the likenesses were great, and it was assumed that there would be very similar species on both and therefore similar poisonous ones as well.

It was felt certain that animal life of some sort did exist, and the assumption that the seas would be the prime provider seemed logical. Because of the way in which the transporter affected the environment in which it arrived, with the electrical field it produced giving a sharp drop in temperature, it was assumed that any living things would automatically lie low, taking the alteration in their surroundings as a threat. It was not therefore expected that they would see anything close to, and the few distant sightings of movement were too far away to confirm as animate. There was some disappointment expressed that there were no confirmations, tinged with relief that possible 'nasties' may not be present either.

As he left and walked back to lunch, Mark tried to fully open his mind to the prospects that lay before him. He wanted to think

clearly, and understand, but knew that the drugs would still muddle him slightly, and stop him seeing too clearly.
Asif met them with the good news that the afternoon was to be spent in being updated on the new planet, and where they had got to in deciding what the settlers would need.
Maureen would take Mark. Asif would be with Nicky, and Elena would have Brian.
Mark could not believe his ears, and neither could Nicky when she accused him of splitting on confidences as soon as Asif was out of earshot. He denied the charges, and as Asif returned, asked him who had picked the pairings.
'Why, are you not happy to be with Maureen?' his dark eyes flashed.
'You know I am, I just wondered,' said Mark tamely.
'It was probably Joanne,' Asif told him.
Suddenly it was clear to all three of them. No-one had to say anything at all, and she would understand. At least it's a step in the right direction, thought Mark. It must mean at the least that Asif and Elena were not attached emotionally to someone else.
Asif looked directly at Nicky. 'I hope that the arrangement is O.K. with you?' he queried.
Mark could have written the next line of the script himself, and imagined his temperature had risen from the heat of the red face next to him.
She did not lift her eyes as she murmured 'Was it what you wanted?'
Together their eyes met as they simultaneously said 'Yes.'
'Come on,' said Mark to Brian, 'I can see we are not wanted here.'

‘Hang on,’ said Asif, taking his eyes from Nicky, ‘Elena and Maureen are coming to pick you two up. It's probably easier to work at home through the network for any bits and pieces that you want, rather than disturb the present working sessions.’
As he finished speaking, the two ladies in question entered the room.
Brian was now the one to colour up, and the first one to speak.
‘Hello Elena. Please get me away from this insensitive lot, especially Mark.’
Mark tried to look aggrieved, but instead burst out laughing.
Elena and Brian hurried away as Maureen asked, ‘what was all that about?’
‘Guess who picked the pairings for this afternoon,’ said Mark.
‘Oh, I see what you mean. I hope she's right.’
‘She is here, and I hope she is out there for Brian's sake,’ Nicky was holding hands with Asif as she spoke.
The four of them left together.

J

Brian and Elena made a striking couple as they walked to her home together. He was tall and dark; she was only five centimetres shorter, with blonde hair that cascaded down her back.

The conversation didn't flow, as Brian, although pleased to be alone with Elena, felt terrified at the thought of spending time with her. Twenty four years old, he had never been alone with a woman in his life apart from his mother. None of the instant feelings that had made Mark's first kissing session such a sensation had arrived in his body yet, although he desperately wanted to try and discover some of the love that he now knew was possible between man and woman.

Elena, only one year younger, had enjoyed time together with the other men in the group, although none had attracted her enough to even lead to a kiss. She was fond of Brian, although how much was genuine, how much was because she had found him, and how much was because she needed a man to share her life she was not sure. Her main work in the group had been on the analysis of the results to find out who was capable of producing children, and she was heartbroken to find that she would never conceive. The second test completed had been for Maureen, and for a time she had let her bitter feelings get the better of her. It seemed so unfair that she had nothing, and Maureen would have everything. She was not worried about becoming a pioneer on the new planet, just wanting to be a mother. Until all the results were available Joanne and her were the only ones who knew anything, and she made a mental note to apologise to Maureen at that time.

Thus it was that they were both wrapped in their own thoughts as they arrived at the apartment door.

Brian was going through a hundred opening lines and scenarios just to make an opportunity to get closer to Elena without being rejected or made a fool of.
Much the same thoughts held the attention of Elena, who although wanting much more than Brian at this stage, knew how the drugs would still be holding him back. The first kiss had done nothing for either of them, but she was anxious to try again.
They sat next to one another in silence as Elena called up the new planet onto the screen. Brian felt his breathing becoming strained and his temperature start to rise as the need to touch her seemed to consume his brain. Which approach should he make? What could he say to start? Suddenly everything rushed out like air from a balloon when the neck is released. 'I can't sit here all afternoon trying to take in stuff from the screen, when all I want to do is... My head aches, my chest hurts...'
Elena took both his hands in hers, and standing, gently pulled Brian after her. As they were upright she buried her lips into his neck. Brian's muscles, so tense up till then, all relaxed, and as their lips met he experienced for the first time how wonderful that first real kiss can be. Neither of them wanted to stop; Brian because he was hanging on to so much pleasure for as long as possible; Elena because of the kiss itself, and the hope that Brian may be ready for something more. She nestled her body tightly against his, and though the fire in her craved attention, knew as she pushed herself against him, that today he was not yet ready.
For Brian, a whole new world had suddenly arrived. He beamed at Elena in contentment. 'Are you a bit like Joanne, and see my thoughts?'
Elena kissed him on the end of his nose. 'I'm a bit like every woman when it comes to thoughts like that.'
'But I just wanted, and it happened,' for all his serious nature, Brian had been opened up as easy as opening a purse. 'And now some learning had better happen so you can catch up with the

rest of us. Excuse me just a minute.' Elena was damp and uncomfortable, but soon returned to restart the new planet sequence.

Unlike Brian and Elena, Nicky and Asif didn't stop talking all the way back to his home. Like their friends, however, they felt the same mix of emotions in wanting something to happen that only one was ready for. Nicky was quite happy to wait for her love life to start, but he, like Elena, had all the pent up feelings that he had not been able to release.

They mixed some cold drinks, and settled down to the lesson. All three would be shown the same footage to bring them up to date.

They started with a brief résumé of the details on the new planet, including size, distribution of land mass, temperatures etc., much as they had seen before. They then went over the details of the six sites identified as possible, but excluding the views that were with the original notes.

The rest was split into two distinct areas: absolute necessities that anyone would need, and variations depending on who and how many would be going.

Nicky could understand the frustration that must have built up in the rest of them as they time and again came back to the question of who could most guarantee to survive and inhabit the planet. Until Brian, Mark and herself were tested, everyone else was waiting to see the results of the best gene matching.

Decisions that had been taken related mainly to the fact that any children were to be shielded from their origins. This meant that the freighter or freighters that went to the new world could only be used for a relatively short time before being destroyed, along with all traces of the previous life. It would be impossible to explain the presence of space age technology in a Stone Age existence. Half-truths would be used to explain their life, to produce a similar grey picture to the one that had been in existence on the old world. Prime importance had therefore been given to selecting sites which contained fresh water, natural food or the possibility of growing it, flint to produce fire and tools, and timber to make a den.

As no one was to return in case of contamination, any physical help had to be used in constructing items which would be of use on the new planet before the settlers left. The old freighters had a huge capacity, as their main purpose had been to haul metals and chemicals, so a vast amount of material could be taken. Some of the twenty were at present constructing items for this purpose, which explained why some of the trees had suddenly gone missing.

Nicky asked how many freighters there were available.

'Twelve,' replied Asif, 'and we can't build any more. Most items we have can be replicated, but a number of materials needed in spacecraft construction are not available here.'

'What are the chances that the first settlers will be wiped out by a disease for which they have no immunity?' Nicky was probably taking the same train of thought as the others, but would try and cover everything anyway.

'We have no idea at all.'

'So we can really only spare one ship, in case there is failure.' It didn't seem much to start a new world, and Nicky's previous desire to be one of the passengers dropped a couple of notches.

'It's not just failure that concerns us, but the way we should use the others anyway. If the new planet is a success, then it may be possible to extract the materials we need to make more ships. If the new planet does not contain all of them, then we will have to try elsewhere,' Asif added sadly, 'we may only get twelve shots.'

'So we pick just one site, or will it be possible for the ship to drop at more than one place.'

'Theoretically that is possible, but the balance of opinion is that the freighter should be used as an initial den, until the eldest child is say ten years old. It can also produce a protective field

round the site chosen, until everyone is happy that there are no dangerous species present.'
'What happens to it then?' Nicky asked.
'It's loaded with all the modern equipment and has a quick last flight to the bottom of the deepest ocean.'
'Surely that's a waste,' protested Nicky,' if by then the settlers are still O.K., we could bring it back.'
'Some deadly diseases have incubation periods of years, and we have pledged never to endanger the Happies. If we fail totally, then don't forget that they are the future. Nothing and no-one will come back here. We can remain in touch through the transporter. As that cannot alter anything, whoever goes must come back exactly the same. Even the smallest germ couldn't affect them, as an altered state cannot be returned.'
'How dangerous is the transporter?' Nicky asked.
'They are the safest form of travel that there is, because nothing alters, but of course you can only materialise for a few moments at the other side before you are pulled back. That is the affect of the fact that an altered state would fail.' Asif had worked widely with Greg on the use of the transporter, and new his facts.
'But if you did alter, then it would fail,' Nicky couldn't quite grasp the idea.
'No, that's the wrong way to look at it. It's another ring. Because you are using it to go, you are also using it to come back. The one is the same as the other. Greg took those views, which covered up to five hours for each half hour slot, by not materialising at all, so he wouldn't be pulled back immediately.'
'So how long was he away?' Nicky knew this really wasn't part of preparation for the new planet, but needed the answer.
'He wasn't; he enters the transporter and gets straight out again as far as those here are concerned. Because he is coming back at the same time he is going, then he isn't gone at all in our time.'
'I knew I was going to have trouble with this before,' said Nicky, 'you are talking about time travel.'

'Not really,' Asif replied, 'because he doesn't travel through time, he just loses some, or gains it, whichever way you look at it. True time travel is not possible using this computer, because it is not factually possible. We know it is, but try to write the programme that it will accept.'
'Like I said, I knew I was going to have trouble with this,' Nicky smiled.
'If trouble gives you smiles like that, I hope you remain troubled.'
'So you only like me when I smile,' teased Nicky.
'No, I didn't mean that. It's just that you are so beautiful normally, but when you smile it's as if a lovely picture is lit up.'
Nicky needed no second invitation, and their lips met in a fierce and passionate kiss. Time and again she kissed him, each one as powerful as the last. A small part of him just in front of the bottom of his spine ached and spread. He knew the only way he could be satisfied, but he also remembered Joanne's warning to everyone as they came off the drugs. 'Sex with a Happy, or someone still on drugs, of whichever sex, is rape. Those of us who are free can consent if they want to. Those who are not free are ours to protect.'
He made his excuses, and as he washed himself and changed, felt relieved that he had stopped in time. Less than a month, he told himself as he mixed them some more drinks and took them back into the lounge.
Nicky was back to her old self. 'I'm so sorry, attacking you like that. I know it's not fair on men.'
Asif smiled at her. 'Feel free to attack whenever you want. And believe me, it gets better.'
'Nothing could be better than that, surely?' she asked.
'Maybe one day we'll find out, but now back to work.' he replied.
Maureen and Mark had reached the stage of the programme which listed out all the items considered necessary for survival

on the new planet, and Mark was impressed at the amount of thought that had gone into each area of survival. They then came to the plants and animals which were to travel with them. Li Po had originally held an imprint for every known species, and a lot of the plants had been used for their present life. Some of them had been 'improved', but there was basically the same available as had been brought from the old world. Opinion was fairly unanimous that plants for food and beauty should be transported. None carnivorous insects and birds presented no great problems. The assumption had been made that there should be sufficient seeds and berries for them to survive. None carnivorous marine life could be released and take its chance in the same fashion. As the present species could be divided and re-created again, they would not actually lose any of the huge range, although a fair number would not make it in the new world. When it came to animals was where opinion was at present divided. Everyone could see that it was no use having carnivores until there was a sufficient population of available food, although one or two thought it was unnecessary to ever introduce them. There was, however, majority agreement that everything from the old world should be given its chance in the new. If these had to compete with anything already there, so be it. For the herbivorous animals, however, feelings were fairly evenly divided.

If they were to compete for some of the available food, it seemed stupid to take competition with them. If there was already competition there, it could make matters worse. No one could envisage ever killing an animal to eat it, but it was generally accepted that this could well happen in the future. It was also generally felt that other animals should be released in the distant future, when it was certain that no fatal diseases could be brought back. If they were to come in search of the minerals needed to complete more spacecraft, then they would be able to do two jobs with one flight.

Maureen and Mark sat staring at a blank screen for a couple of minutes.
'Having second thoughts?' she asked.
'It's not so easy and romantic as when you first hear about it,' Mark was still looking at the dead screen
'But would you still like to go?'
'If I could look on it as going away to live with you, with the beaches and the sunsets, the animals, and everything else that I love, then it is everything I want. It's when the responsibility of creating a whole new world is added that it becomes a bit frightening. To a certain extent we would be living in a goldfish bowl. Every one of our actions can be seen and documented, and nearly all the time we would know nothing about it. Then, probably just when we thought we had done something right, we would most likely be instructed to do something else. I want going away with you to be something magical. I want to make love to you under the stars. I want us to swim together, out to that tiny island in the bay. I want us to hold hands when we walk to the other side of the island. I want it to be real, not a story that we create on stage because we are looking over our shoulders.' Mark had turned to look at her.
'So you don't want any interference from this world.'
'Well, at times it would be necessary, but if we could control the viewing times it would be better,' Mark was concerned at the lack of privacy. 'And you have decided on site E, even though it might not be the best,' she took his hand as she spoke.
'Like I said before, I want it to be magical, special.....Oh, I don't know. It seemed so easy before. Why can't things be straightforward and easy?'
Maureen smiled. 'You mean life as a Happy. Let someone else do the thinking.'
'You know I didn't mean that. It just seems so difficult now.'
'To get the best out of life you have to put the effort in. Try to imagine what we will be able to accomplish together. Our own

house, our own family, our own everything. So what if someone is looking over our shoulders. They might be now for all we know. You were the one who suggested this may be the third chance, not the second,' Maureen moved closer to him as she spoke.

'But that's different. We don't know for certain. It's just a possibility,' Mark was defensive.

'We won't know in the future. Sometimes there will, sometimes there won't,' Maureen squeezed his hand.

'I know. It's just that when I kiss you it's for us, not for everyone else.'

'Our kisses have been the most talked about thing in our relationship, so they can hardly be private,' she teased.

'Yes, but its only talk, not watching,' Mark felt he was arguing a lost cause.

'If we are happy with the way we live our lives, then I don't think we have any reason to worry,' Maureen felt so sure.

'Well if just part of the time we could be totally alone,' Mark knew now he was losing the argument.

"You believe in a God." Maureen took his other hand in hers.

'Yes.'

'God can see, hear and feel everything.'

'Yes.'

'You likened Joanne to playing the role of God.'

'I know, but...'

'But nothing,' she interrupted, 'if you can live in the knowledge that your every action is being seen, then why worry who it is that actually sees it. If I kiss you like this, then the entire world can see as far as I'm concerned.' With that she knelt on the floor in front of the settee, and pulling his head down, kissed him with all the passion she could feel. She moved the top of her body gently, then more fiercely across his chest.

Mark could feel everything at once. All the ecstasy of those first kisses returned with interest. His hand coursed up and down her spine, pulling her ever closer to him. His whole body ached with the pleasure of being so tightly pressed against her. His other hand, held tightly behind her neck, felt the flesh of her shoulder as he slipped it inside the neckline of her top. As they parted from that single kiss, he was trembling violently, and Maureen looked at him with eyes wide open.

'Are you unhappy for others to see how much in love we are?' she gasped.

'I could shout it from the mountain tops,' he agreed.

The six of them met that evening to discuss the progress that they had made with the new world, and though all of them wanted to tell the world about their love, not one of them mentioned it.

K

‘Where are the freighters kept?’ Brian opened the conversation.
‘They are all kept outside, as they do not deteriorate with no atmosphere. They are kept apart from one another, just in case a meteor hit wiped out all twelve, although that is very unlikely.’ Asif’s dark eyes flashed as he spoke.
Mark realised that he was still not thinking totally freely. ‘What if a meteor hit the city?’
‘A large one would wipe out civilisation as we know it. Smaller ones are sensed way out and a deflector beam alters their trajectory, although we think that has only happened twice.’ Elena smiled as she spoke.
Mark was not sure if he detected an inference in her 'civilisation as we know it'. ‘Is it possible that there is another civilisation out there from the original planet, or a similar one from somewhere else?’ he asked.
‘We don't know, although we believe another group from the original planet is extremely unlikely. We feel sure that Li Po would have known about it and recorded it. It's a bit like your theory about us being attempt number three instead of two, we think it's very unlikely, but possible nevertheless,’ Elena replied.
‘When will we be able to see the freighters?’ Brian returned to his original subject.
‘Now, if you feel like a trip outside,’ said Elena, ‘and we should be able to catch the sunset as well.’
Five heads nodded in agreement, and Elena punched a number into the videophone. Cocho's face appeared on the screen, with his normal serious expression. ‘Would there be any problem in six of us going out to look at one of the freighters?’ Elena asked.
‘No problem at all,’ Cocho registered a tiny smile as he replied. ‘I would be happy to show you round. Number AA is the nearest, so shall I meet you at the airlock in fifteen minutes?’

Elena glanced round and nodded in agreement, then checked the airlock location with Cocho.
He was waiting for them as they reached an apartment on the perimeter. They went through the familiar routine of using a code on part of the wall, and all passed silently through to an area which afforded a view out across the flat landscape. It was dominated by the largest, ugliest spacecraft that Mark could imagine. He was not sure what he had really expected, but this was certainly not it. The thing was monstrous, and instead of being smooth and rounded, appeared to resemble an apartment block that someone had painted with the dreariest dark green imaginable. Unknown bits and pieces seemed to be stuck on all over the place, and if you tried to imagine being the captain of the vessel which was to start the next new world, then you would have picked something totally the opposite.
Cocho smiled round at them. 'I can tell by the silence how impressed you all are. Struck dumb by the beauty in front of you,' he burst out laughing,' if you think that this is grim, wait until you see the others.' As he spoke, he was walking, and Mark could see that the tunnel curved round and out to the freighter.
'Is it safe?' Nicky asked.
'The freighters were the safest of the lot,' explained Cocho. 'They were purely for transporting huge amounts of very expensive materials. Speed was fairly inconsequential, so size and reliability were everything. The cost of them was enormous, but was insignificant compared to the cargoes, so the firms that owned them took every precaution to ensure that those goods would be delivered.'
As they walked in a slight curve, the name of the company which had owned this one came into view, emblazoned down the side of the ship in white, with the initial letters picked out in a brilliant yellow. 'Amalgamated Removals Corporation', with the number AA following in small print.

‘We call this one number one because it is the biggest,’ explained Cocho without being asked.
They proceeded into another air lock and through into the ship itself. A lift took them rapidly upwards, and Cocho gave a brief idea of the areas that they passed, most of which were for storage. ‘And so to the bridge,’ he announced as the lift stopped.
The best part by far was the view outside, as although the window was relatively small, from forty stories up they could see far more of their world than ever before.
Inside were four armchair type seats, and a surprisingly small number of dials and controls.
‘You mean this is it!’ Brian exclaimed,’ you run this giant from here?’
‘Most of the controlling is preset into the computers, before the journey begins. The bulk of the controls are for internal use, and to allow manual use of the weapons systems...’
‘I thought this was a transport freighter for moving commercial cargoes, not a warship,’ Nicky butted in.
‘In the old days they were so paranoid about war, that all spaceships were armed, just in case the little green men tried to capture them...’
‘Who were the little green men?’ Nicky interrupted Cocho again.
Cocho sat down in one of the armchair type seats. ‘As you come off the drugs, you will notice that anything that you cannot specifically see, or look up, you will form in your mind. Say that someone you had not met before came on the videophone, but that the video link was down, so you just heard a voice. From just a few words you would form an impression in your mind of what that person looked like. This happened all the time in the past. The main problem came when someone then put this impression into print, or onto a screen. The bulk of the population accepted what they were told or shown. The first comic writer to invent alien life forms decided that they were

little green men, so most of the population then had that impression in their minds. There was no logical thinking behind the description, but nevertheless the impression was maintained. Taking Mark's theory about the possibility of us being the third chance, it makes you wonder if the old population were like the Happies, as the bulk of them never queried anything at all, and most of those who did accepted as fact what they were told. Whole countries survived on lies told to them by the government, and I believe that most of the governments didn't realise that what they were telling was untrue. They were fed information by a relatively small band of experts, accepted the information, and ran the country accordingly. They were really no better than dictatorships, which used exactly the same type of small band of experts. I'm sorry... it's just one area of the past that gets to me, and 'I tend to get on my soap box' as they said in the old days.'

'No, please go on.' said Mark, glancing round at the others for encouragement. No one disagreed, so Cocho continued.

"One of the finest features of man is that he can query anything he does not fully understand, and then try to work out a sensibly reasoned answer. One of the worst features is that he does not want to be different to the rest of mankind. If the current way of thinking is that blue is a good colour and that purple is a bad colour, then the bulk of the population will avoid purple. They will not query the fact that a colour cannot of itself be good or bad, in case they are made to look foolish by not understanding the properties of colours. For anyone to make a radical change to an established way of thinking took a huge amount of courage, and very often that person was ostracised, and sometimes put to death. The people who wielded the power realised this, and worked the system to their advantage. They could provide an expert to back their opinion if necessary, but mostly the views that they put forward did not seem to matter a great deal, so they went unchallenged and became in time a sort of truth. They were the ultimate in advertising agents. They could sway whole populations into believing or doing virtually anything, and the bulk of them never appeared, and were mostly unknown. They could start and finish wars, elect and reject politicians, create and destroy religions, and most of their work was never challenged at all.'

Mark had studied history, but it had never been like this. 'But surely people would not go to war, where their life was at risk, without first questioning why?'

Cocho grinned. 'But you would be the first on board a ten thousand year old freighter to go to a planet that may kill you on day one, because a few friends say it will be O.K.'

Mark looked suitably admonished, and Cocho continued, 'But in your case you can be forgiven because of the drugs still in your system. The people in the old world - shall we call them Oldies - presumably had no such excuse. They stood by and watched year after year as wars continued, mass starvation continued, the planet became more and more polluted, and whole species of plants and animals were wiped out. A few brave souls tried as hard as they could to reverse some of the dreadful things that were happening, but could never convince the rest of the population. Either the relatively few who controlled the world were incredibly clever and evil, or Mark was right, and the masses were drugged into submission all the time, and ended when the final drugs went wrong. The Oldies were just like the Happies, they didn't care.'

Elena was suitably serious as she spoke 'Now you three can see how hard we are trying to set the parameters for the new planet in such a way that the same thing can't happen again. The problem is that man has to try to acquire knowledge to create a better future, but he automatically links that with acquiring possessions, and it becomes like a drug, so the more he has the more he wants. When he has everything he could want, someone

invents something that is worthless, but tells him it is valuable, and so he wants it.'
Brian looked shocked. 'Surely no-one could want more than was necessary in life.'
Asif took up the story. 'Competition is one of the ways forward for mankind. If you can produce something better than your neighbour, you will succeed and he will fail.'
Nicky interrupted. 'Everything you have just been telling us relates to money! But money was actually worthless, it was only a means of moving goods and services about.'
'Not exactly,' Asif continued, "man wanted to be rich in possessions, but he was not content with that, he had to let everyone else know how rich he was. He had to have the biggest house, the biggest car, the most beautiful wife...''
Nicky's eyes blazed as she butted in. 'A wife is not a possession."
'In a lot of cases she might just as well have been, and the reverse was true for rich women. They had to have the biggest and best jewels, and the best looking man to escort them. There comes a stage when you cannot get any more or any better. So how do you tell people that you are richer, and therefore better or more stupid, whichever way you look at it, than other people? You advertise the fact. Some of this you will have seen in the Memory Builders, but it shows how stupid man can get. If food is short, then get as fat as you can to shout out ' I am rich.' Let the rest starve. People might not recognise that your clothes are the dearest, as they are no better than most of the others. So the firm that sells the dearest puts their name on the outside of the garment. The rich fool gets what he thinks he wants, and the manufacturer gets free advertising. But I think my favourites are the ones where something of absolutely no value could be talked up to huge values. It was especially prevalent in the art world, where the work of untalented people could change hands for huge amounts, and number plates were another prime example.'

'What were number plates?' asked Brian.

'Cars and other forms of transport had to have a number plate to identify them in case of accidents etc. If you had the most expensive car available, there was not much else you could do to it to show how rich you were. So someone decided on what a 'smart' number plate should be. So you could then put the most expensive number plate on your car. The sums involved could be a thousand times what someone else could earn in a lifetime.'

Nicky's lips trembled. 'I bet the most expensive one was 'Here comes the biggest idiot'.' The others joined in as she burst out laughing.

'It sounds far fetched, I know,' smiled Maureen, 'but it goes to show how silly man can be. He can concentrate on his own tiny world and ignore the disasters around him. If the new planet goes like that, do we interfere? You can see why the discussion goes on.'

'Talking of going on, it's time we did the same,' Cocho was the only one facing the window, and the rest followed his gaze. Once again Mark held Maureen's hand as they watched the sun go down from their lofty viewpoint.

'However rich you become, you can only watch the same sunset,' he murmured.

They descended in the lift in silence, and made their ways home, each one of them thinking of the potential for triumph and disaster on the new world.

L

It had been agreed that the results of the compatibility studies would be issued at the time the three newest members were finally free from drugs. Their tests would be carried out in the final week, as the dosage in their bodies would by then have no effect on the outcome.

There were now only two weeks to go to that time, and Mark's body craved more and more for Maureen, and his mind seemed to become more and more illogical. His previous logical and carefully controlled existence had given way to one in which he had to make his own decisions. When he was with Maureen, and sometimes when he was apart from her, he wanted nothing more than to spend his time with her, just being together in love for eternity. At other times he wondered if she was not to go to the new world, who he would be paired with, and what it would feel like to try and fall in love with someone new. In his darkest moments he was the one to stay behind, while Maureen went, paired with someone new.

The three of them now spent less and less time in the Memory Builders, and more time working with the other members of the group, manufacturing the items that the new settlers would need. The basic shape of the accommodation had already been agreed upon, and was in the form of a log cabin on a stone base. The logs had been produced; each carefully finished giving the impression of having been cut with an axe. Most of the small tools necessary had been created from flint, stone, wood, clay, etc., each rough in appearance, but functional. The materials would not exactly match those available on the new site, but were considered near enough so that any future suspicions would not arise.

The timbers and stones were not put together for transport, but were carefully labelled in conjunction with a master plan. There was still some discussion about using animal based material in the manufacture, but the general opinion was that those animals which would normally be used for clothing and food in the old days would eventually die, and could then be used rather than totally wasted. In the meantime a number of similar synthetic materials had been tried and tested, with the theory that they could be replaced in time.

Mark felt a little uneasy about the future use of animal parts, but could see no logical alternative, so went along with the general wishes.

So with two weeks to go the three of them once more headed for the Memory Builders. Tanya had given them the tabs for the morning session, and had wished them good luck as she left them.

Mark was feeling content with life as he pushed the tab in the slot. He was in love, felt happy rather than scared about the future, and was optimistic that in a fortnight he would be on the list to go.

He was once again by the small wooden style leading past the cottage and along by the river. He stopped again to make a fuss of the dog, but this time the programme took him into a field behind the cottage, with half a dozen goats as company. As before, the Builder created the scene directly into his brain, so that he was part of the programme, and learnt directly. He was given a brief history of the goat, and its normal life cycle. It was explained that they would use goats in preference to sheep at the start in the new world, as their eating requirements were far easier. Sheep would be introduced later. A demonstration was given on milking one of the nanny goats, and he was taken through cheese making. Mark was fully aware as he took in all the information, but a small part of him was already racing forward to the future, running through the names to call their goats. The programme proceeded to helping with the delivery of a kid, and Mark felt just a little bit queasy at the sight, but decided that if it became necessary, he would be able to cope.

Some of the possible illnesses were explained, together with the remedies that would be available from the different herbs that would go on the spacecraft, both for immediate use and planting for the future. Again Mark felt uncomfortable at some of the sights, but just managed to keep on top of the situation.

He was just starting to congratulate himself on having absorbed the knowledge to become a goat herd when he was plunged into despair.

The programme went on to show how the animal could be butchered at the end of its useful life to provide a skin for clothing and bedding, meat for consumption, bones to make into rudimentary tools, and the number of processes that the innards could be used for. Mark missed everything after the initial blow to the animals head, and the sight of a sharpened flint axe approaching its neck.

He was kneeling on the floor just outside the Builder, the nauseous waves sweeping over him as they had done before. The vile taste of vomit was still in his mouth, but he knew there was more to come, as the heat of his body and the sweat on his brow kept that dreadful feeling of near sickness in him. Once again he retched, and tried to push himself backwards, away from the encroaching edge of the stain on the floor.

Although the Memory Builders taught by living through the experience, you still had the feeling of being slightly apart. The previous sight of the war ravaged woman and child had made him just as ill, but this time was worse because he knew that this was part of his future, where the previous one was never likely to happen.

As his thoughts started to come back to him, he began to realise how much he had to learn to be able to start to survive in a new and hostile environment.

What if Maureen became injured and he had to treat her wounds? The present world was built to reduce the chances of damage to anybody to a virtual zero, but everything on the new

world would be a potential disaster. Even small things like splinters could become infected if they were not dealt with properly. They wouldn't even have a plaster.
He managed to roll back into a sitting up position, leaning against the door of the Builder, although his head was still hung down close to the floor as he tried to make the blood flow back into his brain.
Maybe Maureen would be able to look after the animals as far as anything nasty was concerned. If he could only learn enough first aid to get through, then maybe things would be O.K.
As his breathing started to ease, he let out a big sigh, and started to raise his eyes. From a pair of shoes, his eyes worked their way up to Maureen's soft features smiling gently down at him. 'I didn't know whether to disturb you or not. I was afraid you might collapse altogether if I touched you,' her voice was very easy.
Mark felt very embarrassed by the whole situation, and it was only the lack of blood in his face that saved him from turning crimson. 'I feel rough,' was all he could manage.
Maureen bent and put her arm across his shoulders.
'What are you doing here, anyway,' Mark felt angry that his failure to cope with the programme was being witnessed, especially by the woman he loved.
'I knew what today's programme was, that's why Tanya wished you good luck when she left you.'
'So you came to see me make a fool of myself?' Mark was starting to feel a bit better from the sickness, but couldn't hide his feelings.
'I came because I love you as you are. Remember, you went this way before, and it is because you have such a gentle nature that you cannot cope with programmes like that. It is because you have such a gentle nature that I love you so much.'
'I'm sorry. It's just that it feels so awful to be like this, and for

you to see me seems to make it worse,' the anger subsided as quickly as it had risen.
Maureen helped him to his feet, and used a videophone to request a robot cleaner to freshen up the area.
They headed for Maureen's apartment. Mark washed in cold water, and after carefully cleaning his teeth felt he could start to cope with life again.
'I think it may be very difficult for me to cope with life on the new world,' his face was very serious. 'Until now I had only been looking at the good points, and couldn't wait until we got out there.'
'That's because you are a true optimist. Everything will be O.K. tomorrow. That's another of the reasons why I love you,' Maureen smiled as she made some drinks. 'But don't forget that everything is a ring. If nothing happens, then you stay at the same place on the rings, and life goes on just the same, but that is very rare. If tomorrow is to be better, then you, or someone, has to do something to alter your position on the rings. That alteration, of course, makes life better and worse, because as you know, you are always getting nearer to both. Today's experience made you feel worse, but made the chances of you being able to cope better. I know it's a rough and ready way to think of it, but that's how it happens.'
At last Mark started to smile. 'When you are knelt down wishing you could die, it's not easy to work out that things are getting better.'
'The Oldies had a saying. 'The darkest hour is just before dawn.' That neatly explains a ring. The worst moment is the one just before it starts to get better. I wonder who thought of it, or if it was given to them,' Maureen had been wondering about the possibility of the old world being one that was overseen.
'Say that we hit the jackpot and go there together. Do you think that we will be able to cope with everything?' Mark ventured.

'You mean will I be able to deliver the baby goats and make sure they are O.K,' Maureen smiled.
Thinking he was making progress, Mark put his arm round Maureen and moved his body closer to her on the couch.
'I will be able to sew up a wound in your leg if you fall on the rocks and cut it badly,' she was still smiling.
Mark knew that they could survive together. 'We will be a great team.'
'Just the two of us, alone together to create the new world,' Maureen's expression hadn't changed.
'It will be paradise,' Mark murmured as he softly kissed her cheek.
'And I suppose you will be able to cope with childbirth by the time you have delivered our eighth. No way, you cope from day one,' Maureen pulled slightly away from him as she spoke. 'If it's me who is injured, then I have to depend on you totally for my life. I will need your help in childbirth. Don't forget how many generations have passed since women gave birth naturally. It is not going to be easy.'
Mark felt his temperature rise, almost as it did when he felt so faint. 'But you don't understand how bad it feels.'
'I know it is dreadful for you, but it's the only way forward. To me the most terrifying thought in the world is going on that freighter. I just cannot bear to think about the days cooped up in that old lump of metal. It doesn't even look as if it will take off.'
'But I will be there to hold your hand and look after you. I will make sure you are alright,' Mark took hold of her hands as he spoke.
Maureen smiled inwardly. 'Then I will do the same for you. We can use the Memory Builders together. Going through them again will be a refresher course for me, and I will be there for you. Together we will win,' as she finished talking she hugged Mark tight and kissed him full on the lips.

Mark was caught between heaven and hell. He knew that he wanted her more than anything in life, but he also knew the pain and sickness he would have to endure to be with her, unless neither of them went. He couldn't start to contemplate that, and before his thoughts could continue he was again reduced to that wonderful, almost semi conscious state that she could induce in him. The tip of her tongue traced its way round the opening of his lips, and as he pulled her to him, entered his mouth fully. He leaned slightly backwards, at the same time pulling her with him, and as she leaned more heavily on him he became very aware of how her breasts felt pressed against his chest. Her lips now left his mouth, and were concentrated against the bottom of his neck. The feelings going round his body and through his mind were overwhelming, and following her lead, he dropped his mouth to the crook of her neck and shoulder. As he pressed his lips hard against her, she gave an involuntary shudder, and gasped 'Oh, Mark, I love you so much.'

She reached down, and taking his hand, spread his fingers across her right breast. Through the soft thin material top that she wore, Mark could feel the softness of her, and was amazed at how hard and erect her nipple felt. He gently caressed her between his thumb and forefinger, and felt her start to tremble. She suddenly let out a huge gasp of air, and breaking herself away from him, rushed into the bathroom.

Mark felt as if he were coming out of a trance, and not wanting these sensations to stop, called out after her. 'I'm sorry if I did something wrong, please come back.'

Maureen's face appeared round the bathroom door. She looked very flushed, and at that moment more beautiful that Mark could ever have imagined. 'You did nothing wrong, it was me. We were getting too far ahead of ourselves.'

'But those were the most magical moments of my life. I didn't want them to stop. Please come and sit down again.'

'Let's hope those sorts of moments stay with us forever,' Maureen smiled as she disappeared.
Mark heard the shower start, and for just a few moments was tempted to go and see her naked body.
Part of him yearned to see her, touch her, and hold her close again, but his whole life and upbringing new that it would be an invasion of privacy. In the world of the Happies, nothing was done without consent.
As his feelings subsided, he made the decision to succeed in the learning that would be necessary in the new world.
'Have you any wine left,' he called, 'I think we should celebrate something or other.'
Maureen came out, and walking past him, took a canister from the shelf and poured it into a jug. She fetched two glasses and when they were full, turned to him, and saying 'Here's to our future,' they drank together as friends and lovers.

M

After a small lunch they made their way back to join the others. Joanne took charge of the session, explaining that although there had been lots of input into which site should be chosen, and what should happen to secure the future on the new planet, it would be up to whoever went to decide the final details. She nodded at Mark as she went on 'Those of you who have looked at history may have seen that the minimum for a settlement which incorporated fishing was four families, because it took four men to crew a decent fishing vessel. That was to allow some of the catch to be traded for other things the families needed. Although there will be no one to trade with, so the boat could just as easily be handled by two, I think the basic concept is correct. Four families can watch out for one another, and work together towards a viable future. The main thing is that whoever goes must want to go, and conquer all the problems that will crop up. No one should feel pressurised into going if they are not fully committed. We will soon know who we think is fertile, and who isn't, but that should not by itself be a bar to going, as we can still rely on doing what we do now for the first few years. In just over a week we will know the possible natural parents, and I want you all to try and martial your thoughts into deciding whether you want to go or not. Those who decide to stay behind will form a team who will give every possible assistance to the new settlement. How long that will last for remains to be seen, but I would guess at a minimum of twenty years. It will not be a case of being a lesser group because of staying here, as the future of our new world will be reliant on the information, and possibly practical help we can give. Much of the time will be spent looking intensely at the surroundings of the site chosen. I am very excited at the prospect of being part of that group, and from that statement you will know what you have already probably guessed. I will be staying here.'

'So the idea is to put all the eggs in one basket,' Mark was not too sure.
'It's something that has been discussed a lot,' Joanne replied,' but going back to what I said before, it will be up to the ones who go to make the final decision.'
There was a lull in the conversation, and Joanne spoke again. 'I propose that we take the rest of the day off, and concentrate on what we love about here, and what we love about the new challenge. Only remember that when the freighter takes off, you will never come back. I don't expect you to finally decide today, but try to get into your mind and think what will be best for you. Only when you are sure can you go one way or the other, but decision time will arrive sooner than you can possibly imagine.'
Murray partially stood as he asked 'Do we need to set a timescale, as up to now we have been sort of doing the work without pressure.'
Joanne nodded at Cocho. 'I think you are best to answer that.'
He smiled. 'Most of the freighters were relatively short haul and big payload. They could travel at any time as the routes were fairly simple. We will be travelling longer, and consequently it is a more complex route. The optimum time is when we can use the pull of the stars we pass. There is a two week window coming up in just over four months which would suit us perfectly. The next good opportunity would be just over a year. There is no reason we can't be in a position to take the earlier time. I will be onboard, so two of us are now decided. If there are no objections, I suggest we agree to that timescale.'
No one at the meeting raised an objection. Joanne suggested they meet again tomorrow.
Outside, Mark and Maureen walked in silence for a while. They sat in the park and eventually Maureen spoke. 'Are we still both committed to the new earth?'
'You sound as if a small doubt has crept in.' Maureen made a face. 'Up to now I hadn't really thought about who else might be

going. It's just that Elena was very difficult with me, and I am not sure that whatever the problem was has gone away. If she goes it might not be so easy.'
'Any other problems?' Mark queried.
'No, I still want to go, so I suppose we vote to go and see who else we get,' she squeezed his hand as she spoke.
'Let's wander right round and soak in everything so we can hold it in our memories.'
It was late afternoon when they were passing the entrance to one of the tunnels.
'Let's go see the sunset, to put us in the mood,' Maureen seemed to have lost her earlier worries.
Mark punched in the code, and they sat in wonder as the sun went down, and the stars exploded across the night sky. 'If it can look this wonderful from here, just think how good it will be in the new world.'
'Probably not as good, because we will be looking through an atmosphere, but it will be where we are looking from that counts more than what we are looking at,' Maureen seemed reassured that their decision was correct. 'I suggest that tomorrow we commit to going.'
That night Maureen fell asleep thinking how much she loved Mark and how much she wanted his children.
The next day the atmosphere seemed more highly charged. The factor of the target date seemed to have increased the intensity of getting on with everything else that needed to be done. Maureen announced that she and Mark wanted to go to the new planet.
Joanne accepted that Mark was sufficiently free from drugs to know his own mind. 'I think none of us doubted your intentions,' she laughed.
Sue also said she would like to book her seat early if possible. This really lifted Mark and Maureen, as she was one of those perfect people who work hard, and only see the good points in

all the people round them. Sven also asked to go on the list. Again, Mark and Sue were pleased as he was so easy to get on with.
Sheila said she would be staying. 'I think I might want to spend too much time enjoying myself, and not enough time working, and I think it may be fun back here. We will eventually have to recruit our own replacements.'
Wendell made the same decision. 'My talents are not the ones you need to start your new lives.'
Tanya agreed with him for the same reasons.
So although they had more time to think about it, nine of the twenty had already made up their minds, with five going and four staying.
Joanne took centre stage once more. 'I suggest Nicky, Mark, and Brian form their own little group, and someone can take them through all the work that has been done so far, while the rest of us concentrate on what else is needed.'
Asif immediately volunteered to be their helper.
Maureen smiled to herself. Nicky was certainly onto a winner.
'Before we go off, can I leave the rest of you with one of my worries?' Mark was smiling as he spoke. 'I dreamt the other night that I swam out to the little island in the bay at site E. That just gives me one little problem.'
'We hadn't thought of that one,' Sophie nodded in agreement. 'I would love to learn how to swim as well.'
'The only place is in the water holding tanks, so anyone who wants to learn will have to really freshen up first. We had better make flotation devices of some sort to help,' Joanne was her usual practical self.
'And some bathing costumes,' added Sophie. 'I can do that, so let me know who wants to learn and I will take measurements.'
Mark wondered how many things they would not have thought about when they got to site E, and why Sophie wanted to learn how to swim, unless she had decided to go as well.

For the next week the four of them buckled down to patiently going through the huge list that had been put together. They thought about every item, and how they would use it, and whether it could be bettered.
On the following Friday, Joanne had an envelope each for Nicky, Mark, and Brian. 'Here are your fertility results. Have a look, and we will then all look at the full results.'
Mark was first to read his result, and his huge grin was repeated by Brian and Nicky. They followed Joanne into the meeting room, and she read out the names of the thirteen who were thought to be fertile:

Mark
Brian
Greg
Clive
Asif
Cocho
Sven
Nicky
Maureen
Cynthia
Sophie
Sheila
Sue

Nicky immediately realised that Elena was not on the list, and glanced at Brian. He squeezed his eyes tightly shut, then looked across at Elena, and walked across and kissed her. He whispered something to her.
Asif and Nicky were holding hands, and after a few quiet words announced that they would like to go to the new world.
Sven had moved round to stand next to Maureen. 'How do I go about speaking to her?' he whispered. Maureen was giggling as

she looked at him. 'Ask her if she fancies going to the new world with you?'
'What if she says no?'
'Believe me, it will be a yes,' Maureen confirmed to him.
'How can you be so sure, and anyway I haven't said who it is yet'' Sven looked puzzled.
'Sophie, have you got a minute?' Maureen called.
Sophie walked over to them.
Sven was always quiet, but this time the emotion in his voice carried right round the room. 'Sophie. I love you.'
There was an explosion of clapping and cheering in the room, and Sven went scarlet.
'How do men manage to take so long to get round to what has been on their mind for months?' Joanne queried.
Amidst the general laughter Sophie planted a huge kiss on Sven's lips. 'I hoped if I waited long enough you would get round to it. I suppose that means we will be on the freighter as well?' Sven had a smile so wide it seemed to go on past his ears.
'Wow,' said Joanne, 'that means we already have eight going, four staying, and eight still to decide. If the eight of you that are going can get together, I suggest you try and agree on where to set up camp.'
Brian was still standing with Elena. 'Can we join that group as well? We assumed we wouldn't be able to go as Elena can't have babies, but if we can still use the same system, we may want to tag along. We can decide later if we want to go.'
'That's fine,' Joanne looked pleased
Elena walked over to Maureen. 'My apologies for how I behaved before. It was when I got the results, and knew I would never be a mother. I was jealous of all the other women who were fertile, not just you. I was wrong.'
Maureen hugged her, and little tears formed in Elena's eyes. 'I wanted it so much,' she snuffled, 'I wanted it to be so perfect with Brian, like you and Mark'

Maureen didn't know what to say that would help. 'Is it possible you could be implanted with an egg, like in the old days?'
'I might give it a try, but I just wanted my own,' with that the tears flooded down.
Greg confirmed that he would join the stay behind list, and continue to visit the planet when necessary.
The eight who were going gathered together, and were joined by Brian and Elena. They found a separate room, and Sophie suggested they should have a leader, much as Joanne had led the whole group, and added 'I think Maureen would be good, because she has some of the same quality that Joanne has in knowing what people are thinking.'
'I thought it was only my brain she could read,' Mark thought Maureen was a good choice, and seconded her. A quick look round the table confirmed everyone agreed.
'I will try to be like Joanne, and interpret what I think the group feels, instead of making suggestions, and of course the first one is the choice of site.' Maureen was pleased to have been elected leader.
'Please count us out of the important stuff, as I do not think we should vote unless we fully commit to go.' Brian spoke and Elena nodded her agreement.
'For what it's worth, I can navigate easily to any of the sites we have looked at, so I am relaxed,' Cocho always seemed very serious.
Sophie smiled at Sven. 'I think I probably favour site E, not only because of sitting with Sven, watching the sun go down, but because the island is small enough for Greg to do some intense searches and try to ensure it is safe.'
Sven added 'If we are going to build a boat big enough for ten of us, then it should be able to reach other islands when and if we need to. Site E for me as well.'
Mark nodded. 'As you know, Maureen and I favour E as well, and I like the idea of Greg looking hard at it first.'

Nicky and Asif looked at each other, and Nicky spoke. 'Site E it is then.'
'I suppose I had better keep a few notes,' said Maureen, 'any objections to site E? No, then I take that as unanimous. Now housing. We can live in the freighter for a while, but need to establish a base. One large place or four or five smaller ones?' she glanced at Brian and Elena.
A quick discussion decided that separate houses were better, and Cocho asked if he and Sue could withdraw for a moment. When they came back in they were both smiling. 'I didn't like to assume that Sue would share with me without asking her. Obviously, everyone loves her, so I had no problem, but…..'
'Are they all the same?' interrupted Maureen. 'Everyone knows except them?'
'Knows what?' said Mark.
'How Sue feels about Cocho, sorry,' said Maureen, 'everyone except Mark.'
'And Sven,' said Sven.
'And Asif,' said Asif.
Maureen shook her head. 'I am sure the men will have some uses in the new world.'
'My first use will be to suggest we have a name for the settlement, rather than new world, or new planet. A name that means something,' said Cocho
There was silence round the table until Sophie spoke. 'As we are building our dens on site E, I suggest we call it Edens.'
A quick glance round the table, and Maureen noted the new name.
The rest of the afternoon was spent discussing lots more detail about the new site, all of which Maureen recorded, and when they called time everyone was very upbeat that the future together looked good.
Mark and Maureen walked hand in hand back to her apartment. They were both feeling elated from the meeting, and ordered a

light supper. Sat next to each other, Mark felt new warmth in their relationship, as if they had settled down together, rather than being two separate people.
With the meal over, Mark put his arm loosely across Maureen's shoulders, and she snuggled closely against him. Turning her face up to his, she kissed him lightly at first, then more deeply and passionately. She stood, and pulling him to his feet, gently removed his top, and then did the same with hers. Mark could not believe the effect this produced in him. Every nerve in his body was working overtime, and he clasped her to him. Step by step his emotions were rising. Maureen gently moved her breasts against his chest, then leaned away and placed his hands there. Mark stopped thinking, and succumbed to all the pleasures his body was feeling. She eased her hand inside his pants, and gently squeezed. The rest of their clothes were discarded on the floor as they lay together on the couch, and Maureen guided him inside her. Stars were racing round Mark's head and when he eventually climaxed, Maureen was with him all the way.
They lay wrapped in each others arms for some time, then showered together and dressed.
'So,' Maureen smiled at him.
'I don't know how to describe that,' Mark replied. 'Every bit of me was on fire. My brain saw continuous shooting stars, and the intense feelings of pleasure in all my lower body were beyond anything I knew existed. Fantastic or wonderful does not do it justice.'
Maureen kissed him very gently on the lips, murmuring 'Much the same for me, and they say it gets better with age.'
That night Mark went to bed and tried to re-live the evening in his mind. Everything was there, except the incredible sensations, but he drifted off to sleep a very happy man.
Next morning Joanne addressed the meeting. 'Maureen has given me all the decisions made by the pioneers, who have

chosen sight E and named it Edens. We had vaguely decided beforehand that it would be best if we looked at who would be the best cross matches to start the new race. The group of eight, or ten, seem to have already decided who is with who. Although this may not be perfect, I think it may be the best way forward in what will be a close nit community. Unless anyone has any argument with this, I propose we let nature take its course, and only assist where any couple cannot reproduce.'

No one disagreed, and the work of listing all the necessities, then checking them again continued for the next few weeks. Cocho decided that freighter AH was the best one for the job, as it was built as a long range vessel, but still had an enormous cargo capacity. Like AA, it was another of the ARC vessels, and loading started immediately that one had been chosen.

For Mark and Maureen, life was like one long honeymoon, and they kept postponing how they would explain to their parents as long as possible.

The ten of them were still working well together, although Elena seemed to be getting more and more depressed. Although she was very fair, she seemed even paler than normal. One or two people had remarked to each other that she looked unwell, but put it down to the strain of being unable to have the baby she so desperately wanted, and being undecided if someone who was not a natural mother should go to Edens. She had explained that she felt her infertility may go through to any children she conceived artificially. With just over six weeks to go to launch date, Elena fainted in the tunnel out to AH. Wendell and Sophie were the ones to deal with the problem, as they had the most medical training.

Next day, as the twenty gathered, Elena looked just as bad, but walked with Brian to the front of the room. Turning, she managed a smile. 'Will the freighter be OK to take ten and a half?' Maureen rushed over and threw her arms round Elena. 'You clever thing. How did you manage that?'

Brian blushed, and stammered 'How do you think?'
By then everyone realised what had happened, and congratulations were showered on the lucky couple.
'I think we need to review our fertility checks,' Joanne seemed really pleased for Elena and Brian. 'Can I leave it up Sophie and Wendell to look at the previous tests, and the current state of play?'
Sue was as red as a beetroot, and her freckles really stood out. 'We weren't going to announce it yet, but as everyone is so happy, make it ten and two halves.' Cocho stood beside her and couldn't stop smiling.
Maureen was very pleased for the two couples, but wondered why nothing had happened to her. She brought it up with Sophie when she re-tested for fertility. 'So you have discovered the joys of sex,' Sophie smiled, and her long black curls shook as she burst into laughter. 'I'm not pregnant yet either. It doesn't happen to order, just takes time. But remember, practise makes perfect,' she burst out laughing again.
As the time for the flight drew nearer, Maureen asked Joanne for advice on how to tell her parents. 'I'm afraid it will be a lie, but I suggest we up the drugs substantially for a couple of weeks before the ten of you tell your parents, so that they will be numb and just accept the fact that you are going.'
Joanne discussed it with the others, and they all told their parents on the same day and it went very smoothly.
And so the great day arrived, and the ten and two halves left for Edens. Mark Eve and Maureen Adams travelled together with the others in a freighter with the yellow letters ARC standing out on the hull, together with the identification No.AH. They prospered in the new world, and the stories handed down to their children and grandchildren were allowed to become twisted as Adam and Eve arriving in Eden, and Noah's Ark transporting all the animals.

END

Chapter 2

Michael put down the pages.

He stretched, trying to undo the muscles that had seized up as he sat immobile while devouring the contents of the buff envelope. For a minute or two he wasn't sure which world he was living in. The one that had been destroyed sounded identical to the one he lived in, but according to the information, the inhabitants were long gone. So he was descended from the original inhabitants of Eden, or did that world already hold a population? Had more eventually joined the original ten and two halves? Did Rui and Jean come from the planet where the Happies lived? Or was Eden somewhere else?

His reading had produced more questions than answers, and his sleep that night was as restless as his mind, with the questions piling up ready for the morning.

Wednesday dawned bright and clear in New York. It was three days until he visited Hampton, and Michael wondered if he would be able to contain all the questions he needed to ask Rui and Jean until then. Tuesday had really been one hell of a day in his life, and so much had changed that he didn't know where to start. He was the first one up and quietly helped himself to some grapefruit juice from the huge fridge in the kitchen, and took it through to the pool. A few lengths made him feel more awake and relaxed, and he decided that he would just have to go with the flow. Bob Haynes had set down the next three days for learning some more about the business and Michael wondered if he knew that his parents were still alive. He decided to talk it over with Jessie, as he felt she would know more than him. In the meantime he would learn as much as possible, and try to get away with saying as little as he could.

'Good morning,' Peter followed Mary into the pool area, 'let's hope today is just a little less active than yesterday. We are still trying to come to terms with everything that happened.'

Mary smiled. 'Have you given any thought as to how you see all this working out?'
Michael nodded at his mother. 'I have given it plenty of thought, but haven't a clue as to any of the answers. I think we should take the rest of the week as it comes, and see if we are any nearer a sensible decision by the weekend.'
Peter stepped down into the pool. 'Although I am sure we could get used to the lifestyle here, I think I really belong back in Suffolk.'
Mary nodded in agreement. 'Hopefully we can return early next week.'
Michael laughed. 'You are both going to keep on working, even though you are multi millionaires!'
Peter gave a rueful smile. 'You know perfectly well that I would teach for nothing, although Mary has agreed to cut down slightly on her work. She would like to be involved in your new empire from a distance if possible. Presumably you will stay on longer than us?' Michael nodded his agreement. 'I will have to return to Cambridge at some time, but I am sure they will be extremely sympathetic, especially when they realise that I am now very wealthy. I would still like to complete my studies if it can be worked out.'
As they had breakfast Bob Haynes phoned to check what time they would be arriving, and arranged for the chauffeur to collect them at nine thirty.
Peter felt that he would not have much interest in the business discussions, but wanted to tag along to try and understand what it was that Rui and Jean hoped to accomplish.
Just before they were due to leave Michael was using the bathroom when what he later described to himself as a feeling that Rui came into his head. 'Are you going to see Bob and Jessie today?' Although he received the question, it was like before, almost wrapped in cloud. He tried to reply, but Rui willed him not to try and reply, but just to picture himself in

Bob's office talking to them if he was going there. 'Try not to think it, just see a picture and do nothing with it,' encouraged Rui. 'So Peter and Mary will be there as well.' Again, it was more like a dream as Rui made contact once more. Michael realised that they were in the picture he had created. 'Don't try anymore,' came the message, 'we will see you on Saturday. I have left some details on your computer.' Suddenly his brain cleared, and he was looking at the bathroom wall, seeing with his eyes rather than with whatever was giving him the messages. As they went down in the lift, Michael was starting to realise what a massive advantage Rui and Jean had if they could see what other people were thinking, especially from a distance. He wondered if he could do the same, and tried to picture Rui, but nothing happened, except Mary asked him if he was OK, as he was screwing his eyes up so tightly.

Michael smiled. 'I'm fine, just trying to remember everything that happened yesterday and decide what is the most important, and how and in what order to deal with it.' Even as he spoke, he knew that Brenda Casey was number one on the list. He would also have to do something about Mikey Spinetti to avoid looking over his shoulder all the time. Maybe Bob could suggest something about both. Rui and Jean would have to wait until Saturday, but he would quiz Jessie a bit more about them. Starting to learn about the business would have to roll on at its own pace.

He punched the buttons for the top floor and the one beneath, explaining to his parents that he would call in and say hello to Jessie, then join them one floor up.

Jessie gave him a huge smile when he went in. 'You must fancy me to bits. Can't wait to see me in Bob's office,' her eyes were twinkling.

'You see straight through me. I thought using the excuse to check my computer would be my cover,' Michael poked his tongue out at her.

Jessie burst out laughing. 'You are as soft as me. I think we are going to get along just fine. Just wish I was thirty years younger and looked like Brenda.'

'Yeah, that's something I need to deal with today,' Michael grimaced.

'My best advice would be not to get involved, but as I know that is not an option, I will do whatever I can to help,' Jessie looked more serious.

'Thanks, I know you will,' Michael hugged her, 'and now to business.'

Going through to his office, he saw that his computer was already on.

Jessie had followed him in. 'This is the password combination,' she hit the keys quite slowly so he could memorise the sequence. 'This is probably what you need,' she opened a page that contained half a dozen instructions from Rui. They were all details of what shares to buy, 'do you want me to action these?' she looked up at him.

'How can you be certain these are from Rui?' Michael asked.

'See the sequence of numbers at the top? We each have a list of randomly produced numbers that we use in sequence. If anyone found the list, it would mean nothing to them.'

'Then action away,' Michael smiled, 'or have you already done that?'

'We are not going to be able to fool one another, are we?' Jessie looked up at him.

'No, and I want to ask you about this mind thing, and also about Jean and Rui. Can we meet for lunch, just us two?'

'There you go again,' laughed Jessie, 'a girl isn't safe when you are around. I can fix something in the office when we decide to break.'

They took the lift up, and entered Bob's office dead on ten o'clock.

Again, the four of them sat facing Bob.

‘Any thoughts before we get down to business?’ he asked.
‘I wondered if we needed to do anything about Mikey Spinetti?’ Michael had a serious face.
‘You have had a couple of top minders looking out for you from the moment you left The Sandstone,’ said Bob, ‘and Marcel knows the situation and how to handle security inside the hotel. We can take it further if you want.’
Michael nodded. ‘The other thing……’
‘Try not to get involved is the best advice,’ Bob interrupted, ‘but I guess that is not what you want to hear.’
Michael winced. Could Bob also read his mind? ‘It’s very hard to explain. Something really bad has happened, and she is not to blame. I know it sounds stupid, but I have no option.’
Bob nodded and picked up his phone. Punching one of the buttons, he said. ‘Hello Paul, please go ahead and find out everything you can. Many thanks.’
Looking at Michael, he tilted his head slightly. ‘We need to tread carefully if we are to get her out of Century Fields. Can we speak about her and Mikey later on?’
Michael nodded his agreement.
They started with the two banks, and by the lunch break had taken in one of the oil companies as well. ‘Three down out of one hundred and forty seven, but it will get faster as we go,’ Bob rose from his chair.
‘I am having a passionate rendezvous with Jessie in my office, if that’s OK with the rest of you,’ said Michael.
‘Then meet back here in, say, half an hour?’ Bob raised his eyebrows.
‘So it’s not going to be long and passionate then,’ Jessie winked at Michael and burst out laughing.
Back in Michael’s office she buzzed for some food and drink, and then turned to look at him. ‘Rui and Jean, where do you want to start?’

‘Start with Peter’s question, what were.....are they trying to achieve?’
‘You know that they are not from here.’
Michael nodded.
‘Wherever they come from has been monitoring how earth has been getting on for thousands of years. A number of them are becoming concerned that the earth is heading for disaster unless it can be altered. Rui and Jean are two, although I think there may be more, who are trying to do something about it. They are trying to support good governments, and help good oppositions overcome bad governments to try and improve life for the underprivileged minority. They have already spent billions, and have had some success, but nothing like they hoped for. I think they are becoming a bit disillusioned.’
‘So they interfere with the politics of the world,’ Michael frowned.
‘To a certain degree, but obviously not enough,’ Jessie looked very serious.
‘I am not sure it’s what they should be doing.’
‘So they shouldn’t interfere?’ a flicker of a smile crossed Jessie’s face.
‘No, or at least I don’t think so,’ Michael was not totally sure of his reply.
‘So you shouldn’t have interfered with Jamie Spinetti yesterday, or is it like father, like son?’ Jessie’s smile widened slightly. ‘It’s just that you correct the world from one person up, whereas they try to correct it from one country up. And don’t say ‘that’s different’.’
Michael bit the words back, and shut his eyes.
‘You saw a problem and dealt with it, and have already taken on a perceived problem with Brenda Casey,’ Jessie shrugged.
‘Touché,’ Michael knew when he was beaten. ‘Right, this mind thing. First of all, can Bob see into my mind?’

'He has tiny little flashes, but nowhere near as much as me. I think because I work with your parents very closely, it has somehow rubbed off more on me. The big difference is that they can control it, whereas mine seems to come and go,' Jessie looked puzzled.
Mark remembered Joanne in the file that Rui had given him. 'They have had a hell of a lot longer to practice.'
'I know that they were born like that. Jean mentioned that bringing up babies is easy when you know exactly why something upsets them.'
'So how much are they able to do?' Michael was still trying to understand.
'It's not just how much they can do, but how much they can understand it. If they were in a room of fifty people, and they 'listened with their mind instead of their ears' as they put it, they would know the thoughts of those fifty people all at once, but their brains are able to hold the information apart, but also put it together if it is relevant. Imagine if you listened to fifty people talking at the same time. I barely scratch the surface,' Jessie shrugged, 'it's a huge business advantage, but they also have incredible brains. A long time ago one of my best friends was nearly court-martialled out of the forces. He hypnotised an entire parade ground, and the officer in charge was not amused. He obviously had some power, but nothing like Rui and Jean.'
'I suppose we had better return to work,' Michael got up as he spoke.
'Just let me smudge my lipstick, to make them wonder,' Jessie smacked his leg as he walked past.
Michael laughed. 'I don't know why I love you but I do.'
'My favourite song,' replied Jessie.
'Just one other thing,' Michael turned, 'does Bob know Jean and Rui are alive?'
'Yes, anything I know, he knows, and vice versa.'

Back in Bob's office, Peter had excused himself and gone sightseeing for the afternoon, and the four of them gradually worked through more of the businesses.

It was nearly six when Peter returned to collect Mary. 'Are you calling it a day now?'

'I have just a few points to go through with Bob,' replied Michael. 'I will be back at The Sandstone by about seven thirty, so see if you can book us a table somewhere please.'

When they were alone Bob started the conversation. 'Your mother is one very smart woman.'

Michael smiled. 'She is lovely, but I had no idea how good her business brain is.'

'I think she will be a huge asset to you and Jessie, even if she wants to work from the UK.'

'I think it may be the safest place for her, at least until the Spinetti problem is sorted.' Michael's face was very serious.

'We have to talk about that, and also the possible threat hanging over from Rui and Jean. They staged their accident because of real and perceived threats to them, mainly from the Middle East and Africa, where their support for the underdogs has not been fully appreciated by some. We made sure the crash had worldwide coverage, but any reprisals may possibly be carried over to you and Jessie. Even to me I suppose,' Bob looked a little sad. 'I suggest fairly tight security for all of you, probably over and above that currently in place, so we can cover both threats, I guess Spinetti will act quite quickly, if at all.'

'Can you arrange that for all of us, please, Bob?'

Bob nodded. 'That's not a problem.'

'Now Brenda.' Michael got up and walked to the window. 'I have to sort that out so I am able to fully concentrate on the business.'

Bob buzzed on his phone. 'Would you like to join us, please, Paul?'

Paul came in, not much taller than Bob, but much thicker across the shoulders. Probably in his mid thirties, with short fair hair. He walked quickly across to Michael, and they shook hands.
'Brenda Casey. Where would you like to start?' he sat down, and Michael took the seat next to him.
'I know it sounds stupid, but I bumped into her in a police station, and she asked me for help without speaking. Just seemed to beam straight into my head, twice. Just from that I know she is not insane, and not guilty of murdering her daughter, which was confirmed by the station sergeant. I know I shouldn't get involved, but I'm stuck with her. Take it from the alleged murder,' at last Michael felt there was something he could at least try and do since his arrival in New York.
Paul smiled. 'I will go back just before that. She was a very beautiful girl, but from the wrong side of the tracks as far as her husband's family were concerned. The Jepsons are one of the richest and oldest American families, and Greg was not supposed to marry anyone like Brenda. She was twenty-one when they married, and just twenty-two when Abigail was born. At that stage everything seemed to be fine. When Abigail was three, she was found on the family estate very badly beaten and died later that day in hospital. Greg's mother and father testified in court that they had seen Brenda beating the child, but had got to her too late to save Abigail's life. They also explained that Brenda had suffered very badly from postnatal depression, which had got worse and worse over the years. That fact was confirmed by the family doctor. In court, Brenda could not have been a worse defendant. She could not remember anything about the incident, and was extremely vague in her replies to questioning. She was convicted of murder, but placed in Century Fields instead of prison. Nothing has happened since. We have been through all the trial papers, and the evidence was insufficient, and the verdict definitely worthy of appeal, although the Jepsons would be very difficult opponents. Two

interesting points. The Jepsons own the hospital where Abigail died, and Century Fields. Also, there was no independent autopsy. I am not sure where we go from here. Greg divorced Brenda soon after the trial, and she reverted to her maiden name.'

Michael had been studying the ceiling right through Paul's statement. 'First, thank you very much. That is an incredible amount of information in such a short space of time.'

Bob coughed gently.

Michael dropped his eyes and smiled at him. 'I know, that's what we pay for.'

'I'm so glad you understand,' Bob was nearly smiling.

'Second,' Michael went on, 'I know exactly how to proceed from here. Again, Paul, thanks very much. A super job.'

Paul asked Bob if there was anything else. 'No, off you go home. Well done.'

Bob was biting at his top lip. 'Second.....Rui?'

'Exactly,' said Michael.

Bob picked up his phone and punched in a fast code. 'Hello, Rui, it's Bob. I have Michael here for you.'

Rui was laughing. 'Phones are so cute, aren't they? Of course I will take a look into the minds of Henry and Marion Jepson. Greg as well, just in case. Your mind is overflowing with it. You shouldn't really have got involved, but she is gorgeous, so I can understand why.'

'I didn't realise you had seen her,' Michael could still not get to grips with the mind thing, and wasn't sure if Rui had been speaking to him or not.

'Your head is full of her, and I was speaking,' Rui laughed again, give me ten or fifteen minutes.'

Michael asked Bob if he was OK for another ten minutes. He nodded. 'I could use a cold beer, you?'

Michael nodded his assent.

He sipped at the Budweiser, again going through the events since his arrival in New York, but every time his mind slipped back to Brenda Casey. He was certain she hadn't killed her baby.
What if Greg had done it? His parents would want to protect him. 'No, it wasn't Greg, it was Henry.' Rui was back with him. 'He walked her down to the stables and raped her so savagely she was virtually dead. He then beat her with a shovel in the stables. It was not the first time in his life that he had raped a child, but he has such power over his wife and son, that they went along with his lies. Marion harbours suspicions, but Henry stuck by his story that he saw Brenda do it. Greg believed his parents rather than his wife. Let me know if you want me to do anything further.' Rui was gone.
Michael was shaking, and jerkily told Bob what had happened over a year ago.
'It will be a difficult appeal,' said Bob.
'Can you find out if Abigail was buried or cremated?' asked Michael.
'No problem. Same time, same place?' asked Bob
'Yeah,' muttered Michael, thinking hard.
'You pay me a lot for advice,' said Bob, 'don't do anything in a hurry. Especially don't go near Henry Jepson. Think hard for a couple of days. Also, don't go near Brenda. Time and knowledge are on our side, so don't screw up our advantage.'
'But….' Michael shrugged, 'yes, you are right.'
'Come on,' said Bob, 'I will drop you off on my way home.'
They were very quiet in the taxi, and Bob's parting words stayed with Michael. 'We will skin the bastard, one way or the other, but we will do it together, in our own time.'
Michael entered the penthouse, and Mary glanced up at him. 'What's wrong?'
'Christ,' thought Michael, 'everyone can read my mind.' He went through the story of Abigail.

His mother shuddered, and his father sat shaking his head. 'At least we now know you were right about Brenda, and can try to figure out what to do.'
Michael put his head in his hands. 'Big mistake,' Rui was back with him, 'they buried Abigail. I saw you ask Bob, so just checked up for you. Good night son. Try to sleep well.'
'They buried Abigail,' Michael explained to his parents, 'we should be able to find proof if we need to.'
'I have a table booked downstairs,' said Mary, 'do you feel like eating?'
'I actually feel sick,' replied Michael, 'there are some shit heaps in the world.'
Mary raised her eyebrows.
'Sorry,' Michael glanced up.
Mary smiled at him. 'No problem. That is mild compared to what we are all thinking. But you should feel good, your perseverance against all advice has at least given us a problem we can deal with, and probably saved Brenda from spending the rest of her life in Century Fields.'
'Come on,' Michael glanced at his watch, 'let's go eat.'
As they descended in the elevator, Rui was back with Michael. 'I forgot to mention, I am keeping tabs on Mikey Spinetti. If he decides to try anything on with you, I will give you plenty of warning, or stop him if necessary. See you on Saturday.'
That seemed to lift Michael's spirits, and he explained to his parents that they could ignore one possible problem for the time being.
In spite of himself, Michael actually enjoyed the meal that evening. The three of them chatted like old times, and Peter went through all the sites he had seen that afternoon. He had enjoyed himself so much that he asked for the next day off as well.

Chapter Three

Thursday and Friday followed a similar pattern to Wednesday, and Peter managed to go sightseeing on both days. The more companies they went through, the faster it became, and whole sectors of business needed just one explanation, which covered all in that group.

Jessie managed the buying and selling according to Rui's instructions and net worth continued to rise.

It seemed that Mikey Spinetti couldn't care less about the death of his brother, although Rui kept an eye on him just in case.

Bob had somehow managed to fix it so that if and when the Jepsons fell, he had the necessary paperwork to legally remove Brenda from Century Fields to a place of safety. He was starting to put together an appeal case, making sure that nobody was alerted as to what was going on.

On Saturday their now familiar chauffeur delivered Peter, Mary and Michael to Hampton.

After coffee Rui and Michael split from the others and sat down near the lake at the bottom of the extensive grounds.

'Well done, son, you were right about Brenda.'

Michael nodded. 'We just need to work out exactly how to deal with it.'

'Would you like my help with that?'Rui was smiling, as if he relished the thought. 'We can fix it tonight if you like.'

Michael jumped to his feet like a small boy. 'Oh, please dad. How do we do it?'

Rui laughed. 'Let me tell you about your mind. You read through the notes I gave you about how this world was created. Everyone in the old world could communicate by thought transfer. The polite way was by acceptance, then Joanne took it one stage further, and quickly everyone became 'open minded' which was the term used to describe a situation where your mind was projected for all to see. Initially it caused problems, because your mind cannot lie, unlike your mouth. Having started down that route, it soon became apparent that in spite of the faults, it was good for society as it removed all lying. It made for some interesting relationship situations at the start, but as everyone, except the Happies got on board, it became the norm. When the ten plus two halves arrived, funny how that name stuck for something so momentous, they carried on being open minded. What they had not realised was that there was already a small population on this earth, which we called new earth, but we now call earth two, and over the centuries the two groups produced the civilisation we have today. So some have the inherent ability to be able to use thought transfer, if they are descended in any part from the original group. Some of them use about one per cent of their ability to understand the thoughts they have. They could develop to the state that we and your mum have, but it would take thousands of years of evolution.'

'So my mind is the same as yours?' Michael interrupted.

'Exactly, it just hasn't practised as much yet. On earth two, most of the population use about twenty per cent of their brain. Of that twenty per cent, about eighty per cent is used to interpret what they see; so about four per cent of brain power is actually being used for anything other than sight. That is why a lot of people shut their eyes when they concentrate, and why dreams are often so brilliant. The part of the brain used to interpret sight is being used for something more constructive. We use about eighty per cent of our brains, and only twenty percent of that is used to interpret sight, so our brains are about sixteen times as efficient as those on earth two. That's why you could hear Brenda, because receiving is the easy part. You are open minded, which is fine, but to actually go into another mind is the more difficult bit, unless that person is open minded, although you will soon master it. You probably tried to answer Brenda in thought, but I would suspect you failed.'

‘So how good is Mary, because she is Jean’s sister?’ Michael asked.

Rui continued. ‘We came to earth number two twenty five years ago, and needed a history. We altered a few records here and there, and one of them was a ‘long lost’ daughter for Mary’s mother. We used Peter and Mary because they are inherently good. We knew we would need someone to bring up any children we had in the normal earth two way, because up till now we have only dabbled in trying to help on earth two. It was suggested that we needed someone with our abilities, but who was earth two wise, so that hopefully they would be more in tune to what was actually needed here on earth two. We have interfered on earth for thousands of years, but never managed to make it the paradise it should be. We have helped along the way, mainly by using the transporter, so whoever uses it has less than a day to have an effect. It used to be seconds, but that is one area that has vastly improved. So we could give direction to people like Leonardo da Vinci, hoping they would push the world forward in the direction we wanted. I suppose over time, hundreds of thousands of trips have been made. As a matter of fact, that is where ghosts come from. It is easier to use the transporter to go to the same references on earth two that have already been used, depending on which area you need to be. We use ley lines, something like airport landing lights, so if someone spots a visitor from our world, it is often in the same place. If it is in a house, and the furniture has been moved, then it can be a bit noisy. In that case we are called poltergeists.’

Michael grimaced. ‘So we are sixteen times as intelligent as the locals, but we have not managed to sort out the problems here.’

Rui closed his eyes. ‘To a large degree we have handicapped ourselves. At the very outset of populating earth two there was a difference of opinion as to how much we should help. Some voted not at all, so it ended up that we could suggest, but not force.’

‘So how do you differentiate between a strong suggestion and a weak force?’ Michael pressed the point.
‘I will demonstrate that tonight. I think it will be just within the guidelines we use, although I may be bending them slightly. I will face the consequences if necessary,’ Rui opened his eyes and smiled at his son, ‘anyway it will be in a good cause.’
‘To do with Brenda?’ Michael asked.
‘Wait and see,’ said Rui. ‘Going back to the problems of earth two, we are now convinced that it was the population already here that we knew nothing about that was the cause.’
‘Of course,’ said Michael, ‘if you have a problem, blame someone else.’
Rui smiled, ‘Possibly, but now that earth three and earth four are running like the paradise earth two should have been, and they are populated solely by people from my home, then it seems that is the case.’
Michaels’ eyes went wide. ‘So there are two other populated planets.’
Rui nodded. ‘And the computers have identified another three potential sites.’
Michael shook his head. ‘So paradise exists, and you want to turn us round to the same ideal.’
‘That was the original intention.’ Rui looked quite sad. ‘Because Jean and I felt so strongly about it, we were given the chance to try from the inside, rather than via the transporter. We aimed to help elect governments that could really make a difference, and thought our biggest breakthrough would be here in America. I think the new president can and will make a difference, but unless minds change massively he will not get the support he needs. Basically the population are greedy for themselves, rather than for mankind.’
‘And you cannot change minds?’
‘Not enough minds,’ agreed Rui.

'Have you tried before ; were some of the population in the past ours or yours?'
'Such as?' queried Rui.
'Like Jesus and Mohammed. People who managed to rise above the general level.'
'I see what you mean,' his father replied. 'I will let you know on that one.'
'So what is to become of earth two?' Michael suddenly felt a chill run through him.
Rui screwed up his eyes, and then looked out across the lake. 'Scenario one, it self-destructs, which is getting more likely every day. Scenario two, we destroy it. Scenario three we save it, which is looking less likely every day.'
'How do you contemplate scenario two?' Michael asked in horror.
'Using our freighters, earths three and four and our home planet are all within thirty days travel for us. We do not believe that this planet has the technology to make that flight at the moment, but it is getting too close for comfort. We cannot allow this world to infest ours.' Rui was firm with his reply.
'But surely you can monitor the situation.' Michael felt his world was under attack.
'Not closely enough. We cannot see everywhere at the same time. We are not Gods.'
'But you are prepared to destroy a world and everything in it,' Michael was feeling angry.
'If necessary, as a last resort. Probably it will self-destruct first. So that is why Jean and I came here, to try and prevent both. Now it is up to you,' Rui looked his son straight in the eye.
Michael's head dropped. 'I don't think I can take that on.'
'Do you have any choice? Jean and I will help you all we can, but so far we have failed. You are the in-between. You have our brains, but earth two experience, which is something we could

not totally learn,' Rui was still looking intently at Michael as his head rose. 'I don't know of anyone else who can do it.'
'What happens if I fail?'
'We bail out, and it is the end of this world.'
'Who are we?' Michael asked.
'You, Jean and I,' Rui replied, 'we would transfer to world one, and then on to three or four as one shuts down. Maybe even five, six, or seven.'
'So your home is going as well,' Michael looked at his father.
'Yes, it has served its purpose. The Happies have all gone, and it is now little more than an outpost. Still the same original dome, still perfection, but nothing like living on a real world.'
'And Peter and Mary?' Michael thought that he already knew the answer. 'So I guess failure is not an option.'
'Come on, time to get changed and go out,' Rui seemed to have raised his spirits a little, but Michael's were still on the floor.
They wandered back to the house. 'I have booked us a table at nine, but we will have a drink on the way, and try to help Brenda.'
'How….?' Michael asked.
'Wait and see,' Rui smiled at his son, and Michael felt his heart lift slightly that at least they were going to do something right.
The five of them left the house soon after seven thirty, and just before eight the chauffeur pulled the limo into the drive of the Lakeside Golf Club. They went through to the main bar, which sat above and looked out across the restaurant to the eighteenth green. Rui spoke to one of the stewards, and he pointed them across to a table at the edge of the balcony. Mitch Cameron got up to greet them.
'Hello Mitch thanks for coming. I couldn't get a table here, so we will have a drink and then go on to The Fortune Restaurant,' Rui turned towards Peter. 'I thought we should buy Mitch a meal as a thank you for his help.'

They all sat down, and Rui ordered drinks. Michael looked around, and sure enough, the restaurant was pretty full. He turned round to Rui, and was about to speak when his father smiled and winked at him.

Rui was in his mind again, and he knew Jean was there too. 'See the big fat guy over there by the window at the table for eight.' Michael looked across. 'That is Henry Jepson, Marion on his left and Greg next to her. On his right is the owner of the golf club, then his wife. The other three are friends.'

Suddenly Henry Jepson got to his feet. He picked up a spoon and hit it forcefully four or five times against a bottle of red wine. The restaurant and the bar hushed, although Michael felt Rui had something to do with that as well. He could feel Rui almost talking through Henry, and holding Marion and Greg as well. 'I have an important announcement to make,' Henry's eyes looked glazed. 'I raped and murdered my three year old granddaughter Abigail. That was dreadfully wrong, and not the first time I had done such a thing. I blamed my daughter-in-law, who was not there at the time.' He sat down, amongst almost a hiss of surprise from the other diners.

The hiss died to complete silence as Marion stood up. 'I was not there, and lied when I said Brenda killed her daughter. I thought at the time it was Henry.' She sat as Greg rose.

'I knew Brenda didn't kill Abigail, but my father said he would disinherit me if I objected. What could I do?' he asked as he sat down.

Michael felt the emotion in Rui. 'They are telling the truth, although they would never normally have admitted it. Was I right to do it?' Michael knew that he was.

Mitch Cameron rose, and nodding at Rui said 'I had better take care of this.' As he walked down into a dazed restaurant, he was using his mobile phone to call for back-up.

Rui was also using his phone, and Michael overheard 'Go ahead now, please, Bob. It's all taken care of this end.' He came

straight into Michael's mind. 'Bob Haynes is now releasing Brenda with the papers we had already prepared. He will take her somewhere safe.'
Michael's mind was in turmoil. He knew that what Rui had done was probably wrong, but it had the correct result. His elation at the release of Brenda mingled with thoughts that if he had the same powers as Rui, then he could do anything. He felt Rui again. 'Careful Michael, it is a dangerous gift. Jesus didn't have enough time to cure all the sick people. How many wrongs do you think you can right?'
'At least I can bloody well try,' thought Michael.
He looked down into the restaurant again, where the sounds of conversation were fairly loud. Mitch, together with the owner of the golf club, was ushering the Jepsons towards a door near the back of the restaurant. Michael noticed that Marion Jepson was crying.
'Let's go get some dinner,' said Rui, rising and leading the way back out to their car.
On the way, Michael was wondering when he would be able to see Brenda again. Rui replied almost immediately. 'Always remember, Michael, she may not want to see you, but I will give Bob a ring and find out the latest situation.'
He phoned Bob, 'Hi, Bob, how did you get on at Century Fields? That's fine. I'll have a word tomorrow. Give her our love.'
'Bob and his wife have collected her. He took our doctor, and a couple of assistants, and they are currently on their way to Bob's home. The doctor will examine her then, and probably give her something to help her sleep. Bob's wife says she can stay as long as she needs.' Rui delayed for a few moments, and then turned to Michael. 'She also says many thanks to the nice young man with all the hair.' Michael could feel the colour coming to his face, but was so happy he didn't care. Just for a couple of

minutes he could forget all the other problems that were mounting for him.

At the meal that Saturday evening the conversation flowed freely, although Peter, Mary and Michael all reflected individually how much had happened since they touched down in New York just a few days ago.

Jean had already apologised profusely to her 'sister' for putting her through the agony of the funeral, and Rui brought up the subject again during coffee.

'I think this weekend we all need to take stock of where we want to be and what we want to be doing from Monday on. There are some big decisions to be made. Jean and I need to be less visible in view of our recent deaths, as we do not need more and more people to find out we are still around.'

Michael butted in. 'How did you manage to avoid the neighbours, etc., etc.?'

'We had prepared for quite some time, and already had a different address, cars, clothes, passports, bank accounts and all the other thousand and one things sorted out. There are less than thirty people who know we are alive, including present company, so it has not been too difficult. But any of those thirty might slip up in the presence of the wrong people, so we intend to drop out of sight. That is us taken care of. What about you, Peter?'

'Definitely back to Suffolk for me. I have enjoyed nearly every minute of this trip, but honestly need a quieter existence. I would also like to remove Mary from any perceived danger.'

He glanced at his wife, who smiled back at him. 'That's not a problem. I would still like to be involved with Jessie, but we can do everything we need via computer. It's not the making money so much as the being involved in the decisions that I find stimulating. So that just leaves Michael.'

All eyes turned to him and he smiled. 'Sorry I can't join you on the return trip, as the police still have my passport.'

‘I can sort that out for you on Monday,’ said his father.
‘No, it’s not a problem,’ Michael replied.
‘But leaving Brenda here might be,’ Rui laughed.
‘I just want to be sure that she is OK,’ he whispered.
‘And in the meantime, you can kiss her better,’ Jean was laughing now.
Michael nodded and the meal ended with everyone in a good humour.
On Sunday morning Michael spoke to Bob Haynes very early. He told him that Brenda was fine, and that she would probably be sleeping for most of the day. The doctor had taken samples from her, as although he had the notes from Century Fields, he was worried that she might have drugs in her that had not been recorded. He was pressing for the results to be available later that day. He suggested that Michael brought his parents round for a meal that evening, and he could see for himself how Brenda was.
He phoned Jessie, and she said nothing was going on, so why didn’t he take a break and do a bit of sightseeing with Mary and Peter. She suggested a break from the last hectic few days would do him good.
Mary and Peter agreed, and they enjoyed the day out together.

Chapter Four

Back at The Sandstone, Michael showered and changed, but by the time they were collected he was trembling with anticipation. He sat in the back of the car, his head in his hands gently shaking side to side.
Mary smiled at him, 'love hurts.'
'It's still a great number,' her son replied as he looked up,' but how can I be in love with someone I have never spoken to?'
'So will you know for sure when you speak to her?' Michael knew she was gently taking the Mickey.
'I really haven't got a clue what's going on,' Michael confessed.
'So it's true love then,' Mary started laughing. She squeezed his arm. 'Just relax, everything will be fine.'
'Relax,' said Michael, 'my heart is doing a thousand miles an hour, and I can't breathe properly.'
Mary was giggling. 'I am going to really enjoy this evening, whichever way it goes. Anyway, the evening starts now, as here we are.'
Bob welcomed them into his home, and seemed really pleased to see them. His wife Shauna was a delight. Even smaller than Bob, she had beautiful red hair, set off by a shimmering green silk dress, and matching emerald earrings. She took Michael to one side. 'Brenda asked if she could meet you alone before we ate. She wants to thank you in private for rescuing her from Century Fields.' She took Michael's hand and led him through a couple of doors towards the back of the apartment. 'Stop trembling,' she whispered, 'she's not a dragon, she's really lovely.' Shauna knocked on the door in front of them, opened it, and pushed him gently inside.
Michael was in a study that had a huge picture window looking out down the Hudson River. It was dark enough for most of the lights to have come on, and was an imposing sight. Brenda had her back to the door, silhouetted against the view.

Michael stopped dead. The trembling was worse, his heart had doubled its speed, and he couldn't breathe at all. Suddenly into his mind came 'you love me.'
Brenda turned as she opened her arms and they met in the middle of the study. He held her as tightly as he dared, their cheeks touching. Suddenly she started sobbing. 'Please don't cry,' he whispered, 'everything will be fine from now on.'
She leant away from him and looked deep into his eyes. 'I wanted so much for you to love me, but every time I told myself it was impossible. I so much wanted you to say it, but you didn't have to, I just knew somehow. Please tell me I am right.'
'You know you are,' Michael spoke very slowly and quietly, 'I loved you as soon as I saw you.'
'I feel the same,' the sobbing had stopped, 'I just didn't believe this was possible. When Bob arrived and told me what had happened, it was like a fairytale, with you as the handsome prince.'
'I think we had better get you some glasses,' Michael suggested.
Brenda started to giggle. 'I can't believe how much my life has changed. I really was so low, and now everything is perfect.'
Michael thought how everything in his life had been perfect, and how much it had changed. He also knew that everything he had been through was worth these few moments.
'There,' said Brenda, 'you just did it again. Were you thinking that this moment is the most wonderful in your life?'
Michael nodded.
'How do you do that?' she asked.
'It's a long story, and I have the rest of my life to tell it to you. My God, I can't believe I just said that. It is so corny,' Michael blushed.
'But you feel it is true,' Brenda was shaking her head slightly, 'can you see what I feel?'
Michael nodded again, 'everything.'
'That's frightening,' Brenda stared at him.

Gently, Michael held her hands, and even more gently kissed her lips. They stood for over a minute, neither of them daring to move, or break the spell that had been woven.
A cough outside the door brought them back to reality. 'If it's OK with you two, we are about to eat.'
'Just a minute Shauna,' Brenda spoke to Bob's wife, 'I just need to check my hair.'
Shauna smiled to herself as she went to the dining room.
Brenda dabbed at her eyes and lips, and the two of them followed.
Michael was slightly disappointed that they had been placed opposite one another at the table, but he soon realised that maybe being able to look at Brenda full face was probably even better than sitting next to her.
Polite conversation seemed to be the order for the evening, although time and again thoughts passed between Michael and Brenda that none of the others knew anything about. Bob had a word with the doctor after the meal, but there were still a couple more results to come, which he had been promised overnight. He would call fairly early tomorrow to see Brenda and update Bob on the medical situation.
Back at The Sandstone Mary smiled at Michael. 'I'm glad you ignored all the advice and got involved.'
'I had no choice,' Michael replied. 'I have felt things all my life, especially if there was something really important going on. I often knew things before they were announced. I just wrote it off as one of those things. When I saw Brenda at the police station, and she looked me in the eyes, there was no way I could not act, but I'm glad I did,' he added.
On Monday morning he went with his parents to Bob's office. Bob confirmed that Brenda was indeed doing well, and that the doctor was correct in his assessment. She had been given drugs that were not listed, and had not been given some of the drugs

that had been listed. She would need time and medication to recover, but guaranteed that eventually she would be fine.
Peter and Mary had managed to book flights back to Heathrow taking off that evening, so Mary wanted to spend most of her time with Jessie, working out the best way forward in running the group. Probably against Peter's wishes, she agreed that they would return for the memorial service. Her argument was that how could they miss seeing such a collection of stars when they had the opportunity. He gave in gracefully.
Michael told Bob that it would be best for him and Jessie to go ahead and arrange the service. They talked for a while about all the stars that would want to be there, but realised that a lot would not be able to break arranged dates to join them.
Bob had a list of all their main clients, most of whom he hoped would be able to attend.
When Peter looked down the list he whistled, 'I am glad you persuaded me to agree to come,' he said softly to his wife.
Michael looked at Bob. 'It will be more like a concert than a service if even half of these turn up.'
'At least you can look forward to something that is normally pretty sad,' Bob commented, 'and looking forward, what about you, Michael? Rui and Jean stepping into the background, Peter and Mary back in the UK. How do you want to proceed?'
'The funds created by the group are more than useful, but we need to succeed more in influencing the direction this planet is taking,' Michael wasn't sure he understood the way forward. 'You know the whole object is to make for a better world.'
Bob smiled in agreement.
'How much input have you had in deciding which way forward is the best?'
Bob was still smiling, 'none so far. My remit was to carry out the distribution of funds within whichever area Rui and Jean decided so that we broke no local or international laws.'

‘Would you be willing to work with Jessie, giving your thoughts on how as a group we can improve the future?’
Bob agreed, ‘my thoughts may not be in line with yours. Also, I don’t know how to put this, but I don’t know if you will have the ability that Rui has to accomplish things. I’m sorry to sound rude, it isn’t meant.’
‘I know exactly what you mean,’ Michael was honest.
‘For example, that scene at the Lakeside Golf Club. I guess somehow that was something to do with Rui being in control of the situation.’
‘I guess the same,’ Michael laughed. ‘Rui assures me that I have exactly the same abilities as him, I just need them sharpened up a bit. That’s why I intend to take time off from the business until I am up to speed. I have agreed to live with Rui and Jean until I am ready and able to concentrate on where we go from here. If you and Jessie can come up with your ideas, at least I will have something to start with.’
‘Is it essential?’ queried Bob. ‘I always had the feeling from Rui that it was of paramount importance, but he never confirmed it.’
‘Believe me Bob, it is the most important thing you and Jessie will ever do in your lives. This world has one last chance, literally. We truly have to save it from itself. Failure means it is the end. I don’t just mean global warming, although God knows that is bad enough, but the whole system of greed, man’s inhumanity to man, war, injustice, violence, drug abuse,’ Michael was shaking his head. ‘It’s a hell of a list and a hell of a fight. How we do it I have no idea, that’s why I’m asking for your input. Time is not on our side. Please help me.’
Bob looked straight at Michael. ‘You already have a lot of the power from Rui. Go get the rest. You know Jessie and I will do everything we can.’
‘I personally think we are the perfect trio,’ Michael lightened the tone.
Bob smiled back.

‘Now I’m just going to pop over to your place if that’s OK,’ Michael looked a bit sheepish.
Bob glanced at his watch, ‘you have done well to hold out this long. I’ll order a taxi.’
Five minutes later Michael was on his way to see Brenda.
‘I can start saving the world tomorrow,’ he thought, ‘even Superman has to have some time off.’ He started shaking again.
‘OK, so I’m not Superman,’ he thought, ‘but at least I don’t have to wear that crummy costume.’
Bob must have phoned ahead, because Shauna was expecting him, and took him out onto a balcony, where Brenda was waiting.
She smiled as he sat down next to her.
‘How are you feeling this morning?’ Michael asked.
‘I’m still quite tired, but the doctor says that will last for a few weeks, until the drugs clear through my system. Each day I should be a bit better than the last, as there is no permanent damage of any sort. Shauna fusses round me like a mother hen, she really is lovely,’ Brenda smiled at him, and took his hand in hers, ‘thanks for coming again so soon.’
‘Bob has had a word with the police about the way you were treated at Century Fields, so they are tagging that onto the whole enquiry about your ex father-in-law.’
‘What exactly happened at the golf club?’ Brenda queried.
‘The place was packed, and suddenly Henry got up and confessed to murdering Abigail.’
‘You had something to do with what happened, I can feel it,’ Brenda turned slightly to look at Michael.
‘No, I knew something was going to happen, but I believe it was my father, Rui, who triggered the whole sequence. He has a very powerful mind,’ Michael was unsure how much he should tell about Rui and Jean and also how much Brenda could read from his mind. ‘As you get better, I will tell you the whole complicated story. At the moment it doesn’t have an ending, but

at least I have you, which is more important than everything else going on.'
She squeezed his hand. 'So are you are staying here for some time, as I hear Peter and Mary are back in the UK tonight?'
'Yes, he wants to get back to his beloved teaching, and Mary will stay in contact with Jessie to keep the business ticking over. Jessie is my right hand woman, although in reality she knows ten times as much as I do about what is going on. I think I am actually her assistant,' Michael was telling the truth.
'I heard Bob describing how good she was. He said he always wanted her to work for him. She sounds really good fun.'
'She is great, 'replied Michael. 'Brilliant brain and sees the funny side of everything. I will be staying with Mum and Dad until I get up to speed on the business. They want to take a back seat, and drop out altogether before too long. I will have to pop back to Cambridge at some time to sort out my future there, but shouldn't be away too long.'
'It must be a beautiful place to visit,' ventured Brenda.
'So why don't you come with me when I go, it really is a special place. By then you should be feeling a lot better, and a punt on the Cam will be just the thing to make you feel on top of the world.'
'What are punts and Cams?' asked Brenda.
'A punt is a type of boat, and the Cam is a very pretty river that goes through the centre of the city. Cambridge means the bridge over the river Cam.'
'Then let's make a date, as long as you do the rowing,' Brenda couldn't believe that they would be going away together.
Michael laughed, 'no rowing, as there are no oars and no engine.'
'So how does it get along?'
'Wait and see,' said Michael.
'At the moment, everything seems the wrong way round,' Brenda was a little bit more serious. 'Usually you meet

someone, and learn all the little things about them, and then fall in love. I never believed in love at first sight until now. It's just that we know nothing about one another, and I worry and feel nervous when you are not around, but when you are here, everything seems perfect. I suppose I can't believe how lucky I have been, coming out of that twilight world into your arms. I keep thinking I will wake up and be back in Century Fields.'

It was Michael's turn to squeeze her hand. 'There isn't a lot to tell, really. I am at Cambridge studying history and economics. I was brought up by my aunt and uncle in a beautiful little village called Grundisburgh, which is not far from the Suffolk coast. It is like a picture postcard, with a small stream running through the village green, which is set in front of the very old church. Nearly opposite is the village pub, The Dog, where they serve proper beer, and have a brilliant restaurant. We also have a shop and post office. It's surrounded by fields, and you can wander for miles sometimes without seeing anyone.'

'Can we go there when we go to Cambridge?' Brenda butted in.

'Of course we can. Peter is a history teacher in Woodbridge, which is a very pretty town set on the river Deben, just five minutes away by car. Mary does some consultancy work in London, which is just over an hour away by train. We have more than ten lovely beaches within an hour's drive, and Cambridge is also about an hour away,' Michael nearly felt homesick it sounded so good.

'I'm not surprised Peter and Mary have gone back. Compared to New York it sounds like paradise. How come you are staying here?'

'I get to take over the family business. In theory it can be run from anywhere, but I think Jessie is New York through and through. She is so important that the business runs from where she lives, basically. Mary will help from Suffolk, so there is really no reason why I couldn't do the same from Cambridge once I know what it is I am actually helping with. Bob is also very important to the business, so it works very well that Jessie and him are separated by just one floor,' the more Michael learnt about the business, the less he felt he knew. 'So what about you?'

'I'm like Jessie, New York through and through. My mother died a couple of years ago, she'd been ill for some time, and I think seeing Abigail gave her the energy to hang on for another twelve months. I never knew my father, and she never spoke about him. She was a nurse and worked all the hours she could to raise me and give me a decent education. It couldn't have been very easy for her but she gave me the best life she could. I met Greg when I was nineteen and he lived in a very different world. I was easily seduced by it. At first everything was fine but as our relationship grew more serious, his family became more and more against me, especially his father,' Brenda looked bitter as she remembered.

'He doesn't seem the nicest guy in the world,' Michael ventured.

'You can say that again, he threatened to beat me with his riding crop if I didn't leave his son alone. When I got pregnant, Greg was so terrified of his parents he didn't tell them until I showed so much it was obvious what had happened. It was a low key wedding but I was never forgiven for 'ensnaring his son' as Henry put it. Abigail was a beautiful child but by then I was spending more time with my mother than with Greg. I had sufficient money but no love from any of the Jepsons. By then, his parents had turned Greg against me. I used to take Abigail over to see Marion from time to time, as she really loved her, but never when Henry was going to be there. The day she died Henry turned up unexpectedly. I should have known something was wrong when he offered to take her to see the horses and didn't want me or Marion to go as well.' Tears were falling down her cheeks and Michael put his arm round her.

'I should have stayed with her.'

'I can never bring her back but at least I can put some love back into your life,' said Michael, as he pulled her closer to him.
Brenda turned her face towards him. 'I was so lost before, you don't realise just how much you have given to me. Oh my God, you have done it again. You do realise, don't you. How do you do that with your mind?' she kissed him, softly at first, and then more passionately, and the salt from her tears on Michael's lips made him realise how totally she depended on him.
'I can do it, like my Dad, only he can do it all the time.'
Michael so wanted to keep on kissing Brenda, but also knew that she was still very vulnerable, and pulled back. 'I will call again tomorrow, but now to lessons from my parents.'
They kissed again, long and tenderly, before Michael was on his way again to Hampton.

Chapter Five

Rui and Jean were pleased to see him and they had a light lunch together.
'The bad news,' said Rui, 'is that Mikey is thinking he should do something about you. He has been asking around for information on you or your family. Peter and Mary will be off tonight, so that just leaves you and possibly Brenda, although he knows nothing about her yet. The good news is that we are one step ahead of him. All we have to do is set a little trap. Are you happy for me to take care of it?'
'That's fine,' Michael replied, 'just make sure Brenda is not exposed to danger.'
'No problem,' said his father, 'now, how good are you at the mind business?'
'It has always been there, although I didn't know what it was. It's become stronger since I came over here, probably through meeting you and Mum. Brenda can sometimes feel my mind if I am thinking intensely. Jessie even more so. I tried with Jessie to put my thoughts into her head, but failed miserably.'
'I can understand Jessie,' said Rui, 'she has been with us and exposed to it for a long time. I know Brenda really loves you but even so it's unusual that she can feel your mind so quickly. I suppose these things sometimes happen.'
'Right. Lesson number one. To start with, you can't force your thoughts. I know it sounds ridiculous, but you almost have to not think in order for it to happen. I will go blank in my mind. Try to send me a message of anything but don't think of doing it or whatever the thing is. Try concentrating on something else and then imagining what you want to transfer as almost a shadow on the edge of your vision. I know it sounds stupid but it is the fastest way forward when you start.'
Michael thought of him and Brenda floating idly down the river Cam on a hot summer's day. The University Backs looked

particularly beautiful, but he couldn't take his eyes away from Brenda. On the edge of his vision one of the colleges slid into view. He could imagine Rui stood looking across at him from a window at the college. His mind went almost immediately back to Brenda, who was trailing her hand in the river.
'What the hell is that on your head?' Rui was laughing.
Michael felt his head.
'No, on the boat,'
'I transferred a picture?' Michael was thrilled. 'What did you see?'
'You were on a boat with Brenda, wearing a red straw hat, which seemed to have a thick fishing rod hung down from it,' Rui looked perplexed.
Michael was puzzled. 'The boat, which is called a punt and Brenda are correct. I would have a straw boater on. I guess it may have had a red ribbon, but no fishing rod. How thick was it?'
'No, it was too thick for a fishing rod. I guess maybe two or three inches in diameter.'
Michael laughed when he realised. 'That's the pole that I was pushing the punt along with.'
'Then that's a pretty good start,' said Rui. 'Normally to start, you get what the person 'sees' but in your case, in your mind you had the red ribbon and the pole, although you couldn't see them. You have grasped the main thing, which is not to think directly at the start. That will come with time. At the moment you almost have to dream it. Now try a message to Brenda.'
Michael tried the same trick again. He was in Grundisburgh, walking past the bench at the side of the green. He looked towards the church and from the corner of his eye could see Brenda walking over the little bridge next to the ford. 'Help! Phone me as soon as you can.' He stopped at the little church gate.

'Bloody hell,' Rui said, 'you terrified the life out of her. That's lesson number two. Now you have passed lesson number one, don't send out false alarms. I have told her it's OK.'
Jean came in, holding a phone. 'Brenda,' was all she said.
'Are you OK?'
'Yes, I'm fine,' Michael was almost stuttering.
'I think Rui told me that you were, but I just wanted to check. Grundisburgh looks beautiful. That huge weeping willow in front of the church looks gorgeous. And your parents got married in that church. It looks so cute.'
'How did you know that?' Michael was amazed.
'You were thinking it when you looked at the church, just before you asked me to phone. Michael, I love you,' Brenda had never sounded happier.
'That's lesson number three,' said Rui. 'Try to control what you send. It's supposed to be a snapshot, not a Michelangelo,' he shook his head as he finished. 'In less than fifteen minutes we have arrived where I hoped to be at the end of tomorrow,' he looked very pleased with himself. 'Let's just try one more. Jean is out in the garden,' he nodded towards the window. 'Convince her she is a ballerina. Remember, it is not a message from you. Keep it on the edge of your mind again. You are just trying to convince her she wants to dance, not pass a message. For this, you will probably find it easier to look at her.'
Michael looked at Jean, and then pictured himself going to the theatre in Cambridge. He was at the first night of Swan Lake. He watched the principal dancers, and there on the edge of his vision was Jean, in the chorus line. She danced in perfect unison with the others, and the applause from the audience was deafening.
Jean stopped her dance in the garden, and waved to them through the window. 'That was a very good attempt,' came into the minds of both Michael and Rui. 'I had the power to easily resist it, but anyone else would have been compelled to dance.

Well done, Michael, but next time I would rather be a principal dancer.'

Michael waved to her out of the window.

He turned to Rui. 'How much power have you got, and how much do you think I will have?'

'You will have at least as much as me, and that power is frightening. I don't use it for personal gain, although there was a lot of satisfaction when I outed Henry, but the bastard deserved it. Sometimes it is very tempting. Do you support a football team?'

'Yes,' said Michael, 'Ipswich Town.'

'Imagine they are playing in their most important fixture ever, and they are losing one nil with ten minutes to go. Could you resist making a few of the opposition players make errors to give your team a couple of goals. Might be difficult.'

'So you can control people, like a hypnotist?' Michael was trying to understand.

'A little bit like that, but anyone being hypnotised has to be willing for it to happen, and expects it. With this, they have no option, and think it was they who wanted to do it when they reflect on it afterwards,' Rui was nodding. 'However, I am not supposed to do it. The code is that I do not force anything on anyone, and I do not cheat. Think how much money you could make by betting on the results of sports fixtures.'

'But you cheat a bit in your financial dealings,' insisted Michael.

'Not really cheating. If you point out to a struggling oil company exactly where a massive find is located, and at what depth, they are very pleased. If I happen to own shares in that company, then it is my good luck,' Rui smiled, 'it's a thin dividing line.'

He glanced at his watch. 'We had better get going. I have arranged a meal with Peter and Mary, and then we can see them off at the airport.'

The three of them met Bob, Jessie, Peter and Mary at Seventy Three. The food was as good as ever, and the atmosphere around the table was very friendly and relaxed. Michael had secretly wished that Brenda would be there, but even he was still pleased with how their spirits had been lifted in such a short space of time.

They all went to the airport, and said their goodbyes as Peter and Mary walked through to departures, but not before Mary had taken Michael to one side and asked him to make sure he took good care of himself. He promised that he would, and she winked as she told him she thought Brenda was lovely.

Rui suggested they went back to Bob's office before they split up, just to tidy up a few points.

Over some coffees, he explained the possible threat to Michael from Mikey Spinetti. He tapped his son on the shoulder, and said 'we will sort that one out between us later. Assume for now that he will not be a threat in the future. As you know, Jean and I will be moving soon, probably in the next two or three months. Michael will be our main point of personal contact for the foreseeable future, although any business suggestions we may make will be sent to all three of you as normal. Jean and I have not changed the planet in the way we wanted, and Michael may decide on a different approach to solving the problem, possibly in a way that we were not able to do. This may mean that assets will be sold off, and the value of the group will decline. Bob, I need you and Jessie to ring fence her two and a half billion, so that she can take it when necessary.'

'I need nothing like that,' interrupted Jessie, 'ten million, the same as Peter and Mary, is more than plenty. I would give the rest to charity anyway.'

Rui nodded. 'Much as I expected, Jessie, thanks, if you get stuck, it's easy to make another few hundred billion anyway. You only have to ask if it's essential. If it comes to winding up

the group, you take ten million personally as well, Bob. I really appreciate how you have helped.'
Bob smiled. 'I have more than I will ever need, so that can go to charity as well. I'm like Jessie; I just enjoy the buzz that the work gives.'
Jessie nodded her approval.
'So, if it's OK with you, Michael, Jessie can take out her ten million net now, and the balance of the company if it is wound up goes to charity. Michael will be working mainly with us two for some time, so will be splitting his work between here and Hampton, and I guess we can head off there now if there is nothing else,' Rui rose.
As they made the journey to Hampton, Michael was wondering at the way such huge sums of money seemed to have had so little impact on the team in the office. Almost as if money had become unimportant to Bob and Jessie. They both turned to giving to charity, and he wondered if some of the lifestyle Jean and Rui were trying to create for the world was rubbing off on them.
'What do you want to do with Mikey?' Rui asked his son.
'You said he was pretty nasty. How nasty?'
Rui made a face. 'Ten murders, sixteen rapes, multiple GBH and ABH, and plenty more.'
'So he should be dead,' Michael was not entirely certain, but the words came out anyway.
'If that's what you really want,' Jean looked serious.
'I think that is what he deserves, but I suppose we should keep within the law wherever possible. I've killed already; although I'm not sure I meant to do it.'
'So gaol it is then?' Rui asked.
'If it's for long enough,' said Michael. He suddenly realised, 'you will get him to confess, just like Henry did.'
'No,' replied Rui, 'that was a one off. I am not supposed to affect the world like that. All I can do is help people to try and

make the world better, but you can send him to gaol if you think that is the best plan.' Michael nodded.

'Another five minutes and we will be home. We can try then,' said Rui.

Michael knew he had managed to get Jean to dance, and had contacted Brenda across a fair distance, but felt nervous at what he was about to try.

Indoors, they sat together in the lounge, and Rui opened the conversation. 'Go ahead. Remember that you are still working on the edges, but I will be there to give you help if necessary.'

Michael stared out through the French windows. He thought of the police station where he had first met Brenda. The same Station Sergeant was still on duty, drinking coffee as he looked through some paperwork. He had a quick look round the rest of the station. Mitch Cameron was just leaving his office, on his way home. Quickly Michael was in his mind. 'Stop and have a chat for a while, someone is coming in and will need to see you.' Mitch immediately stopped at the desk, and started discussing the state of the New York Yankees. Michael imagined Mikey looking in through the window, and almost immediately he was in Mikey's mind. He was in a nightclub. Get up, go outside and get in to a taxi. Mikey rose, and without saying goodbye collected his coat, exited and got into a taxi. Michael suggested where the taxi should be going, and ten minutes later Mikey was entering the police station.

Mitch looked up. 'What a pleasant surprise, Mikey. Come to rob us?'

'I need to write something down,' Mikey didn't look happy.

Michael gave Mitch a little jolt.

'Come with me,' he led the way to an interview room, and gave Mikey a pad and a biro.

'Everything you have ever done wrong, and everything anyone else you know has done wrong. Get writing,' Michael couldn't think of anything else at the moment.

Mikey picked up the biro, and started on his life story, telling it to Mitch as he wrote. Mitch switched on a recorder, headed the interview and let it run.
Michael was still looking out of the French windows as he let go of the scene in the police station.
'That was just about perfect,' Rui was really impressed, 'especially the bit about anyone else he knew.'
'I thought while he was doing one, he might as well do them all.'
Two hours later, before they retired, they had a quick look back in the interview room. Mikey was still talking and writing, but now had another couple of policemen in the room with him, who, like Mitch, had expressions of amazement written across their faces.
Next morning, Michael had a quick look round the police station. Mikey was in a cell asleep. It was a different Sergeant behind the desk, but his mind was full of the nights' main event. Apparently Mikey had implicated over one hundred other criminals, and a large operation had already started to bring them all in.
Satisfied with his work, Michael switched his thoughts to Brenda. She too was sleeping, and he left her undisturbed, but not without leaving the thought of how much he loved her.
At breakfast, he felt on top of the world, and his high spirits seemed to affect both Jean and Rui.
'Mikey really went for it,' laughed Rui.
'It seemed so easy,' replied Michael.
'Don't get too carried away,' said Jean, 'remember it's you versus the world, and it's one hell of a population.'
'At least I've made a start,' said Michael.
'You had better start building some more prisons if you continue in the same vein,' Jean was laughing as well now.
'Seriously, Michael, this is one of the reasons Jean and I are not allowed to change minds, only help. We wanted to have world

leaders who could make the lives of everyone better. The problem is that ninety nine percent of the population only see 'better' as relating to themselves. If they have children they want free education. If they are retired they want higher pensions. If they are ill they want free and better health care. Financially, the politicians cannot provide everything everyone wants, but the next politician can, so he gets elected, and the merry-go-round sets off again,' Rui was more serious.

'So how does it work on worlds three and four?' Michael asked.

'It's the mindset of the people that is different,' said Jean. 'There are pockets of people around the world who would originally have fitted into those worlds with no problems. In Africa, there were tribes who never took more than they needed from the earth. In Poland, any traveller could cross the country and have food and shelter freely provided if that was what he needed. In the Outer Hebrides a village had to have sufficient fit men to put a fishing boat to sea, so they all looked after everyone else to make sure they all kept well. There are hundreds of examples like that, but unfortunately the great greed seems to have taken over. Most people look at what's in it for them, rather than what's in it for everyone else. Also don't forget that on average the inhabitants have sixteen times more brain power, so they more easily recognise and solve problems.'

'On your world there is no sickness,' Michael stated.

'There are very few people left to be ill, but yes, illness was eradicated centuries ago,' Rui agreed.

'And on worlds three and four?' Michael queried.

'Exactly the same,' said Rui, 'there were a few inherent diseases when they were first set up, but those were easily wiped out.'

'Crime?' asked Michael.

'No crime either,' Jean chipped in. 'Remember, the populations of those planets all have open minds. It was not easy to begin with, as you know, but if you did something wrong and everyone else knew about it immediately, it would be pretty pointless. It's the same with acting fairly, everyone else knows if you don't. If you ever did anything wrong, it would be with you forever, and visible to everyone else forever. There is no hiding place, because you have your dirty baggage with you forever, in full view. As you know from the old earth, cash was the root of ninety percent of crime and greed. Ban cash and life gets a lot easier.'

'So if I fail, we three go to wherever, and for the rest of the population?' Michael was not looking forward to the reply.

'The easiest by far is to divert a giant meteor to hit,' Rui said the words with no emotion. 'Either this world sorts out its problems, or we sort them. As I said before, other worlds cannot be infected.'

'But some of the people on earth are actually perfect, and could fit into three and four without being a threat.'

'Like Brenda?' asked Jean. 'So do we take people who are ninety nine point nine percent perfect, but not those who are ninety nine point eight percent perfect? And who makes the decision anyway? Imagine what it would be like if you were put into a new school where everyone was sixteen times brainier than you. No one else travels.'

'Back to the realisation that failure is not an option, I'm afraid,' Rui looked grim.

'It will take a lot of thought,' Michael spoke very quietly. 'What if I could make it impossible for anyone to leave earth for outer space? I don't know how, but I'm sure it's possible. At least we could muddle along as we do now. We wouldn't need to be exterminated.'

'Don't forget, you are on a downward slope at the moment, and the gradient is getting steeper. Our estimate is fifty years maximum, possibly as low as twenty. To be honest, you are killing the planet, and it will not survive without major surgery, and you are the surgeon,' Rui's expression had not changed. Michael was thinking about Brenda. Maybe twenty to fifty years with her would be better than the fight. He sneered at himself. That was the attitude that had landed us in the shit now. Look out for yourself and sod the rest. He slowly shook his head, 'I don't have an option.'

'Son, if you pull this off, you will be the saviour of the world, and no one except us will ever know,' Rui's words sent a shiver down Michael's spine. 'Think by all means, but think as quickly as you can.'

They finished breakfast, and Michael continued with lessons from Rui. He improved, so that he was starting to bring the images that he wanted to affect closer in to his line of vision. Just before lunch, he set off for the office, but via Bob's house.

Chapter Six

Sat in the back of the limo, Michael was already thinking hard about the future. He set the options out in order:

1. Alter mankind sufficiently quickly to stop it from being exterminated by outside forces.

2. Alter mankind not quickly enough for one above, but gain more time by not allowing anyone to leave the solar system.

3. Go on from two above to alter mankind sufficiently for it to survive on this planet longer than the predicted end.

4. Convince Rui and the rest that some from the earth should be able to take over the old world that was to be abandoned.

5. Convince Rui and the rest that Brenda should be allowed to accompany him to earth three or four.

6. Do nothing.

He turned the options over and over in his mind. Six was a none starter. Four and five would have to be last minute plea bargaining, but he felt the odds were stacked against him. Whilst one was the preferred route, the timescale made it virtually impossible. Two and three combined were all that was left. He decided that he would have to aim for one, switching to two and three if time ran too short. If, however, he could somehow put back inter stellar exploration, and prove to Rui that it was currently impossible, then at least it would give him a twenty to fifty year timescale to get earth back on track. Even that, when looked at sensibly, was an impossibility.

He was still checking the options over and over when Brenda opened the door for him.

She kissed him quickly on the lips. 'I could feel you arriving,' she beamed at him.

For Michael, all the options went straight onto the back burner. All that mattered at the moment was the young lady in front of him. Everything about her was just perfect, even down to the slightest of lisps, which was more pronounced when she was excited. He loved her so very much.

'And I love you just as much. I can really feel everything today,' Brenda stepped back and looked up at him.

Michael immediately concentrated on a fire engine rushing down a street.

'What was that?' Brenda asked.

'Just making sure you really can't feel everything today,' laughed Michael.

Brenda took his hand, and led him out onto 'their' balcony.

They sat side by side in the golden silence that only lovers can create. Neither of them wanted to break the spell they were under by speaking. Both of them were comfortable in the knowledge that they were in the company of the one they loved. They were still holding hands, and both turned together to kiss, lightly and tenderly. Michael let go of Brenda's hand, and went to move his left arm round her back. The back of his fingers barely brushed across her right breast, and Michael felt her tighten.

'Sorry, I didn't mean that to happen.'

'I know,' whispered Brenda, 'this seeing into your mind is a funny thing to live with, as I know when it happens, but I can't make it happen. Where does it come from?'

The moments of magic had disappeared as quickly as they had arrived. 'Apparently some of our ancestors had what they called 'open minds', so that anyone could see everything another person was thinking. Anyone descended from those ancestors has the ability to read minds to some extent. Practice makes it better I believe.'

'I wish I could do it all the time,' Brenda looked dreamily at him, 'then I would know all the time that you really loved me.'
Michael squeezed her, and suddenly added number seven to his list. If he could get Brenda to an open state of mind, then there would be no reason for her to be refused entry to world three or four. It would be difficult, and might be impossible, but it was certainly worth a shot. He knew that, saving the world or not, he would never leave her behind.
'How will you save the world?' Brenda asked innocently. 'I'm sorry to sound so strange, but I keep getting little bits of your mind inside me, and why does it have to be you?'
'Do you think there is any chance of a cup of tea?' Michael stalled.
'I will go make one for you,' said Brenda, with a puzzled expression.
Michael immediately contacted Rui, and explained what had happened with Brenda, emphasizing that she was still ill according to the doctor. He wondered if it would be possible for Brenda to become open minded, and how much he was able to tell her about what had happened, and what was about to happen.
'Give me just a minute,' Rui replied.
Michael was then party to Rui contacting Brenda, and flying through all her thoughts. He acknowledged Michael, and spent maybe thirty seconds in her mind. Dropping Brenda, he came straight back to Michael. 'Brenda is not quite what she seems. I don't know what it is, but it appears she is more attuned to mind transfer than the normal population. She is probably on par with Jessie. If that has happened since you met her, then it is an extremely fast process. She has a very fine brain, which is underused as you would expect, but could improve greatly. I think it unlikely that she could ever be open minded, but it is a remote possibility. She has nothing but good in her mind. And yes, if she ever became open minded I would recommend that

she be allowed onto earth three or four. For that reason, you can tell her the truth about the past and the present, but do not go into too much detail, and remember that she has been ill, so slowly and gently will be best.'

Brenda came back in with the tea. 'Were you and Rui talking about me?'

Michael remembered an old-fashioned comedian that Peter used to like. 'I'm going to tell you a story,' he started, 'none of the details, because it is scary enough without. Rui and Jean are not from this solar system. They live in a perfect world, and some of their ancestors settled on earth. Others now live on another two perfect worlds, where there is total harmony. No wars, no illness, no greed, nothing bad at all. They have become concerned that we are sending our planet into oblivion, but are worried that some will jump ship if they can create the necessary technology. They intend to stop that happening, because they do not want their worlds contaminated. Rui and Jean have spent twenty five years here, trying to alter governments so that earth could end up as it was meant to be. They have had limited success. Now it is my turn. They estimate the maximum length of life on earth to be another twenty to fifty years, before we make it uninhabitable through pollution, or blow it to pieces. They will return to their world. I can go as well. No one else can go. You cannot repeat this to anyone.'

Brenda stared at him, and Michael lowered his eyes. 'Look at me,' she demanded.

Michael looked at her, and noticed that tears were welling in her eyes. Suddenly she burst out crying. He grabbed hold of her and she flung her head onto his shoulder. As she cried, her body almost convulsed in time to her tears. She turned her head and whispered into his ear, 'I thought you meant that you were going to go and leave me here. I couldn't imagine life without you. Oh, Michael, I'm so sorry that I doubted you.'

This time when they kissed the whole world stood still. Her tongue explored his mouth with a frenzy he had not known was possible. He physically wanted her then more than anything in his life, but pulled back just in time. She was still drug dependant, and this was not the moment.

'I want you to help me in this. Whichever way it goes, I will be with you,' Michael rose, and bending to kiss her, tenderly this time, he left for the city.

At Bob's office he quickly realised that he was more of a hindrance than help, and decided that he would spend more time with Rui and Brenda to try and get her and himself up to speed.

He asked Jessie and Bob if they had come up with anything they thought the group could do for the future of the planet.

'In order of importance then,' said Jessie.

-Reduce the population by half

-Find another cheap source of energy

-Cut global warming completely

-Get rid of all nuclear power.

-Get rid of greed.

-Get rid of crime.

-Eradicate poverty.

-Eradicate illness.

'So, not a lot of problems for us to solve,' Michael knew they were right.

'While I think of it, Iran has another nuclear facility besides the one they admitted to,' Bob shrugged.

Michael just let his mind wander for a moment. Sure enough, there he was. 'They have another two besides that one,' said Michael, 'that Mahmoud Ahmadinejad is one awkward man.'

Whether it was because the two names were similar in his mind he did not know, but Michael was suddenly looking at Abdelbaset Ali Mohmed Almegrahi, the Lockerbie bomber. 'And Almegrahi didn't blow up the Pan Am flight over

Lockerbie. Nothing to do with what we were talking about, just thought I'd let you know.'

Bob looked straight at Michael. 'You can do the same as Rui.'

'Not yet,' Michael replied, 'but it's coming along. Anyway we have made a start on crime with the Spinettis and their friends.' He instantly flicked to Mitch Cameron. 'They have over one hundred in custody at the moment, all on serious charges.'

'Christ,' said Bob, 'if you can turn that brain of yours to major problems, then there may just be a chance.'

'You two concentrate on the business. I will start having a go at the list. Anything else you can think of, or any possible solutions, just shout. Thanks for the list, I guess I knew what was needed, but it's always good to get confirmation.'

Michael lay awake for a long time that night. By the time he went to sleep he knew the action he would try and take, but wasn't sure if he could, or would be allowed, to carry it out.

At breakfast the next morning, he went through the list with Rui and Jean.

'We agree with all those points as starters,' said his mother. 'They all need direct intervention. We have persuaded the others to let you have a crack at it. They were very negative at first, as you know we were forbidden to interfere directly, it all had to be the wish of someone born on earth. Because you were born here, they have decided that you can try to save the planet directly.'

'When Li Po didn't allow anyone to come from the old earth, he saved mankind. There were two chemicals released into the world that caused the catastrophe. Would it be possible to obtain or manufacture enough of either to slow the growth? And manufacture the antidote?' Michael added speedily.

Rui laughed. 'That seems the obvious, but I'm not sure it should be number one on the list. Just say that you pull this off, and bring the earth to paradise. It should be able to support the current population. Animals in the wild have more babies when they can be supported and less when they can't. If only a few of a litter survive, they have more and bigger litters. If you can eradicate infant mortality in countries where it is high, then there will be fewer children produced. If in the rich countries, you cut out the benefits of having children, it will have the same effect. Britain is now heavily overpopulated, and yet your government pays women to have babies. So, cut illness and poverty and you may not have to cut the population. Also, and here I am really going to never-never land, if you succeed, we will need volunteers to populate earth five onwards.'

Michael nodded, feeling a little deflated.

'I would start with number two, cheap energy,' Rui continued.

'So, where does that come from?' Michael asked.

'For it to be cheap, it has to be produced by natural movement that is already taking place,' Rui nodded at his son.

'Like wind power,' Michael was not impressed.

Again Rui nodded. 'Think bigger.'

'Lots of wind power?' Michael ventured.

'Bigger,' said Rui.

Michael thought the winds were bigger than the oceans, but suggested 'wave power?'

'Bigger,' Rui was laughing.

'The sun,' said Michael.

'To do with the sun, certainly, but not the sun,' Rui flicked his eyebrows.

Michael was stumped.

'The biggest thing is the earth itself. Spinning round a core of metal, with a magnetic pole at each end, it is one huge generator,' Rui was sure of himself. 'It's what we use on three and four.

'Bloody hell,' Michael was suitably impressed, 'how is it done?'

'Not as difficult as you would think. Of course, there are still costs of distribution, but there is no fuel to purchase, and no pollution. I can have all the details ready for you later today. The big decision is who you give the secret to, and how you

protect it from the energy suppliers, who will try for all they are worth to stop it,' Rui smiled. 'It's going to be fun, isn't it?'
Michael was shaking his head, totally amazed at this turn of events.
'It will also really upset your friend from Iran. When no nuclear power is needed for energy production, there can be no excuse for producing it,' Rui laughed out loud.
'But you will still need airline fuel.'
'Not really,' said Rui. 'They can also fly round the world on electric power. Again, it's not difficult, and don't forget the massive effect on global warming. Just that alone will send it into reverse.'
'But how much energy would the revolution of the planet produce?' Michael suddenly felt he was sticking in too many buts. 'Sorry, Dad, you are so far ahead of me.'
'It will produce about one hundred times the power that the earth currently consumes, and will last for about five hundred million years, give or take. It's somehow linked to the effect of zero point energy. Good, isn't it,' Rui was still laughing.
Michael was finding it hard to take in such a huge amount of information. 'Why haven't you done this before?'
'We have only ever tinkered at the edges. If someone had a new idea, then we could improve it for them. This is a whole new ball game. I think it is because of the impending doom of a world, rather than protecting our worlds from being infected by this one. I think for the first time they are really trying to help. Now go over and see Brenda. Talk it over with her and see who she thinks would be the best person to approach. Don't forget, whoever it is, you will need to vet him or her down to the n'th degree, to ensure he or she will carry it out for the benefit of the world,' Rui looked at his son, and for the first time felt that he might have the smallest of chances. 'By the way, I have already told Jessie and Bob to get rid of our oil companies, and all our interests in power production.'

Brenda was expecting him, as before. 'You are really excited, have you discovered something?'
Michael pictured the earth spinning.
'Use the earth as the source of all power. Why has no one ever done that before?' Brenda asked.
Shauna stuck her head round the door. 'Hello Michael would you like tea or coffee with your lunch, or you can have a cold drink if you like?'
Michael realised that he had no idea what time it was. He glanced at his watch. Nearly one thirty. 'A cold drink please, Shauna. You look really lovely today.' And she did.
'Why thank you, sir,' replied Shauna, pretending to curtsy. She headed for the kitchen.
'Was that flirting?' asked Brenda.
Michael laughed. 'Have a look at my mind.'
Brenda started laughing. 'It wasn't was it? You were just telling the truth.'
Michael nodded. 'Don't forget, if ever we get to open mind status, then you would know if I was flirting, or even if I thought another girl was pretty.'
'I'm not sure I really want to go that far,' the smile had left Brenda's face.
'Also, of course, I will know if you are flirting with anyone, wherever you are. No secrets.'
The smile returned to Brenda's face. 'No secrets at all?'
'If we end up on worlds three or four, no secrets from anyone,' said Michael.
The smile disappeared again. 'I'm not sure about that one.'
Shauna called them in for lunch.
They made small talk while they ate, and after they had finished, Michael spoke. 'Ladies, if you had some information so important to the world, and had to trust the secret of it to one person, who would that be?
'What can the information do?' queried Shauna.

‘Replace all the sources of power with a free, totally reliable, and continuing source of power,’ Michael said proudly.
Shauna whistled. ‘It exists?’ she asked.
‘It can do, if we think it’s a good idea,’ it was Brenda who answered.
‘So it needs to be someone with the technical knowledge to do it,’ Shauna was quite excited.
‘And it needs to be provided extremely cheaply, then carried at a reasonable price all over the world,’ said Michael.
‘Then whoever transports it needs to be controlled,’ Shauna smiled. ‘I guess whoever produces tells them the end price. No agreement, no power. How is it produced?’
Michael realised that it was something he hadn’t asked. ‘I get the full details this afternoon.’
‘It’s not easy to pick someone,’ said Brenda, ‘the power that person would have is immense.’
‘Don’t forget, as a last resort, we are able to control him or her. Remember Henry,’ said Michael.
‘So it was you who did that. Well done,’ said Shauna.
‘It was Rui actually,’ said Michael, ‘so come on, ladies, who is your choice?’
‘I think the President could be trusted to carry it out, but as part of the administration, he may get bogged down, and may not be a popular choice in other parts of the world,’ Brenda was dismissing him as a possibility.
‘I think maybe we can count out politicians,’ Shauna seemed quite certain. ‘Let’s face it, if you can’t do it, teach it, and if you can’t teach it, be a politician.’
‘Who said that?’ Michael queried.
‘I did,’ said Shauna, smugly.
‘So no politicians, what about scientists?’ Michael asked.
‘How many of them do we know enough about? I think the only one I have ever heard of is Stephen Pederson, and all that I know about him is that he was described on television as the

most intelligent man on earth, so that should be a good recommendation,' Brenda, like most people, had a lack of knowledge when it came to this area.'

'Is he the one with the wheelchair?' asked Shauna.

'Yes,' replied Brenda, 'but that doesn't seem to have held him back.'

Michael thought about it. He was obviously brilliant and well respected throughout the world. Would he be fit enough to do it?' Would he want to do it? 'Would you just have a look on the web, and see what it is he suffers from?'

Shauna headed for Bob's office.

Brenda looked across at him. 'How are you managing to cope with all this? Last week life was easy. Studying at Cambridge with hardly a care in the world. Now you have all the problems of the world.'

Michael shrugged. 'Somehow it doesn't seem like that. If I have a problem, someone else always seems to deal with it.'

Shauna returned. 'He broke his spine in a motorcycle accident. He has no movement below his neck.'

They all realised that he may not be able to complete the task.

Michael took out his mobile phone. He wanted Shauna to listen in to the conversation. 'Hello, Dad. We are thinking about Stephen Pederson, but are concerned about his spine.' Michael filled Rui in on the details. 'Any chance of a cure?'

'As you already know, we have eradicated illness in all the worlds except this one, and accidents are extremely rare, so I don't think his condition exists anywhere else. It would have been sorted immediately after he had the accident. Just hang on a second... we can repair the damage and degeneration, but it will take time for him to regain use of all his muscles. The process of recovery can be speeded up. Probably less than twelve months for a full recovery. Don't forget, you need to check him out before getting involved.'

Michael explained Rui's reply to the ladies.

‘Would he want to do it?’ Brenda asked, ‘it’s not really in his field of work.’
‘If he gets cured, would he really have any option?’ Shauna countered. ‘How come Rui can cure Stephen Pederson, when he must have had the best medical attention possible?’
‘Ask Bob. He will tell you that my Dad is pretty special,’ Michael was relaxed about involving Shauna in any conversation. He knew from his father that she was as trustworthy as her husband.
His mobile interrupted him. ‘Hello Michael, it’s Mitch Cameron.’
‘Hello Mitch, great to hear from you. We still owe you a slap up meal, after you put business before pleasure last time. What can I do for you?’
‘I really don’t know how to put this. You know when Mikey turned up at the police station, and confessed to a lot of what we knew but couldn’t prove, and a hell of a lot we didn’t know about.’ Mitch went silent.
‘Yeeeeees,’ Michael knew what Mitch was trying to get round to. He helped, ‘wouldn’t it be great if other criminals did the same.’
‘God, you must be reading my mind.’
‘Anyone in particular?’ Michael asked innocently.
‘Toni Brunni,’ said Mitch. ‘Four times we have had him, and four times he has managed to get off. Witnesses have disappeared; jury members have been got at.’
‘Whereabouts is he at the moment?’ Michael asked, as he looked at a description of Brunni in Mitch’s mind.
‘In New York.’
‘Shall I try for about one hour’s time?’ asked Michael innocently.
‘How do you do it?’ Mitch replied.
‘Just a little persuasion,’ said Michael, ‘I hope he will see the error of his ways.’

He concentrated for a couple of minutes, and was happy that Toni Brunni was on his way to see Mitch.
'Who is Toni Brunni?' asked Brenda, although Michael had been careful not to mention his name.
'One of the bad guys,' replied Michael, 'like Mikey Spinetti, only ten times worse apparently. He wants to go and see Mitch at the police station. That's very nice of him don't you think?' He was feeling really pleased with himself.
'Smug expressions don't suit you,' said Brenda, and then burst into a fit of giggles.
'Just sometimes I like to feel smug,' Michael answered with a smile.
'Are we talking about another situation like your ex father-in-law?' Shauna looked at Brenda. Brenda nodded.
Michael changed the subject. 'So we are agreed on Stephen Pederson as the first choice.'
'Or the only choice if you put it another way,' Brenda was still giggling a bit.
'I'm going to have some coffee,' said Shauna, 'anyone else?'
Brenda and Michael both said yes.
Michael looked at Stephen Pederson. He was amazed at the power and content of his mind. If he could use as much of his brain as Rui, or if someone with Rui's ability had a brain like Professor Pederson, that person would be truly awesome. Even as he regretted that would not be possible, all Michael saw was goodness dominant in the Professor's mind. He would be a great choice if he could be persuaded to do it.
They finished their coffees, and Shauna asked to be excused. 'I promised to go over and see old Mrs. Green this afternoon. It's been lovely seeing you again, Michael, and thanks for letting me in on the discussions.'
After she had left, Brenda smiled. 'I wonder if old Mrs. Green exists. Shauna is really so sweet.'

'I was too polite to have a look,' admitted Michael, 'although I did think about it.'
Again the kisses were both long and magical. Their minds intertwined, and they were both in that state of happiness that comes to so few. They didn't want it to stop, but didn't want it to go any further that afternoon. They both seemed to be saving themselves for some special event at some special time, although neither of them knew what it was.
Mitch phoned to say thanks, Toni Brunni had just arrived.
Michael returned to Hampton that evening feeling as happy as he had ever been, Brenda was improving every day, even faster than they had hoped, and they had possibly made a start on changing the world.
As promised, Rui had the details of how to obtain energy from the rotation of a planet. Michael looked through the dozen or so pages, but hadn't a clue what it was all about.
'Stephen Pederson,' said Rui.
'He's fine,' Michael was certain. 'What would we have to do to turn his problem round?'
'It's fairly straightforward to reattach all the nerves endings correctly. About ten injections into the spine over ten days. Not nice, but he shouldn't feel the first half a dozen anyway. The drugs are being manufactured at one of our hospitals at the moment. They should be available tomorrow. Then it's up to the physiotherapists. How do you propose to handle him?'
'I think I will have to meet him face to face,' replied Michael. 'If I suggest he sends me an invitation to meet him in say Cambridge, I could kill two birds with one stone.'
'And then?' asked Rui.
'I suppose I tell him what we want him to do, then show him how to do it. How I get the drugs into him I'm not sure, but I think we should cure him whatever the outcome.'
Rui nodded his agreement. 'Try not to get too involved. One of the reasons we didn't interfere directly was to avoid these sorts

of situation. If it becomes known that you cured Stephen Pederson, you will be in demand worldwide.'
'Yeah,' said Michael, 'it happened earlier today.'
'Mitch?' queried Rui.
Michael nodded.
'Hard to refuse isn't it. So easy to spend time on specifics, when the whole is what needs curing.'
Michael felt suitably admonished, but Rui came in quickly to say it wasn't an admonishment. He would have done the same thing.
Michael contacted Stephen Pederson, who asked his secretary to contact Michael Kelly in New York to try and fix up a meeting with Stephen as soon as possible. He left Rui's phone number. He then checked on available flights to London for tomorrow.
Within half an hour the phone rang, and Rui handed it to Michael, whispering 'Stephen's secretary.'
A very efficient lady spoke to Michael, explaining that Stephen Pederson had asked her to fix a meeting with him. Michael suggested the day after tomorrow. She agreed to a two o'clock meeting at Cambridge University, adding that she would have to cancel a very important engagement for Stephen that day. Michael thanked her and said he would look forward to the meeting. She stalled, and then said sweetly, 'Stephen forgot to tell me the reason for the meeting, and I always put the details in his diary.'
'Did he?' Michael smiled.
'So could you tell me what to write in his diary, please?' she asked.
Michael thought for a couple of seconds. 'The effect of zero point energy on severed spinal nerves. The meeting shouldn't take more than half a day.'
She thanked him profusely; although she had no idea what he was talking about, she could fill in her diary.

‘Are you going over to Cambridge on your own?’ asked Jean. ‘I know Brenda would love to go there.’

Michael laughed. ‘It’s very tempting. I had a word with her doctor earlier, and he said if it was essential, she could make the trip, but if not she was getting on so well it seemed pretty pointless to upset the recovery plans. I hope we will have time later, as it is a beautiful place. I guess this trip will be just one ticket.’

Rui and Jean agreed, and he booked a return flight for the next evening.

Rui said he would get the drugs delivered by express air to Cambridge so Michael could collect them the morning after his flight. ‘They won’t let you take them on the plane,’ he explained, ‘although we can fiddle it if you think it would be easier.’

Again, Michael found sleep hard to come by that night. His head was buzzing with so many things, and top of the list were greed, crime and poverty, which he had not even thought about how to tackle. He tried to convince himself that everything had to be dealt with in order, and that he should concentrate on his present problems, but each time he tried, those three returned to his mind, almost haunting him.

Next morning Bob called. He had set the date for the memorial service for just over one month’s time. He said everyone he had contacted had promised to make it by fair means or foul. ‘I guess they all really loved Rui.’

‘I know illness is at the bottom of the list, but we will end up helping Stephen Pederson whatever,’ Michael looked at his Dad. Rui nodded.

‘And the rest of the world?’

‘I would guess that if we can get the immediate problems out of the way, cheap energy worldwide, no nuclear power, and start reducing global warming, then the world at least has a chance. Let’s get those well under way, then we can turn to medicine,

and start sorting out the other three.' Although Rui was going slightly against what had been his mandate for the last twenty five years, he was really enjoying the current situation, and living the excitement of it through Michael. 'You know, Jean and I are starting to believe that it's a possibility. The line we must never cross, however, is the self glorification one.'
Michael knew exactly what he meant.
It would be so lovely to see a child on her deathbed with some terrible disease, and cure her, then accept the thanks of her parents. He knew, however, they would have to deal in bulk, hidden from the people they helped.
For the rest of the evening they played mind games together, all the time strengthening Michael's brain. He could almost feel his mind power expanding, as memories became clearer. He mentioned to his parents that he felt his brain was becoming more powerful, and that he seemed to remember more and more from the past.
'OK,' said Rui, 'you are studying history.'
Michael nodded.
'Pick one aspect of it that really interests you.'
'The rise and fall of Greece,' Michael suggested.
'Pick a lecture you attended that meant something to you.'
Michael nodded again.
'Now, from the beginning, give the same lecture to me,' Jean smiled as Rui spoke.
Michael started repeating the lecture, and he knew it was word perfect. He interrupted himself. 'How the hell….'
'You should be the best student ever,' Rui laughed.
'So is this my brain expanding sixteen fold?' Michael asked.
'No, it's only just starting. Memory is one of the most noticeable. Pick your first girlfriend.' It was Jean speaking this time. 'Now remember your first ever kiss.'
Although that kiss had been quite a tame affair, Michael felt that same intensity that coursed through him all those years ago. He

immediately switched to the first kiss with Brenda, and relived every minute detail and feeling.
'You really do love her, don't you?' said his Mum.
Michael blushed slightly. 'She is just so different to any other girl I have ever known.'
'The downside can be that you remember everything,' Jean continued. 'The normal human brain blocks out the exact memory of pain to stop you from going mad. You can remember an accident, or illness, but not the feeling of the pain associated with it. At the moment you will remember something exactly as it felt, but you also have the brainpower to reduce or over ride the feeling.'
Michael could not resist. He remembered dislocating his shoulder in a football match, and gasped as the pain seared through him. He struggled for a few seconds, then brought the pain under control, and quickly removed it.
Jean watched him. 'The second good thing is that you can also control the pain as it actually happens. If you accidently cut yourself, you can remove the pain. Just don't forget to put a plaster on, because you can only stop the pain, not the bleeding.'
'So I can remember everything?' Michael quizzed his parents.
'Totally,' said Rui, 'in exact and minute detail.'
'How far back can I go?' Michael was intrigued.
'Try it,' said Jean. Michael went further back, and every feeling, every sight was there. Jean joined him in his thoughts, and together they lived his time as a baby, getting smaller and smaller. Suddenly Michael realised that he was being born. He could remember being in the womb, and the desperate fear that something was happening to disturb his world. As he suddenly rushed out into the light, all he wanted was to be back, held tight and warm as he had been for all those months. He was quickly wrapped up and cuddled by his mother. He relaxed, and soothed by the close contact, went back to sleep again.

His mother smiled at him. 'I sometimes relive it, without the pain of course.'
'I thought natural childbirth had been replaced long ago?' he was puzzled.
'We thought I couldn't conceive. The rules had been relaxed on our world as the population gradually decreased. We were allowed to try and have a baby, but nothing. We came to earth, didn't bother with any precautions, and you were born soon after.'
Michael knew in that instant how important he had been to his parents, and then felt the sadness they shared when they were instructed to have him raised in a more natural environment. They understood the reasons, but were not spared the agony.
'That's why we had no more children,' said Rui, 'there was just no way that we could give another one away.'
Michael thought he was starting to realise the brainpower that was possible, and he felt slightly apprehensive about what was happening to him.
'Let's try one little adventure together,' said Rui. 'It's early for you, but we can see how far you have come in such a short time. Don't be afraid, just go with it.'
He opened his mind to Michael. 'See my memories,' he told his son. Afterwards Michael always thought about the experience as watching Niagara Falls, but full of memories instead of water. If he looked at any particular memory, the full details of it exploded into his mind, and straight into his memory. As the cascade stopped, he realised that his own memory now contained the full memories of his father. Suddenly he was jolted as he also realised that he had all the memories of everyone that Rui knew.
He could run through tens of thousands of memories containing the knowledge, experiences, and everything else their brains contained. They were all catalogued neatly for him, ready to recall in an instant.

'You'd be a wow on Mastermind,' Rui was smiling, 'and it brings a whole new world to the expression 'I'll phone a friend'. Bit of a waste, though, as you could see all the answers anyway.'
'It's mind blowing,' said Michael.
'No,' said his mother, 'you will also be able to remember all your dreams, and all the dreams of anyone you are interested in. That really can be mind blowing.'

Chapter Seven

As Michael again lay in bed, waiting for sleep to overtake him, he thought of his meeting with Stephen Pederson. Would he be able to understand the details of the notes he would give him? He suddenly realised that he knew the full document off by heart. He couldn't yet understand it fully, but knew for the first time, that understanding would come. Comforted by that thought, he drifted into sleep.

Next morning he was eager to find out more about his brainpower. 'When you said memory was the easiest, how easy is it compared to everything else?'

'It's only easy because it is already there,' Rui told him, 'all you have learnt to do is retrieve it. You have always been able to learn and remember. Some people specialise, and remember everything about a particular subject, much like Mastermind that we mentioned last night. Few can remember lots of different subjects in detail. I would guess that you are working at somewhere between a quarter and a sixth of what is possible. You still have a heck of a long way to go.'

'So the other five sixths contain what?' Michael asked.

'Power, and not a lot else really,' his father told him. 'You can have all the knowledge in the world, but if you do not know how to use it, then it is pretty useless. To be able to use it is what you are aiming at. To be able to use it well and wisely is the ultimate pinnacle. To do that, you have to consider the chain re-action to every decision that you make. That takes all the brainpower you will ever have, but we both think you can do it.'

'What shall we work at today?' Michael was excited at the prospect.

Jean shook her head. 'Just get to grips with yesterday first. Try out some dreams as well, that's really weird.'

‘I can’t remember most of my dreams,’ said Michael. ‘I wake up and know I have been dreaming, but can’t remember about what.’

‘Everything is there,’ Jean replied. ‘Think about dreams, then any subject and it will all be there. Of course, everyone else’s dreams will be there as well. Try to work out on the plane exactly what having the entire knowledge means. There are no boundaries. When you have worked out what it all means, then you will start to be able to use it. Now go and see Brenda, and explain to her why she is not going to England. Also pick up your passport, or you won’t be going either.’

‘Unless you want to cheat,’ said Rui.

‘Go on Dad,’ said Michael, ‘you said that last night about the medicine.’

If you get to passport control, you just instruct the officer that you are to be escorted through immigration. Same with anyone else. You can give them a banana and tell them it’s a passport. No problem,’ Rui shrugged.

‘You can actually do anything,’ Michael suddenly realised.

‘That’s the problem. We couldn’t. That’s why you have to succeed. Give all our love to Brenda,’ Rui looked slightly sad.

As Michael arrived to see Brenda, his mind was full of what he had learnt. He expected his brain to be overflowing, as if it was a suitcase that had been over packed, but instead it felt much the same. Just that everything was there, available, and it seemed he could see it all a lot more clearly. As if in the past he had been looking at his memory through a fog. Now a breeze had taken every last remnant of mist away.

Brenda looked stunning. She smiled as she recognised his feelings. ‘Thank you,’ was all she said.

Michael knew she had felt what he thought, but said it anyway. ‘You do look absolutely gorgeous.’

‘Shauna and I went to the hairdressers, beauty parlour, and then clothes shopping,’ she confessed. ‘It was brilliant. Don’t forget,

nearly all my clothes are in the old house. No way am I going back there.'
Michael looked at the pale pink lipstick, and imagined himself kissing it all away.
Brenda giggled. 'Anyway, I needed something to cheer me up after you being so particularly nasty to me.'
'I could never be nasty to you,' Michael protested.
'So we are going to Cambridge?'
Michael groaned. She entered his mind. 'I felt your mind, even though you were all the way over in Hampton.'
'The doctor thought it was a bad idea.'
'I know,' said Brenda, 'but he would probably have thought shopping, and the beauty parlour were a bad idea, so Shauna didn't bother to ask him. I'm glad I have got one really nice friend, who looks after me.'
Michael started to protest, but Brenda interrupted. 'I'm sorry, but I couldn't help teasing you. You are probably right, but I do seem to be recovering extremely well.'
Michael smiled. 'I'm only spending two days in Cambridge, so I'll be back soon.'
Do you have a girlfriend there?' Brenda asked shyly.
'Yes, she is terrific. Really dark black curly hair. Gorgeous crimson lips. Laughs a lot. Really great fun to be with. And tomorrow night will be just amazing.'
Brenda knew he was lying, so hit him, a bit harder than she intended. 'Don't you ever lie to me,' she said, 'especially about something as important as that.'
Michael burst out laughing. 'So you can tease me, but….'
'Quite correct,' he was told, 'I am to be kissed, not teased.'
Michael duly obliged, and they spent a couple of hours together.
Michael thought about taking her memories into his own mind, but realised that would include her making love to her ex husband, and possibly more. He felt that they could only share

those sorts of secrets if they could both do it, and he was afraid to bring up the subject.

After one long, last, very intense kiss, he left to go and collect his passport in readiness for the trip to England.

Chapter Eight

The plane for England left on time, and Michael reclined in his seat and closed his eyes. He wanted to run through in his mind how to approach the meeting with Stephen Pederson. He started just over a week ago, when he had first landed in New York with Peter and Mary. Every detail of what had happened was available, and he found that he could skim over the bits that didn't matter and drill down into the ones that did. He also realised that he could look at the bits of his life when Rui was there from Rui's perspective. This of course also meant that he could look at himself through the mind of anyone else.

A stewardess offering free champagne interrupted his thoughts. He refused, but asked her brain what she thought of him. The answer was fairly noncommittal. He was nice looking and polite. She didn't think he would be any trouble on the flight. She wondered what sort of job he had that enabled him to fly club class. He reminded her a bit of her husband, who was better looking and had a decent hair cut. Her mind switched to the next row of seats.

Michael was just slightly miffed that she was not more interested in him. He then laughed to himself. If every woman on the planet thought he was the most desirable man ever, it wouldn't be easy to handle. He was tempted to make himself more interesting in her mind, but told himself to concentrate on the large picture, rather than the particles of life.

He went back to running through the events in New York. As he went through the enormous changes that had been made to his life he was amazed that he had coped so well. Considering what had happened, he was relaxed, confident, and focused. He knew he was laid back, but not that laid back.

He contacted Rui and queried if he had been given just a little bit of help along the way. Rui confirmed that he and Jean had been looking out for him, and sent their congratulations on realising it so quickly. 'Just keep thinking about what it all means,' Rui suggested. 'You will have it all in the end, although there will be plenty of times you wish you hadn't.'

He thought about Brenda. She was having a meal with Shauna and Bob. She sent her love to him, and told him to enjoy the trip and hurry back to her.

He thought about Jessie, and although it probably took thirty seconds, she suddenly realised he was there. She was still at work, reducing their interests in anything to do with power production. She sent her love, and wished him well.

That was when the first inclination of what it was all about hit him. If he could get into their minds from thirty thousand feet, Rui could get into the pilot's mind and do whatever he wanted. All the airport security in the world counted for nothing if anyone who had the inclination could tell the pilot and the co-pilot to crash the plane. Or possibly do the same to a super tanker. Or a nuclear power station. Or all the rockets round the world that had nuclear warheads available to them, all without a trace of how it had been done.

He shuddered at the thought of his, or especially Jean and Rui's brainpower, in the wrong hands. What if terrorists used blackmail, or forced him to do something against his will. If Brenda was threatened, how could he cope? Almost instantly the answer came to him. Just stop their brain from carrying out the threat. So keeping this brainpower in check was paramount. Bob and Jessie had a small amount of ability, but not enough to alter someone's mind. Brenda had already overtaken Jessie in her abilities, which was not logical. Rui had expressed concern about her, but on the other hand Michael knew her mind. He was sure she had no malice in her at all.

So it was basically him and his parents, and they would be leaving soon.

He went back to thinking about tomorrow's meeting. He knew the notes off by heart, and went through them again. This time he understood more than the last time. He was able to see better how some pieces of the equation affected others. He worked through what he knew, and realised that although one plant could provide the energy for the planet, the present distribution system could not cope. It relied on lots of small sources of energy providing what the infrastructure could cope with. Did they need to alter the present system of overhead wires and underground cables?

Again he was back in touch with Rui. 'Good thinking,' he was told. 'Try contacting Maria Leskow on planet four. I will stay with you to help.' Michael thought about planet four, although he had never seen it. His father helped with that bit. He then thought about the distribution of electricity and Maria Leskow. Suddenly Maria was there. 'Hi there, pleased to meet you. I hope we can meet in the flesh one day. You must have really interesting stories to tell about life on earth. I believe it is pretty dreadful. You want to know about distributing electricity. We have the simplest form here that has so far been found. This planet is about the same size as yours, with oceans and continents fairly similar. We have found that two to three production sites per continent work well. The distribution is then by power wave, so there is no hardware involved. We actually use two hundred and fifty volts as standard, so all necessary appliances run directly. Any increases or reductions in voltage are taken care of at the point of use. Of course, we have no one trying to interfere with the system, and it is free. I'm sorry, but you will have to work out those bits for yourself. What is that noise I can hear? Oh. I forgot, your planes still have mechanical engines. You would at least think they could be soundproofed. There again, I know nothing about those problems.' Michael asked if they had planes. 'Sure,' came the answer, 'battery powered. A one hundred kilo pack will fly a plane round the world none stop. Whatever size pack does whatever size job. The planes could tap into power waves, but it's easier and more efficient to use batteries. I will download all the data you need to convince Professor Pederson. Good luck with your meeting tomorrow.'

Michael had no idea where planet four was, and how he was able to communicate with Maria over what must be a huge distance. Rui was still with him. 'Everything is a ring. It is like visiting that planet by transporter. You may be gone for an hour, but because coming back is the reverse of going, all you do is step into the transporter, and step back out again. Much the same as thinking. Stick with it son, it will all seem logical in the end.'

Michael went through the information he had received. Production of the power waves was fairly straightforward, although there were still blank areas in his understanding. He knew that the rotation of the earth produced the initial continuous power wave, and that the zero point energy somehow increased the use of that power and transmitted it as a more powerful wave. There were no moving parts at all. Michael saw the funny side of the fact that lots of scientists had been experimenting with wave power, when they should have been looking at power waves. At the receiving end, instead of an appliance being plugged into an electricity socket, it had a receiver. Maria said that for the original experimental ones, all they did was wire a receiver onto about two inches of cable. The newer appliances had the receiver built in. Michael started to think about the politics of installing the system worldwide. If they built say three production sites in Europe, would there be a problem if say one was in Holland, one in Poland, and one in Italy. Would Germany be happy to rely on power supplied by Poland, and vice versa? Payment would be a pain, especially across borders, so supplying the electricity for free made sense. Would Poland be happy to cover the cost if it was supplying Germany for nothing? He realised he had not yet thought about costs. He asked Rui. Assuming thirty production sites worldwide, to give an extra bit of power for any problems, the

current production cost for the lot was going to be less than one million dollars. 'What do you think?' Rui asked, 'we pay for installation, and then the countries involved can sort out running costs, which will be negligible?' Michael agreed.
Michael was still concerned about the politics of the situation. In the Middle East, if a site were built in Israel, would it supply the rest of the area? Would it cut off power if it hit trouble? If it did that, it would also cut off its own power. That was when he had a second thought about the power he had available to him. He remembered the story about the guy who had hypnotised a complete parade ground. He had nothing like the power that Michael could generate. If a government was meeting, then he could control all their thoughts, so they would unanimously vote the way Michael wanted them to. Or the United Nations, or any other group of people.
Suddenly his flesh tingled. He was dictator of the world. He was God.
How could he be trusted to make the right decisions? Did he really know better than anyone else? Were the people out there happy as they were? Self doubt flooded through his mind. What if I get it wrong?
Suddenly Rui was there with him. 'You have to find it out for yourself. No warnings, just you discovering. Now you are starting to see why we had reservations about how much we should influence this planet. Do you still want the job?'
'Excuse me sir, are you OK? You have gone very pale.' The same stewardess had touched his arm.
Michael shook his head. 'Thank you, but I'm fine.' Her consideration was part of the job, but in her case it was primarily because she actually cared about a fellow human being. Michael could feel the basic goodness in her. Suddenly he was lifted. She was surely more representative of what he was trying to save. 'I have a very important meeting tomorrow, and you have just

given me the inspiration I needed to carry it through. Thank you very much again.'
The stewardess looked puzzled. 'Is there anything I can get you?'
'Coffee latte would be really welcome,' Michael smiled up at her, and just glimpsed a touch of sadness in her eyes. Instantly he felt her mind. She also had an important meeting tomorrow. She was unable to have children, and had a meeting scheduled with her husband at an adoption agency. He felt the sadness in her. Quickly he asked Rui if he could help.
'Glad to see you are sticking to the big picture,' Rui told him. Michael shrugged in his mind. 'OK,' confirmed Rui, 'just let me have a look. No problem. Tell her to postpone the meeting, and see her doctor instead. He now knows how to treat her. Glad to help, son.'
As she returned with the coffee, Michael looked up at her. 'The meeting you have tomorrow. Postpone it and see your doctor instead.'
'But how do you know about my meeting?'
'Sorry,' replied Michael, just putting a little pressure on the stewardess's mind. 'I just realised who you are. It's a long story, but my Dad, who is an expert, knows your gynaecologist. He has some good news for you.' As he spoke, he implanted in her mind that the conversation was perfectly normal.
Holly Vanes was a confused lady. Now thirty seven, she had been trying for ten years to have a baby. Here was a perfect stranger telling her to go and see the gynaecologist who had told her only six months ago that there was no hope. Yet she knew he was telling the truth. She would not get excited, but she couldn't wait until tomorrow.
'Yes,' Michael thought, 'I do want the job.'
Next day Cambridge was bathed in soft sunshine, and looked at its best. Michael was happy that he understood enough about the project, and was looking forward to meeting Professor Pederson.

After a pleasant lunch, he wandered along St. Johns Street in the direction of the college where they had arranged to meet. He still loved walking through this beautiful city, and was in high spirits when he entered the room where he was to meet Professor Pederson. He was introduced to Stephen, his nurse, and a young gentleman who was described as his carer. Michael smiled to himself, as the young gentleman was obviously a minder.

'They thought it best I had someone to look after me.' Michael smiled as he detected the irony in Stephen's voice.

'That's not a problem,' Michael was already taking a liking to this man.

'So, zero point energy and my spine; I invited you here to discuss it.'

'Yes,' agreed Michael, 'although the link is somewhat tenuous. May I start with zero point energy? I have a wad of notes here about how it can be used to provide free power. What is the easiest way for you to read them?'

'Just put them through that scanner and it will show them on the screen,' Stephen told him.

For the next hour the great man was silent. Michael read through the notes, and fed the pages through the scanner as he finished them. For five minutes after he had finished, Stephen Pederson still said nothing.

Then, 'You didn't write those notes.'

'Correct,' replied Michael.

'Elsie, would you leave us alone please, and take John with you.'

Elsie started to protest, but Stephen was firm with her. 'None of us have anything to fear from this man.'

When they were alone, Stephen asked. 'You know this works; I can see it in your mind, but I don't understand how you are certain it will work.'

'It is already working.'

'Not in this world,' the professor was certain.
Michael entered his mind. 'My apologies for the intrusion, but just in case we can be overheard, there are three inhabited planets where it does work.'
Stephen let Michael know that he had felt the same sensation of a mind within his brain before. 'Was that why he had agreed to the meeting?'
Michael apologised again. 'I am on a fairly short time scale, and needed you on board as soon as possible.'
'So I can assume that this is fully operational,' Professor Pederson spoke again. 'How is the power distributed?'
Once again, Michael entered his mind, and transferred the full details. 'Would you like the full details on the power plants?'
'No,' replied Stephen, 'believe me when I say I will never forget a word of what was written there. You can take it away with you, and it is probably best to destroy it. So what is it you want of me?'
'We, that is my parents and I, need someone to oversee the entire project. We do not trust any government or corporation. We need someone who has no political or financial motivation, but will do it to provide free power to the world. Someone who has the respect of the world, and who would not be bullied by the fuel suppliers, who will go out of business fairly quickly. We could think of no-one better.'
'It's a long term project, and I am a fairly short term bet,' the Professor was brutally honest.
'That's where the other half of the equation comes in,' said Michael. 'You can be cured. It will take about a year, and will involve lots of muscle rebuilding, but it can be done.' He looked down at the floor. 'Of course, even if you decline the project, I can still give you the cure.'
'So it was meant to be a bribe?'

'Only for a very short time. Yes, I do have faults,' admitted Michael. 'If you would rather not be involved with the project, would you be able to recommend someone please.'
'You already know I can't refuse. Just open the door and shout for Elsie to bring us tea and cakes. It should be champagne, but God knows we need clear heads to think this through.'
Michael did as he was told.
'So, thirty power wave plants dotted round the world. I guess we skip the major oil producers. The other problem area will be governments losing tax income. Have we got a cost estimate?
'Around one million dollars US,' Michael told him. 'I can provide the funds, that's not a problem.' He realised he had not thought about the tax implications.
'Production?' queried Professor Pederson.
'Already in progress at two plants I own. The plants are not a problem, and we are churning out the receivers by the shed load at the moment, and packing them together with multilingual notes on how to fit them. We will supply those free of charge,' said Michael.
'OK, so I am on board; can I pick my own team to do the actual work?'
'Of course, I will pay all the salaries, including your own,' Michael was elated. This had turned out better than he could have hoped.
At that moment Elsie came in with a tray.
'Before you feed me, go give that young man a large kiss, he deserves it.' Michael could hear the emotion in the strong voice.
Elsie stared at Michael. 'I don't know what you have done to him, but whatever it is you deserve much more than a kiss.' With that, a large, matronly fifty year old planted a resounding smacker on Michaels' lips. 'Please can you stay around and keep him in this sort of humour.'
She gave Stephen some cake, and a drink of tea.

Michael handed Elsie the small parcel he had brought with him.
'Elsie, can you please organise for Professor Pederson to have injections for the next few days. Full instructions are included, and as a competent nurse you will be able to administer them.'
Elsie looked at her boss.
'If that's what the man wants, then that's what the man gets.'
Stephen burst into laughter as he looked at the expression on Elsie's face.
'How do you know they will do you any good?' she asked.
'I know for certain they won't do me any harm.'
'The drugs will halt any further degeneration immediately, and start to reattach nerve endings in three or four days. There should be sensation within a week, and assuming that happens, then it will be daily exercise, increasing for the next year. At that stage, he should be as good as new.' Michael handed Elsie his card. 'Just shout if you need any help. Only one other thing, Elsie, this is a secret between the three of us. There will be plenty of time in the future to cure other people, but for the time being, we have larger problems to take care of.'
'Who exactly are you?' Elsie asked as she read his card.
'I am a Cambridge student, reading history and economics. Tonight I will sleep at home near Woodbridge in Suffolk. Tomorrow morning I will see the principal of my college to ask if I can take time off to work in America, and finish my studies later. I fly back to the States tomorrow evening.'
'Which principal?' asked Stephen.
Michael told him.
'Then I will take care of that. There is no problem. Return when you want. I need you here tomorrow. Are you staying with your parents tonight?' Stephen was taking control.
'They are my adoptive parents in Woodbridge. My real parents spent their time in New York.'
'Spent?' queried Stephen.
'Kind of complicated,' replied Michael.

'I can imagine,' said Stephen.
'Tomorrow you have….'
'To see Michael, here,' Stephen interrupted Elsie. 'Cancel everything for the next two months, I have work to do.'
Elsie shook her head. 'I had better get started. Shall I postpone?'
No, cancel. Tell them I will re-arrange as soon as possible.'
Elsie left the room, and Stephen asked Michael if his adoptive parents knew anything about what he was doing.
'Not in any great detail,' he replied.
'Then you get off and see them. I need time to go through all this from every angle. I then need to start building my team. Can we meet tomorrow at nine?'
'That's fine, and thank you for taking a great weight from my shoulders. It's really been a huge pleasure,' Michael smiled.
'Believe me when I say, probably for the first time I have ever said it and meant it, the pleasure is all mine. Give Elsie a shout, and she will see you out.'
Michael got to the door just as Stephen spoke. 'What is the power of your brain?'
Michael smiled to himself. 'Mine is still developing, but my parents brains are about sixteen times as powerful as the average guy.'
'Impressive,' was all that the professor said as Michael left the room.
That evening, it was lovely to see Peter and Mary again, and they enjoyed a delicious meal at The Admirals Head in Little Bealings, just a few miles from their home. Michael was surprised at the choice, but Mary explained that their local, The Dog, had been fully booked, and that they had always had very good food at The Admirals Head.
That night, for the first time in a while, Michael was asleep as soon as his head hit the pillow. The alarm woke him just after six and he felt really refreshed, and looking forward to the challenge.

Cambridge was, as ever, a nightmare to drive into, but he was in plenty of time as he entered the same room as yesterday.
Professor Pederson was already there, and he was obviously pleased to see Michael. 'I know the drugs haven't kicked in yet, but I feel better than I have done for years. It's either the expectation that I might one day be free of this bloody wheelchair, or the excitement of the project, or both. Are you able to tell me the whole story from start to finish?'
Michael nodded his agreement. 'I will try to shift it all into your mind, from arriving in New York up to yesterday.' He arranged his thoughts for a few moments, and then looked at the Professor.
'How the hell did you manage all that without going mad?'
'I know my parents gave me a lot of help, though I didn't realise it at the time,' Michael admitted.
'When will you have the first plant ready for testing?' Stephen asked.
'Next week,' Michael fished about in his pocket. 'This is one of the receivers.'
'It doesn't look much,' Stephen commented.
'It isn't much,' said Michael, 'just a receptor fitted to some wires, covered in plastic.'
'That's one area we haven't spoken about'' said Stephen. 'We will still need an oil industry for all the things made from fossil fuels, such as plastic.'
'On world four, there is no oil, or coal for that matter, so they have to get by without. Most products are based on treated soft wood. There are various different ways to alter the values of it, mainly by injection, to give it the versatility of plastic, at a lower cost, and more sustainable.'
''So you pretty well have it all sorted,' the deep strong voice sounded sceptical to Michael.
'No. The progress we have made is incredible in the timescale we have allotted to us, but we are tackling the easy things first.

From our list, you are taking care of cheap energy, which will make nuclear energy redundant, and should start reversing global warming. Illness we can get under way quite quickly, I think. We still have greed, crime and poverty. I can't think how to start on that in a global way. You know how we dealt with specific cases by getting them to admit to their crimes. We haven't the time to deal on an individual basis. I worry that we will run out of time before we become a major threat to the other worlds. I will probably have to try and stall somehow to accomplish everything. If I could work out how each country could provide enough good food for its population, then we would at least be some way to dealing with poverty and illness.' Michael was feeling just that little bit more optimistic than before. 'Worlds three and four were started by pioneers who already had open minds, so most of the problems of this world never existed there.'

'It might still be worth asking advice,' countered Stephen. 'If you want to achieve perfection, then look at perfect. Anyway, back to the current problems. We have ten more people on the payroll, and I think they will be able to accomplish everything. I suggest we install the first unit here. We understand all the laws here, and the country is very stable. My only worry is the tax implication. I will start looking for a suitable site, it that's OK with you.'

Michael nodded his agreement.

'How long will you test for?'

'Less than one day. There are no moving parts, so it's really turning it on and then seeing how far away things will work. If they work on full power at two thousand miles, then I can see no problems. We are building in a fail component, which will need a bit of testing to get it right,' Michael had insisted on that.

'What is a fail component?' Stephen queried.

'If someone tries to replicate what we have built, there is one essential component that will destroy itself if it is opened. I can't

see why anyone would want one if they can just get free electricity anyway, but just in case. I suggest all the sites are well protected and guarded, just in case.'
'What about the batteries? How difficult are they to construct?' Stephen was looking ahead.
'They are called batteries, but energy store would be a better description. The name battery was borrowed because of historical usage. Again, they are not a problem. Size is just linking them together. A typical car, for example a Ford Focus, would have a battery weighing about two kilos. That size would give it a range of about one thousand miles without charging. Speed and acceleration would be about the same as for a standard one point five litre petrol engine. Again, like planes, it could pick up power waves and recharge as it went along, but stopping to recharge is easier. Take out the engine, gearbox and clutch, and link up a battery to the drive shafts. We will release the battery details to the motor manufacturers, and they can get under way making conversion kits and new models as soon as they like. I guess a two kilo battery should retail for about two hundred pounds, and last for about fifty years. Free fuel for fifty years for two hundred pounds. Sounds good.' Michael was feeling even more positive.
'And boats and planes would follow in due course.'
'And tractors, earth movers, if it's got an engine, then change it,' said Michael. 'There may even be a case for replacing overhead lines on railways with battery driven trains. A lot more reliable. All running for nothing.'
'Keep in touch, Michael.' Stephen's eyes were sparkling. 'I will concentrate on this project alone, but no doubt I will have other thoughts, probably about getting rid of illness. I will call you if I think of anything worthwhile. Thanks again for having faith in me. I will make sure this works.'

‘Thank you for taking it on. The only problem is that you may have to postpone your dream of flying in space if I have to ground all space flights to give us more time to cure our ills.’

Michael called Elsie to let her know he was leaving, and he made his way down the M11 and onwards to Heathrow.

Chapter Nine

Back in New York, Michael made his way to Hampton. He had kept Jean and Rui up to date with progress, and they were really pleased to see him back. Everything seemed to be going to plan.
Toni Brunni had admitted to over fifty murders, plus hundreds of other criminal acts, and had given Mitch a list of major crimes committed by over three hundred other criminals. They had already picked up most of them. Mitch sent his thanks.
Bob was making good progress with the memorial service and had the three hundred guests that they had limited the service to.
Jessie had got rid of all their interests in power production and had taken on another two manufacturing companies in the Far East, which were churning out receivers twenty four hours a day, seven days a week. She and Bob were negotiating for two major battery manufacturers, solely for their names. They would continue the old torch battery type of business, but in the meantime start building the new type batteries and storing them. They had also bought a small car manufacturer in Malaysia, and the staff there were designing a new vehicle around the specification of the battery, as well as working out conversion kits for the old models.
'All in all, pretty good progress,' Rui was pleased.
'Yeah, all the easy stuff is running well. Stephen reckons twenty years and the world will be running totally on power waves. Are we able to produce better and cheaper end products at all?' Michael asked.
'I know what you mean. Have really cheap effective fridges in the middle of deserts, jungles, whatever, so that medicines could be stored, and food kept fresh.' Jean joined the conversation. 'Lighting, computers, radios, televisions, cookers, water pumps, filtration plants, anything that improves life for not much money.'

'I guess it's back to asking on world four for the latest technology. Shall I have a word with Maria, to see if she knows who we should contact?' Michael thought it was the best way forward.

He contacted her, and she seemed really pleased to hear from him again. 'You want Eddie Phillips, just hang on and I will bring him into the loop.' Eddie seemed to be one of the nicest guys he had ever spoken to, and immediately understood what Michael was after. He explained that they had all been told about the plans for earth two if everything failed, and they were all hoping Michael would succeed. He explained that the cheapest result was always to do away with moving parts. Not only did it reduce cost, but improved longevity immensely. He would chuck across all the latest technical data. Michael thanked Maria and Eddie, and they asked him to contact them at any time, and told him that they would also let him know of any improved products.

'They are really nice people,' said Michael to his parents.

'Don't forget they have no stress, no problems, and no illness. They live in paradise, so it's very much easier to be a nice person under those circumstances,' Jean smiled at him.

As Jean spoke, Michael's mind began to fill with details of every conceivable electric item. All basic, but doing a perfect job. He glanced at his parents, and they nodded that they were receiving the same information.

'How is manufacturing of the power wave plant going?' Michael asked.

'The first one should be finished this week,' Rui replied.

'So how big is it?'

'Go on, guess,' Rui laughed.

Michael had seen power stations before, but knew it would be a lot smaller. 'About the size of this house?'

'Much smaller than our car,' Rui replied.

'And that can power everything within two thousand miles?' Michael was truly amazed.
'That's in a heavily built up and industrialized zone. In open country, ten thousand miles,' Rui told him, 'but don't forget, it's not manufacturing, just transferring none stop energy.'
'What about in mountainous areas, will they be able to receive the power waves?' Michael suddenly saw a major problem.
'The power waves go straight through everything, just as they come straight out of the ground at the moment. It's not like mobile phones, where you need a pole on every corner,' Rui reassured his son.
'Can we prove that it's not harmful?' Michael asked. 'There are bound to be people who have a go at it.'
'It's actually less powerful than radio waves, and don't forget it is a natural phenomenon that occurs anyway. Compared to fossil fuels, it is actually beneficial. It will have to be a hard argument to be able to go against it,' Rui convinced his son.
'Before I start looking at cheap basic fridges, I am going over to see Brenda. Can I use your car please Dad, I thought I would take her down to the coast.' Michael usually used the chauffeur and the limo.
'Of course. Remember we drive on the proper side of the road here,' his father joked.
Michael enjoyed the drive, as it made him concentrate on something other than all the business in hand. The roads were relatively quiet, and as he pulled up outside Bob's apartment, he could see Brenda waving down to him. Shauna welcomed him in, but Brenda was right behind her. They had tea together, discussing the way things were going, and then Michael suggested that he would drive Brenda down to the coast.
'We might not have been in, you know, Brenda chided.
'You were looking out of the window for me before I set off from Hampton,' Michael laughed.

'I know, I felt you. That's how I guessed how long it would take you to get here.'
They travelled in silence for a while, both just happy to be with one another.
'You have never asked me about my past,' said Brenda softly.
'I know, but I have been tempted. When I want to know everything there is to know about you, then you must know the same about me. In the meantime, I am happy to listen to any bits and pieces you would like to tell me,' Michael was not sure where the conversation was going.
'When I was pregnant, I decided that I would try and find my father,' Brenda started. 'I thought it would be lovely if my baby had two grandfathers. I didn't like to trouble my mother, who by that time was quite ill. So I did my own investigating, on the web, that sort of thing. I kept it secret from Greg, as even by then he was a bit ashamed of my family, or rather, lack of it. As far as I could make out, my mother was probably an illegal immigrant from South America, and at that stage I couldn't find a trace of my father. Not much of a background, is it?'
Michael smiled at her. 'Nothing about your past worries me at all. All I care about is now and the future. I love you as you are.'
He parked the car, and they sat looking out over Long Island Sound.
'Are you a virgin?' Brenda looked into his eyes.
He could feel himself blushing. 'Yes, as a matter of fact, so please be very gentle with me.'
'It's not funny. You shouldn't joke about it. I'm not a virgin.'
Michael burst out laughing. 'I know. You had a baby. It doesn't matter.' He turned and put his arms round her.
Brenda burst into tears. 'You just don't understand how much I love you; I want to be perfect, like you. I always think I will not be good enough.'
He pulled away just enough to be able to look into her eyes. 'I am not perfect by any means. I think, because of the way our

civilization evolved from the original ones with Li Po, and babies only being produced on the death of someone, and those babies not necessarily being from their parents, we somehow stalled a bit on love. Don't forget, for all those years my ancestors were drugged. It has taken a hell of a long time for that to work through. I just never fell in love before. I have dated some beautiful girls, and kissed most of them, but I think I was always waiting for the moment that usually only happens in the movies. That magic moment. The moment that arrived when I met you.'

Then they kissed. At that moment Brenda was ninety nine percent sure that he would love her forever, although Michael was the full one hundred per cent.

When they came up for air, Michael was aching. He had a lump in his trousers and wanted nothing more than Brenda, there and then. Once again, wrong time and place.

'Let's have a walk along for a while.' He managed to adjust himself as he got out of the car.

They walked hand in hand, looking out over the Sound. Lights were starting to come on across the water.

He turned towards Brenda, and took her other hand in his. He pulled her very gently towards him, and kissed her, just as gently. She let go of his hands, and put hers behind his back, pulling him even closer. His hands tightened behind her back. He could feel the outline of her body against him. He moved, ever so slowly, like a half speed waltz. She responded to his body, and tilted her head towards him, looking forward to the kiss still to come.

Instead, Michael moved his mouth towards her ear. 'Brenda, will you marry me?' He whispered so softly that for a few seconds she was not sure what he had said.

She put her hand round his head, and pulled his lips to hers.

Sometime later, as they drew apart, she murmured 'Yes, Oh yes.'

They kissed again, and Michael fished in his pocket.
'I found this in Cambridge,' he explained and opened the small box.
He slipped a platinum ring, with one solitary emerald, onto her finger. 'I thought it was beautiful. It reminded me of you.'
Brenda started crying again, but this time the sobs came from a smiling face. 'Oh Michael, it's really gorgeous.'
She looked down at her finger, then back to his face. 'I love you so much.'
Again they kissed, then wandered slowly back towards the car.
Stars were just beginning to appear, and he pointed to one. 'Somewhere out there is another world. When we have seen everything this one has to offer, we will go there. To paradise. I will prove to them that you will never be a threat.'
As they drove home, they felt that their futures were both happy and secure. They determined together to try and make the future for everyone else just as wonderful as it was for them.
As soon as they went in Shauna spotted the ring. She let out a scream of delight and kissed Brenda more times than Michael could count, then turned to Bob.
He sat bemused. 'I see my wife is pleased to see you home. Have you been gone for a few years, or have I missed something?'
Shauna pointed at Brenda's ring. 'They are engaged,' she shouted at him.
Bob rose, put his arms round Brenda and kissed her. He shook Michael's hand, and congratulated them both.
'This calls for champagne,' he announced.
'Not for me, thanks. I've got to drive back.'
'Nonsense,' Bob told him, 'the limo can collect you.'
'Don't bother with that, you are staying the night,' Shauna declared. 'The guestroom needs some use, and don't even think of arguing. I'll just go check everything is in order.'
Bob went out to collect the champagne.

Brenda stood and giggled.
'I don't know who's more excited, you or Shauna,' Michael smiled at Brenda.
'She really is great, just like a mum. She might be excited, but I'm the happiest,' Brenda looked really radiant.
Bob and Shauna came back together, and they all stood to toast the engagement.
The Dom Perignon was excellent, and the second bottle was just as good.
'We were intending to eat out tonight, but if it's alright with you two, I will order something in. I'm not too good at drinking without something to eat,' Shauna was already slurring her words just a little.
'It sounds a good idea to me, if you two are in agreement,' Bob backed his wife.
Michael and Brenda nodded their agreement, and Bob suggested Thai cuisine, as there was a very good restaurant nearby that did deliveries. Everyone thought it was a good idea.
By the time they started the third bottle, the food arrived.
As is often the case with takeaways, there was far more than they needed, but there was a large variety, and the eating took precedence over the drinking.
It was just before midnight when Bob and Shauna retired.
Left alone, Michael and Brenda wandered out onto the balcony with their drinks, and sat very still, looking up at the moon and the stars. Michael looked at his watch. Just after midnight. 'We have been engaged for two days now, and it still feels great.'
'It feels the best ever feeling I have ever had,' Brenda yawned as she smiled.
'Then let's follow Bob and Shauna, and maybe your dreams will be the best you have ever had.'
At breakfast next morning, Shauna was still buzzing after the news of the engagement. Michael thought how correct Brenda

had been with her description of Shauna being like a mother hen.

Doctor Myers called in as they were finishing, and gave Brenda a quick once over. 'You really are doing very well. I see no reason for you not to take up life in full again. Just ease yourself into it, rather than jumping in at the deep end.

'What does today hold for you two?' Shauna asked.

'I need to go through more bits and pieces with Rui, and I had better take his car back. I thought we should both go over, and announce our engagement to them officially. They already know, but I think it's the right thing to do,' Michael looked at Brenda.

She nodded. 'I won't be a minute.'

Bob flicked up his eyebrows. 'That means about twenty minutes in the female mind. When we are going somewhere, I always tell Shauna we need to set off twenty minutes early, then we have a chance of setting off on time.'

Michael laughed, and picked up a paper.

Bob was right, and twenty minutes later Michael and Brenda left for Hampton.

Jean opened the door, congratulating and kissing them both. 'It's such wonderful news, Rui and I are thrilled to bits.'

Rui offered his congratulations, kissing Brenda, and shaking Michael's hand. 'The even better news is that we know you were just made for one another.'

Michael looked at Brenda. 'When Dad says he knows, then you can believe it's a cast iron guarantee.'

Jean took Brenda's hand. 'Come on, we have so much to talk about. Let's leave these two alone.'

Michael made them a coffee each. 'I have a concern about tax.'

Rui nodded. 'I agree. If we start in Britain, the implications for the Chancellor will be massive, especially with the current state of the world economy. On the other hand, manufacturing will receive a massive cost saving, although I guess it is relatively small in the UK. There will be savings in all state run enterprises, and higher profits for major electricity users, so higher taxation revenue. He could always increase the cost of road tax. I think we have to let the economics shake itself out.'

'Is it possible for the power wave to be traced back to its source?' Michael was exploring every option.

Immediately Rui saw where he was coming from. 'I'll put it to Maria.'

Rui sat and finished his coffee. 'Apparently we are probably about fifty thousand years ahead of ourselves with being able to use power waves. If someone with a really good brain devoted himself to the task of tracing the source, he might just possibly crack it in less than one thousand years, so the answer is no.'

'So is it best to not release any details of the plants?'Michael felt sure he was on the right track. 'If the receivers take all the credit for tapping into the natural phenomena, then no one will ever start looking for the plants.'

Rui nodded. 'If we start with just the receivers for electrical appliances, we can get the thirty plants in place round the globe. Then release the receivers for lighting systems. Then the batteries. Large tax implications will then be at the end of the chain.'

'I will suggest that to Stephen,' Michael entered Stephen's mind. He immediately understood the problems. If they are the size of cars, why not build them into vans. We can then just park them in garages, and move them if it becomes necessary. 'Nothing better than a nice white Transit van,' he joked.

'He really is enjoying this, his mind is so excited,' Michael was pleased with Stephen's response.

'So we construct them to fit inside a wooden case based on a pallet that will go into a standard Transit van. We export them as machine tools on the pallet, then fork lift them into a van, and take it wherever necessary. Switch it on and we are up and

running. I will give instructions to Bob and Jessie. They are testing today,' Rui added.
'Can the batteries, when we get that far, take in power waves, or do they need to be plugged into a socket?' Michaels's head was full of thoughts.
'They can receive power waves, but it is a lot less complex to receive them when the battery is not being drained. At the moment, the design is that the battery takes in power when it is expending less than the power coming in. So if a car stops at traffic lights, it will take in power until the accelerator is pressed. If the driver stops for a coffee, then the battery will fully recharge. You will never have to actually do anything. With planes and ships, it's slightly different. They will normally only recharge at the airport, or in port. The largest plane would take less than one hour, and the largest ship about four hours. Both done automatically. It was one of the areas I had already queried,' Rui replied.
Bob phoned. 'We will be ready to test in about one hour.'
'Do you fancy a trip to the factory?' I know we won't see anything, but just feel we should be there for the start of the whole thing,' Rui asked his son. 'It's just North of New York, so not very far.'
The ladies were discussing far more important things, so just the two of them made the trip to see the test.
Bob and Jessie were already there, and they all shook hands. 'I hear congratulations are in order,' Jessie whispered to Michael.
'Yes. Thanks Jessie,' Michael replied.
'Oh, I'm not congratulating you, I thought you were saving yourself for me,' she looked straight at him with as cold an expression as Michael had ever seen, then burst out laughing. 'It's wonderful news,' she hugged and kissed him.
When they went through to the factory, Michael felt a bit disappointed.
'Doesn't look much, does it?' Rui echoed his feelings.

The engineer in charge of the project looked round at them. 'We haven't had time to put any go faster stripes on it. Sorry,' he turned back to the machine.
It sat on two workbenches backed up to one another, and was basically a metal box, just under a metre cube.
'OK, who would like to do the honours?' asked the engineer.
'Ladies first,' said Rui.
'What do I have to do, Bill?' asked Jessie, the only female present.
Bill, the chief engineer, moved a small cover on the machine. 'Press that button and hope.'
He looked over to some screens on the wall behind them, and nodded. 'Number one is in Orlando, number two is in L.A., and number three is in Thunder Bay.'
Each screen had just one person visible, and they all acknowledged Bill as he spoke.
'Go ahead,' he nodded at Jessie.
'May God bless, and all that,' said Jessie as she pressed the button.
Nothing happened.
Bill looked at screen one. 'OK, Barry, switch on.' Barry turned and switched on a television behind him. After a couple of seconds the picture appeared, and they could hear the western that was in progress. Barry lifted the lead at the back of the screen, showing the receiver. He looked down at a small hand held device. 'Full power,' he announced. Screens two and three gave similar results with a fridge and a drill.
'Thanks guys. Come on home when you are ready. We won,' said Bill, pressing the button on the machine.
It was almost an anticlimax. It seemed that everyone knew it would work.
'All staff here will each receive a fifty thousand dollar net bonus, and our immense thanks,' Michael announced. He

wanted to keep this team together, and not have them taking their knowledge outside the company.

A big grin crossed Bill's face, and was quickly followed on the three screens.

'Thanks very much, can we make something else please?' Bill laughed.

His laughter instantly broke the atmosphere in the room, and they all congratulated one another.

'When can we complete production?' asked Rui.

'We are doing fifteen here, so will two weeks be OK?' asked Bill, still grinning like a Cheshire cat.

'That's fine,' Rui confirmed.

'How come it didn't make any noise?' Jessie asked.

'It's male, not female,' Bill replied.

Jessie hit him on the arm.

'No moving parts,' Bill told her. 'It's really simple, but to be honest, I still can't explain why it works.'

'Can you organise the next one off the line to go to Stephen, please,' Rui asked Jessie.

'Do you want it accompanied, by airfreight?' asked Jessie.

'No, send it with our own line. Just explain it is priority,' Rui replied.

'Collect the day after tomorrow?' Jessie asked Bill, and he agreed.

Rui and Michael thanked everyone again, and then left for Hampton.

On the way Michael confirmed the test results to Stephen, and told him when to expect the plant at Stansted airport. They would also ship one hundred thousand receivers, all set for two hundred and forty volts.

Back home, Jean and Brenda had cooked supper together. Michael and Rui explained to them about the test, and how they were shipping the stuff into the UK.

‘So when do we start?’ asked Jean.

‘It’s all up to Stephen Pederson now. He will keep in contact, but it’s up to him and his team to start the revolution,’ Michael replied.

‘I like that,’ smiled Rui. ‘The revolution of the earth starting the revolution against all the problems mankind faces.’

‘So how long do you think?’ Jean insisted.

‘Certainly less than a month, but we will see.’

After the meal, Michael ran Brenda back to Bob’s apartment.

‘Wouldn’t it be easier if you moved in with us at Hampton?’ he asked her.

‘Easier for what?’ she replied.

He could see what was in her mind, and laughed softly, but as they kissed goodnight, they both knew that their special moment was going to arrive soon.

Chapter Ten

They were still having breakfast when Stephen made contact. He had had what he laughingly called a brainstorming session with his team, and they had gone right through the programme together.

Everyone had then spoken, some at length, on the best way to launch free electricity. They had worked through all the possible pitfalls, and decided that a press launch by Stephen to coincide with the trials would reduce the risk of a backlash. Anyone who wanted to speak out against it would be speaking against the bulk of public opinion. This would take place as soon as the thirty plants were installed worldwide. They had already picked the areas, and would send the list so shipment could start as soon as they had confirmation from their contacts.

For the initial installations, they were recommending that the three pin plug was taken off, and the receiver attached. That would give the impression that it was a trial, and that the plug would be replaced if the experiment failed. They were going to contact enough qualified electricians to find fifteen who would be willing to take part in the experiment. They would not be told in advance, just asked to change a three pin plug in a customer's house for a receiver, in front of a television crew. The hope was that it could happen at six fifteen in the evening, prime news time, but they still had to check that out with the broadcasters. When all fifteen were ready, one for each television area, unknown to anyone else, the plant would be switched on. The effect should be spectacular. They also planned to have a couple of really remote outdoor sites boiling electric kettles with no electricity, just for effect.

Stephen and the team would then answer questions, just withholding details of the plant. They would also explain that three factories were working at full capacity, manufacturing the receivers, which would be delivered worldwide at zero cost. They intended to bring more factories online, and would welcome any aid from manufacturers with spare capacity who could help in production. Their costs would be met by the foundation who had first devised the scheme. They would also express the hope that anyone who tried to sell receivers for financial gain would be prosecuted.

'We also need to have some sort of regulation on the price electricians will charge to fit receivers,' Rui commented.

'We are working on suggesting that there is going to be a massive amount of work for electricians in the future as everyone, private, business and state will want to change from gas, oil, coal and wood to electric appliances. Anyone overcharging will be named, shamed and banned from future participation. We are sure the television companies will help with the whole package,' was the reply.

'I will have a word with the two plant manufacturers and get an exact timescale,' Michael promised. He knew it was stupid, but he really wanted to get this whole thing underway as soon as possible.

They promised to speak again later that day.

'Have we made any progress on lighting circuits yet?' Michael asked his parents.

'All the suggestions so far involve electricians, because people will still want to press the switch when they enter the room, but have the light come on in the normal place. The obvious way is to disconnect the lighting circuit and replace the connection with a receiver, but it is quite a task. We are still working on that one,' replied Rui. 'For new builds, receivers can replace the socket the bulb goes into, together with a remote control. The lights can then be put literally anywhere, as there will be no electrical circuits. We will sort it.'

'On world four?' Michael asked.

'All new builds, which does make life simple,' Rui replied.

Michael phoned the factory they had been to for the test, and spoke to Bill, asking about production. 'Now we have the first one up and running, it's all a lot easier than we thought. All the plans are laid out in the system, so it's really just the manual assembly, and we now know the best way to do that. To test, we just turn on, and if our TV comes to life, that's it.'

'So timescale?' Michael asked.

'Five a day in comfort, or fifteen if we work a twenty-four hour shift. After that bonus, everyone will happily do a full day,' was the reply. 'Ivan over at the other place is already two ahead of us.'

'Five a day is just fine,' Michael told him, 'I should be able to let you have shipping instructions soon.'

He thought about the proposed test day. 'Do you think we should go global from day one?' he asked his parents.

'Snap,' said Jean, 'when they mentioned the remote locations, I wondered if we should go for somewhere in the Sahara desert, or a yacht in mid Pacific.'

'I was on the same lines,' admitted Rui. 'I think if we supply all national television stations worldwide with receivers and tell our TV producers to link up worldwide for the broadcast, then they can replicate the show at home whenever it suits them best. I'll check with Stephen when he calls later today.'

'Those countries can also start manufacturing if they want. There are no patents, because as long as we give them away, the patent is worthless. As long as we cover the production costs, there shouldn't be a problem. But we know that there will be problems,' Michael added.

The next few days were a whirl of activity. Rui couldn't resist buying some electrical appliance manufacturers. He told Michael that he felt it necessary to keep making money as fast as his son gave it away. Brenda was feeling better every day, and the doctor had given her the all clear. The plants had all been completed and distributed. Tens of millions of receivers were now being produced and despatched daily to warehouses around the world. Tomorrow was the day of the launch, and Stephen or one of his colleagues was in touch almost constantly as the great day approached.

At lunchtime in the UK, on the day of the launch, Stephen was back on the phone. Michael could feel the excitement in his voice. 'Guess what?' and Michael knew straight away. Stephen had managed to move his hand. Only the tiniest amount, but he had done it himself. 'All the radio and TV channels are buzzing here. We have really caught their imagination. Elsie sends her love. She thinks that you are the nicest man on earth.'

Michael smiled. He knew that was not what it should all be about, but he still loved to help.

The television news in the US carried pieces referring to the experiment that was to take place in the UK that evening at 18.15 hours, as had been hoped. CNN would be taking coverage to see what it was all about.

Sure enough, they were all together for the big event. The electricians all went into action, while high on Ben Nevis, a young mountaineer sat with a kettle and a fridge. The screen went back to Stephen Pederson, surrounded by his team. 'And now for something really great.'

As they flashed round all the locations, in every one of them the electrical appliance was working, unconnected to the electricity supply. By the time they reached Ben Nevis, the kettle was coming to the boil, and when the fridge door was opened, on came the light. The mountaineer smiled as he explained, 'I do like cold milk in my tea.'

Back at base, one of Stephen's party was organising the questions from the media. The first one, quite naturally, was how it worked.

Stephen was the one to answer. 'As a lot of people know, the earth has a metal core, with magnetic poles at either end. It spins, which produces electricity in the form of power waves.

We have managed to capture those power waves, and push the power through the receivers you saw the electricians fit to the appliances.'

Question number two referred to how much power was produced. One of the team answered. 'Currently about one hundred times the maximum usage world wide.'

Question three, answered by a different member of the team, was how long it would last. 'As long as the sun exists, or more probably as long as the planet lasts.'

And the questions came, one after the other. The news programmes ran way past their allotted times, as the implications of what had been shown were announced, and CNN stayed with it all the way.

Summing up, the anchorman asked the team. 'Is it possible for the whole world to have free electricity and to run everything currently run?'

'Yes, and a lot more,' was the answer. 'All the places on earth without electricity or a generator can now run any appliance with a receiver. Put a fridge in the middle of the jungle, or the desert, and you can keep medical supplies and food at the correct temperature. You can run pumps for water, and boil that water without chopping down trees for firewood. Let's hope that all the nations on earth will let their people choose to take advantage.'

'I have been told that we will keep with this subject to answer viewer questions if we can.' The anchorman glanced at his watch. Most of the questions were fairly repetitive and went from some viewers who were worried that they were interfering with God's laws, to someone who wanted to know if Tesco would reduce its prices as it would save a lot on its electricity bills, and another gentleman who wanted to know if he should sell his shares in his electricity supplier. Mostly, people wanted to know how soon they could get receivers, and how they could get them fitted.

As the show eventually closed, the general consensus was that the whole thing had been a resounding success, and they closed with an old lady sat in front of an electric fire, wrapped in a blanket. 'Thank God and Stephen Pederson. I have been able to turn the fire back on.'
'I suggest we should all go out for a celebratory lunch,' suggested Rui, and the agreement was unanimous.
Before they left, Michael checked on Stephen. The team were still answering press questions, and were reconvening the next morning, when the Prime Minister and the leaders of the opposition parties were to join them.
'You mean they will actually be talking to one another? Opposing politicians? I thought we had worked one miracle, but that beats it all ends up,' they were all laughing as they left for the restaurant.
That evening, Michael had a date with Brenda at Seventy Three, just the two of them. They were both on top of the world from the success of the day. The meal and the wine were excellent, and two very happy people sat in the back of the limo on the way to Bob's apartment.
When they got there, Bob asked Michael to come in for a moment. He had the final list for the memorial service. 'Yes, your two favourites are coming, to save you looking right through.' Michael skimmed through, and recognised well over two hundred names on the list.
'Many thanks, Bob; it's a really great turn out.'
'What is it?' queried Brenda.
'Rui and Jean's memorial service guest list,' said Michael, handing it across to her.
'I keep forgetting they are supposed to be dead,' said Brenda, as her eyes grew wider and wider. 'When is it?'
'Two weeks time,' said Bob, 'will you be able to make it?'
'Of course I will,' said Brenda, and then flashed her eyes as they all burst out laughing.

On the way home to Hampton, Michael felt the world couldn't get any better.
Next morning the session with the politicians had finished when they met for breakfast. They had mentioned that they would be losing VAT income on free electricity, but were comforted by the fact that all the government controlled property would have no power bills eventually. They wanted to know about converting buildings the size of hospitals, and things like powering electric trains and the underground. They also agreed that they should get together with the electricity industry, and get all the staff that wanted to be retrained sorted out so they could get the whole country totally converted.
Stephen's group had not got much sleep as they answered questions from around the world. The thing that surprised Stephen most was that no one had mentioned fuel and transport, except to assume that lots of people would be buying electric cars. They thought the retraining, together with the electricians who would have more time to spare because they would have no rewiring and correcting faults in property, could get the project well under way.
There had been huge interest from around the world, most of it congratulatory. Concerns about different voltages were quelled, and although most countries had decided to see their own demonstrations that had been promised first, a lot of countries had asked about obtaining receivers, and all wanted plans for manufacturing, which were duly emailed. Major manufacturers wanted to know about rejigging their appliances to run on receivers. The call centre that they had used for the expected flood of calls had managed to answer over ninety nine per cent, and had mainly let through just governments and large corporations. There had been the cold shoulder from some of the countries who were not in favour of either the USA or Britain, but that had been expected.

Michael looked on these as a challenge, one that he was quite happy to handle personally, although he suspected that Stephen was probably the better diplomat.

Stephen thought that they should let some of the alterations, especially the large capital projects, get under way before they brought up the replacement for the internal combustion engine. He thought it would be good fun to invite along some of the top motoring experts to the meeting, but in the meantime, could they produce a replacement car so they could present it at the release to the media?

Michael agreed that would be fine. They already had one quite well developed in Malaysia, and were experimenting with two or three standard cars in which they had placed different sized batteries. He guessed that a couple of weeks would see something available.

Stephen went on, 'I think we will probably spend the next fortnight dealing with the fallout from the television programmes. We want to keep the momentum going on this, and encourage worldwide take-up. We are stressing the reduction in global warming that can be achieved from this one piece of scientific change, so at the moment we hold all the aces. I think we should be available, and will drop members gradually so they can take up their motor engineering posts. And I could move just a little bit more today. It's not so much that, which is absolutely wonderful, but the fact that there is suddenly hope instead of an ever-decreasing pinprick of light in the distance. Thanks again, Michael, to you and to all who helped me.'

'It was well worth it, just look at the first results we have achieved. Thank you very much, Stephen.' Michael now spoke to Stephen as a friend.

Michael asked his father if anything could be done to produce a 'special' car for the launch of the battery powered motors. 'If we take one of the lighter sports cars and replace all the bits and

pieces with say a six kilo battery pack, which is actually lighter than a normal battery, it should really go,' Rui replied.
'Let's see if we can get a Lotus prepared in the UK that we can show alongside the basic models.'
Michael agreed, and his father said he would get something sorted. He would also keep on top of the other cars to make sure they would be ready on time.
As reports came in from around the world that day it was obvious that cable free electricity was the huge success it was intended to be. There were still some sceptics, but they were in the tiniest of minorities. Among the bizarre pictures that arrived were a camel train trekking across the desert. One camel had what looked like a rusty old caravan fridge strapped to its side. The old man leading the caravan opened the door, on came the light, and he beamed at the camera, showing the only two teeth in his head. He took out a bottle of Coke and took a noisy swig. Some nomads in Mongolia were shown sitting round an old three bar electric fire in their tent. The interpreter said they had also arranged to trade a goat for an electric oven with two hot plates. The wife told the interpreter that she normally spent half the day collecting enough firewood for cooking and heating. Although both of these had obviously been stage managed by the television companies for maximum effect, they were still a joy to watch.
There were also new ideas coming in from across the globe. Heated outdoor clothing seemed to be one of the favourites, along with heated bandages, sleeping bags, and even carpets. Desalinisation plants were being talked about with renewed interest. Fresh water for virtually nothing was too good to be true. The ingenuity of man seemed to know no bounds as ideas bounced about the web, radio and television.
Michael took stock of what they had achieved so far. In maybe a couple of weeks they would release the car batteries topped up

by power waves. They would point out that the same batteries could replace the engine in anything. The shipping and aircraft industries could then work out their own futures, together with every other manufacturer of something that required power.

He could tick the boxes for cheap energy, where they had substituted free energy worldwide, nuclear power, which would become redundant, and global warming, which should now start to decline as carbon use was dramatically reduced. He checked the original list in his mind. Cut the population, stop greed, crime, poverty and illness.

He still wanted to tackle illness next. It was often linked to poverty, so would help in that direction as well. He knew from the reaction of the airline hostess, and Stephen, how much happiness could be created around the globe.

That evening he took Brenda out, and they sat again looking out over Long Island Sound. It was totally silent apart from a pair of owls calling to one another. They sat holding hands, both content to relax in each other's company.

Brenda came into his mind. 'Who do you most want to meet at the service?' Michael immediately thought of his favourite singer, whose hairstyle he had vaguely copied.

'Why did I expect him, although I admit he is brilliant on stage,' she was still in his mind.

'You have seen him on stage?' Michael blurted out loud.

'Twice,' Brenda replied.

'Remember one performance for me,' Michael thought.

Immediately, they were in the theatre as the rock legend took the stage. Brenda could remember the whole show, and for the first half Michael was enthralled at how good his hero was.

At the interval, Michael broke the connection. 'You can remember the whole show perfectly, Brenda. Who are you?'

'Does it matter?'

'Not really, it's just that Jean, Rui and I can do the same thing. Maybe there are others on earth that can do it as well.' Michael

knew that Brenda didn't really want to discuss it yet. 'Have we got time for the second half?'
Brenda nodded, and Michael was almost praying that the last number would be 'Always.'
Sure enough, the second half was even better than the first, and as the final notes of 'Always' left his mind, Michael opened his eyes, and looked at his fiancée. He had goose pimples everywhere, and the hairs were standing up on his arms.
This was truly paradise; sitting with the one he loved, having just watched that performance.
'Life just doesn't get any better,' he murmured.
'It will do,' giggled Brenda, 'I'll just make sure 'Always' is playing in the background at the same time.'
They kissed, long and passionate, and were both content with that for the moment. It was almost like waiting for Christmas, the expectation sometimes exceeding the actual moment.
On the way home, Michael mentioned that at some time he wanted Brenda to see inside his entire mind.
She replied that she needed to explore her whole mind first, so she could give it to Michael, but that she had to pluck up courage to do it. 'I am frightened of who I will turn out to be,' she whispered to him.
They kissed goodnight, and Michael made his way to Hampton. He puzzled over how quickly Brenda's brainpower was catching his own. Suddenly a chill struck him. What if she was from another planet, like his parents? He knew that somehow he would have to see her whole mind.
The days passed by with even more bizarre uses of how cable free electricity was being used. Massive projects were being completed, including hospitals, universities and factories going on to power waves one hundred per cent.
The cars were all on schedule, but Michael still kept nagging at the problem of sickness. He knew that once again he would have to seek outside help, but decided to put it on hold until the

battery project was up and running. They had agreed to take things one step at a time, and it was actually at the bottom of the list. The memorial service was to be this Sunday, and Wednesday had been chosen for launching the new and improved cars. Stephen had all the news channels on standby again, and they were already making sure that viewers would be watching their screens at eighteen fifteen GMT.

He had been through the service two or three times with Bob and Jessie. He purposely excluded his parents because they weren't supposed to be there, although he couldn't ignore some of the suggestions they had made. Christian Baddow was to make the first reading. He was the first truck driver that Rui had employed when the whole thing started. He was now managing director of that division. Six foot nine, with striking ginger hair, he knew virtually all the guests, and they had a similar affection for him to the one they had for Rui and Jean. Bob would also speak, and Michael would finish up. He knew he would struggle, as he always did at these types of service, which seemed crazy when there hadn't been a death, so he decided that short would be the best way for him.

Rui had sensed his struggle. 'Can I give you a few words of advice on the service?'

'Any help would be much appreciated,' Michael confessed.

'Nearly all of them think they are the greatest in their field,' Rui tilted his head. 'Some of them are. I was able to be successful because I gave them what they wanted, straight into their minds. A little peek told me how they most wanted to be admired. They believed that I held them in the highest regard for their music, voice, looks, whatever, sometimes all three. It's a huge boost to be told that you are loved, but if you can be convinced that you are loved, then you are really on a high. Any you meet before the service, just see what they want and give it to them. When you speak in the service, love them all.'

'All three hundred?' Michael queried.

'You could do a crowd of eighty thousand in the Giants Stadium with no problems. If you told them to clap, boo, stand up, or buy popcorn, then that's what they would do. Three hundred will be a doddle.'

Michael shivered. 'How?'

'The same as any other,' his father replied. 'In your mind see the whole crowd, from inside or out it doesn't matter, and let them know what you want. You don't even have to be there. Let's give it a try,' he turned on the television. 'There must be a game on somewhere, here, this one will do.'

There was a minor football game being screened, with just two or three thousand watching.

'Look at the area in your mind, taking in all the ground, even though you can't see it. See all the fans.'

Michael did as he was instructed. 'Now, whatever you want.'

Michael thought for a few seconds. Something simple. He pictured the crowd waving, and sure enough it happened, just for a few seconds. The commentator was puzzled. He asked his co-commentator what they had missed, as everyone had waved. They decided it must have been pre-arranged for a particular time.

'You can make them do anything,' Rui laughed, 'but never get carried away.'

Suddenly Michael realised his worry about speaking at the service had been greatly reduced. If he could control the crowd, he should be fine.

Sunday quickly arrived, and he went with Bob, Shauna, Jessie and Brenda. They had agreed before that it should be a service of happiness and humour, and had asked all the guests to dress up, avoiding black, to smile, and really enjoy the occasion.

People were already gathering on the lawns outside, small groups chatting to one another. Michael noticed that there seemed to be an abundance of large gentlemen standing around, chatting to no one, and only watching. He assumed it came with the fame. They wandered towards the doors.

'Hi, Bob,' came a voice from behind them. They all turned as one of the greatest rock musicians in the world walked across the grass. He shook hands with Bob, and kissed Jessie on both cheeks. 'Still as sexy as ever, I see.'

'You'll get your chance one day,' Jessie smiled at him.

'Can't wait,' was the reply.

Michael suddenly realised that he had stopped breathing.

Before he could think he found himself shaking hands with a superstar, and realised that that was exactly what he had sent into his mind.

'Hello, it's really good to meet you, I'm so glad you could make it,' was his rather stilted opener.

'Wouldn't have missed it for the world. We all really loved Jean and Rui. They just seemed to know every one of us.'

'He is really genuine, and means what he says,' Michael was thinking freely.

'My God,' he exclaimed, 'you really are their son. They could both do that.'

'What's that?' Michael asked innocently, his brow slightly puzzled. He was starting to regain some control.

'You don't have to talk, I just know you are one of the good guys,' he shook Michael's hand again. 'This time I am really pleased to meet you.'

'So this is Michael. Don't keep him all to yourself.' Michael knew the voice, and turned to be face to face with one of the all time greats. Both singer and actress, she was so perfectly beautiful. How could you get that voice and that face all in the same package? She turned her cheek just a fraction, and he felt her mind inviting him. A peck on each cheek, and she looked him straight in the eyes. 'It would be oh so easy to fall in love with you,' she smiled.

'Thanks, it's really special that you could come,' Michael said quietly.
'And this is your fiancé,' she turned to Brenda, shaking her hand. 'You are one lucky lady.'
'I know, but thanks for confirming it,' said Brenda. They both laughed, as they seemed to share a private joke.
The megastar turned and spoke to both Bob and Jessie.
Michael looked at Brenda. 'I can see inside her mind,' was the thought, 'just like you.'
'This is becoming surreal,' thought Michael, 'two down out of three hundred.'
'It's probably best if we go in, then hopefully people will follow,' said Bob, glancing at his watch.
Michael had one last look round, recognising most of the faces, and then followed his small group in.
They were in the front row, and Michael was too embarrassed to look round, thinking it would somehow not be fitting.
The service proceeded as planned. Christian and Bob both spoke well, and suddenly it was Michael's turn.
He ascended the short flight of steps, and looked out across the sea of faces. There was his hero, and for a couple of seconds he caught his breath. Regaining his composure, he smiled and the thought went out, 'Rui and Jean loved you, and I know why. You are talented, wonderful, honest people, and that is why I love you as well.' There was a slight stir among the crowd as he looked down on them.
'My parents were unusual.' There was total silence. 'They were unusual because they believed this world of ours deserved to be a better place, and they were prepared to do something about it. You are all lucky, because you have the talent to make people feel better. You can perform, and set free the magic that everyone needs to lift them above the everyday humdrum of life. They didn't have that talent, but it didn't stop them trying. In

twenty five years they donated over two hundred billion pounds to good causes.' There was a small gasp as the figure hit home. 'Obviously they cannot be here today, but if they were, I would say thanks, Mum and Dad. You done good. You'll be a hard act to follow, but Brenda and I will give it our best shot. Thank you all for being their friends.'

'Clap and holler, cheer and shout,' thought Michael, and they did. It was just like the end of a performance by any one of them. He descended the steps to thunderous applause, and joined Brenda. Together they led the way back outside. As they walked Michael thought again of his hero, and the greatest female country and western singer, who was also there. 'Please find me outside,' was the request, and they both did. Within five minutes Michael was talking to the two of them. He found it easy to talk to them, as the feelings he sent out were genuine, and they felt them and knew they were true. It made life so much easier when you speak face to face and know that the other person is telling the truth.

He promised to see the next performances by both of them, and agreed to meet them back stage after the show.

Making their excuses, Michael and Brenda did the rounds. It was a mind-blowing time for both of them, as all the celebrities found them so easy to chat to. Eventually people started drifting away until just the five of them were left.

'They responded to you two just like they did to Jean and Rui,' Jessie had really enjoyed the afternoon. 'I think I spoke to everyone, and they were all relaxed and pleased to be here. I think I guessed who your favourite was, Brenda.'

Brenda smiled. 'She is my favourite of all time. Every time I hear 'I will always love you' I get goose bumps.'

'It was really nice of her to come and talk to you,' said Jessie, a slight frown crossing her face.

Michael squeezed Brenda's hand. 'If you can do it, then so can I,' she thought.

Jessie came into their thoughts. 'Both of you asked your favourites to come and see you. I felt it happen. I didn't realise you could do that, Brenda.'
Brenda shrugged. 'I guess it's being around Michael so much.' But the three of them all felt that wasn't the case.
Later that evening, Michael and Brenda sat watching the lights twinkling over the Sound. 'At some stage I will have to find out about my father,' Brenda felt sad.
'What do you want to find out?' Michael asked.
'I don't know, I always feel afraid when I think about it, as if he was someone who was wrong. I need to know, but I also don't want to find out.'
Then leave it until you are sure you want to know,' was all Michael could suggest.
On Monday morning they were getting very close to the battery launch, and they all knew that life would now get a lot bumpier. A lot of countries and companies would see their wealth disappear before their eyes.
'I'm glad Stephen was the choice. I can't imagine anyone who could attack him in any way,' Jean was pondering on the problems.
'I can think of a few who will speak without thinking,' Rui was wistful.
'We could always alter what they say,' Michael looked for the easy option.
'Don't always look for the easy way out. It sometimes doesn't pay dividends. I think the rest of the world will be the best judge.' Rui was sure.
Stephen came on the phone, and Michael felt, or imagined that he was just a little bit better. 'We are all set for Wednesday afternoon. The show is coming from Silverstone racetrack. We have our usual team, plus three guys from one of the motoring programmes. We are already testing the Lotus, and the results look good. Our car from Malaysia is being air freighted in today.

We have converted two cars, one artic, and a bus. They are all at Silverstone already. The TV stations are going to run the same formula as before. Free electricity was such a huge success that they can't resist this one.'

'Thanks very much, we are all looking forward to seeing the results.' Michael was impressed with how Stephen and his team were able to organise things so well in the timescale available.

They kept in touch throughout the rest of Monday and Tuesday, and suddenly it was Wednesday. They finished lunch, and then settled down to watch the evening news from London.

At 18.15 GMT, the screen moved to Silverstone, where Stephen Pederson was waiting to greet them. He was turned slightly away from the camera, and very slowly turned his head the two inches he needed to look into the lens. At the same time he lifted his hand and touched his cheek.

'He was keeping that secret very well,' Rui remarked.

'Continuing the progress from our last programme, today we are looking at modifications to transport,' the deep voice opened the show. 'We hope you will find it very interesting.'

The view changed to outside, where the three mainstays of the television motoring show were talking to some mechanics.

One of Stephen's team took over the microphone. 'We have invited these experts to test three cars for us today. For those of you who have not seen their programme, it is devoted to the car. We have altered the cars for the better, or so we think. Gentlemen, please take your seats, do one circuit and let us know your thoughts. By the way, they are all automatic. Just push the accelerator.'

A camera and microphone inside each car gave the reactions of the drivers. There were various comments from the three, but the opinion was that they were no different to normal, just automatic instead of manual.

As they came to a stop, three puzzled drivers got out.

'Can't see any improvement at all, except maybe a bit quicker,' commented the leader.
'Just the same as before?' asked the team member.
'Exactly, except for the total silence. Are they all electric?' asked the quiet one.
Mechanics opened the boots and bonnets, and the cameras looked in.
'That battery was driving that car?' the leader asked. 'It's smaller than the normal battery you would use to start it. So you have invented a car that runs from a smaller battery. That is clever, but I expected something more than that.'
'That battery will retail at less than two hundred pounds, runs on power waves, and should last over fifty years,' the team member played his trump card.
The silence was deafening.
Eventually the small one spoke. 'You have just changed the world again, so how does it work?'
'Once the battery is activated, it is charged by power waves every time it is not using its full power. Pull up at traffic lights, and it starts charging. A full charge will take it over one thousand miles, although in effect it will go for ever, as you would never drive that long without a stop,' the team member replied.
'So two hundred quid for fifty years is about four pounds a year for fuel, drive as far as you like?' the leader of the three looked impressed.
'Put more batteries in and get more power, or move bigger loads,' was the reply. 'Try out the Lotus, but be careful as it has three batteries. Maybe you two would try out the truck and the bus.'
The format was the same, with the reactions live on screen.
The Lotus driver was in his element. The reduction in weight and the increase in power gave him the ride of his life, and took

him off the track three times. The other two were less spectacular, but just as impressed.

'Ships, planes and trains will use bigger battery packs, and recharge only when they are in dock, in a station, or at the airport. In an emergency, they can recharge while travelling, but not normally,' they were told.

Suddenly the Lotus driver was laughing. 'You haven't just changed the world; you have invented a new one. We now don't need any manufactured power. No fossil fuels, no nuclear power stations.'

The quiet one looked delighted. 'You will have made even more friends than before.'

'And a few more enemies, I think,' the small one added darkly.

The scene returned to the studio, and Stephen Pederson. 'Again, there is no reason why this new piece of technology cannot be used worldwide. The benefit for global warming is total, as the carbon footprint will be zero. The arguments over nuclear power can stop, as it will be redundant. Costs will be reduced dramatically. On the downside, most countries will have to look elsewhere for taxation, and there will have to be massive retraining in the carbon fuel industries. I believe the gains will outweigh the costs.'

The programme then followed the same format as before, with a general discussion followed by questions and answers.

Rui, Jean, Brenda and Michael felt just a little deflated. 'I suppose it was too much to ask, that there would be the same euphoria as for the last one,' said Rui. 'We could almost predict the result from what happened before.'

'It is almost as if something bigger, more revolutionary was expected,' said Michael, 'and no one even remarked that Stephen had actually moved his arm. That on its own would have been a remarkable event.'

'It is massive,' said Brenda, 'everyone just needs to start working out exactly what it means. The end of the world has been put on hold. Give them a few days to work it all out for themselves.'

Michael made contact with Stephen, and congratulated him on the presentation.' Has anyone asked how you moved your arm?' he asked.

'You are the first one,' Stephen confirmed.

'So how is the back overall?'

'Gradually gaining in strength, as you said it would. Still feels marvellous to have hope.' Again Michael thought he sounded better, but was sure it was wishful thinking rather than fact.

'What is your opinion on today's effort?' Michael asked.

'The media are incredibly supportive, probably more so than before. They have grasped the global warming issue more quickly than anyone else, but I suppose they have been leading the push to do something in the past, so it is only to be expected,' Stephen told him.

'Have any problems been made apparent from oil rich nations, and oil companies?'

'No,' Stephen replied,' not a word, which is surprising. I believe that for the first time they are thinking before speaking. From the way the press have reacted, I believe at the moment they would give a really hard time to anyone who objected. I suppose the moans will come, but I think we have all the ammunition we need to take them down.'

'Please ask the team to stick with it to try and ensure that the benefits spread round the world. If we can get desalination coupled with cheap to run agricultural equipment, I'm sure lots of areas will be able to feed themselves in the future. They will also be able to use reduced transport costs to move any excess production,' Michael was starting to feel a bit more optimistic on the results of today's broadcasts. 'Hopefully the next project for the team will be illness. If you could start thinking about the possibility of curing virtually all the illness in the world, I would be grateful.'

‘’I already have,’ came the deep voice, and Stephen put down the phone.

Chapter Eleven

'Greed, crime and poverty are the next three on the list,' Michael wanted to push ahead, 'but I would like to start with illness.'

'Then you really need to start thinking it through,' his father responded. 'So far we have taken one concept, power, and given it freely to the world. How many different types of illness are there, and how many different types of doctors would we need to treat them? It is the largest of all the projects. I will see what I can find out from our friends.'

Michael felt frustrated as he wanted to dive straight in, but the more he thought about it the bigger the problem became. The probability was that individual types of illness would have to be treated separately. He realised he should wait until he had a response from Stephen and his father. He nodded his agreement.

Knowing everything was on track as far as power was concerned, he checked with Bob and Jessie that they were happy with everything and decided it would not be a problem if he took Brenda over to see Cambridge.

She was delighted at the idea, although Shauna insisted that she had no clothes suitable for the trip, and they would have to go shopping. Michael managed to organise flights for the next day. When he spoke to Mary, she said that it would be perfect as she had business in London that day, and would collect them from Heathrow.

The flight was uneventful, and Mary was very pleased to see them as they came through the barriers. Michael drove, while Mary and Brenda chatted away in the back like mother and daughter. It was Brenda's first time in England and she was amazed at the difference to America. They were in Grundisburgh by seven thirty that evening, and Peter was already cooking supper for them. The conversation was relaxed, with the main topic being what Stephen Pederson had managed to organise. They were very impressed with what had been achieved already.

Peter said he wanted to catch the news headlines at ten, and put the TV on. Michael glanced up as the programme started, and was sickened to hear the story of a nursery worker who had committed acts against children and babies so vile that they could not be described on television. She had then shared the images she had taken on the internet. Two men were also in custody. He could not understand the depth of the depravity that had occurred, and missed the rest of the headlines as his mind focused on what had happened.

The four of them discussed how such a thing could happen, and what could be done to stop it happening in the future. They concluded that it was a very difficult subject to deal with, and Mary and Peter went to bed just after eleven.

'Come here,' said Brenda, holding her arms open. Michael turned and kissed her. 'You can't do everything, you know,' came into his mind. He broke the kiss. 'Sorry, it's just something like that is so horrendous. There must be something we can do.'

'It's crime, so it is on the list. Maybe not the type of crime we were thinking about, but crime none the less,' Brenda spoke very gently. 'We cannot look into the brain of everyone to see if they are fit to live here.'

'Just say that we could,' Michael was thinking out loud. 'Say we could somehow know if people were evil or not? No, the size of the problem makes it impossible.'

'So logically, if a problem is too big, then we reduce the size of the problem.' Brenda flicked her eyebrows. 'Money is the root of all evil,' she sang a snatch from the old song.

'So getting rid of money is your answer,' Michael did not sound impressed.

'Getting rid of cash might be a better way to put it.'

Brenda hinted at what she was thinking of. 'Drugs, prostitution, muggings, most robberies were for cash, or to steal something that could be sold for cash. That must take up most of the time that the police and social services have.'
'Plus all the income that people never declare for tax, and all the benefits that are fraudulently claimed. Our countries are in huge deficits, and need every cent they can get hold of,' Brenda was still on American money.
'So we would replace cash with……'
'Electronic purses,' Brenda sounded as if it was the easiest thing in the world. 'That's how they first did it before. Rui and Jean were talking about the old days, and that was how they first dealt with cash. Eventually they were discarded when everyone had open minds.'
'Of course they did. You could download money from the bank, or anyone else, then spend it just like a debit card,' Michael remembered bits from the minds of his parents.
'So somehow we need to have a record of the transactions. Put a future date on the purse, so that it has to download, say every month. It would be no more hassle than going to the cash point, or collecting a pension from the post office,' Brenda could see clearly what they needed.
'And who would have access to the information?'
'Obviously the taxman, social services, police, in fact any government department that needed to know someone's income. Civil liberties would strongly oppose it, and it would be a brave government who brought it in,' Brenda knew what was needed, but could also see problems.
'Governments are not a problem, I can fix them,' Michael's brain was stepping up a gear.
'You are starting to think you are God,' his fiancée replied with a smile.
Michael laughed. 'I know, but we have to do something. The United Kingdom would be a brilliant place to start, because we

have a currency limited to an island. Everyone has to pay their cash into a bank, as they did when we went decimal, but instead of new currency they get an electronic purse. So everyone has to have a bank account. Visitors to the country would change their currency for an electronic purse instead of pounds, and exchange it back when they go.'

'Are you sure that you can get the government to impose it?'

'That's not a problem. I just need to get some prototypes for private individuals and businesses. All it will do is replace cash, so it's not really something new,' Michael felt confident.

'If you really want to hit hard, you need to do it very quickly from announcement to completion. Any cash people don't want to bank for whatever reason has to become worthless.'

'There will be lots of cash that misses the cut-off, like people being abroad, but that can be dealt with on a one-off basis. I really can't see any problems that will stop it,' Michael was nodding to himself.

'I think we may see a mass exodus of criminals from the UK.'

'Then that will prove it works, and I can then persuade other governments to go down the same route. After all, we are trying to change the whole world,' Michael shrugged.

They both smiled, and kissed again, this time with more feeling. Other thoughts were banished as they concentrated on the pure pleasure that they enjoyed. Still the time was not right, and they went their separate ways to bed.

Next morning Michael took Brenda for a walk round the village while Peter and Mary made breakfast. She loved the old timbered buildings, especially the ones with haystacks on the roof, as she described the thatched cottages. They collected a paper from Forge Stores, and wandered back home.

Over breakfast, Michael brought up the main subject of last night's news. 'Would you bring back hanging?' he asked. 'No,' was the unanimous reply. 'Say someone murdered Mary?' Michael spoke very slowly and softly to Peter.

‘I’d kill the bastard personally.’ Peter exploded.
‘So you are against capital punishment, but not totally,’ Michael looked at Peter.
‘I guess I am like most people. Don’t get involved until it becomes personal.’
‘And the children you teach?’ Michael persisted.
‘Yes, I guess you are right, but the government will never vote for it,’ Peter was certain of that fact.
‘Just a thought,’ said Michael, ‘prisons overcrowded and the costs of locking someone up for life when we have no money. Just a thought.’
They left for Cambridge soon after breakfast, as Michael had arranged to see Stephen at ten thirty. He was already looking a lot better, and moving a bit more every day. He explained how far they had got with power and batteries, and was genuinely surprised at the lack of opposition to the schemes. The main feeling was that most oil would be running out in about twenty years, which would give them time to replace oil-based items. The longer reserves would give them the extra time for items that were difficult to make from another source. There would still be some small-scale production of fuel for museums, old cars and motorbikes, but it would be insignificant.
Michael asked for his thoughts on illness. The team had been thinking about it, but had only really got as far as suggesting that they tackled the problems one at a time. Start with the biggest killers, and work your way slowly down the list. They were still devoting time to it, however. Michael and Stephen thanked each other, and Brenda left with her fiancé for his college.
They were all very pleased to see him, explaining that he could return whenever he wanted. Over lunch, his Principal couldn’t help remarking on the coincidence of Stephen Pederson asking for time off for Michael, then launching a programme that must be costing someone billions of pounds. Michael laughed. ‘I suppose stranger things have happened.’

'Whatever,' he was told, 'it's the most fantastic scheme ever. If you have anything to do with it, we are all mighty proud of you.'
'That would be a lovely thought,' was all Michael said.
He showed Brenda around his college, and the sights of Cambridge. She was thrilled at what must be one of the most beautiful places in the world.
Mary had managed to book a table at their local pub, 'The Dog', for that evening, and the food and service were as brilliant as ever. They all had slightly too much to drink, and really enjoyed the atmosphere. Next morning Michael asked Peter who he thought would win the next election. 'God save us from any of them,' was his reply, 'how do we nearly always end up with idiots running the country?'
'You already know the answer,' Michael winked, 'if you can't do it, teach it. If you can't teach it, be a politician.'
'Then I suppose I am lucky I can teach, if the only other option would be to enter politics,' Peter laughed.
Brenda asked if they could have another walk round the village before they left. As they strolled, she asked if Michael intended to go ahead with his plan for electronic purses, and he confirmed that he would.
'Then would it be better for us to be over here than in America when you start?' she asked.
'Probably, I could cope from New York, but here would be a lot easier. Why do you ask?' he queried.
'I think it's absolutely stunning over here. Mary was showing me some photos of The Cotswolds, Cornwall, The Lake District and the Scottish Highlands. I would love to see them all,' she told him.
'Then see them all you shall. Talking of stunning, let's go look in the church,' Michael took her hand as they crossed the road and walked up the path to the church. As they entered he said 'look up at the roof, all the angels.'
Carved wooden angels were at the ends of all the roof beams.

'What a place to be married,' said Brenda, 'all those angels looking after you. When they talk about a marriage made in heaven, I guess this is what they have in mind.'
Michael smiled at her. 'Shall I put this one on top of the list?'
'Can I still wear white?' Brenda blushed as she asked.
'Of course you can,' he squeezed her hand.
Mary insisted on coming to Heathrow, and with Michael driving, the two ladies again sat in the back. Brenda told Mary how beautiful the church was. 'I know,' she replied, 'we were married there.'
'We are thinking of doing the same,' Brenda admitted.
'Let me know when you have a date, and I will organise it with the vicar. She is really lovely. Where do you think we should have the reception?'
'I will have to leave that up to you and Michael, as I have no idea.'
At Heathrow, they said their goodbyes, but not before Mary had again told Michael how lucky he was to have met Brenda.
'Don't you mean how lucky she was to have met me?' he ventured.
Mary nipped his arm. 'No I don't. I just hope you realise how lovely she is.'
Michael was suitably admonished. 'I do, I really do.'
Back in New York they checked how things were going in the office, and then returned to Hampton.
'How were things in the UK?' Rui asked.
'Fine,' Michael replied, 'we saw Stephen and the team. They are making progress worldwide, with very little opposition. Everyone seems to have taken the changes to heart. The university are happy with my continued absence. They hinted that I may have something to do with Stephen, and said they would be very proud if it was correct. Mary and Peter are well, and Brenda has been discussing wedding plans with Mary.

‘And I thought she was going to marry you!’ Jean laughed, ‘have you thought about a date yet?’
‘No,’ Brenda replied, ‘it was because Grundisburgh church is so lovely, with all the angels looking over you, and that was where Mary and Peter were married.’
Rui looked a bit sterner. ‘I’m afraid that is one of the things we will have to miss. Besides the obvious reason, we will be returning to the old planet next week. There is no problem at all in you two taking over from us, but now that you are getting closer to directly interfering in the politics of the world, it will be best for us to be at a distance. The chances are that the longer we stay the more likely it is that we will be recognised. All the legalities of the crash and the deaths have been completed, and you now have total control of the way forward. We thought that giving you to Mary and Peter so that you would have the upbringing of someone born on this planet, but with our knowledge was the hardest thing we have ever done, but now having really got to know you, leaving is going to be even harder.’
Michael swallowed hard, and didn’t trust himself to speak.
Jean put her arms round him. ‘Don’t forget about open minds. Anytime, anywhere, you can enter our minds. You can see what we see, so we will never be far apart, and every day we will do the same. At some time in the future you will leave this planet, by which time we will be on planet three, four, or whatever. We are already looking forward to seeing you again.’
Michael nodded. He had known this time would arrive, and hugged his mother. ‘When do you go?’
‘Wednesday morning. One of the transporters will land just after eleven.’
‘Whereabouts?’ Michael queried.
‘About sixty miles north of here. It’s the same site as before,’ Jean replied.
‘How is it not detected, something that large?’

Rui replied, 'When the freighters were used for transporting very expensive commodities, they needed as much protection as they could get. They developed a system that puts a sort of photo taken from one side of the ship onto the other side, so if there was just darkness behind, you saw all darkness. In effect, anyone looking would see nothing. If you knew where to look, then you could spot the fake, but by that time it was long gone. Coupled with detection jamming devices, it is pretty invisible to everything. There is a bit of damage done where it lands, but nothing much. One or two sites around the world have been found, but nothing has ever been seen.'
'Rendlesham forest in Suffolk?' Michael queried.
'That is one,' Rui agreed. 'Anyway, to cheer us up, tonight we are eating at Antonios. It has a very good reputation.'
The days passed quickly and Michael spent most of them refining the plan he had for the United Kingdom. Rui and Jean said their goodbyes to Bob and Jessie. On Wednesday morning Michael and Brenda drove his parents for their final trip on the planet. The freighter had arrived one minute before them. Final goodbyes were said, and Michael managed to hold back the tears until the ship had gone.
Brenda kissed his tears. 'You swapped them for me.'
Michael managed a smile. 'Then I did the right thing,' he whispered.
That evening, for the first time, they were alone at the house in Hampton. Everything was going to plan on both sides of the Atlantic, so the decision was made to start the next phase of the programme in England.
Brenda was looking forward to the sightseeing. 'Will we have much spare time to see around the country?'
'Yes, once I have started the ball rolling, it will only need some little tweaks. Production of electronic purses has started, and conversion kits for tills have already been tested. There may be

a few minor points to start out, but of course, Rui and Jean will always be there to help.'

Michael slipped his arm round her waist.

Brenda turned slowly towards him, and they kissed long and tenderly.

Suddenly, all their defences dropped, and their minds merged. Each of them knew what was happening, and what the other wanted to happen. It was like being directed in a slow motion play for two people, except that they were the directors as well. They held back, and held back, but when the play reached its climax, the thrill, passion and intensity of feeling they both felt was doubled as each of them experienced their own and their partners orgasm. As the curtain dropped, they relaxed in each other's arms. It was some time later that they went upstairs to share a bed for the first time since they had met.

Next morning they made love again, and Michael knew they were right for one another. Their open minds meant he could experience everything that Brenda felt, and she could also feel exactly everything he felt. Whatever each of them wanted from the other was provided, and the intensity increased and increased until that final moment of doubled pleasure exploded within them. They both felt totally at ease with each other. The trust that open mind creates was already there for them.

Michael had felt the power of her brain. He picked out an extremely difficult algebraic equation, and put it into her mind. Instantly she had the correct answer.

'Your brain is far beyond any that started life on this planet,' he challenged.

'I know. So did Rui and Jean. Sometimes I'm a bit frightened by it, but at other times it seems to bring me closer to you. I feel that I am closer to being your equal, and that gives me an advantage over other women who you may find more attractive than me.'

Michael laughed. 'Still that tiny bit of self doubt.'

‘I think that came from my marriage, Henry made it so difficult.’
‘You never have to doubt me, you only have to look into my mind,’ Michael looked her in the eyes.
‘I know, I’m just being silly. I should have no doubts.’
‘I’m glad you have. Every time you talk about it you wrinkle your nose just the tiniest little bit, and that is the sexiest thing I have ever seen,’ admitted Michael.
‘Like this,’ laughed Brenda, wrinkling her nose.
‘Just like that,’ Michael grabbed her.
‘So every time I want you, I just do this?’ again she wrinkled her nose.
They made love again, but this time laughing all the way through.

Chapter Twelve

Back in England on Friday, they booked into their hotel suite in London. Parliament was about to return from the summer break, and Michael wanted to get the plan under way from day one. Peter had managed to obtain a pair of tickets to the visitor's gallery for the first day of the new session.

That evening they had tickets for the stage show Mama Mia, and like the rest of the audience came out of the theatre with huge smiles on their faces. They ate late in Chinatown, and after a couple of drinks, a very tired pair hit the pillows.

Next morning they had breakfast served in their room, and while they ate, Michael went to work. First he contacted the Prime Minister, suggesting that a temporary political truce with his opponents for the sake of trying to resolve the financial problems that still beset the country as a result of the banking crisis was a good idea. Then on to the leaders of the other main parties, suggesting the same thing, and asking them to call the Prime Minister, and arrange a meeting that afternoon at Westminster. Michael thought half past two would be good.

They wandered in the morning sunshine through Piccadilly Circus and along to Trafalgar Square, arriving at Horse Guards Parade in time for the changing of the guard. Brenda's camera was working overtime. Then on down to Westminster Bridge and across the river for a ride on the London Eye. They grabbed a quick lunch, and were back over the bridge by two thirty.

Leaning with his back to the river, Michael picked up the three minds. The Prime Minister was the first to speak. 'I believe we need to come to some sort of agreement on the way forward if we are to gain control of the country's finances.' The opposition figures nodded in agreement. 'Would you both be in favour of getting rid of cash, and substituting it with an electronic system that we will be able to monitor?'

'Exactly what I had been thinking of,' both his companions

spoke as one, and the leader of the opposition went on, 'I believe a system has already been tested in Malaysia, called the electronic purse.'

'That's the one I'm in favour of,' his companions echoed.

'Apparently there is already sufficient kit available for it to cover the whole of the country,' one of them suggested.

The Prime Minister continued. 'We need to bring in a law next week that everyone in the UK has to have a bank account, so that their cash can be paid into it. All bank accounts, credit cards, and investments will then be open to scanning by the civil service, whether it is the tax office, social services, or the police.'

This was agreed upon.

'Once that is completed, then we must act swiftly to swap cash for electronic purses. Any Sterling cash not deposited in time will be subject to intense scrutiny.' Once again the Prime Minister's companions nodded.

'I suggest that we re-enable post offices to handle bank accounts, and give everyone who has no bank account at all say a one hundred pound deposit when they open the account. I will bring this up on Monday if we are all agreed?'

The three of them agreed on the course of action, and were convinced that it was correct.

Michael and Brenda spent the rest of the weekend sightseeing, and Brenda voted Windsor Castle as her favourite place. The weather was kind to them, and they were the typical tourist couple.

On Monday, they were there for the opening of Parliament, and took their places in the visitors' gallery.

After the ceremonial opening, and while the chamber was still full, the speaker rose and asked for silence for the Prime Minister. All eyes were on him as he rose, 'during the recess I spoke with the honourable leaders of the other two main parties, and we have agreed that there is too much cash being kept insecurely in houses, especially by older people, providing a temptation to criminals. In the past this has often resulted in violence towards those people, sometimes for quite meagre sums. We have agreed that everyone in the United Kingdom should have access to at least one bank account. Anyone without a bank account will be denied access to any services provided by government. The post offices will be able to act on behalf of the banks, and everyone who has no bank accounts will have one hundred pounds credited to their new account, tax free, by the government, as long as the account is opened by Friday week. We feel that the sum of money involved is relatively small compared to the safety that will be brought to our people.'

Michael was already working, and everyone was silent until the Prime Minister sat down, then they all joined in the cheering and clapping.

The motion was proposed, and everyone filed out in order to register his or her vote for the ayes. No one was surprised by what had happened. Everything seemed perfectly natural.

Brenda looked at her fiancé. 'So far so good.'

'It's a start,' agreed Michael, but I will just need to persuade a few of the financial and political commentators. I think it should be easy compared to the next phase.'

By the time of the television early evening news, everyone who mattered was on board. Even the supporters of civil liberties were convinced that the benefits outweighed the downside. People were asked to start opening their new accounts from Wednesday onwards.

There was the inevitable rush to take up the offer on Wednesday, but the banks and post offices up and down the country had all been primed on Monday afternoon, and they had a full complement of staff to handle the situation. Checks were made to confirm that applicants were truthful about not having another account already, and a second check was made before the one hundred pounds was credited to the account a week later. A number of people who tried to cheat the system by attempting to claim two lots of one hundred pounds were swiftly prosecuted, which deterred others from attempting anything similar.

Brenda and Michael passed a busy bank in Bourton on the Water, and smiled as they continued their sightseeing tour. From the Cotswolds, they went on to Devon and Cornwall, all the time keeping tabs on the political situation, and making little adjustments to the thoughts of anyone protesting about the scheme. By now, Brenda was as adept as Michael at the process. They spent a couple of Nights in Ilfracombe, and loved the walks along the cliffs, then went on to Woolacombe, which Brenda thought had the loveliest beach she had ever seen. They walked the length of the two mile beach and ate a lunch of cod and prawn fishcakes outside the little café at the end. They were delicious.

They came back along the south coast of Cornwall, and then spent three nights in Lyme Regis before making their way back to London. By Friday evening, the government estimate was that there were less than four million people in the UK who did not have a bank account, plus an unknown quantity of illegal immigrants for whom they had no records. Michael commented that they would soon all come to the surface, or emigrate.

On the Saturday, Michael again called the three main party leaders together. They were pleased with the success of the scheme so far, and the Prime Minister then suggested stage two. The Malaysian company who produced the electronic purses had eighty million in warehouses across the UK, plus another twenty million slightly larger ones for business use. There were enough replacement ATM machines that would download into electronic purses instead of paying out cash, and at the same time upload the transactions already stored in the purse. He suggested that the ones for business use and the new ATMs be distributed in the early part of next week, so that they would be ready for the following Monday. Seventy million of the others would be sent to banks and post offices. On that Monday they would again ask the members of parliament to vote. This time it would be the more controversial end of cash. The three of them agreed it was the way forward.

Michael and Brenda went north, stopping off at Stratford on Avon on their way through the Peak District and into the Lake District. Again the weather was kind to them, and as they travelled they both kept in touch with the electronic purse situation. The theory was implanted that it was just a test for an alternative and more secure way of paying for goods and services. Once again, critics were persuaded to change their opinions.

By the weekend they were again back in their London Hotel, and the three leaders were at their now regular meeting. They went through the speeches they were to make on Monday, and were satisfied that the chamber would be as full as possible, and that they had covered all events. To emphasise that it was a cross party agreement, the leader of the Liberal Democrats would make the opening speech.

On Monday the press were trying to guess what the next announcement would be. They knew that nearly all the MPs would be there, but didn't link it to the electronic purses. They were, after all, just part of a trial.

The speaker asked for silence, and the leader of the Liberal Democrats rose. Michael and Brenda were there to watch.

'Honourable members, today I propose that we take the largest step ever to improve the way we tackle crime in this country. Ever since cash was invented, it has been by far the largest source of criminal activity in the world. We are fortunate that the United Kingdom is virtually an island, and that we have retained a separate currency to the rest of the world. Today I propose that this week we get rid of cash.'

There was a sharp intake of breath, and a few members attempted to rise, but Michael and Brenda soothed them into submission.

'This week, everyone with sterling cash can deposit it into their bank account. They will be given an electronic purse, or epurse into which they can receive an amount from their bank account, or ATM machine, or from another epurse. This will be solely for their use, activated by a pin number, which they will receive at the same time as their epurse. They will have to take it to the bank, or an ATM, at least once every month for the transactions to be uploaded into their account. That will be no more arduous than currently going to pay in or withdraw cash. The epurse will be totally secure, because any money paid out from it will show which account it has gone to. Any account that receives cash will record which epurse it came from. That information must be transferred to the bank within a month, or the epurse will not be useable. Unlike cash, which can be stolen, money from an epurse will be totally traceable. I would now like to pass you to the honourable leader of the Conservative Party.

There was total silence in the house as he rose.

'Our estimate is that over eighty per cent of crime is because of cash. No cash means no drugs, no illegal prostitution, no illegal workers, and no theft of goods to sell for cash, no avoidance of VAT and income tax, and no dodgy expenses claims without proof.' The last one produced a flicker of emotion. 'Our police force, social services, and relevant government departments will have their workload eased substantially. Instead of reducing staff, we will maintain current levels, which means that they can turn their attention to none cash related crime, and to crime prevention. Those same staff will have full access to the records of all bank accounts, which will have attached all epurse transactions, and will contact the account holder who will have to explain any undeclared income. The black economy will no longer exist within the UK. And now the honourable leader of the Labour Party will sum up.'

The stunned silence was maintained as he got to his feet.

'I apologise in advance for the queues that are likely to occur in the next few weeks. It is, however, a small price to pay for the benefits that will accrue to our country. The disturbance should be no more problem than when we changed over to decimal currency. We will contact all foreign governments and currency holders, and request the return of all cash by the end of this week. From today, they will not be able to exchange more than one thousand pounds into their own currency without permission from the Bank of England. They will have to take and submit a full record of the customer with the cash. Anyone without a bank account will now have to open one, and will have to show a good reason why the opening has been delayed. Anyone unusually paying more than one thousand pounds into their account will have to explain the origin of the cash, and have it confirmed by the person who gave them the cash.

There are going to be a substantial number of people who will not like the new system. They are the ones who have broken the law in the past. They have a choice. They can stay within the law, here in the UK, or they can continue to break the law somewhere else. For far too long we have tolerated crime. Honourable members, I ask you to back us.' Michael and Brenda orchestrated the applause that echoed round the walls of the House of Commons for a good five minutes.

Again, the vote was one hundred percent in favour.

The next few days were fairly hectic, and most of the banks and post offices increased their opening hours. Brenda and Michael struggled a bit to persuade anyone in opposition to change their minds. They planted the idea that anyone objecting to the new procedure either had something to hide, or was trying to protect criminals. In three cases, seemingly innocent and upstanding pillars of the community expressed such strong feelings against the new law that Michael had a peek inside their minds. He was amazed how people so depraved had managed to avoid being arrested. All three voluntarily walked into police stations, and made full confessions of their crimes, which included murder, and listed their accomplices.

By Thursday, electronic purses were being used freely, and the general feeling seemed to be that it was easier than cash, and a lot more hygienic. The display showed how much you had, or at the press of a button a tinny voice said how much the amount was. Still the bulk of transactions were by credit and debit card, which were unaffected.

There were massive seizures of drugs being exported from the UK, as they became valueless. Michael got the people arrested in the major ones to fully co-operate with the customs authorities and the police. One downside was an increase in break-ins at chemists and hospitals as users tried to continue their habits. Most of them were by then desperate, and made so many mistakes that they were soon arrested. Drug rehabilitation centres started to fill very quickly, although most of the heavy users seemed to have crossed to the continent. Again, the customs authorities were able to spend more time on searching users bringing back enough for their own consumption, as the drugs coming in for resale stopped.

Prostitutes controlled by pimps were either shipped out of the country, or left to fend for themselves. Most of them were arrested on the way out, as they had no legal passports or documentation. Police and social services started to switch their resources from crimes that had stopped and problems that had disappeared to people who were penniless. The vast majority were illegal immigrants who had been working for cash. This problem started to grow at an alarming rate, but as they wanted to co-operate to ensure that they were fed, they did not need to be locked up. A lot of them were living in squalid conditions in houses owned by absentee landlords, so they were given help to improve the way they lived until they could be processed.

By the end of the following week, things had calmed down considerably, and the system was beginning to cope again. Another million bank accounts had been opened. Government estimates of illegal immigrants had been revised upwards to between two and a half and three million. They also thought that up to seven million people had possibly disappeared. Taking into account the number thought to be out of the country, there were still seven million epurses that had not been taken up. The Bank of England estimated that there was still over three hundred billion pounds of sterling in circulation somewhere.

The European Union had at first raised objections to what the UK was doing, saying that EU permission was required. Michael had adjusted this to a wait and see attitude. There were now considerable calls for it to be taken up in the lands of the euro. Not only did they have their own criminals, they now also had most of those from Britain. They had lost the opportunity provided by being first, so rendering a lot of cash worthless, but they still favoured getting rid of their criminal element. Meanwhile, America was considering the same sort of solution.

Very quickly, other countries got on the bandwagon, as they did not want to become a haven for the world's crooks.

Michael decided it was time to push on a bit further, and called the three party leaders to another meeting.

The Prime Minister opened proceedings. 'I had grave misgivings about the possibility of carrying out the plan in the time scale we set, so I am really delighted at how smoothly things have gone. We now seem to have a set of circumstances that we can take advantage of for the financial benefit of the country. The first one is that there will be a large amount of unexplained cash in people's bank accounts. Second, there is the missing three hundred billion or so that seems to have been lost. Third, there are believed to be millions of accounts holding cash where the person who opened the account has disappeared. Fourth, there are a substantial number of premises and goods that appear to have been abandoned. Fifth, the three VIPs who handed themselves in to the police were in the top one hundred richest people. I propose amending a law already on the statute book, so that on top of the appropriate gaol sentence, the government takes all the property of any criminal who has used force, or the threat of force, in his or her dealings. I interpret force as any form of physical or mental abuse, breaking and entering, carrying a gun, knife, or any other weapon, or causing other people to do the same. For other crimes we take fifty per cent, or the total identified as being the proceeds of crime, if it is greater. So, if you are convicted twice of shoplifting, you lose everything. I think we can leave the details to the judiciary if we set out the basic boundaries. I expect to see a substantial drop in the prison population as the major criminals are forced to stop or flee. They may well be replaced by people without possessions committing crimes. Your thoughts, gentlemen.'

Both agreed, but suggested that they go one step further, and one of them proposed 'I believe that for some crimes we should bring back the death penalty. Murder, rape and violent sexual assault to start with. Why should the taxpayers cough up to keep murderers and paedophiles behind bars, when one injection will do the job? They are all people who we do not need in our future society. I believe the country will be behind us.'

All three agreed that Monday would bring another vote.

Once again the outcome was one hundred percent in favour.

Michael and Brenda asked Jean and Rui for help to control and eventually snuff out the expected resistance to the new measures.

An opinion poll on bringing back the death penalty suggested that the population was eighty per cent in favour, eleven per cent undecided, and nine per cent against. One well known civil rights leader was outraged by the thought of the death penalty.

Michael let his televised interview go on for five minutes, and then prompted the question of whether he would be prepared to put his money where his mouth was.
He asked,' what are you talking about?'
'You and your supporters can take over and run a prison solely for people condemned to death. You can substitute death for imprisonment for life, but the whole cost will be down to you. The penalty for allowing anyone to escape will be draconian.'
'But that is ridiculous, the state should pay.'
'The taxpayers no longer want to pay, so it is up to you.'
Michael tweaked a little, and the civil rights leader backed down, suggesting that death was probably a better solution.
Brenda proposed that it was time to go and see Mary and Peter, so that evening saw them back in Grundisburgh. They were welcomed with open arms, and while the two ladies set about fixing a meal, the two men sat with a cold Stella Artois each and chatted about the recent upheavals in Parliament.
Peter was broadly in favour of everything that had happened since Stephen Pederson had started the fuel revolution. 'All the electrical appliances have been sorted. We are on the waiting list for the local builder to alter the lighting circuits to power waves, and they hope to be here in less than three months. I've even managed to get the car converted. Best two hundred pounds I ever spent,' was his judgement. 'I have a nagging feeling that somehow everything is linked to what has happened with the economy. Suddenly we lose a huge amount of tax revenue, and then just as quickly we seem to be regaining it through people having to pay the correct amounts of tax and VAT. If we do manage to get rid of the black economy, together with power waves we should actually end up better off.'
Michael nodded. 'It seems to be working out well; shall we have another beer?'

'Good idea. You know where they are,' Peter agreed. 'A funny co-incidence that you are over here when everything takes off,' he mused.
Michael smiled.
'So you are involved. What about Brenda?'
Michael nodded very slightly. 'I hope the economic situation can spread round the world.'
'I suppose I am probably middle of the road when it comes to politics. Always think political parties spend too much time flinging mud at each other to get anything worthwhile done. Look at what the three stooges have achieved in a few weeks. Pity they can't keep the government as one body all the time.'
Michael nodded again. 'I can go along with that.' Peter looked at him for fully a minute. 'I'll go and open a bottle of champagne,' he left the room.
One bottle of champagne became two as the meal progressed. Michael and Brenda lowered their guards slightly as the alcohol took effect, but they also knew that their hosts could be trusted more than anyone else in the world.
Eventually Mary asked, 'what happens next?'
Michael and Brenda looked at each other, and then Michael spoke, 'a good start has been made on crime in this country, but it needs to be a worldwide solution, so that will be another ongoing task. We then need to tackle greed. In my mind that is linked to crime. If you have far more wealth than you need to be comfortable, but spend your time trying to increase that wealth, while there are children starving in the world, then there is almost a case for calling you a criminal. Say someone rang the doorbell tonight, and when we opened the door there was a baby laid on the porch. Would you bring the baby in, or close the door?'
Peter and Mary spoke as one. 'You already know the answer.'
'So why do so many people close their doors and their minds to the problems of other people? They can make all the standard

excuses, but at the end of the day they are just another example of man's inhumanity to man. Let someone else take care of the problem. If you look at the list of the richest people in the world, then alter it to the list of the greediest people in the world, you end up with the same list. Because it is not a crime to be rich, it will be so much harder to tackle. We can conquer crime if the world co-operates. If the rich can see that any help they give to the poor becomes worthwhile, then I think that it can start to become a self-fulfilling thing. At the same time, we have to ensure somehow that the poor spend their increased resources well. Giving a beggar money to buy a bottle of wine is throwing it away. Giving him food or shelter isn't. A lot of poverty is because of overpopulation, and that is often caused by illness. If an animal, or a person, loses a high percentage of their offspring to sickness, then they will have even more. So crime, poverty, greed, ill health and overpopulation are all linked to one another. Ill health is probably the hardest to tackle, as it takes so many forms. We are still taking advice on it.' Michael picked up his drink.

'How much can you see into, and how much can you affect other peoples' minds? Mary asked very gently.

Once again Michael and Brenda looked at each other, but this time it was Brenda who spoke, 'It is possible for the human brain to reach a state called open mind. It means that anyone can see everything in your mind. Your past, your dreams, your hopes, everything. Just think of the consequences for a moment.'

'Everything?' Peter asked, 'no secrets at all? That is impossible.'

'For the current population, but not for us,' Brenda replied, 'we are the same as Rui and Jean.'

'So you can look into my mind, and see everything?' Mary was wide eyed.

'Anyone, anytime, anyplace. We can also alter what they think, say and do,' Michael smiled.
'So you could alter the mind of Osama bin Laden, for example?'
Michael nodded, and thought of the leader of Al Qaeda. There was nothing. 'But the chances are that he is dead. I can pick up nothing at all, so that is the only reason I can think of.'
'But anyone that is alive, you can alter?' Mary persisted.
Michael nodded. 'Except for people like Brenda and I. If you were born into a society where open mind is the norm, then you grow up and automatically become a near perfect citizen, because that is how that society operates. Totally changing the mind of someone to open mind would be possible in theory, but in most cases would cause a mental breakdown. It has to evolve over probably tens of thousands of years. Changing the minds of individuals, or groups, is relatively easy, but not making them open minded to everyone else. They do not know that their mind has been tweaked. Remember that Brenda and I only became open minded as far as Rui and Jean are concerned, our thoughts are not available to anyone else on this planet.'
'So you could start with the richest, and make them give their money to the poor.'
Michael laughed. 'If you wanted me to, but I'm not sure that is the way to proceed. Somehow we have to get the world worthy of being helped. So much aid goes to the wrong people. The two of us cannot convert everyone.'
Mary asked, 'how does Brenda manage to have this ability?'
Brenda butted in. 'We don't know yet. At some stage we need to investigate exactly who my parents were. It may take some time.'
Peter queried, 'everything seems to have started to happen at a terrific speed, almost as though there is a race against time.'
'To a certain degree there is. The world can only continue along its present course for a finite time. Global warming is not the

only problem we need to solve. The other problems we have been talking about are just as important.'
'Or someone else will but in,' Peter stated what was on his mind.
Michael and Brenda nodded in unison.
'Because that world of open minds exists already somewhere else?' A frown crossed Peter's face.
Again two heads nodded their agreement.
'And they know what's best for us?' The frown increased.
'To a certain degree they don't care. Although we are partially descended from them, they will let this world end to protect the worlds that they inhabit.' Michael was equally serious.
'Worlds?' asked Peter, emphasising the plural.
'Yes, and they do not want to be infected by us,' Michael admitted.
'So the nearer we get to possible space travel, the more of a risk we become. Why not just stop us from going into space?'
'If we thought that dogs could wipe out the whole population, would we keep a watch on them, or eliminate them?' Michael asked.
'Not a nice comparison, but I see what you mean.' Peter looked very sad.
'Looking on the upside, if we can change the world to be a perfect place to live, then the nearer we get to that, the better the possibility we will be left alone. I believe we could reach a compromise solution, whereby if any space travel we undertook did not threaten any of the other inhabited worlds, we may be left alone. If, however, we went in all guns blazing, we would not last long. Unfortunately, our history is against us. Every new place we have gone to, we have managed to end up fighting. You can see why we are not thought of as the perfect neighbour.'
'So we are back where we started,' ventured Mary, 'why you are trying to cure the ills of the world.'

'Yes,' Michael agreed. 'It's just that we are not sure of the next step. On a happier note, can you ask the vicar if she will allow us to get married in Grundisburgh church, please?'
Brenda squeezed his hand as Mary replied, 'of course I will, any particular date in mind?'
'We intend it to be a small affair, so anything she can do in the next three or four months.' Michael turned to Brenda, and she nodded in agreement. 'You fix the date, and we will work everything else in around it.'
Mary smiled. 'Come on Peter, it's always best to go to bed on a happier note.'
The next three months were a time of hard work for both Michael and Brenda. They got involved far more deeply in promoting the end of cash and crime across the world. As more and more currencies followed suit into being cash free, crime fell dramatically. Money and assets were being moved into rapidly diminishing areas in the hope of saving ill-gotten gains, or abandoned altogether. Those areas kept reducing as the leaders realised that they had only one solution. Most of these countries were the poorest in the world, and ended up with a vast wealth owned by criminals. It was likened back to the time when Germany converted from the deutschmark to the euro. All the black economy cash spent on property, especially in Spain, ended up being traced and taken back. In the current cases, the governments involved had the option of seizing the assets, seeing them returned to the country of origin, or seeing them moved on into the ever-decreasing cash economies. In all cases the criminals were going to lose, so most countries started suspending any suspicious dealings they came across. The sums involved were truly staggering. Conservative estimates spoke of thousands of billions of dollars being on the move, or being frozen. Some of the countries were dealing with sums far in excess of the value of the country, and had to ask for help from outside. The whole process was starting to collapse inward on

itself. Michael and Brenda gained great pleasure as the men and women involved in this movement of funds were identified, and they were able to get them one after the other to admit to what they had, and how they had acquired it and who had helped them.

The United nations met to discuss what should happen to the proceeds of crime, and Michael suggested that a fund be set up to administer the vast sums involved for the benefit of the poorer countries in the world, which was, of course, agreed.

The saddest fact was that so many of the people involved were previously thought of as world leaders. Some of them had been thought of as possible criminals in the past, but had always managed to be one step ahead of the law. As they named accomplices, it was like a line of dominoes falling one after the other.

While they worked, Brenda was also making plans for their wedding. With Mary's help she had organised everything in Grundisburgh. Some of her old friends were flying in from the States, along with Bob and Jessie. Michael's school and University pals made the number up to eighty.

Michael knew that Peter and Mary's honeymoon had been at Lefkos on the Greek island of Karpathos, and he had booked an apartment for them, overlooking the three horseshoe bays that made up the resort. They had both rejected a hotel, as they wanted the intimacy of their own place.

The wedding was like one from a fairytale, with everything going to plan, right down to the last detail. The reception was perfect, and they eventually retired to their suite just after two the next morning.

Next day they travelled to Athens, and on to Karpathos. As the taxi came round the headland, they had a view of Lefkos spread out beneath them, and Michael could understand why it had captured Mary and Peter's hearts. The sea was that perfect Grecian blue, the sands golden, and the few buildings seemed to have been placed round the bay by an artist. The sun was just commencing its dip towards the horizon, and the water was beginning to reflect its colour. By the time they walked out onto their balcony, the sea was starting to turn to gold.

They held hands, and then held each other tight. Kissing, they felt each other so much in love that they thought their hearts might burst.

'If only it could be like this forever,' Michael thought, and Brenda agreed with him.

'We will come back again when all the problems have gone,' she whispered in his ear.

He nodded, knowing that even as they honeymooned together, a watch would have to be kept on the rest of the world.

That evening they ate in one of the tavernas on the seafront, and it was just for them.

Later they made love, and for a time forgot the worries of the world.

In their fortnight on the island, they explored every inch, and were enchanted by the friendliness of the locals, wherever they went.

'This is how the whole world should be,' Michael suggested. 'They are just so lovely to be with. Maybe we should make this the model for everything we do.'

Brenda laughed. 'I think that in another time I could live here, but whether that will ever be possible is up to us.'

All too soon they were back to Athens and on their way to New York.

They checked up on the office, where Bob and Jessie were still keeping a tight watch on the business.

Back at Hampton, it didn't somehow feel like coming home. It was not 'their' house, although it was a lovely place to live.

Michael spoke to Stephen Pederson, who was starting to get more movement in his arms and legs, and was delighted with the

progress that had been made. They discussed the way forward on ill health, but were still stuck on taking one illness at a time.
Together with Brenda, Michael decided to ask Rui and Jean to speak to their colleagues for their best suggestions on how to progress.
There was just a faint feeling that they were coming to a halt, while everything they had started was still moving at an incredible pace.
That night they made love as before, their minds entwined, feeling each others' pleasure. Afterwards, they lay with their arms around each other, and Brenda whispered, 'have you ever gone right back to the time you were born?'
'Yes, and before,' replied Michael, just as quietly.
'What was the actual birth like for you?'
'I felt the emotions of Jean, mingled with what was happening, and actually experienced the birth. Why?'
'You actually felt what Jean was going through?' Brenda persisted.
'I could feel her emotions, not the pain directly, but I knew that pain was involved.'
'I felt nothing. It was just as if I was in one place, and was then lifted up. Would you go with me, and see if it was anything like you describe?' she asked.
Michael joined her mind as it went to the time before the birth. Brenda was in the womb, and he remembered the familiar comfort and noise. The noise gradually subsided and stopped. There was a gap in time, which they sped across, before the sensation of being lifted up.
'Do it again, but start back a bit further if you can. Experience the emotion from your mother. Again they went back, and suddenly Brenda went rigid, and broke the sensation.
'What's the matter?' Michael asked.
'That wasn't my mother, it was someone else,' Brenda blurted out.

'That was your mother, the person you grew up with wasn't,' said Michael, feeling sure. 'Whoever your mother was, I think she died before giving birth.' Michael held her tightly.
'So I might be someone completely different. My parents may have been from the same world as yours.'
'Or somewhere else,' Michael reminded her, 'just let me check something with Rui.'
He thought of his father, and asked if there had been a woman from the old world who had died on earth twenty six years ago.
'The couple that we replaced were killed in a road crash about then. A genuine crash, unfortunately, in South America. Their names were Tony and Janet Haskin.'
'Was she pregnant when she died?'
'I have no idea. I can try to find out; her parents are probably still alive. Why do you ask?'
Michael glanced at Brenda, and she nodded. He told his father to look with Brenda back to her birth.
'I would say it's a good chance, and it would explain Brenda's powers. Leave it with me and I will find out.'
Suddenly Brenda was sobbing gently in Michael's arms. 'I may actually have a family somewhere,' she stuttered through the tears.
'Let's wait and find out for certain.'
That night they were very restless as Brenda's mind explored every possibility she could think of as she tried in vain to sleep.
The next morning they had finished breakfast, and were sat looking out over the grounds as they had a second cup of coffee. Rui came to both of them. 'I think we are ninety nine percent certain. Janet was indeed heavily pregnant when they crashed. A local doctor who was giving his nurse a lift home discovered the accident. He reported that the baby showed no signs of life, and was cremated along with the parents. If you let me have your DNA, I can confirm what happened. I'm sure I could find it

from here, but the police there must have it on record. I hope it will be good news, but let's confirm it first.'
Brenda was straight on to the police department concerned, and within one hour they were looking at the results.
Rui checked the result through Brenda's mind, and then fed it into his computer. The instant decision was that her name was Brenda Haskin.
Rui smiled. 'Look straight at your wife Michael.'
Immediately Brenda could see her maternal grandparents, and they could see her. There were tears all round as they explained that she also had another grandmother, two uncles and an aunt, and three nieces. Initially it was very tense, but this soon eased as they put the twenty six year gap behind them. Eventually they passed her over to Tony's mother, who was just as surprised and delighted.
When they broke off, Brenda couldn't stop talking. 'They are all on earth three. We could go and see them sometime,' was one of her remarks.
'It's not quite as simple as that. We would have to go back to earth one and be quarantined for quite some time before we could go on. The whole process would be close to three months. We can still contact them at any time.'
'We can contact them, but I need to hug them as well. To kiss them, to touch them, to just do everything that I can't do at a distance.'
Michael knew what she meant. 'I intended to stay on this planet, because when you were assumed to be from here, the only way I could take you away was if I could cure everyone on the planet of the problems that affect them. Then travel would have been possible for you. Once, I was sure that I could do it, but just lately I have been having doubts. Now you are cleared, we could go at any time we like.'
'And stay there?' Brenda asked.
Michael nodded.

'Abandon this world?' Brenda frowned.
'It is a thought. A very pleasant one at times. Even on our honeymoon, we spent as much time thinking about the problems as we did thinking about each other. Just imagine being on honeymoon for the rest of our lives. We could explore worlds three and four, and even have a look at five, six, and seven. Just the two of us.' He looked at his wife.
This time, Brenda nodded. 'That would be brilliant.'
They looked into each other's eyes, and knew that it was not going to happen. They would have to try a bit harder first.
'There is one other possibility.' Michael contacted his father, and asked if there were any others likc them on earth. 'No,' came the reply. 'The general opinion is that you will be the last. You have made enormous strides towards your goal, but the underlying mindset remains amongst nearly all your population. I think 'sod you, chum, I'm alright' sums up a significant proportion of the people.'
'Have you any idea how to alter it?' Michael asked.
'We can, of course, reduce them to Happies. They served a purpose in saving the human race, but everything was done for them. I think the world would eventually die, as there would be no-one able to meet any challenges. For most it would be a long and painful way to go. It would stop them from going into space, but would have the same ending as finishing it all suddenly.'
'Have you anything which will only destroy greed, crime and those sort of things in the mind. Something like medicine?' Michael queried.
'No, we have a number of cures for illnesses on earth, including mental ones. All these can be administered to everyone with no ill effects. So you can wipe out cancer and a whole list of things by adding cures to water, but not the underlying bad bits of the human mind. Is it worth doing one without the other?' Rui asked.

‘Can you stick everything you have onto the computer in the library here, and at least it will be available if we go down that route. Thanks Dad.’ Michael felt quite downhearted as he broke the connection.

Brenda had been part of the conversation. ‘Let’s look at it logically. In evil people, it is the brain that is evil. We know that we can change them on a one at a time basis. What we need to do is change them on a national basis. Rui said that they had cures for some mental illnesses that can be cured globally. If we can somehow work out what we can do individually and tie it in to what can be done globally, it must be worth looking at.’

‘It’s not an easy one,’ said Michael, ‘a lot of crime is definitely bad, but in varying shades from nearly white to pitch black. There are a lot of things that are considered wrong by some, but right by others. Although the consideration comes from the brain, who decides what is right or wrong? Take Communism and Capitalism. Once they were so far apart that being a communist in some capitalist societies was considered such a crime that it warranted the death penalty. Now they jog along together, as both sides have got closer to the middle ground. If a man’s family is close to death from starvation, because the rains didn’t come and the crops failed, and he steals bread to feed them, is he a criminal? Yes by one set of rules, but not by my rules. Euthanasia is a prime example. Probably something like a fifty fifty split. Some people consider it to be murder. Some see it as affording dignity and relief to people who want it to happen. If we could alter that part of the mind that would allow us to commit murder, we would then stop euthanasia, if indeed it is classed as murder. But if euthanasia is correct, then we have stopped something which is seen by many as a mercy.’

‘The same as hunting for pleasure. I abhor fox hunting, but to some people it is considered perfectly OK,’ Brenda chipped in.

But fox hunting is to control the population of foxes,’ Michael protested.

'In your dreams,' Brenda smiled sweetly. 'It's done for pleasure. If the people who hunt are so stupid that in this day and age they can't protect their livestock from a fox, they certainly shouldn't be allowed to be in charge of anything, even a horse. If they want to get rid of foxes all they have to do is put a bounty on their heads, like they did for coypu. They would be extinct in two or three years. But they don't want to do that, as they enjoy hunting them to death.'

Michael spotted that he had touched a raw nerve, and decided to avoid the subject. 'So what we are saying is that we become Gods, and decide what is good and what is bad.'

'Or what is acceptable to the other worlds.' Brenda countered.

'Again, not so easy. Don't forget that they have open minds, so every possible thought is shared with everyone else. There is no daily struggle, as life is very easy. There is no point in bucking the system, because the system is what everyone agrees on. They don't have poverty, or greed, illness or crime, so they start from a different place to us.' Michael felt that he was missing something, but couldn't put a finger on it.

'I'll see if Rui has sent us anything yet,' Brenda suggested.

Michael glanced at his watch. 'I'll give Stephen a ring and tell him we are thinking of starting worldwide cures.'

A slight frown crossed Brenda's face.

'Aren't we?' Michael asked.

'Yes, but I have no idea in what order we do it.'

'True,' her husband agreed, 'let's see what Rui has got first.'

Sure enough, Rui had sent through page after page of illnesses and the specifics for their cures. Each had full details of timings, frequencies, and quantities required. The first batch all referred to cures that could be obtained by being added to water.

Michael and Brenda thought of how the old world had been destroyed by two compounds being added to the waters of the world at the same time. They skimmed to the end of the batch,

and there was confirmation that none of the above would re-act in any way with each other.
'So do we spread the cures as they did before? Lob it in the water supply, and let it be taken round the world?' Michael queried.
'I think that now is the time to call Stephen,' Brenda suggested.
Michael called his friend and explained that they had the remedies for lots of the world's illnesses. All they had to do was produce enough medicine, and get it into the water supply. They were wondering about the best way forward.
'Are you able to send me the details?' Stephen asked.
'Should be with you in a couple of minutes,' Michael replied as he pressed send on the computer. 'Although in theory they could all be sent out at the same time, we believe it's probably best to take one at a time so we can measure the results. Just a case of which should be first.'
'I think they are just coming through,' Stephen went silent as he studied his screen. 'That is some list.'
'Does it seem possible?' Michael asked.
'Some of the ingredients are difficult, but all of them are possible. Give me an hour and I will call you back. Just before I do, are all these guaranteed to work?'
'You didn't ask me that when you started having injections.'
Stephen laughed. 'They were just for me, this is for the world.'
It had really cheered Michael up to hear his friend in such good spirits.
Brenda was reading through the part of the list that covered mental illness. There at the top was Alzheimer's disease, followed by schizophrenia and depression. She made her way down to obsessive compulsive disorders, and under that title found extreme greed, over eating and under eating, as well as the things she normally associated with OCD. 'Look at this,' she called Michael, 'Rui said they couldn't do the bad bits, but extreme greed would be a hell of a start.'

Michael looked at the screen. 'I suppose greed stems from the time we were hunters, and you always took what you could, because you didn't know if tomorrow you might be hungry. We have always devised ways of keeping food so it could be used in the future. Now we still do it, although everything is available all the time. Get more money, because money buys food.'

'And get fat to advertise the fact that you have money.' Brenda added.

Stephen phoned back. 'We think it's probably best to start manufacturing everything as soon as possible. Can we still use your funds and production facilities?'

Michael agreed straight away.

'Then I propose we start to distribute a soon as we have the first one available in sufficient quantity. Can your group handle the distribution as well?'

Again, Michael agreed.

'Are you proposing to make all of them?' Brenda queried.

'Yes,' was the reply.

'Then can we release one medical and one mental at the same time?' she asked.

'No problem with that. The results shouldn't interfere with one another,' replied Stephen.

'I have particular interest in OCDs.'

'Especially greed?' Stephen queried.

'You bet,' said Brenda.

'We will try to get that one well up the list, if it's not too difficult,' he replied.

Michael called Jessie in New York to check how the business was standing up. 'Stephen will be spending a hell of a lot from now on.'

'We are fine at the moment, in fact with the last deals Rui made, we are now more cash positive than ever.'

'Let me know if we start dipping too much, and I'll pull some more in, but it's pointless having it sit there doing nothing,'

Michael suggested. 'How is staff morale in the different businesses?'

'They are like most people at the moment, so happy with free fuel and electricity that it carries them through the day. Staff turnover is at its lowest ever, and we make sure that everyone who goes has a genuine reason, rather than not liking the job. All in all pretty good. What is the next project that the money is going on?' Jessie asked.

'Illness, but it is huge because it has so many different areas to tackle, hence the expense.'

'What are you tackling first?' Jessie asked.

'Stephen is working on that at the moment,' Michael told her.

'Get him to put getting slim without having to do anything at the top of the list.' Jessie burst out laughing. 'Then I will love you forever.'

'I love you just as you are.' Michael knew how to keep her sweet.

'Wait till you see me at one hundred and ten pounds,' Jessie countered.

'I'll tell Stephen it's a priority,' Michael joked.

He put down the phone, but the call to Jessie had set him thinking. He turned to Brenda. 'I think that we may be missing a trick here. All the staff, and pretty much all the world, I suppose, are feeling better because of the energy situation. I suppose it's like Christmas and birthday rolled into one. If they are feeling better, then I assume they are nicer to other people, who are nicer to other people, and so on. Why is that?'

'For the bulk of them it's because they have had a worry removed. It is one less bill to pay. Don't forget, on the other worlds there are no bills to pay. Poverty is one of the items on the list. So we shouldn't be surprised at the result. We get rid of poverty and we get rid of a lot of worry.' Suddenly Brenda stopped. 'We need to tackle other everyday worries as well.'

'Jessie wants to lose weight,' Michael was speaking his

thoughts. 'If she weighed one hundred and ten pounds, she believes she would be happy. There must be lots of things like that we could help with. If we believe that making someone happy spreads more happiness, do we need to do some research in that area?'
'Like Mama Mia,' Brenda suggested, 'everyone comes out with a big smile on their face. Sort of don't worry, be happy situation.'
'That song wasn't in Mama Mia,' Michael smiled, 'but yes, something like that.'
'Why don't you get one of the phone in radio hosts to ask people what would make their life more pleasant. Not cash, or curing illness, but ordinary things. Offer a prize draw with the lucky one getting their wish. See what happens,' Brenda suggested.
No time like the present, Michael thought. He picked the most popular radio DJ in New York, and with a little bit of mind control got through to him. Thinking the suggestion as he spoke, agreement was almost instantaneous. 'I'm happy to pick up the tab for the prize, or top ten prizes to make it more appealing.'
'That would be brilliant. I will announce it at the start of the five o'clock show. Thanks for the offer, it should be interesting.'
Later that day, Stephen called. 'We think the most effective way we can run this is to pick one that is both easy to produce and carry out, effective very quickly, and then launch it in one place. Can you get the government to agree to it?'
'That's not a problem,' Michael assured him.
'Why did I know that would be the answer?' Stephen laughed. 'It is schizophrenia. All the ingredients of the cure are readily available. One dose is all that is required, and we could make enough for the UK within a month. Differences will be noticed within a week, huge improvement within a fortnight, and complete cure within a month. So two months time and there will be no schizophrenia in the UK. Because of the results, we

can then launch worldwide, and get ready for the next one. Acceptance will be that much easier from then on.'

'Which will be second?' Michael asked.

'Diarrhoea,' was the reply.

'Oh,' Michael did not sound impressed.

'I know, AIDS or Cancer would be more of a headline grabber, but trust me, we have picked correctly. Again, it is a single dose, and fast.'

'Then that is number two,' Michael agreed as he put the phone down.

Brenda smiled. 'Not what we would have picked.'

'I suppose that's why we got someone else to choose. Let's put the radio on and see if we get any responses.'

After the normal headlines, the DJ announced the competition. The calls came in thick and fast.

'I can't believe the number of tiny things that people are so upset about,' Brenda was stunned.

Most of the calls were about appearance, especially weight, and then came noise. Fear covered a big range, from going out, to spiders, dogs and flying, being assaulted or mugged. The people manning the telephones did a good job of vetting the calls, which were mainly about money or illness, even though those had been specifically excluded. They listened to the hour long show, and at the end the DJ announced that they intended to run it for a week, as so many people had been unable to get through.

'Don't forget you can write, email or text us with your problem if you don't like to talk about it.'

Michael looked at the clock. 'Come on, we need to get ready for tonight.'

'What's happening tonight?' Brenda asked.

'Surprise,' said Michael, 'but you need your best dress.'

Later they were at the big rock concert in town, and after touring back stage, went out for a meal at Seventy Three.

'What an evening,' Brenda was still high on the music as she got into bed, 'he can certainly put on a great show.'
'And such a down to earth guy, it really was a great time.' Michael went to sleep that night with 'Always' running through his mind.
For the next week they listened to the show at five, and were quite saddened at the things that upset people, some of which were quite easy to rectify if anyone bothered to do something about it. Unfortunately, a lot of the problems were still related to money. Personal disfigurement that needed expensive surgery, poor living conditions, and in some cases no accommodation at all.
'It is still poverty and illness, however it is disguised,' Brenda remarked.
'At least they are on the list,' Michael replied.
As is the way with commerce, the DJ had announced that the draw would take place over the next ten programmes, ensuring a huge audience for the next two weeks.
Michael smiled. 'It may be easier to handle that way.'
On the Monday, they listened in, and at the end of the programme, the winner was announced. A fourteen-year-old girl with a harelip. Whilst it was not exactly what he was aiming for, Michael agreed that it was not an illness, and therefore within the prize limits.
He organised a visit to one of his own hospitals, and a week later the young lady was operated on very successfully.
The Tuesday show ended with a more difficult case. In a rundown part of New York, a seventy eight year old African American had not been out of his first floor apartment for four years. He had lost his lower legs to gangrene, and couldn't make it up or down the stairs. His wife looked after him, but his biggest wish was to sit outside, and just watch life go by.
'So we can put in a lift, or a chair lift. Move him to a ground floor apartment,' Brenda remarked.

'We could actually go and see him,' Michael suggested. They had never met the girl with the harelip.

The next morning they parked in an area that Michael would have found very scary a year ago. The old houses were very run down, and there was rubbish scattered everywhere. His expensive car looked out of place, and drew a gang of youths who blocked the path to the door they were making for.

'You're in the wrong place,' the self styled leader spoke.

'That's number two hundred and twenty two behind you,' Michael nodded.

'There's nothing there for you.'

'That's where Sam Stokes lives. I need to see him,' Michael was quite polite.

'Who the hell is he?'

'So you don't live round here,' Michael countered.

'This is my territory, and I know everything that goes on,' was the reply.

'Your chick is sure my kind of girl,' one of the others giggled.

Michael resisted the urge to use his mind. 'My wife is very beautiful, and is my girl.' He looked directly at the man who had spoken.

'You got guts, man; I'll say that for you.' The leader was obviously impressed.

'Not really,' Michael smiled as he spoke. 'I just need to help someone. No one who was somebody would stand in the way of that, so I just guessed that you might help.'

The leader looked confused. 'Why should I help you?'

'I don't know. Let's go and find out what the problem is, and then see if you can help. What's your name, anyway?'

'Denzil.'

Michael took his hand and shook it. 'I'm Michael and this is Brenda. Now let's go find Sam Stokes.' Michael took Brenda's hand and the bunch parted as he moved towards the house.

Denzil joined them. 'You stay here, I will deal with this,' he showed his authority to the rest, 'and look out for his motor,' he added as an afterthought. He took the lead up the stairs.
Down a dingy corridor, they found the door they were looking for, and Denzil banged on it.
The door opened an inch, and Michael could see a face that looked old and tired.
'Your name Stokes?' Denzil demanded.
The face nodded.
'Then you got company.'
The tired eyes looked at Michael and Brenda.
'The radio show. We are here to try and help Sam,' Michael smiled.
Mrs. Stokes shut the door, unhooked the chain, and opened it. Denzil hesitated.
'I'm Michael, this is Brenda, and this is my assistant, Denzil. May we come in please?' Michael was still smiling. All three of them entered.
'My name is Annabel,' announced Mrs. Stokes.
Sam was sat in a corner of the room. Michael glanced round, and inwardly shuddered at the state of the place.
Denzil looked at Sam. 'I know you. You used to sit outside and moan at me. How come you're never outside now?'
Sam looked down at his empty trouser legs, and crumpled one of them in his hand.
'Shit, man, what the hell happened to you?' Denzil was very loud.
'Got an infection, got gangrene, they cut off what they couldn't save.' The old man sounded like a broken engine. 'Can't make the stairs now.'
'So is this why you are here?' Denzil asked Michael.
'That's right,' Michael nodded at him.
'Why?'

'There was a radio show where people phoned in and said what would make their lives better. Sam wants to sit outside again on warm days and watch the world go by, but he can't make the stairs. He was one of the winners, so we're here to see if we can do anything,' Brenda explained.

'So what you gonna do about it?' Denzil was still loud, as if he was running the show.

Michael spoke softly. 'Don't know. A lift. A stair lift. Both difficult. I suppose for the time being we could find someone strong who had time to spare. He could lift Sam up and down. Sit him outside in the sun for a while. Don't suppose there's anyone round here though.' Michael knew he had Denzil on a hook.

'Don't give me that crap,' said Denzil, 'you want me to do it.'

Michael shook his head. 'What I want is not important. What Sam wants is important.'

Denzil walked across and picked up Sam as if he was a child. 'Don't weigh much do you. Must be having no legs.'

Sam laughed, a noise like a rusty saw blade. 'You sure have a nice turn of phrase.'

'Don't mess with me, or I may drop you down those stairs.'

Sam burst out laughing at that, and Denzil followed suit. They disappeared down the stairs.

Brenda looked at Michael, and he nodded.

'A ground floor apartment would be better.' She looked at Annabel.

'Kinda used to this place.'

'It could stand a lick of paint, maybe some new bits and pieces,' Brenda suggested.

'I could stand a new dress, and there's just as much chance of that happening,' Annabel looked sad.

'Let me see what I can do.' Brenda gave Annabel a hug.

They went back down the stairs, and found Sam sitting in an old wicker chair with cushions on it. Denzil and his gang were sat on the steps.
'Where did the chair come from?' Michael queried.
Denzil nodded towards the next property. 'The landlord for this block lives there.'
'What's he like?'
'Miserable old buggar, but not too bad, he lent us the chair for Sam,' Denzil screwed his face up. 'Did you know Sam used to play in a blues band?'
Michael shook his head. 'What did he play?'
Sam looked up. 'Guitar, but we pawned it and couldn't afford to get it back.'
Michael looked at Denzil. 'Come and introduce me to the landlord.'
Denzil nodded and followed Michael next door. The landlord was nearly as old as Sam, and just as black.
Michael opened the conversation. 'Denzil thinks it would be a good idea to get Sam's apartment decorated.' Denzil looked puzzled as Michael peeped into the landlord's mind.
'Tenants do all the interior decoration, I do the outside,' Michael could see everything. Eighty of the one hundred and four apartments were rented, but the rents barely covered the mortgages, never mind doing up the exterior.
Michael started again. 'So you would have no objections if we organised to do up the whole block?' He nodded at Denzil as he spoke.
'Why?' asked the landlord, 'I can't afford expenses at the moment.' Michael knew that this was true.
'It's a long story, about a radio show, and Denzil, and spare funds, but mainly it's because it's needed and it's free.'
The landlord got up and shook Michael's hand. 'Pleased to meet yuh, I'm Joe.'

'Hi Joe, I'm Michael, and thanks for the chair for Sam. Come on Denzil, we need to do a bit of shopping.'
He threw the car keys to Denzil. 'Let's go to the Old Times pawn shop.'
Denzil looked at the keys, then at Michael.
'You can drive?' Michael asked.
'Sure, but you'll let me drive that?' He pointed to the big Lexus.
Michael glanced at Brenda. 'Are you OK with the guys for five minutes while we go shopping?'
Brenda mentally agreed as she spoke. 'That's fine, see you soon.'
They set off down the street, Denzil at the wheel. 'What the hell is happening?'
Michael smiled. 'What do you want to happen? You live here. If you don't care what happens here, then who the hell will? And don't tell me it's not up to you. You do something or you do nothing.'
They pulled up outside the pawn shop. Inside the place looked like a rubbish dump. 'Have you still got Sam Stokes guitar?' Michael asked.
The owner nodded and grunted, 'Got the ticket?'
'No,' Michael had forgotten about the receipt. One little tweak.
'No problem, I know where it is anyway.' He disappeared through to the back of the shop, and returned a couple of minutes later. 'There's a hundred and twenty dollars owing.'
Michael thought the instrument looked worth less than half that, but got out his electronic purse and paid.
On the way back, Michael outlined his plan, without any pressure.
Outside the apartment, Denzil presented Sam with his guitar, and the look on the old man's face was worth the one hundred and twenty dollars. While he tuned up, Denzil turned to face his gang. 'Here is the plan. We will set up our own decorating business. To start with, we are doing this lot, inside and out. My

man Michael is funding the cost, all the materials and our wages.' Michael eased the minds just a little.
'I know nothing about decorating,' one voice spoke out.
'For the first month we will have someone showing us how to mend, plaster, paint, the whole thing. Then it's up to us.'
'I used to do plastering,' another voice.
'That's good,' Michael nodded. 'No one has asked about wages. Shall we agree on five hundred dollars a week each gross, and see how it goes. I can organise all the bookwork, and it's up to you guys to do the rest.'
They all looked at Denzil. 'Michael had the guts to drive down here. Brenda even more guts to stay without her husband. If they can do that, then we can do anything,' he turned to Michael and shook his hand. 'We are in business.' He looked past Michael. 'Shit, here comes trouble.'
A black Pick-up pulled in behind the Lexus. Five big guys eased their way out. The obvious leader opened his mouth to speak, and Michael could see the trouble that Denzil was talking about. He dived straight into all five. The leader blinked. 'Hi, Denzil, how's things?'
Denzil was wary, but Michael prodded. 'Hi Clay, things is fine. We're starting a new decorating and repair business. First job, this apartment block.'
Clay looked at his men. 'You'll need a set of wheels,' he nodded at the Pick-up, 'will this one do?'
'Fine, and?'
'We do the outside, three of us were scaffolders, and you lot do the insides.'
Denzil looked at his men. 'OK, guys, your first business decision. Let's vote on whether Clay and his boys join.'
All raised their hands, and Denzil and Clay, although looking shell shocked, shook hands.
'Right, the same terms all round, five hundred dollars a week,' Michael took charge. 'Today is Wednesday. I need to sort out all

the bits and pieces like insurance, so start here Monday morning at eight. Remember, everything you do has to be as good as it can possibly be. You have to build up a good name, and this is your chance to do it,' he laughed as he spoke, 'and talking of names, you also need to decide on one.'

'Denzil started it, so how about Denzil's Decorators?' Clay looked pleased with himself. 'Imagine that on the side of the Pick-up.'

Everyone agreed, and suddenly all the previous tension dropped. Michael knew it was because suddenly their cash only lives had been transformed. The only option was getting a job, which was difficult with the world financial climate, or getting whatever charity they could.

Sam had silently watched the proceeding, and suddenly his guitar came to life. The rusty saw blade voice rang out, and although old, he was still good. Other people came out to see what was going on, and what started as a business meeting turned rapidly into a party.

Michael helped it along a bit, and then turned to Sam. 'You have a picture of Hawaii on the wall. Ever been there?'

'No,' replied Sam, 'we cut it out of a magazine. Everyone has to have a dream.'

'OK,' Michael whispered. 'We will start with your apartment, and then do the empty ones, so we can move people in and out as we go. This weekend you and Annabel fly to Hawaii for a month, and she can have a new dress.'

'I heard that,' said Annabel, stepping out of the doorway, 'can it be green?'

'Whatever,' Michael agreed. 'I will get my best mate Jessie to come round and organise everything.'

He turned back to Denzil's decorators. 'Any questions?'

'Why?' asked Clay.

Michael looked at Denzil.

‘Because if we don’t sort out this neighbourhood, no one else will, and we aren’t going to live in crap for the rest of our lives. Even if it needed a limey to show us the way.’
Michael gave him a business card. ‘It’s not going to be easy. Any problems, you can always call.’
Brenda and Michael left after much handshaking.
‘My God, but I feel really good,’ said Michael as they drove away.
‘They think you are God,’ his wife replied. ‘Do you think they will make it?’
‘I really have no idea, but at least they have something, and can try.’
Later that day they listened in again. Someone had a dog next door, which barked all day while they were out at work.
Early on Wednesday morning Michael was on the doorstep, and a middle aged woman answered his knock. ‘You have a noise problem. I’m from the radio show.’
‘Come in, it’s next door. They put it out in the yard when they go to work,’ she checked her watch, ‘in about ten minutes.’
‘And you have spoken to them?’ Michael asked.
She shook her head. ‘I’ve never met them. I don’t like to interfere. My husband misses the noise because he is at work.’
‘So let’s go meet them,’ Michael used his mind as he spoke.
Next door a young man came to the door. ‘I believe you have a dog,’ Michael quickly eased his mind.
‘Yes, is that a problem?’ he asked as his wife joined him.
‘When you go to work, the dog barks all day, which means the dog is upset, and so are the neighbours.’
‘Oh, I’m so sorry,’ said the wife. As she spoke, a Collie appeared behind her.
Michael bent down on one knee, and made a fuss of the dog. The woman he had first met bent down, and started stroking the dog, which licked her hand. ‘What’s his name?’
‘Her name is Susie,’ said the wife. ‘I’m Olga, and this is Paul.’

‘I’m Joy,’ said the woman, I live next door.’ She was still stroking Susie. ‘She is really friendly, would you like to leave her with me for the day, and see if we can get on together? I can take her for a couple of walks. I could really do with the exercise.’

Olga looked at her husband, who nodded. ‘I’ll get her lead, bowls and some food.’

He fetched them. ‘Are you married?’

‘Yes,’ Joy replied, ‘my husband is out at work all day.’

‘Then bring him round for a drink tonight, about eight, and you can tell us how you got on with Susie.’

Joy beamed. ‘See you when you collect her.’

In her house Joy turned to Michael. ‘I can’t thank you enough. I should really have done it myself, but I don’t like to cause trouble.’

‘No problem,’ said Michael as he left.

Each day a winner was picked, and each day Michael sorted out the problems. By the end of the fortnight he felt he knew more about the problems of daily life, but still couldn’t really understand how the problems were left to drag on and on. It was that same problem that dogged mankind, ‘I’m the best, to hell with the rest.’

He was sat with Brenda, their thoughts entwined. Rui and Jean joined them, asking how it was going on earth. ‘We have made progress, but keep returning to that same old problem. Ninety nine per cent don’t seem to care about anyone outside their immediate family and friends. The rest of the planet’s inhabitants don’t seem to matter to them. We’ve got energy sorted, and crime, poverty and illness are not insurmountable, but it seems to be that ‘don’t get involved’ attitude that is the brick wall. Don’t do anything, and it can’t go wrong. We still have to find a way round that.’

‘I wish we could help, but it’s always been beyond us,’ Rui admitted. ‘We hoped that you being brought up in a normal environment would give an insight into how it could be altered, but maybe our genes held too much sway. We have decided to live on earth four, so we will be leaving in the next few months. It is now virtually certain that this one is going to be mothballed. Everyone has been drawn by the beauty and freedom of the new worlds, and less than twelve months will see it shut down. It will be left in a state where it can be restarted, just in case of emergencies, but it will be uninhabited.'

Michael wondered how it had taken so long for the entire population to move from there.

Rui agreed with him. 'One little problem might be raising it's head in the Middle East. On a normal surveillance sweep of decision makers, we have found that a few leaders are looking to the future of the planet, and trying to insure themselves against the forecast disasters. Their main worry was climate change, which now looks less of a problem, but the secondary one was the world being blown to pieces. They feel that some of the leaders and governments are so unstable that if they get hold of the necessary nuclear technology, they could easily wipe out the whole planet. They intend to fund research into finding a suitable alternative home, and the means of reaching it. We could, of course, take them out now, but the basic rules apply. If someone is thinking about it, someone else is doing the same thing. If they get close to discovering the concept of everything being a ring, and using that information to start travelling, then we may be forced to take action. At the moment we haven't anything concrete to go on in that area, but some here are getting nervous. You may have to abandon the project before it finishes.'

Michael shuddered at the thought. He knew the ultimate decision would have to be made. He could leave with Brenda, but no one else, or they could stay and face certain death. There was no way that they would be parted.

He felt Rui and Jean nodding. 'Let's hope it doesn't come to that. We had better leave you to try and fix it.'
Michael was feeling down after speaking to his parents. He never wanted to face the possibility of leaving Mary and Peter to their fate. Again he shuddered. Brenda held him tight and whispered,' we may just have to work a bit quicker.'
As if on cue, Stephen called. 'We will have sufficient stocks of the schizophrenia cure to cover the UK by this weekend. It is so simple really. The basic premise should have been looking at it as any other illness, instead of putting it in the specialist area of brain damage. If it had been an illness of the heart or lungs, we would have conquered it years ago. Instead we looked on it as a separate, difficult problem. We need permission from the government to put it in the water supply. Can you arrange that for us, please?'
'Yes, that's not a problem. How are you now, anyway?'
'Heading for one hundred per cent cured. I can walk short distances, feed myself, and do all sorts of thing that were impossible before. Life is great.' Stephen sounded great as well.
'And life may be taken away from us all,' thought Michael. He contacted the British Prime Minister and the leaders of the opposition. Within three hours, they were together, had spoken to Stephen, and a courier was delivering the necessary paperwork to him.
By the end of two weeks, there were reports of startling improvements in patients right across the British Isles. At the end of the month, on cue, there were full recoveries for all those suffering from schizophrenia, and associated conditions. Those who had families able to take them back were reunited amidst scenes of great jubilation. There were many who had been hospitalised for years, and had no known relatives alive. For these, training programmes were started to integrate them back into society so that they could cope on their own. Stephen suggested that some of the abandoned properties could be used

for them, and quickly a Bill was passed through parliament giving people who had been ill with schizophrenia or similar problems the right to that type of housing.

The leaders of the three parties announced jointly that they had approved the use of the drug throughout the UK, and that it would be available to the rest of the world as soon as sufficient quantities could be manufactured. There were the usual groups of critics, but Michael helped a little with these, and the general opinion was that they had made the right decision. Television shots of before and after cases made great viewing, and created a wave of the feel good factor across the country.

The drug was welcomed throughout the world, with only a few exceptions. Stephen explained that these would make no difference, as the normal circulation of water across the planet would carry the drug everywhere. They had batches two and three in full production, and could start distribution across the world. Like the one for schizophrenia, his name endorsed the cure, and the uptakes were exactly the same. Batch two was diarrhoea, and the regular causes such as dysentery and cholera. Batch three was the one that interested Brenda, obsessive compulsive disorder, including greed.

Michael's group was again organising distribution, with the worst hit areas receiving the first batches.

Within a week, the effects on diarrhoea were one hundred per cent in the areas affected. Tests showed that the underlying illnesses were still present, but seemed to be reduced in strength. By the end of the month, there were definite signs of the causes being wiped out.

OCD was not as quick to respond to the drug. People who washed their hands two hundred times a day were dropping to one hundred and ninety times after three weeks, and then down to one hundred and eighty, but the effect of the drug was accelerating the cure all the time. Brenda was looking for any signs of an effect on greed, but at the end of two months, nothing had been reported.

By then lower respiratory diseases, including pneumonia, and malaria were being tackled, as were Alzheimer's, dementia and depression. There were moans from the pharmaceutical giants, as their products were made worthless, but again they were powerless to sway public opinion.

Michael spoke regularly to Stephen, and was happy for him to plough his way through the lists that Rui had sent.

Gradually, there were signs of a possibility that greed was being conquered. One or two philanthropists were suggesting that as the world had been able to make use of energy waves to provide electricity to the poorer countries, who had then converted their cash economies to electronic purses, they were able to send increased shipments of aid that were not stolen to sell for cash. This was fine for basics like rice, but if they sent motor vehicles, these were soon stolen.

Brenda shook her head. 'I think we can conquer the greed bit, but it is being replaced by jealousy, which we didn't even have on the list. If Fred has a car, and Charlie hasn't, then Charlie wants one. I really thought we were on to something, but it is still that underlying bit of human nature. How do we make them happy enough to live as they should? We can cure everyone of illness, give them food and clean water, give them shelter and keep them cool or warm. Improve some lives one thousand per cent, but that is still not enough.'

'I suppose it is how man has progressed,' Michael replied. 'Remember, they started off in Eden, but it wasn't enough. They always have to have more. Bigger and better. I suppose it's partly greed, partly jealousy, but it's mainly wanting what they think makes a better life. There is that little bit of the mind that is in some people who automatically believe that it's better to give than to receive. They don't have to think about it, that's just how they are. They will always be the truly happy ones. Because they are happy, they spread happiness, which makes them even happier. They are the ones who will always help others, not for reward, just because it is how man should behave.'

He made contact with Rui and Jean. 'It wasn't greed alone,' they explained. Michael's parents looked at the problem with them. 'Remember, everything is a circle,' Rui explained, 'there is no on/off switch. You cannot turn on or turn off that little bit of the mind. It is part of a ring, and some people are on one side, some on the other, with the vast majority somewhere in the middle. You cannot destroy or take away the ring. The only thing that works for sure is what we have been through in the past, which took tens of thousands of years to achieve. You have probably five, twenty years to achieve it. I think maybe you should start to consider the possibility of failure.' They were all very serious. Jean tried to lighten the mood. 'Our new home has been completed, and we leave here at the end of the month. We have had a quick consultation, both here and on earth four, and it is OK for you to come here, have fast scans for anything contagious, and join us. Maybe stay for a month or two to give your minds a complete break and a change of scene. Then at least you can return and restart the battle feeling refreshed.'

Michael agreed that the thought was tempting, and turned to look at his wife. She smiled at him. 'There is just one thing,' she admitted.

'It's not a problem, perfectly safe,' came in Jean.

'What's safe?' Michael asked.

Brenda smiled again, and wrapped her arms round him. 'I'm pregnant, but it's a sort of woman thing, that's how Jean knew, but you didn't.'

Michael beamed. 'That's wonderful. I suggest we go and look at their new home before you get too large to travel.' He hugged and kissed her. His parents congratulated them, and promised to organise transport.

By the end of the month they were on earth one and had completed their health checks. They joined Rui and Jean, and another fifty six who had chosen earth four. Besides their personal possessions, the huge freighter carried anything they thought would be of use on the relatively new planet. They left behind just thirty three people who had opted for world three.

Their new home sat about twenty feet above the shoreline of a small bay. As they entered the lounge, the view was stunning, and the setting sun was turning the sea to gold. Brenda squeezed Michael's hand. 'Just like Karpathos on our honeymoon. I could get to love it here.' They stood, transfixed, as the sun seemed to get larger and faster as it dipped into the horizon.

Back on earth one, something of a mini crisis had developed. The regular check had discovered what they feared most. Scientists working for the Middle East consortium had worked out the logistics of how interplanetary travel was possible. They were starting to look seriously for a world that would support life.

Thirty two of the thirty three on earth one had voted on what should happen next. A split vote meant that the then chairman had the deciding vote. After the meeting, he walked through the park with his neighbour, the most experienced scientist left there. 'What do you think we should do about them?' asked the scientist. The chairman had already decided that any decision would have to be passed to the other worlds, so that everyone could vote on it. His current thought was what his recommendation should be, and he was just a little bit annoyed that he could not make up his mind. He only half heard what his friend had said.

As they passed the end of a flowerbed, a small heap of soil indicated that somehow ants had once again managed to breed outside. He flicked his foot at the offending heap of soil. 'Can you organise getting rid of them, please.'

The scientist left, leaving the chairman with his thoughts.